Sexy BEDTIME STORIES

AN ANTHOLOGY
VOLUME 1

Sexy BEDTIME STORIES

AN ANTHOLOGY
VOLUME 1

Alley Ciz, Cambria Hebert, Cary Hart, Harloe Rae,
Hilary Storm, J. Saman, J.D. Hollyfield,
J.L. Beck and C. Hallman, Jenna Galicki, Jennifer Hartmann,
K.K. Allen, Kristy Marie, Laura Lee, Laura Pavlov

Copyright © 2023

Alley Ciz, Cambria Hebert, Cary Hart, Harloe Rae, Hilary Storm, J. Saman, J.D. Hollyfield, J.L. Beck and C. Hallman, Jenna Galicki, Jennifer Hartmann, K.K. Allen, Kristy Marie, Laura Lee, Laura Pavlov, Lena Hendrix, Lisa Suzanne, Mandi Beck, Michelle Hercules, Michelle Mankin, Penelope Black, Rachel Leigh, Rebecca Sharp, Sapphire Knight, T.K. Leigh, T. Torrest, Teagan Hunter, Willow Aster, Yolanda Olson

All rights reserved. No part of this publication may be reproduced, distributed, or transmitted in any form or by any means, including photocopying, recording, or other electronic or mechanical methods, without the prior written permission of the copyright owner and the publisher listed above, except in the case of brief quotations embodied in critical reviews and certain other noncommercial uses permitted by copyright law.

This is a work of fiction and any resemblance to persons, names, characters, places, brands, media, and incidents are either the product of the author's imagination or purely coincidental.

Cover Design: Lori Jackson
Cover Photo: Rafa Garcia
Formatting: Elaine York, Allusion Publishing, www.allusionpublishing.com

Have you ever wanted to go right to the steamy bedroom scene when reading a romance?
Then this is the anthology for you. Wild and Windy Chicago Book Event proudly presents SEXY BEDTIME STORIES. 28 stories written by 28 selected authors attending this signing with all profit being donated to the Chicago Food Bank.

Each of the 28 authors featured were inspired by the title and challenged to write five sexy chapters.

Each contribution is different.

The only theme they share is the challenge to be sexy.

All the authors contributing to this anthology are attending the fifth annual Wild and Windy Chicago Book Event May 12-13, 2023.

Each author has generously donated their story and 100% of the profit from this anthology will be going to the Chicago Food Bank. There are paperback and hardcover versions of this anthology available separately.

The following authors are contributing to this anthology: Alley Ciz, Cambria Hebert, Cary Hart, Harloe Rae, Hilary Storm, J. Saman, J.D. Hollyfield, J.L. Beck and C. Hallman, Jenna Galicki, Jennifer Hartmann, K.K. Allen, Kristy Marie, Laura Lee, Laura Pavlov, Lena Hendrix, Lisa Suzanne, Mandi Beck, Michelle Hercules, Michelle Mankin, Penelope Black, Rachel Leigh, Rebecca Sharp, Sapphire Knight, T.K. Leigh, T. Torrest, Teagan Hunter, Willow Aster, and Yolanda Olson.

Table of Contents

Sweet Paradise - Alley Ciz
Page 1

Melt - Cambria Hebert
Page 29

Perfect Hookup - Cary Hart
Page 65

When the Mood Strikes - Harloe Rae
Page 111

Voyeur by Hilary Storm
Page 133

Forbidden Nights with the Rockstar - J. Saman
Page 161

My Boyfriend's Daddy - J.D. Hollyfield
Page 195

Corium Ever After - J.L. Beck & C. Hallman
Page 237

Love Stinks - Jenna Galicki
Page 267

All Keyed Up - Jennifer Hartmann
Page 319

Mr. January - K.K. Allen
Page 383

IOU - Kristy Marie
Page 415

Bedding the Bossman - Laura Lee
Page 439

Beneath the Clouds - Laura Pavlov
Page 467

Sweet PARADISE

ALLEY CIZ

A BTU ALUMNI SHORT STORY, THAT, LET'S BE HONEST, IS PRETTY MUCH ALL SMUT AND VERY LITTLE STORY.

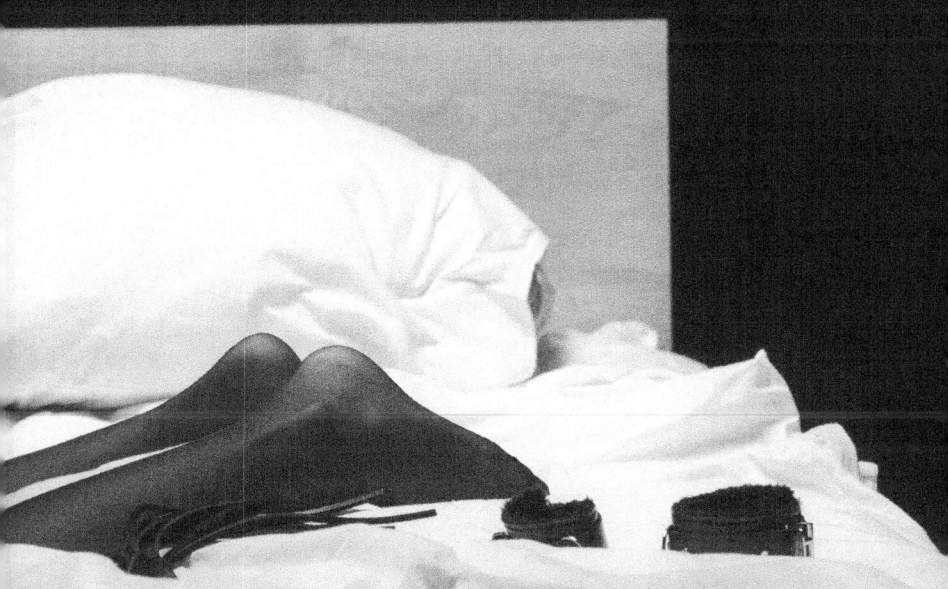

Chapter ONE

Vince

Is it common for a person to be matrimony shamed by their officiant? Because that is precisely what is happening right now. And the worst part? It's delaying me from finally being declared my woman's husband.

"And since you jerks were too impatient to wait and allow me the time to properly plan a wedding..." Lyle says, casting a judgmental frown at my beautiful bride and me.

I give him my most intimidating glower. It's a facial expression I typically reserve for the opponents I face off with inside the octagon, not my friends. But Lyle, a man I would typically call my friend—hence why he is *officiating* my WEDDING—is getting the murder eyeballs because he is KEEPING ME FROM MY WOMAN.

"Not that you're bitter about that or anything," says the woman of my dreams, the mic clipped to her wedding gown allowing all the guests filling this rustic-farmhouse-turned-winter-wonderland despite Lyle's complaints about lack of time to hear her chastisement, causing them to laugh.

"Hush, you." Lyle cuts Holly a glare that would flip my homicidal switch if I didn't know he also loves her unconditionally.

Holly's red-painted lips, the same ones currently requiring my body to work overtime to avoid embarrassing myself in front of all our guests with the erection it's inspiring behind my zipper, part in shock. "You can't hush the bride."

Lyle props a hand on his hip. "Do you want to argue, or do you want me to finish marrying you to this sexy beefcake of a man?" He winks at me, staying on brand by shamelessly flirting with me while he's in the middle of performing my nuptials.

Holly turns to Kyle, who's dutifully holding her bouquet and standing behind her. "How about fulfilling your man of honor responsibilities by getting your husband in check?"

"Ly, babe," Kyle cajoles, a well-practiced affectionate smile on his lips, "they agreed to let you officiate, so don't be a vowblock."

"Vowblocking?" Lyle pauses in his monologue, his gregarious personality not caring that he's in the midst of officiating. "Is that a thing?"

"Only when my best friend allows you to guilt-trip him into letting you perform his wedding ceremony," Jase comments from his best man spot beside me, the jackass doing nothing to hide his *I told you you shouldn't have trusted him to behave* smirk.

"Whatever." Lyle runs a careful hand over the neon green and hot-pink tips of his spiky hair before smoothing it down his green crushed velvet tuxedo jacket. "You guys still love me."

"That may be true." I clap him on the shoulder, squeezing a tad harder than necessary. "But if you don't pronounce my woman my wife in the next two seconds, I'm going to find a new coffee shop to frequent."

Lyle lets out a dramatic gasp, clutching at his chest. "You take that back *right now*, Vincent Steele." He shakes an aggressive finger in my face.

I just grin, letting my threat linger for maximum effect.

Lyle and his husband—because he had no one vowblocking him on his wedding day (the lucky jerk)—Kyle own the coffee shop Espresso Patronum, which my Holly bakes out of.

I used to be grateful for having the greatest coffee shop in all the land across the street from The Steele Maker, my family's gym that I fight out of. For one, their coffee and the baked goodies my future wife creates are hands down the best I've *ever* had. And for another, it's how I met my bride.

Right now? At this moment? While Lyle watches us with that judgmental frown tugging down the corners of his mouth, I'm re-thinking all my life choices that led me to my friendship with him.

He knows damn well it took me over a year to get this damn woman to *finally* accept my proposal. I'm sure as shit not dragging out this engagement any longer than necessary.

"Tell me I can kiss my bride, and I'll consider it." I don't blink, staring my friend down until he gives me what I want.

It was a mistake letting him officiate. He's become drunk on power.

"You know what? Screw this," I declare, done waiting for permission. Hooking an arm around Holly's waist, I haul her in and dip her backward with a not-suitable-for-public-consumption kiss.

Ask me if I give a fuck.

Spoiler alert: I don't.

"Fine, fine, fine." Lyle tosses the leather-bound notebook containing the ceremony dialogue. Honestly, I don't know why he bothered holding it since he's *barely* been reading from it. "I pronounce you man and wife and all that marital jazz. Merry Christmas."

Whoops and hollers cheer on my continuing display of inappropriate public affection. It's only when Holly is breathless that I pull back, letting her body slide against mine as I stand her upright again, pressing my forehead to hers.

"You're mine forever, Holly Meredith Steele."

"Yes, I am." She smiles, her whiskey eyes twinkling like the lights dangling from the exposed beams overhead.

Slipping my fingers under her left wrist, I lift her arm to my mouth, kissing the tattoo on her wrist that proclaimed her as mine long before the rings encircling her fourth finger.

Our friends and family continue to carry on, and it feels like the whole world has paused to celebrate this moment with us, our moment of becoming one. It's chaos, the perfect kind.

Chapter TWO

Holly

I've never been one of those girls who dreamed of what her wedding would be like. Granted, a lot of that had to do with how I grew up. It's kind of hard for a girl to imagine her wedding being the happiest day of her life when the expectations for it trended more toward a spectacle than a special occasion.

Still, it's hard to ignore a day that's at the forefront of almost every other girl's mind at some point, especially when I'd catch glimpses of the fantasy in movies and read about it in many of the romance novels I would devour on the QT. Not that there's anything wrong with romance novels—hell no! I love those sumbitches, even more so now that I get to call one of my favorite authors one of my best friends.

Anyway...we're getting off topic. That's not really the point I was trying to make.

The point is, my wedding was supposed to be some lavish affair planned more for the thousand-plus guests that would have been invited to attend than it would have been for myself and a parental-approved groom.

God. Thank Chris Kringle I *finally* grew a backbone and escaped that life. Sure, *technically*, I ran away, but—and trust me on this—it was the *best* decision I could have *ever* made. If I hadn't risked *everything* to escape the life I had always known, I wouldn't now be married to the man of my dreams, and it sure as Santa wouldn't have happened in the most magical, winter wonderland,

Christmas spectacular wedding ceremony this side of the North Pole.

I can't help but sigh at the perfection of it all.

"Come here, wife."

There's no stopping my smile as Vince pulls me along with him. We've been married for all of thirty minutes, and my husband has called me *wife* roughly one hundred and twenty-seven times. Though, seeing how I just called him *husband* in my mind, I guess I shouldn't judge.

The twinkle lights strewn across the beams above us cast a sparkly glow on Vince's blue-black hair, the blueish hue even bluer with each bob and weave of his head as he searches the ceiling for... something.

"Where are we going?" I ask around a giggle.

My husband—oops, I did it again—electric slides around his cousin Gemma dancing with—

Ohemgee, is that Chance, her kinda-sorta enemy she's dancing with? Ooo, maybe she'll finally hate bang the hockey hunk and the rest of us can stop getting blue clit any time they are in the same room together. Seriously...it's a problem.

"Right here." Vince twirls me around, pressing my back to one of the support pillars at the edge of the dance floor and effectively breaking me out of my musings about my friend's sex life.

My tongue peeks out to wet my suddenly dry lips as he moves in close, one arm resting on the pillar next to my head, my heart skipping a beat as the other bands around my waist, pulling me flush against his solid chest. Anticipation bubbles in my veins as he leans in, his breath teasing my neck moments before his lips do, and I groan at the sensation.

He chuckles into my ear before trailing kisses down my jaw. "I love you," he whispers against my mouth just before claiming it in a passionate kiss meant to seal every promise spoken during our vows today.

His fingers curl around my hip, digging into the soft flesh and making me gasp at the possession as a tingling sensation spreads throughout my body from his touch. My nipples pebble against the soft material of my gown, and I moan into his mouth, still melded with mine.

And then, just as quickly as he started, Vince pulls back, caressing my cheek with a maddening nonchalance like he didn't just set my body on fire and make my panties damp.

I bite my lip and peek up at my husband through my lashes as his gaze roams over me in hungry reverence. That lopsided smile that's been charming me since even before I *wanted* to be charmed by it tugs at his lips.

I narrow my eyes. If I didn't love him so damn much, I could hate him for how alluring that expression alone is. But, alas, I'm head over pineapple upside-down cake for him.

"Ready to get out of here, wife?"

I press my lips together to restrain a grin. It's best not to encourage him if he's already trying to ditch our reception less than an hour into it.

I loop my arms around his neck. "*Some*one's being impatient," I singsong while playing with the hair on the back of his head.

Vince's gray eyes twinkle with familiar mischief as he dips his head again. "Well you see..." I shiver as he trails feathery kisses along my skin. "We have this bridal suite in the back that is completely *empty* right now."

"Mmm." I hum, lowering my chin to recapture his mouth with mine. "You know I *live* for your take-charge initiative." I peck at his lips. "But Lyle's head might literally explode if we cut out early."

"Ugh." Vince drops his head, his forehead resting against mine. "I hate that you're right."

I run my hand along his freshly shaven jaw, cupping his cheek before giving it an affectionate tap. "Better get used to that feeling because you know I'm *always* right." I duck under his arm. "Now come dance with your wife, husband."

I prance toward the dance floor, letting out a screech when he hauls me over his shoulder, smacking my ass in a resounding spank before giving it a dominant squeeze.

"Vince!"

I'm out of breath by the time he sets me on my feet, our friends and family closing in around us in a makeshift circle as my husband pulls me close for his own special brand of dirty dancing.

"I love you so much, Cupcake," he says, lifting my left wrist to his mouth and placing a kiss over his nickname, which I inked on my skin almost a year before I allowed him to put a ring on my finger.

"I love you too, Muffin." There's no suppressing this grin that tugs at my lips at how my UFC champion of a man loves me calling him Muffin on the reg. Though I know that ironclad ego of his is why he preens from it because he knows it's short for *Stud* Muffin.

"I know you do, baby." Vince dips me back, laying his lips on my throat.

"No, no, no, no." Lyle pushes his way into our bubble, physically putting his body between ours and holding us at arm's length. "You're not ruining my wedding day because the two of you don't know how to keep it in your pants. Save that enthusiasm for tonight and keep it out of my wedding."

"*Your* wedding?" Vince's tone is incredulous, but he's chuckling in my ear as he recaptures me in his arms, my back pressed to his front as he sways us side to side.

"Yes, *my* wedding." Lyle squares off with us, his velvet tuxedo jacket gaping open as he rests his balled hands on his hips. "Do you two know the *lengths* I had to go to to be able to plan this"—he flutters his hands at our winter wonderland—"*extravaganza?*"

Outside of the man I married less than an hour ago, Lyle is my favorite human in life, and I know laughing at his typical flamboyant exuberance at this particular moment could be detrimental to my health.

"You'd think we'd committed the heinous crime of eloping like my sister with how he's reacting," Vince mock-whispers into the soft spot behind my ear.

Oof. The glare Lyle levels Vince with makes me think if my new husband isn't careful, I might become a widow on the same day I became a wife.

"*Puh-lease*, Mr. Man of Steele." Lyle rolls his eyes as he emphasizes Vince's fighting moniker. "If life were actually like the game board in The Game of Life, your wedding would be only *one* step past an elopement. So don't act like you had this long-ass engagement with beaucoup planning time."

"Beaucoup?" I press my lips together. "*Really? That's* the value amount you're going with?"

"Hush, Sweets." Lyle attitude finger circles me.

Vince is practically vibrating with laughter behind me.

Lyle flips an enthusiastic bird at my husband. "Now, seeing as *I* did all the legwork for you and your special *special* day, you will keep your sexy asses here until every dance has been danced, and every bouquet has been tossed, and every garter has been removed—"

"Now *that's* a tradition I can get behind," Vince says, cutting into Lyle's run-on sentence.

"*An-y-way...*" The narrowing of Lyle's inky lashes gives away our friend's utter lack of amusement as he continues despite what his glare tells us was a *rude* interruption. "You will listen to every toast, and you will smash your bites of cake, and then and *only* then will we call it a night, and you two can commence with the fucking like bunnies."

"Bring on the honeymoon, baby," Vince declares with a bellowing roar.

Chapter THREE

Vince

With my wife thrown over my shoulder, I climb the staircase to the private plane our friends were gracious enough to let us use for the almost five-thousand-mile flight to our honeymoon. I don't choose my friends based on the perks they come with, but not gonna lie, this is one of those times it's fun being friends with rock stars.

"I'm not sure how I feel about this new habit of yours." Holly slips her hands underneath the bottom of my jacket, lifting the leather above my beltline, the frigid December air blanketing the now-bared skin of my lower back in an instant. "But I'll admit...I'm digging this view."

I chuckle as a hand slides into my back pocket and squeezes my ass.

Tightening the arm I have banded around her upper thighs, I use my free hand to return the favor with a playful spank. "Not as much as I'll be digging mine five minutes after takeoff."

"I take it you want a window seat?"

I pause at the question, returning the greeting from the flight attendant staffed by BoP before moving into the main cabin and setting my wife down on one of the leather couches, making quick work of her seat belt.

Holly pushes her hair out of her face, an adorable frown tugging between her brows as I take the spot beside her and lift her legs to drape over mine. "I thought you wanted the window seat."

"What would make you think that?" I ask, playing dumb.

She cranes her neck, glancing at the small oval-shaped window behind her before returning her gaze to me. "You were talking about the view after takeoff."

My teeth dig into my bottom lip as I bite back a grin. It's cute how even after us being together for over a year, she so easily forgets how my mind forever stays in the gutter when it comes to her.

Slipping a hand over her leg, I slide it up her inner thigh, dragging my thumbnail along the seam of her leggings. "Cupcake..." I let my pet name for her hang in the air and cup her between the legs, feeling the heat of her pussy radiating through the stretchy material of her pants. "The view I was talking about was you." I squeeze, pushing the heel of my palm against Holly's center, not bothering to smother my smug smile at the throaty moan spilling from my wife's parted lips. "More specifically, you naked, bouncing on my cock."

"Vince!" she whisper-hisses, a blush spreading across her cheeks as her eyes dart around to make sure our flight attendant isn't anywhere near us.

"What?" I shrug, letting my hand slip away from her heat to adjust my pants, my dick straining against my zipper painfully.

"I'm not taking my clothes off"—her eyes dart around again—"here."

I crook a finger beneath her chin, bringing her eyes back to meet mine. "Barely married a day, and already you're trying to skirt your wifely duties?"

"Wifely. Duties?" The dropped octave of Holly's voice and the sky-high arch of one of her sculpted brows would each be a warning indicator on its own, but the combination of the two is dangerous. Thank the Dark Knight I know she knows I'm joking and she loves me for my sense of humor. Otherwise, I'd be at serious risk of losing my manhood.

"Mm-hmm." Hooking an arm around her middle, I tug her against me, burying my face in the curve of her neck. "And I promise I won't *stop* fulfilling my husbandly duties until you pass out from the pleasure of it all."

"*Vin...*"

"Yesterday, we were joined together in matrimony. Today..." I bite down on the spot where her neck meets her shoulder. "We join the mile-high club."

"Bu-but what about the flight attendant?"

Holly's tone may be hesitant, but the hand she's slipped underneath my shirt that's now tracing along the ridges of my abdominals is anything but.

"She's been employed by Birds of Prey for years, baby—I doubt seeing newlyweds fucking even rates on her scandalous scale."

Holly loops her arms around my neck, her fingers automatically toying with the hair at the back of my head. "Really?"

"Really, baby."

She giggles against my mouth when I kiss her, her arms tightening around me, pulling me closer. I continue the kiss eagerly, my tongue dipping into her mouth as my fingers fist in the soft fabric of her sweater.

"But don't worry, she won't see anything because as soon as the pilot gives the all clear to move about the cabin, I'm taking you to the bedroom in the back of the plane."

"There's a bedroom?" She abandons me, spinning around and folding herself over her legs to look from a better vantage point.

A chuckle rumbles up my throat. Before fate brought the love of my life into my life, she grew up in a family with more money than God. Money certainly didn't buy my bride happiness in her old life, but the thing I find so special about her is that, despite how common ostentatious displays of wealth were, she still has this pure excitement for an experience like this.

"Guess it's a good thing we aren't traveling with the band because I could guarantee we'd have to listen to Pete go on and on about how BoP is *kind of* a big deal."

Holly's giggles soundtrack the pilot's announcement for preparing for takeoff. "And *that's* why he's Lyle's favorite."

I'm nodding along because I couldn't agree more. The vivacious personality of BoP's drummer was like a friendship homing beacon to our exuberant friend.

"Yes, my beautiful bride, there is a bedroom...a bedroom where we will be *alone*." I emphasize the word to put the last of her hesitation at ease, keeping my voice low and intimate. Besides, despite our penchant for risky semipublic places for sex, I'm way too possessive of her to openly risk any other eyes but mine getting the chance to see her naked.

Emboldened now, Holly glides her hand up my chest, circling a finger around my nipple before scraping her nails down my torso. "And what's going to happen once we're in this bedroom?"

So beautiful. So curious. So intuitive.

"Well..." I skim a knuckle along her jawline, my heart pumping faster in anticipation. "Once you and I are alone..."

Holly's trembling lips part with a sigh as I trail my finger down her body, hooking it into the collar of her sweater.

I lower my voice to a husky whisper. "I'm going to strip you of every stitch of your clothing."

The small movements of Holly's chest rising and falling send a rush through me as I toy with the edge of her scooped collar. The swell of her cleavage taunts me as her breath hitches, but it's knowing she's enjoying the tease as much as I am that takes my grin to shit-eating proportions.

"And while I'm enjoying the *view* of your gorgeous naked body"—my eyes cut up to meet hers again, and they are blazing with a desire that matches mine—"I'm going to touch you however I damn well please." Holly shivers against me as I move my palm up her chest, cupping her throat, squeezing just enough to add weight to my final declaration. "And you're going to let me."

"Is that so?" she challenges.

"It is." My voice is firm and sure, letting her know I won't be deterred from my mission.

"And why is that?" She narrows her eyes, her nostrils flaring as she tries to play tough, but the smile tugging at the corners of her mouth gives her away.

"Because I am your husband, and what I say goes."

A tiny growl rolls around in the back of her throat.

"I'm going to pay for that one, aren't I?" I ask with a wince.

"Oh yeah." My wife nods but leans in, kissing the underside of my jaw. "But I have a *feeling* you can make me come hard enough to forgive it."

"Oh, Cupcake." I use my grip on her throat to bring her close enough for my lips to brush her as I promise, "I'm going to make you come so fucking hard you'll forget you were ever mad at me in the first place."

The jet engines whir as Holly's pulse races under my fingertips. Seconds later, the plane speeds down the runway, my belly dipping and ears popping as the wheels rise from the ground.

As promised, I lead my bride to the bedroom before the captain even finishes giving us the all clear. The room itself isn't much more than a queen-size bed made up with premium bedding, but I don't need anything else for what I have planned.

Holly sits on the edge of the mattress as I slide the lock on the door home, my eyes roaming over her face, taking in the flush of excitement radiating across her skin.

Fuck, she's beautiful.

Beautiful and all mine.

It took me longer than I wanted, but finally, I bound this way-too-good-for-me woman *to* me. By marrying Holly, I am officially—and legally—the luckiest man in the universe. It is now both my duty and my mission to make sure she knows it every single chance I get.

Closing the small distance between us in a single stride, I curl a hand around the nape of her neck, anchoring her for a kiss hard enough to steal both our breaths. Fingers dig into my shoulders, nails sinking into my skin as I sweep my tongue inside her mouth to taste her.

I pull back abruptly before I get completely lost in my new bride. Then, reaching an arm behind my back, I grab my shirt and pull it over my head, carelessly tossing it to the floor.

Holly's whiskey eyes glide over each inch of recently revealed skin. My cock jumps at how her irises darken like the top of the delicious crème brûlée she makes.

No, no. This won't do.

Before sheer horniness can distract me from my plans, I grab my wife around the hips and reverse our positions.

"Strip, wife," I demand, leaning back on my elbows.

Her eyes dilate even more, her pulse jumping at the side of her neck as her fingers toy with the hem of her sweater, anticipation clawing at me as I wait to see what she does.

Her tongue peeks out to wet her lips, and when our gazes clash again, I can see the full weight of my undying devotion to her reflected back at me in her eyes. That, that right there, is why I was hooked on this woman from the jump.

Finally, fucking *finally*, Holly crosses her arms in front of her body and lifts the soft cashmere. Her gaze never wavers from mine as she bends her arms behind her back, unhooking her matching red bra and sending it the same way as her sweater.

The sight of her perfect breasts taunts me enough that I need to fist the duvet in my hands to keep from launching myself at her and taking over the task at hand. Thumbs hooked in the waistband of her leggings, my wife stills, biting down on her lower lip because she *knows* precisely what she's doing to me.

Fi-nal-ly, she shimmies side to side, peeling the stretchy pants over the swell of her hips until they pool around her ankles, the fabric forgotten as quickly as she kicks it aside.

"Fuck, Cupcake."

I stab a hand into my hair, gripping the strands like they are a direct link to the sanity I'm desperately trying to hold on to as she stands before me in nothing but a pair of red lace panties hugging her curves and clinging to her sex.

"I don't deserve you."

In a blink, my wife is directly in front of me, her bare thighs pushing against my jean-clad knees as she takes my face between her hands. "I don't *ever* want to hear you say something like that again." She strokes her thumbs over my cheeks. "You are the best man I've ever known."

No matter how hard I try, I can't look away from those bottomless irises full of love and kindness. The pull of her is stronger than any gravity, and I am helplessly drawn in on an invisible tether.

I grab her by her hips, twisting my fingers in the lace until it snaps. That gasp I live for spills from her lips as I toss away the ruined remnants of her panties.

"If that's the case…" I scoot back on the mattress. "Come sit on my face, wife."

"Vin," she responds breathlessly.

"Don't get shy on me now, woman," I tease as the blush staining her cheeks works its way down her neck and across her chest. "You know I love eating your pussy as much as the treats you bake."

She squeezes her eyes shut, a tiny shudder rippling over her skin as she inhales a shaky breath.

"Now get your fine-ass self up here." I crook a finger. "I need to taste you."

I take her by the hand, helping her climb over me as I lie back on the bed.

"I want to feel you on my tongue."

Her knees bracket my face, and I wrap my arms around her thighs, anchoring her in place, the scent of her arousal making my mouth water.

"I want to hear you moan," I demand, burying my face in her cunt and licking her from back to front.

Holly jerks away instinctively, but I grip her tighter, keeping her exactly where I want her. There's no preamble, no buildup. Instead, I stab my tongue into her entrance then drag it through her folds.

Holly gives me the moans I want, writhing over me in a sensual wave.

"Grab the headboard," I command.

She obeys instantly. With her hands gripping the wood, I reach up, taking her ass in my hands and tilting her cunt for a better angle. Her skin is like warm velvet, her taste the most hedonistic drug.

I bite her clit, and she mewls, my fingers digging into her plump flesh to the point I know I'll leave marks. Holly moans louder, her flesh quivering around my tongue, her muscles contracting under my touch.

"Come for me, wife."

"Vin..."

"I want your orgasm."

I release her ass and plunge two fingers inside of her. She gasps, her head dropping back as I drive them home. Her grip on the headboard tightens as I start to pump my hand, pushing her closer and closer to the edge.

"*Vin*," she pleads, desperation lacing her voice.

I use the flat of my tongue to stroke her, driving my fingers in and out of her until I feel her muscles tightening around them.

"Come for me," I murmur into her flesh. "Come hard."

A shudder ripples through Holly's body as she lets go, her lips parting on a half moan, half scream as her orgasm rips through her.

"I'm coming, I'm coming," she chants, surrendering to me completely.

"Do it," I order, taking her clit between my lips and sucking.

Her back bows, her spine curved in the sexiest arch, her thighs tightening around my head as she rides out her orgasm. I don't stop, refusing to relent until she's breathless and I've wrung every ounce of pleasure out of her gorgeous body.

"Good girl," I murmur, dotting kisses along her inner thigh.

"Holy cannoli, you're good at that." Holly collapses beside me on the bed, an arm thrown over her eyes.

"I know," I say, rolling until I hover over her. "But I'm not done with you yet."

Chapter FOUR

Holly

It's not even noon on day seven of our honeymoon, and already it's shaping up to be another perfect day in paradise. At this rate, I'm never going to want to go home.

Can you blame me though? Here I am, lounging against a stack of fluffy pillows on a king-size mattress inside a private cabana, a frozen drink in my hand, a spicy romance novel loaded on my Kindle, and the gentle cadence of waves lapping in the distance.

Seriously, does life get any better than this?

Just when I think it can't, my stupidly sexy husband comes jogging down the beach in all his shirtless, bulging, inked, muscly glory. It's genetically unfair how attractive he is. And yet...I'm the lucky girl who gets to call him mine. No, wait—I get to call him *husband*.

My heart flutters at the reminder. It's not because he's a seventeen on a scale of one to ten, but because he's five hundred times more amazing on the inside—if that's even remotely possible.

I prop myself up on my elbow as Vince nears our cabana, drinking in the sight of his tanned skin glistening with sweat, his muscles rippling with his movements. His inky-black hair is messy, the undercut swept back hastily from his face, giving me an unobstructed view of his gray eyes drinking me in hungrily.

He jogs up to the edge of the platform I'm lying on, ducking down and holding himself over me by balancing on the shelf of his knuckles.

"Good morning, wife."

He plants a quick, sweaty kiss on my mouth, the slight taste of salt lingering on my lips as he pulls back.

"Morning, hubby," I reply as he plops down beside me.

"Whatcha reading?" He helps himself to my Kindle, slipping it out of my loose grip and taking a gander at the words on the screen. "Is this one of Maddey's books?"

Maddey McClain is one of the handful of amazing women who adopted me into their girl gang, or as my darling husband deemed us, the Covenettes. Before I knew her as a bestie, I knew her as Belle Willis, one of my all-time favorite romance authors. The fangirl in me is obsessed with knowing I have her in my real life and not just on my Kindle, though I suspect it's Maddey who gets the most enjoyment out of our friendship due to how much she gets to tease Vince about how she was the one I loved first.

"Nope." I pop the *p* as I steal my Kindle back. "This gem of deliciousness is *Give Me More* by Sara Cate."

"Oh, *really*?" Vince teases while tracing his fingertips over the jut of my hip bone. "And is it inspiring you to try anything *fun* with me?"

"I don't know..." I toss my Kindle aside, rolling over until we're face to face.

Mischief I'm *more than* familiar with dances across Vince's features. "Aww..." He reaches up, tucking a loose tendril of hair behind my ear. "Don't get shy on me now, Cupcake. You know I love making your spicy BookTok dreams come true."

My nose scrunches when he boops it.

"Plus," he continues, "I fully subscribe to the whole *happy wife, happy life* thing."

I bite my lip, not to be seductive, but to hold back a laugh because I know my sweet, wonderful husband is far too alpha to even let the mere *idea* of what I'm about to tell him be a possibility, let alone actually happen. Not that I would want it—I have my hands full enough with Vincent Steele on his own. Trying to add anyone else into the mix would be utter chaos.

"Well...you see..." I shift until my breasts pillow against his hard chest. "It's about this married couple..."

"How convenient." Vince toys with the strings tied low on my hips. "Seeing as we"—he bounces a finger between us—"are a newly married couple."

"That we are." I casually walk my fingers up the plane of his chest. "But in this story, their relationship doesn't feel complete until they add their best friend Drake into it."

Vince lets out the feral growl I expected he would, the vibration of the sound and the sheer possession in it making my nipples hard. "I love Jase, but I would castrate him with his hockey skate if I suspected he was *thinking* about suggesting something like that."

Vince and Jase have a friendship unlike any I've ever seen before, and I say that as a person whose own best friend is married to Lyle. But, really? Does anything else need to be said?

"Aww, is polyamory the thing that could finally break the most epic bromance of the ages?" I tease, tracing the shapes of the superhero emblems inked down his arm.

I'm shoved onto my back in a blink, a scowling MMA champion hovering over my prone body. Fear is what I should feel given my history, but because I know I'm safe with Vince on a soul-deep level, my pussy clenches instead.

I have no idea where my Kindle went or what happened to my drink. The only thing my mind is able to focus on is the feel of Vince's calloused fingers dragging along my skin as he takes my arms and lifts them over my head.

He laces his fingers with mine, pinning my hands to the mattress. "One week, and already my bride is bored of me?"

I wiggle around for space, but the only thing my efforts get me is Vince planted firmly between my thighs…not that I'm complaining.

Arching my neck, I dot kisses along his chin. "You're a man with Batman sheets on his bed—how could I ever be bored with you?"

My husband's grin is proud, the dimple in his left cheek making a pleased appearance. "Damn right, baby." He slams his mouth on mine.

Our kiss deepens, and I groan as our lips connect, his teeth biting down on my bottom one before he sucks it into his mouth.

"You know I'm all yours, right?" I say when we finally break apart for some much-needed oxygen.

Everything about Vince softens at my words. Well...not *every*thing. His dick is still as hard as my new surname against my thigh.

"Never doubted it for a second"—there's a purposeful pause before he finishes—"wife."

My heart stutters at the reminder of how important I am to this man.

Untwining one of his hands from mine, Vince cups the back of my nape, stretching his thumb up to push against my chin to keep me in place. "And I've always been yours."

Then, as if his declaration didn't just steal my breath, he makes sure to finish the job by sealing his mouth to mine. His fingers flex around me, and I moan as our tongues tangle together, the taste of him addictive, like a drug I could never get enough of.

A warm breeze blows across my overheated skin as Vince's hands slide down my body, his firm grip holding me to him as he continues to kiss me with more hunger than ever before. The warmth of his touch radiates through me, setting off sparks of electricity in its wake.

I can't help but squirm closer, wrapping my arms around his neck and my legs around his waist, wanting more. With a growl, Vince deepens the kiss further, his hand running up my side and over to cup my breast possessively. Through the thin fabric of my bikini top, his thumb circles my nipple, teasing it until it's hard and practically begging for relief.

"Vin..." My voice trails off on a moan as he pushes the triangle of fabric to the side and sucks my nipple into his mouth.

"Fuck, I love the way you say my name, Cupcake," he mumbles around my flesh, his teeth biting the hard nub, making my back bow off the mattress.

"We're on the beach," I warn as he moves from one breast to the other.

"A *private* beach."

I blink, struggling to see through the haze of lust coating my vision as I take in our surroundings. Yes, our bungalow sits on a section of private beach, but that's all it is, a section, one connected to a much larger, much more *public* stretch of sand. But when his palm flattens to my belly and slips inside my bikini bottoms, I couldn't care less if we have an audience or not.

"God*damn*." He drags two fingers through my slit, plunging them inside my pussy. "You're fucking *soaked*."

"I need you inside me."

His fingers still, the tips skimming along my G-spot in the most maddening tease as he arches back to meet my gaze, that dangerous smirk tugging up his lips. "Here?"

I'm nodding before he even finishes asking the question.

"Thank fuck."

Everything after that happens in fast-forward. Vince reverses our positions, hauling me around to straddle his lap in an effortless display of strength. His fingers hook under the crotch of my bikini, pulling the bottoms to the side and slamming me down on his dick. I have no idea when in all the maneuvering, he pulled it out of his shorts, but I'm damn grateful for his Houdini-esque penis-escaping skills.

"Oh my god." I let out a choked gasp.

Vince bands his arms around me, laying his forearms against my back and curling his hands over my shoulders. "*God*, I love the way your cunt squeezes me."

I groan when he swivels his hips, my clit brushing against his rippling abdominals as he slams up into me, sinking himself deep.

"More, Vin. I need more." I tangle my fingers in his damp hair, clutching at the silky strands.

His mouth covers my breast again, his tongue lashing at my nipple as his hips continue their relentless thrusts. Over and over, he pumps, pushing me higher and higher until I'm gripping him for dear life, my touch gliding through the sheen of sweat coating his skin.

His body moves like a well-oiled machine as he takes me, our breaths mingling in harsh little gasps. *Sweet sugar cookie.* I'm *beyond* grateful for all the hours my new husband dedicates to the gym to maintain his reign as the UFC's Light Heavyweight champion.

Vince releases my boob with an audible pop, his hands going to my hips, driving our bodies together with powerful thrusts that leave me clinging to him in desperation.

"You know what I want, wife," he growls against my ear, his throaty exhalation fanning my heated flesh and setting off a wave of goose bumps.

Pleasure crashes around inside my body as his fingers dig into my flesh in a punishing grip, the need to come urgent inside me.

"Vin...Vin..." I choke out between needy cries, begging for relief from this razor edge of sensation.

He fists my hair tightly in one hand, his teeth grazing down the side of my neck. "Let go, baby. I've got you."

That's all the permission I need before ecstasy breaks over me so hard it steals away everything except his name escaping my lips on a broken cry.

I don't know how long it takes until I can do more than cling to Vince, shuddering in his arms as I come down from the high.

"I love you," he whispers against my hair. The kiss he presses to my sweat-speckled temple is so sweet, especially compared to the animalistic way he just took me, and my heart squeezes inside my chest.

"I love you, too." I sigh, my heart still thudding behind my rib cage.

His arms tight around me, I lift my head, blowing a wayward strand of hair out of my face, and meet his gaze with a flirtatious grin.

"What?" he asks, brushing a knuckle against my cheek.

"Can we do that again?"

His answering laugh is pure, unfiltered Vincent Steele. "Hell yeah we can, Cupcake."

Chapter FIVE

Vince

Five thousand miles and six times zones—you would think that would be enough to keep the real world back home from invading our little slice of sweet paradise.

But...

You'd be wrong. There's no amount of distance or time differences that will keep a Coven Conversation at bay.

It was one thing to be rudely woken up by the start of the girls' incessant group chat. That's whatever. I could roll with it. I'm a flexible guy thanks to all the yoga my pain-in-the-ass-because-she's-always-right sister insists on being part of my training.

But the constant bellow of Santa's hearty *ho ho ho* chiming as text after text practically trips over itself to make itself known before the next one is ruining this sexy-time mojo I'm trying to build kissing my wife's bare back.

Cockblocked by text message. *What the fuck?*

"Make it stop," I mumble against Holly's soft skin.

She giggles, arching her back until her delectable ass pushes against the erection already grumbling about these anti-aphrodisiac notifications. "Just let me make sure it's nothing important."

"*Holly*," I whine. She and I both know *important* is a relative term with the Covenettes.

Utterly unconcerned about the growing situation in my groin, Holly reaches for her phone. This time her ass grinds into me, increasing my chances of succumbing to death by blue balls.

To add insult to impending injury, the text thread is filled with speculation about my cousin Gemma's sex life. *Yeahhh*, knowing whether or not my relative took a trip to Pound Town with her would-be nemesis is information I'd need brain bleach for.

YOU KNOW YOU WANNA (Becky): **cropped and circled image of Chance's hand sitting dangerously low on Gemma's back**

ALPHABET SOUP (Rocky): Oooo, I think someone likes you, cuz.

DANCING QUEEN (Zoey): You don't need to like someone to fuck them.

And then, and *fucking* then...Holly starts joining in. Here I am trying to do my best erotically teasing wake-up call for my bride, and she's typing a freaking message to our friends. Ooo, someone is on my naughty list.

HOLLY: OMG, this being 6 hours behind you guys is NOT working for me. I'm missing ALL the things.

PROTEIN PRINCESS (Gemma): You guys are RIDICULOUS. And Holly, you're on your honeymoon. As much as it makes me throw up in my mouth to say *puke emoji* shouldn't my cousin be keeping you too busy banging to text us?

I feel that puke emoji deep in my soul. Brain bleach, remember? Still...my sunshiny cousin's observation is why she is one of my favorite relatives.

It's time to put an end to this insanity so I can put a start to banging my wife.

Holly lets out a yelp of protest when I yank the phone out of her hands and start typing out my own response.

(Me writing as) SANTA'S COOKIE SUPPLIER: THANK YOU! THIS IS WHY YOU ARE MY FAVORITE COUSIN, GEM!

PROTEIN PRINCESS: Hi, Vince.

"Can I have my phone back?" Holly attempts to retrieve her phone, but I roll her underneath me, smirking at the feel of having all her nakedness pressed against me.

"That would be a no." I laugh at the adorable pout she gives me.

(Me writing as) SANTA'S COOKIE SUPPLIER: Don't you worry your pretty little head, cuz. I've been keeping my new wife VERY satisfied.

Holly's eyes go as round as the coconut she drank her piña colada from yesterday. "*Vince.*"

I'm chuckling as I drop the phone over the side of the bed then take her beautiful face between my hands. "It's cute how you think I don't know you well enough to know you'll be back in that chat telling them all about how I fucked you so hard you passed out from pleasure the first chance you get."

"You sound *awfully* sure of your sexual prowess, Muffin." She dances her fingers along the ridges of my muscles.

"Maybe." I ghost my lips across her collarbones. "But I think the number of orgasms you've had since becoming my wife stacks the odds in my favor."

"How do you know I wasn't faking them?"

Her taunt sets off every competitive alpha molecule residing in my cells. I flip her over onto her belly with a growl, blanketing her body with mine and kneeing her thighs apart. "I dare you to fake this."

"Oh, fuck." She moans, squirming underneath me as I slam home in a single, powerful thrust.

"That's it, baby." I drop my mouth to her ear, kissing the soft spot behind it as I move inside her. "I promise you'll only ever have real orgasms for the rest of your life."

She moves with me, meeting me thrust for thrust and panting out, "Now that's what I call happily ever after."

***

Thank you so much for reading! Want to learn how Holly and Vince met and feel in love (*Sweet Victory*)? Or if Gemma finally did hate-bang Chance Jenson (*Defensive Hearts*)? Find out in my BTU Alumni Series. All books are LIVE.

For more information, go to my website:
https://www.alleyciz.com/

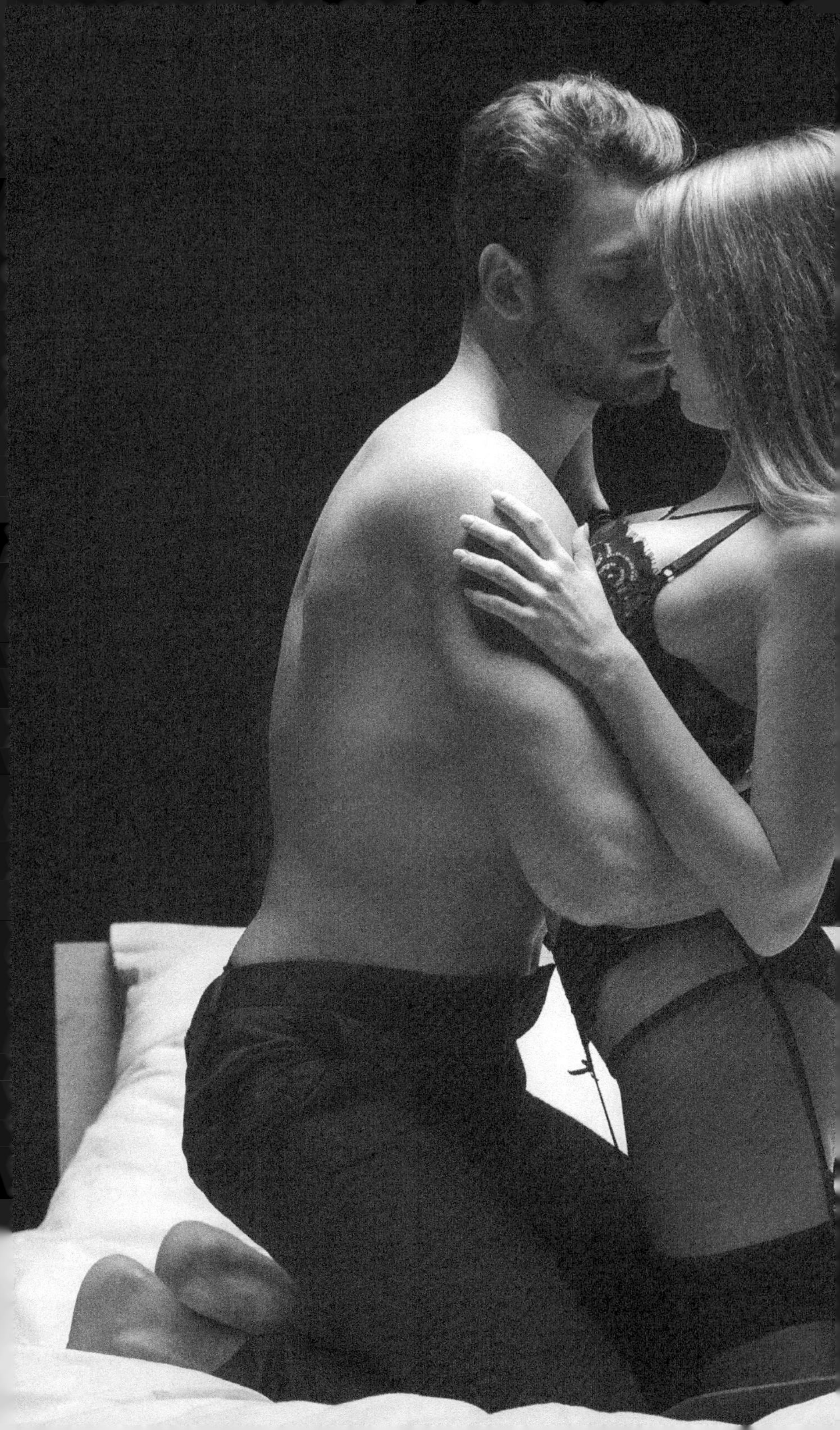

MELT

CAMBRIA HEBERT

LET'S SKIP TO THE GOOD PART...

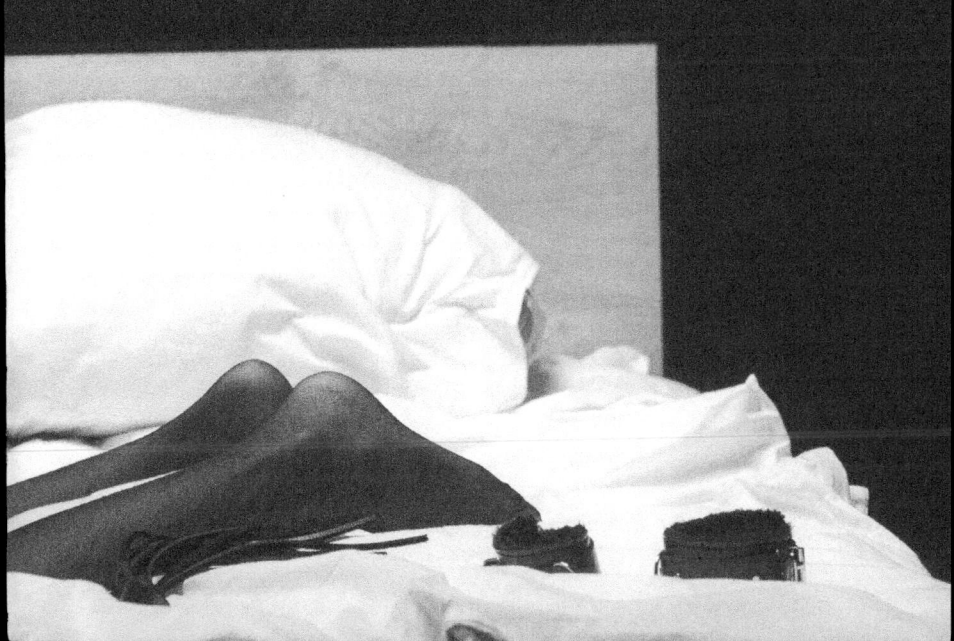

Chapter ONE

Meg

Football is not my thing. Actually, sports in general are not my thing. Watching a bunch of men run up and down a field with a ball is about as fun for me as going camping and having no access to a bathroom or running water, which, by the way, is *none* at all.

And playing sports? I am so painfully uncoordinated that even my high school gym teacher let me sit out and gave me a participation grade anyway. He said it was safer for all involved. He was right.

So what exactly was I doing sitting on a set of bleachers surrounded by a bunch of people who liked football a lot more than me on this crisp fall day?

Making an effort. A herculean one, no less. You know what that got me?

A late boyfriend.

Craning my neck, I looked around for the umpteenth time, hoping to see him striding down the stairs with apology snacks in tow. I mean, the least he could do for stranding me at this testosterone fun fest alone was bring snacks.

The scarf around my neck caught in the wind and blew back when I turned, plastering itself over my face and blocking my view. My gloved fingers struggled to grab the thin material and peel it away, which flustered me, and I tipped backward off the bench seat as I struggled to free my eyes.

"*Ah,*" I squeaked, pitching to the side as I forgot about the dumb scarf and grappled for balance. I was as successful in that endeavor as I was with the scarf and landed in a heap in the narrow concrete section between rows.

The person sitting next to me grunted when I landed on their foot, jerking it back, which took away the only cushion I had against the ground. Wincing, I smacked into the hard surface again as I fought to sit up and peel the scarf back.

Vision finally cleared, I blinked up into the scowling face of the man whose foot I likely crushed. Thanking him for providing my butt some cushion was probably not the way to go here, so I settled for offering him a sheepish smile. "Sorry."

The apology was met with a dirty glare, flared nostrils, and him shifting away from me completely. Guess that meant my apology was not accepted.

Grimacing, I slid back onto the bench, my hip throbbing from the way I'd landed.

Oh, and my boyfriend?

Still nowhere to be seen.

Pursing my lips, I yanked my phone free of my coat pocket. The gloves made my fingers slippery, and the phone went flying... right into the back of the man who was already my victim once.

I watched the device jab itself into the center of his back, bounce off, and land precariously on the seat. I dove to scoop it away from the edge before it could tumble onto the ground and crack.

I'd just replaced the screen. I did not want to do it again.

The triumph I felt upon saving my phone was short-lived because the heated glare lasering from the man's eyes seared it away. Cheeks hot, I giggled nervously—something else about me that was unfortunate, the way I automatically laughed in situations that did not call for laughter.

"I'll just, ah, get a new seat," I told him.

His nose was still flared when I stood.

Without thinking, I said, "You better hope your face doesn't freeze like that."

That only made him look more like a bull.

Giggling again, I hurried past the other people sitting in my row, tripping only once on the straps of a bag before heading up the steps toward the small platform between rows. Once there, I leaned against the railing and typed out a text.

Where are you?

As I waited for a reply, I watched the bleachers fill up more and more, almost to max capacity. I marveled at the fact that so many people wanted to spend their day here. *Is it always this packed?*

The phone in my hand finally vibrated, and I looked down.

What's it matter?

I made a face at his reply. Look, maybe Brent wasn't the most charming, but that was just downright rude.

Considering I'm at the game waiting for you, I'd say it matters a lot.

His next reply was equally unappealing. **You really expected me to come?**

I made a sound. **Considering you asked me to meet you here, yes.**

That was before.

A stone dropped into my stomach, making me squirm a little. **Before what?**

Seriously, Meg? You can't be that stupid.

I sucked in a breath. **Excuse me?**

I can't date someone like you.

That stone in my stomach? It turned into a boulder, and breathing around it was difficult. I thought back to last night, and instantly, my eyes slammed closed. Dragging in a deep breath, I forced the nerves down and reopened them. Sure, things hadn't exactly gone smoothly. But he'd said it was okay. He said he would be patient.

Swallowing, I typed out. **Someone like me?**

An ice queen.

My chest clenched, and the words on the screen blurred a bit as I typed. **I'm not.**

Yeah? Well, last night, you were colder than a witch's tit, and I felt like I was touching stone.

Shame and embarrassment washed over me, the feelings so overwhelming the loud sounds of the crowd didn't even register. I might be standing here in a crush of people, but his words made me feel small and alone. *Please, not again.*

I typed out, **You said**, but at the very same moment, more of his words appeared onscreen.

We're over. I need someone who can handle my needs.

I gasped, and the person passing by rotated to look at me. "Are you okay?"

My lower lip wobbled before I schooled my face and looked up. Plastering on a smile, I said, "Never better!"

Then I turned and fled onto the staircase that led below the bleachers where the concession stand and bathrooms were located.

Sniffling, I hurried past people, bumping into them as I went but not bothering to apologize or make sure they were okay. With the phone still clutched in my hand, I hurried down the long corridor and around the corner away from prying eyes.

Leaning against the concrete wall, I let out a shuddering breath as the tears I'd been holding back dripped over my cheeks. I hadn't realized how cold I was until the water felt warm against my skin.

With my glove, I swiped them away, but more took their place instantly. Lighting up the screen, I stared down at the messages through unclear vision. A sob worked itself up my throat and forced its way past my lips, the sad sound echoing through the empty hallway where I hid.

Leaning a little more heavily into the wall, I dipped my chin toward my chest, the lower part of my face disappearing in the scarf draped around my neck.

An awful pressure squeezed my ribs, making it impossible to draw in a full breath, and my head spun. Misery so strong wailed inside me that I could do nothing more than part my lips and let it out, sobbing in the darkened tunnel.

I wasn't even upset he'd broken up with me. He was a colossal jerk. He stood me up. Called me stupid.

He said he would be patient. Yeah, well, he was a liar too.

If he hadn't broken up with me, I certainly would have with him. Truth was I didn't even like him much anyway. He liked himself enough for the both of us.

So why was I standing here crying as though he'd crushed my heart into a thousand pieces? It was what he called me. How he unknowingly attacked my most private and vulnerable spot.

Ice queen.

I wasn't an ice queen. I wasn't. Except, deep down, I worried...
What if I am?

Here I stood, a twenty-year-old virgin. And sure, in the grand scheme of things, I wasn't that old. But in the terms of the V-card, I felt ancient.

Most everyone I knew had handed in their card in high school. And those that managed to hang on to it lost it soon after going off to college. But here I was, a sophomore at Lincoln U, and my V-card was tucked right beside my driver's license.

FYI, both of them had horrible pictures.

The worst part was I had opportunities. I dated in high school. I even dated here at LU. Sure, not excessively, but I went out. I'd gotten close a few times, but it always ended the same.

Me freezing up. Me going tense. Me unable to relax enough to enjoy it. Or worse... me being indifferent.

Honestly? I secretly feared I was broken. I even considered that I might be asexual. But the thing was I wanted to have sex. I wanted the kind of consuming, overwhelming connection where my body just let go. But my mind and body didn't seem to be on the same page.

Or maybe that stuff didn't exist. Maybe I was waiting to feel something I never would. Maybe I should have just done it with Brent last night even if I wasn't into it. I wrinkled my nose at the thought. No way. He was a class-A asshat dirtbag that did not deserve the honor of being my first.

Ice queen or not, I had standards. And at the top of my standard list was no asshats.

So here I was—stood up, single, and crying at a god-awful football game under the bleachers in the dark.

A rush of anger whooshed through me, straightening my spine off the wall. I was *not* going to stand here and cry over some douchebag. He wasn't worth it.

I started to text my bestie, Kat, and send out an SOS, but my eyes snagged on the previous texts.

Ice queen. I can't date someone like you.

A fresh sob tore from my throat, making it burn. I was still upset. I spun away from the wall and rushed down the empty hall, my sniffles and whimpers echoing behind me.

Tucking my chin low, I hurried deeper into the dark, not bothering to clear my watery vision as more and more tears fell.

It was probably why I didn't see it coming. Well, that and the fact I was a giant klutz.

Slam!

A strangled squeak filled the air when I collided into a massive wall of something and went flying backward onto my butt. The sore hip from earlier screamed again, but I barely registered the pain or the all-too-familiar cracking of my phone as it hit the ground. Instead, I lay there stunned, flat on my back, and trying to catch my breath.

Breath that absolutely escaped me as I stared up at a giant, looming shadow.

Chapter TWO

Noah

"If you're going to kill me, just get on with it," a strained voice groaned from the ground.

I paused, cocking my head to the side. "For someone who thinks they're about to be murdered, you sure don't seem that afraid."

A low hiccup accompanied by a muffled sob brought me up short. "*Fuck,*" I cursed, reaching down to the sprawled figure at my feet. She flinched when my hands closed around her upper arms, but I didn't let go.

"Easy now." I cautioned, effortlessly lifting her off the floor. "Did I hurt you?" I asked, depositing her on her feet in front of me.

Seeing her slight stature made the concern I felt morph into full-blown worry. "Hey," I said again, reaching out to cup her elbow in my palm. "Are you hurt?"

"I'm f-fine." She sniffled.

Squinting, I bent down, pushing my face closer to hers. She recoiled, eyes turning into saucers beneath her askew knit hat. Long blond hair fell from beneath it, waving over her shoulders, clinging to her coat.

Her cheeks were wet. Even in this darkened tunnel, I saw the tear tracks streaking her pink cheeks.

A growling type of rumble vibrated the center of my throat. "If you were fine, you wouldn't be crying."

She yanked her arm free, the force of it causing her to stumble backward.

"Whoa." I warned, avoiding her flailing arms to snake an arm around her waist and pull her in.

"Let go."

I considered it. "No."

The tears on her face contrasted against the incredulous ire lighting those blue eyes. "No?" she parroted. "It wasn't a request."

She started to push away, so I yanked her even closer. Her breath whooshed out when her chest hit mine, her forehead bouncing off me.

Snapping her chin back, she glared at me, the sparks flying in her stare giving me a jolt of anticipation.

I smirked. "You've already hit the ground once, almost hit it again, and literally have tears soaking your face, and I've known you all of one minute. I think I'll hold on to you. You're clearly a danger to yourself."

Her mouth dropped open. Her indignant little growl was cute.

"I wouldn't have fallen if you hadn't mowed me over!"

I lifted one shoulder. "You came out of nowhere."

"Actually, I came from around the corner."

A wide smile split my face.

"Let me go." She tried again.

Bemused, I answered, "No can do."

"I will scream." She threatened.

Raking my stare over her, I took in her narrow, oval-shaped face that tapered into a V. Her eyes were round and wide, oversized compared to the rest of her features. She seemed pale in the dim tunnel, but the tips of her nose and high points of her cheekbones were red from the cold. Or maybe it wasn't the cold.

Lifting my hand, I brushed the pad of my thumb over one of the tears and whispered, "You're crying."

The sound of her swallow echoed above our heads, and her face dipped. "It's not your problem," she said, voice strong compared to how soft she felt.

I opened my mouth to argue, but it was like she knew I would, and her chin rose again.

"I was crying before you flattened me, okay? You're absolved of all guilt." Laying her hands flat on my chest, she shoved. "Now let me go."

It was easy to keep hold of her. "Why were you crying?"

"Pretty sure it's not your business," she said, smacking my chest.

I released her, and she stepped back, the cool air swirling through the new space between us.

After the briefest hesitation, she turned. "I'm leaving."

My gaze settled onto the ground, snagging on her forgotten phone.

"Hey," I called, leaning down to pick it up. "You forgot this."

She glanced over her shoulder, stare dipping to the phone. Heaving a heavy sigh, she turned back. "I think it's broken."

I hit the side button, and the screen lit up, highlighting the large crack down the center of the screen, the corner shattered.

"Yeah—" I started to agree, but then my attention caught on the messages on the screen. As I read them, a warm lick of fury burst in my gut. Fingers tightening on the device, my eyes fired to her. "*This* why you were crying?"

She blinked. "What?"

I held the phone out to show her what the screen seemed to be frozen on.

"Don't read that!" she yelled, rushing toward me with an outstretched arm.

Too late.

Even though the ground was flat and she was not wearing heels, she tripped, seemingly over air, and pitched forward. I slid forward, catching her once more around the waist while planting my feet into the pavement.

Her cheek hit my chest, her arms going around my waist to steady herself. The second she was stable, she jolted back, reaching for the phone. "Give me that!"

"No," I said, holding it up over my head, which was well out of her reach.

She jumped up toward it, and I tsked. "You're just going to fall on your ass again."

"Give me the phone."

Ignoring her, I continued to hold it up so I could read the rest of the exchange on the screen.

Damn. This dude was brutal.

Her fist caught me in the middle, forcing a rush of air out of me. I bent a little, my arm lowering, and she stole the phone from my hand and took off.

I was used to way harder hits than that, and I laughed as I grabbed a handful of the back of her coat and towed her back.

"Ugh!" she spat. "Who the hell are you? Let me go!"

I paused. *She doesn't know me.*

"The next time you punch a guy, don't tuck your thumb under your fingers. That's asking for a broken bone."

She stopped struggling. "What?"

I smiled. "If you're gonna punch someone, at least do it right."

"Whatever."

"Is that why you were crying?" I asked, gesturing to the phone with my chin.

"It's not your business."

"I'm making it my business."

She seemed startled by that assertion, and she fell quiet for a moment.

Reaching down, I took the phone and lit up the screen again. "You dating this jackass?"

"I thought you read the texts." She smarted off.

I focused back on the screen, but her hand came up, not taking it away but pushing it down. "Don't read it again."

The hurt in her voice made my protective instincts roar to life. It made me want to find the asshole who'd sent these messages and pound him into the ground.

"We barely dated, okay? But we aren't anymore."

"Because he broke up with you."

She nodded once. "Stood me up at this stupid football game."

Amusement lifted my lips. "What's wrong with football?"

"Besides being boring as hell?"

I laughed out loud, but it was cut short because I felt her watching me like she was really looking at me for the first time.

"Hi," I heard myself say softly.

I swear the air around us crackled as she visibly swallowed.

What was left of the tears on her cheeks caught my attention, and my heart turned over. "You must have really liked him."

She scoffed. "He was a complete asshole."

Can't say I was sorry to hear that. But still, the tears. "So what's this about, then?" I asked, swiping over the patchy wetness.

She shrugged.

"Is it because of what he said?"

Her eyes flared with emotion, and her lips rolled in on themselves. "I have to go," she said, side-stepping away from me.

As I stared at her retreating back, I realized something.

I wasn't ready for her to walk away. I wasn't done with her yet.

"It's not true," I called out.

She stopped for a few silent seconds. Body rotating, she faced me, our gazes colliding in the distance between us.

"Maybe it is," she whispered, fear and dejection thick in those three words.

Denial rose in me swiftly, so sure and steady it surprised me. "No. No way."

Her head lifted. The sound of her indrawn breath tightened my gut. "And how would you know? We just met. You know nothing about me."

I took a step toward her. And then another. "Oh, I know. I can feel it. The air practically vibrates with it."

She scoffed. "You're imagining things."

"I don't think so," I said, the distance between us growing small.

She took a step back, and another, until her back was pressed against the wall.

I flattened my hand beside her head, leaning to look at her from beneath heavy lashes. "You feel it too, don't you?"

She started to slip away, so I slapped my other palm on the wall, effectively boxing her in with my body.

"W-what are you doing?"

"I'm going to prove that asshole wrong."

"You can't!" she hollered, the protest echoing down the empty corridor. I knew just around the corner was a crowd of people and bleachers without any empty seats. The field filling up with amped-up players.

All of that was just background noise.

"Why can't I?" I purred, easing even closer.

A sob caught in her throat. "What if he's right?" she burst out, immediately slapping a hand over her mouth.

We both froze for a brief moment, and I watched embarrassment flood her expressive eyes, the emotion quickly rinsing away with a new rush of tears.

Humming, I pushed off the wall, reaching around behind me to pull off my shirt.

Her tearful eyes dropped to my chest, taking in my wide shoulders and well-earned muscle. Even though it wasn't necessary, the urge to puff out and make myself look even bigger befell me.

I settled for tightening my abs, feeling a rush of satisfaction when her eyes noticed. Gripping the shirt in one hand, I reached for hers with my other. She let me tug it away from her mouth and tuck it against her side.

Shifting my stance, I widened my legs so I didn't have to bend down.

"No more tears, kitten," I whispered, using the soft material of the shirt to soak up the old and new tears.

Her breathing hitched, but then so did mine when those beguiling blue eyes looked into me. Not at me. *Into* me. Something deep inside settled, and something else rose, wanting to envelop her.

"You gonna let me prove it?" I asked, dropping my stare to her lips.

Her tongue darted out to wet them, and my thumb traced the swell of her bottom lip. I leaned in, and her head tipped up. The hum of anticipation wrapped around us, the base of my spine tingling with awareness. She smelled sweet, a scent not often found where sweaty jocks ruled.

"Say yes, kitten," I whispered.

"Yes."

I covered her lips immediately, eyes sliding closed with my groan. Her mouth was wet and soft, and I sank in wholeheartedly, hoping like hell when I pulled away, my imprint would be left on her lips.

She made a light sound, and though she was soft and open, there was a slight hesitation, the small tremor of worry.

Fuck that.

I scooped her close, going at her like I did everything else, no holding back. My palms swallowed her face, tilting it just the way I wanted, and my body blanketed hers, shielding her from everyone but me.

Thumbs caressing her jaw, I deepened the kiss, licking over the seam of her lips and smiling into her mouth when they parted instantly to let me in.

"Good girl," I rumbled, stroking my tongue over hers. The heat of her mouth was addictive, coaxing another deep moan out of me. She was a craving I never knew I had, sweet satisfaction I never knew I needed. We lapped at each other, my body sinking farther into hers as I buzzed with the high I discovered on her tongue.

Lungs burning, I pulled back only slightly, refusing to take my lips completely off hers.

She made a sound, chasing after me, and smug satisfaction made me smile. "More," she whispered against me, and I swallowed down the plea.

Palming her hips, I lifted, and her legs wound around my waist, ankles locking at my back. Sliding my arms up her back, I pressed us harder into the wall, attacking her mouth all over again.

The sound of smacking lips, breathy sighs, and little moans filled the air around us. Her supple frame arched into me, arms circling my neck, fingers anchoring in my hair. I yearned to feel all of her against my chest, but the layers she had on robbed me of feeling her the way I burned to.

Pulling away from the wall, I started walking, not even needing to see, feet already knowing the way. Her fingers tightened in my hair, prickling my scalp with a pain/pleasure combo that had my footsteps quickening.

"Lose the gloves," I ordered between kisses and she quickly listened, tossing them a place where they'd never keep her hands from me again.

The locker room came into view, and I kicked out, making the door bang against the wall when it flew in.

Startled, her mouth popped off mine, hazy, owlish eyes seeking out mine.

"It's okay." I promised, stroking a hand down the back of her head that caught in her hat, blocking me from all those silky strands. Impatient, I ripped it off, tossing it aside.

Her honey hair looked like sunshine, the strands all mussed from the hat. As I combed my hands into the newly freed strands, my pulse jumped at the way they greedily wrapped around my fingers.

"Where are we?" she asked, her voice breathless.

"Locker room," I said, pulling her from around my upper body to stand her on the bench running between a row of lockers.

"What—" The question died away when I ripped the scarf from around her neck and then yanked her coat off just as fast.

She was wearing a red V-neck sweater that hugged her slim figure. Beneath it, her chest rose and fell rapidly.

She let out a squeak when I caught her around the waist, lifting her again, legs automatically winding around me as though she knew that was where they belonged.

Pressing her up against the row of lockers, I fused our mouths again, sucking her lower lip between mine. Grabbing her chin, I turned her face away, sliding my lips across her jaw and finally down to her neck. I kissed and sucked, the little purring noises she made only spurring me on. Sinking even lower, I pressed into her fragrant skin, latching on to the spot just above her collarbone and sucking with enough force it made her jolt.

Her surprise turned into a moan, and my hair filled her fingers as she kneaded my scalp, urging me on. By the time I unlatched, there was already a mark, and seeing it there turned my hunger into desperation. Reaching between us, I shoved up the fabric of her sweater and latched onto her breast over her bra.

Her back arched, pushing her soft flesh farther into my mouth. Growling, I yanked the cup down and imbibed her bare skin.

"Oh," she cooed, body falling slack against the locker as I sucked her nipple between my lips.

My laugh was husky, and it vibrated her skin, which made her thighs flex around my waist.

I nibbled and sucked, dragging a wet trail over to the other where I yanked away the fabric and did the same. In my jeans, my dick throbbed, so fucking hard it ached. My hips thrust toward her, but she was too high up for me to get the friction I needed.

Releasing her rosy breasts, I pulled back, letting her body slide down mine a bit as I thrust up. My rock-hard dick met her core, and I let out a groan. She gasped, hands settling on my shoulders, fingers digging into my flesh.

I took her lips again, this kiss sloppy and wet. I rocked into her again and again until my blood hammered so hard I felt like I was going to blow a vein.

All at once, I wrenched back, trying to find a shred of rational thought. It was no use because everything I looked at was through the foggy lens of desire, through the overpowering need to claim.

A light touch honed my focus, and I looked down to her slim fingers rubbing over my erect nipple, exploring the skin around it.

I hissed, and she paused. Feeling her eyes, I glanced up, taking in her flushed cheeks, swollen lips, and bruising hickey at the juncture of her neck.

Holding her stare, I pushed my chest closer, and her entire hand covered my pec. Biting into my lower lip, I watched her watch me as she backed away to pinch the nipple between two fingers.

My dick jerked and tried to rip its way out of my clothes.

"I want you so fucking bad." The truth of that statement made my voice gravelly and thick.

The hazy desire in her stare cleared just a little, making way for some doubt. Her small voice did nothing but make me want her even more. "Really?"

"Oh, fuck yes."

"You don't think... I'm cold?"

My laugh was hoarse as I palmed her hip, sliding my hand beneath her sweater to rub over her side. "Cold? God no, kitten. In fact, if you'd let me, I'd shove inside you and watch you melt all over my dick."

She stroked my chest again. "Okay."

A strangled sound forced its way out of me. "Okay?"

"Make me melt."

Chapter THREE

Meg

I didn't know his name.

I didn't know anything about the handsome stranger except that he set my insides on fire and made me welcome the burn. Never in my life had I had such an immediate, overwhelming reaction to anyone.

And I didn't even know his name.

"Kitten."

The rumbly quality of his voice and the way he beckoned me with that nickname made me care even less than I already did.

"Are you sure, sweetheart?"

I was absolutely sure. I was so sure I wondered how I ever doubted this feeling existed.

"Yes," I told him confidently, brushing my thumb against his erect nipple once more.

He growled, a sound that sent sparks of desire shooting between my legs. I wanted him so much it was almost painful, like my body was already clutching at him before he was even there.

Oh my God, I was going to have sex with him. I was going to hand this man my V-card.

My back left the lockers, and he crushed me to him, clutching me like I was something he'd just robbed from someone else. Something he had no right to but wanted so much he would fight to the death to keep it.

He started walking again as if I weighed nothing at all, and the bite of his fingers at my hips promised there would be marks.

Good.

Let there be evidence. Let there be proof I wasn't the ice queen I worried for so long I was.

A door banged open, slamming against the wall inside a vacant room. He strode confidently toward a table in the center of the space.

"PT room," he explained, setting me down on the edge.

His dark-blond hair was mussed, sticking out from my hands, strong jaw locked in concentration as he kicked off his shoes and popped the button on his jeans. His upper body was completely ripped with muscle, his biceps bulging as he shoved the clothes off his lower half.

For a moment, my eyes caught on the sharp, sexy V-shape muscles at his hips before realizing his cock had been set free.

I bit my lower lip, looking at it standing off his body, the tip flushed and glistening. It wasn't the first dick I'd ever seen, but honestly, it was the only one that made my stomach bottom out.

Instead of feeling nervous or even apprehensive, all I could do was feel my empty core spasm as I imagined what it would be like to have that shoving inside me and filling me up.

Suddenly impatient, I reached for my sweater, wanting to peel it away.

"Leave it," he demanded. I glanced up at the gruff order, and he shook his head while tossing away his clothes. "That's my job today," he said, strong thighs carrying him closer as his dick jutted out.

Despite the power in his body, he was gentle when he tugged off the sweater and bra. His eyes simmered with barely contained lust, and I squirmed as slick heat coated my center.

He filled his hands with my breasts, which were already hyper-sensitive and aching, and I moaned under my breath as he rolled and kneaded the burning flesh.

"You are fucking beautiful," he said, dragging his hands down to the button on my jeans.

Instead of watching what he was doing, he watched me as he popped the button. The sound of the zipper sliding down filled the quiet room.

"Lift up for me," he murmured, hooking his fingers in the waistband, and I tilted my hips so he could pull off my panties and jeans all at once. He knelt between my legs, working the fabric over my feet, dropping them onto the floor.

Instead of standing up right away, the pads of his fingers dragged up my calves like they were tracing some invisible path only he could see. I shivered and shook, the sensations he brought out in me so overwhelming I could barely breathe.

When he slid up the backs of my knees, I bit my lip to muffle the moans trying to break free.

Pausing in his exploration, he looked up, his green eyes finding mine. "Don't you keep in those sounds, kitten. I want to hear them. I want to know how much you like what I do to you."

I nodded, and he leaned in to nip and kiss my inner thigh. His body was wide and powerful, making me feel infinitely vulnerable beneath his touch. Just knowing I was at his mercy brought out a breathy moan as I clutched at the table.

Muscles rippling, he rose to his full height, pushing my legs wide, and then hooked his hands behind my knees.

A single tug and I fell back against the table, the mattress not very forgiving, but I was too far gone to care. Still holding on to my legs, he hooked them over his shoulders, which had me lifting my head to see what he was doing.

Sliding his hands beneath my ass, he lifted my lower half off the table and dove in.

My loud gasp echoed around the room as his tongue swiped all the way up my center. Shock warred with desire as he licked again and then again. My hands slammed onto the table, gripping and twisting in the thin sheet that topped it.

"Purr for me, kitten." He beckoned and then buried his face even deeper between my thighs.

I felt like a livewire, shocks of pleasure vibrating my entire body and making my muscles tight. This man was not shy, and he did not hold back. His tongue flirted with my throbbing clit and then unapologetically stabbed into my drenched opening.

The little mewling sounds I let loose seemed to spur him on, but I didn't make them for him. I made them because being silent was literally impossible. I was panting when he lifted his face, the top of his nose glistening with what I could only assume was me.

"Eyes on me," he demanded, and I looked.

His jade eyes held mine captive as he slipped not one but two fingers inside me, pushing deep and then crooking them up toward my belly.

My body bucked upward, and he pushed it down, forcing me still while he worked me from the inside out, doing things to my body I didn't even know could be done. I was straining, near exhausted, when he chuckled, the sound making my muscles clench. He withdrew from my body slowly, teasing, making me want to beg.

"Don't go," I whimpered, my inner muscles clenching as though they could force him to stay.

"Oh, I'm not done with you yet." He vowed, lowering my thighs from around his shoulders, giving my body a hard yank until my ass was practically off the table.

Startled, I pushed up onto my elbows at the same time he thrust in. My mouth opened, but no sound escaped. He grunted, that muscular body quivering, and his hand slapped the table beside me, low swears dropping from his lips.

A moment of panic stole over me as if perhaps I'd done something wrong. A rush of wetness pressed behind my eyes, and the extreme pleasure pulsing through my body warred with the sudden need to be good for him.

I didn't know how to say it. I was afraid to ask. What if he looked at me like I was a disappointment? What if he confirmed the things I'd always been told?

My hand crawled the short distance to his, tentatively covering it, my fingers curling around his.

His eyes flew to where I touched him, then whipped to my face. His pupils were blown, high points of his cheeks splotched with red. The way his lips glistened made me want to lick them and see what I tasted like on his tongue.

For all his power and confidence, he also knew how to be soft. His hand flipped over, enveloping mine. "You're so good for me. So tight. So wet."

I whimpered.

"That's a good girl." He praised more, hips thrusting, burying himself even deeper. Releasing my hand, he palmed my hips. "Wrap your legs around me, sweetheart."

I pushed up into a sitting position and locked my legs around him. Still holding me, he pulled back and then plunged in. The feel of his swollen tip made my head fall back and my inner walls clutch him tighter.

He groaned, his speed picking up as though he couldn't get enough.

"C'mere," he whispered, pulling me in so we were chest to chest, his arms wrapped around me in a hug.

He held me tight, lips playing at my temple while he fucked into me using a steady rhythm that put me in some kind of pleasurable haze. All that existed was his hard body and his equally rigid dick spearing me over and over again.

I clutched his back, digging my fingernails into his spine, silently asking for more. In reply, he lifted me off the table completely, dropping my body farther down on his dick and making me cry out.

A few steps and he had me against the wall, pumping up into me like he had all the stamina in the world. Hot ribbons of pleasure wove around me, bringing me higher and higher with every thrust.

His lips found mine, and we were kissing, my body sliding up and down the wall as he thrust. My stomach muscles clenched, my core pulsing as he drove me closer to the edge. My lips unlatched from his, head falling back as I slit my eyes open to stare at him.

"Look at you," he rumbled. "Melting over my dick just like I knew you would."

I could do nothing but grab his shoulders and grind down on him, crying out.

"That's it, kitten. Give it to me. Drench my dick with all that sweetness." As he said the words, he reached between us, pressing his thumb over my swollen bud and rubbing.

I splintered apart, my entire body going taut, arching off the wall as white light exploded behind my eyes, and the only thing left in existence was the pulsing pleasure ripping me apart and then putting me back together.

When it was over, I slumped forward into him, burying my face in the side of his neck. He crooned in his throat, stroking my back and whispering words of praise I didn't hear, only knowing the sweet sound of his voice.

I didn't even realize we'd moved until my back hit the table, eyes flying wide as he came over me. I smiled, drunk from passion and admiring the way his wide, muscled body blocked out everything else as his rigid dick slid back into my body.

I spread my legs wider and tilted my hips. His eyes flared, and he lost all control, pumping his hips in a wild rhythm. It didn't take long for the tendons in his neck to stand out, his shout filling the room as his body went rigid and his dick flexed and spasmed inside me.

He collapsed, using his elbows to keep most of his weight from crushing me. We lay there spent and breathing heavily as my body drank in everything he'd left behind. His cock slowly started to soften, and then he stirred, lifting enough to look into my face.

In a surprising gesture, he smiled softly, then pressed our mouths together for a tender kiss before pulling back. "Nothing icy about you at all."

Heat suffused my cheeks, and I found it insanely stupid that I would be blushing now.

"Are you shy?" he teased, eyes twinkling.

I averted my gaze, and he laughed.

Leaning in, his lips brushed my ear. "Don't be. That was incredible."

Turning my head, I kissed his cheek, which had surprise flashing through his eyes. Groaning, he shifted, his cock slipping out of me as he gracefully got off the table. Suddenly feeling very naked and exposed, I sat up, covering myself with my hands.

Carrying my clothes over, he chuckled. "Spoiler alert. I've already seen it."

I hit him with my sweater, and his chuckle turned into a full-blown laugh.

We pulled our clothes on quickly, the silence not uncomfortable. But the more it stretched, the more it sank in that I'd just lost my virginity in a locker room to an absolute stranger.

The nerves buzzing around in my stomach settled when he knelt at my feet, holding one of my shoes. Using his shoulder for balance, I let him slip it on and then repeated the action with the other.

Once they were on, he stood towering over me.

Looking a little sheepish, he scratched the back of his head. "So, ah, I actually have somewhere I'm supposed to be."

"Right," I said. Then I was horrified by a new thought.

He must have seen the emotion on my face because he frowned. "What?"

"You don't have a girlfriend, do you?"

His smile was wolfish. "No."

I started to relax, then straightened. "Wife?"

He laughed. "Definitely not."

Relaxing, I found my hat and tugged it onto my head. He opened the door and listened for a moment, making sure we were still alone.

"I don't even know your name," I blurted out.

The lopsided smile he bestowed upon me sent a flurry of butterflies all through my middle. "Does it matter?"

I thought about it for a moment. "No."

His eyebrows lifted his forehead. "No?"

I shook my head once.

"Why not?" he said, almost as though it suddenly bothered him that I didn't want to know.

Stepping close, I tilted my chin back so I could gaze up his body. "Because your name has got nothing on the way you just made me feel."

Something that looked a whole like awe brightened his face before a slow smile took over. "Good answer."

Back out in the tunnel, the crowd seemed louder than before. Music was playing, and from the sounds of it, the game had already started.

"Well, ah... thanks?" I said, suddenly very awkward. Up until a few moments ago, I was a virgin. I definitely didn't know how to handle a one-night stand.

Did this even count as a one-night stand? It wasn't even nighttime. *My God, I just had sex at a football game... in a public locker room!*

He laughed beneath his breath, and my stomach tightened, renewed desire flushing my limbs.

Definitely not an ice queen.

His feet shuffled forward, palm resting against the small of my back. Leaning in, he pressed a kiss to my forehead, and with it, a lump formed in my throat. "You staying for the game?"

I wrinkled my nose. "Ew. No."

He laughed. "See you around, kitten."

"Bye," I echoed, that lump in my throat swelling.

He started away, and all I could do was stand there and watch him go. The farther he got, the stronger the urge became to call him back.

But I had no right to do that.

"Hey," I called out anyway.

He glanced over his shoulder, and more butterflies erupted in my middle.

"Do you go here?"

His lips twitched. "No."

I could only nod. Of course he didn't. I would have noticed someone like him. It was good. Good I wouldn't accidentally run into my one-night stand on campus.

I'd probably never see him again.

The thought had my head whipping up, seeking him out one last time, but he was already gone.

I blew out a breath, not quite ready to make my way through the crowd to leave. Instead, I leaned against the wall and pulled my phone from my pocket.

The cracked screen lit up, and it was still stuck on the text from my ex. Smirking, I tapped the message box and smiled wide when it pulled up the keypad.

Just wanted to let you know that I am most definitely not an ice queen, I typed out. **I just needed someone hot enough to make me melt.**

Which, by the way... is not you.

Holding the phone up, I turned on the camera, tilted my head, and snapped a quick pic using the flash. When it appeared onscreen, I smiled.

Messy hair, swollen red lips, glassy, satisfied eyes, and a very impressive hickey right there above my collarbone.

It was a definite just-been-laid look.

I sent the photo.

I didn't expect a reply. I didn't even want one. It came barely moments later.

What. The. Fuck.

Unable to help myself, I typed out my final reply. **I just need someone who can handle my needs.**

I felt the phone vibrating with a reply as I was tucking it back into my pocket, but I ignored it and smiled.

"Kitten has claws."

Chapter Four

Noah

The second I walked onto the field, the attention of the entire stadium shifted to me. I was used to it. Expected it even.

Everyone here knew my name. Hell, they were chanting it over and over.

I always thought the ultimate rush was to have everyone know my name.

Not true.

Turned out the ultimate rush was to have someone not give a damn what my name was because the way I made them feel was bigger.

Waiving and smiling, I jogged out to my place on the sidelines.

Coach scowled. "Scott, where the hell have you been? You were supposed to be out here before kickoff."

"Sorry, Coach, people wanted some autographs. I couldn't get away."

"Save your bullshit for someone who believes it."

I grinned. "It's not bullshit. You know everyone loves me." To prove my point, I turned around and waved up at the bleachers. Within seconds, everyone was chanting my name again.

"See?" I said back at his side. "Was I supposed to ignore them when they approached? I didn't want to make you look bad."

Coach made a face. "Whatever." He slapped a clipboard and headset against my middle. "Get to work."

I did as asked, getting down to the reason I was here. I tried not to focus on not being the one out there scoring touchdowns. And when I felt the twinges of pain and unsteadiness in my knee, I also tried not to focus on that either.

Until, of course, I realized why my knee was so unsteady to begin with.

Her legs locked around my body as I pinned her against the wall.

Me driving into a warm, wet body.

Me feeling her nails bite into my skin.

Her moaning in pleasure as proof of it coated my dick.

Yeah, the ol' knee held up well today, and the little twinges of ache I was feeling now? Fucking worth it.

The dickbag who told that girl she was an ice queen had no game whatsoever. Me on the other hand? I had so much game it was my full-time job.

Maybe I should have gotten her number...

No. Not getting her number was the best thing. She made her dislike of football clear, and the sport was all I was. 'Course, the way she melted over my dick... maybe she liked football more than she realized.

It didn't matter anyway. I had no room in my life for anything besides hot hookups, which was exactly what that just was.

"Scott!"

My head shot up.

"Get your head in the game!"

I nodded brusquely and turned back to the field.

Chapter Five

Meg

There was an ache *down there.*
Nothing terribly painful, more like a dull throbbing sensation every time I moved. It filled me with awareness and, yeah, maybe a little awe. I'd just lost my virginity to a stranger.

A *hot* stranger.

I could still feel the way his tight muscles bulged and shifted beneath my hands. How he held me up with seemingly little effort while pounding into me skillfully.

Despite the soreness between my legs, I was languid and relaxed, intoxicated from the pleasure he dragged out of me.

I guess it did exist. Overwhelming and all-consuming passion. I didn't know why it took so long for me to find it, but man, it was worth the wait.

I didn't even feel guilty about the hookup. If anything, I was grateful and relieved. It was proof I wasn't an ice queen. Proof I wasn't broken.

I let myself into the apartment, sagging back against the closed door.

"Meg?" Kat's dark head popped up from the sofa, her eyes wide. "I thought you went to the game."

"He stood me up."

Kat sprang up off the couch, her dark hair fluttering around her shoulders. "What?"

I pushed off the door and shrugged. "We broke up."

On my way to the kitchen, I unwound the scarf and tugged off my coat, tossing them both on the small table. Reaching into the fridge, I grabbed a water, jolting a little when I shut the door to find Kat standing right behind it.

"You broke up with him?"

"Actually, he broke up with me. Said he needed someone who could take care of his needs."

Kat's mouth fell open. "He did not."

"Oh. He did. Want to read the texts?"

"He said it over text?"

I half smiled at her outrage. "Yep."

The cool water slid down my throat, and my tongue darted out to swipe over my lip. I could still taste him. Feel him.

Kat's fists landed on her hips as she stared at me suspiciously. "Why aren't you upset?"

"'Cause he's a jerk, and I'm better off?" I asked, taking another sip.

She made a sound. "Well, you aren't wrong." Then, "But still, usually, you'd be more upset. Why aren't you asking me to help hide his body?"

I laughed, turning to face her. "I appreciate your willingness to commit a crime with me, but he's not worth it."

She gasped. Really loud. Blue eyes wide, her hand flew up to her mouth.

"What?" I wondered.

She pulled her hand from her lips and pointed at my neck. "*What is that?*"

Tossing my hair behind my shoulders, I tugged the edge of my sweater farther away, giving her a nice clear view of the dark hickey nestled right behind my collarbone. "Oh, this?"

"*Oh, this,*" she mimicked. "Yes, bitch! That!"

"Just the hickey I got when I lost my virginity."

There was a beat of stunned silence. Then she started to squeal. Did I mention my bestie was super dramatic?

"OhEmGeeeeee." She hopped forward, grabbing my arms. "Are you serious?"

I nodded enthusiastically. "Yes!" I screeched back.

Fine. Maybe we were both excitable people.

We jumped up and down, holding hands for a minute before she stepped back, composing herself. "You mean to tell me you went to the football game to meet up with Brent, he stood you up, dumped you via text, and then you... hooked up with someone else?"

My stomach flipped hearing it all repeated back. "Pretty much."

"I need details. All of them." Grabbing my hand, she towed me out of the kitchen and to the living room and the couch. Blankets were piled all around it. The place where she'd clearly been sitting earlier was still indented.

"Sooo..." She started, dropping back into her seat and tugging a blanket over her lap. I sat on the other side, turning toward her and tucking my legs under me. "Who is it? Do I know him?"

"I don't even know him."

"What?"

"I was upset after those texts from Brent, so I ran off under the bleachers and literally ran into this guy."

"Was he hot?"

"Oh, girl. *So* hot."

"Details!"

I laughed. "Dirty-blond hair. Green eyes. Tall. Muscles for days."

"I'll allow it," she announced.

"Well, it already happened, so..."

"You seriously just ran into some guy and then had sex with him?"

"In the locker room."

Kat's brow furrowed, a look of concern taking over her features. "You wanted this, right? He didn't pressure you?"

"No!" I said instantly. I couldn't stand the idea that she would think badly of him. "Definitely not. I was all in."

She bit her lower lip. "Did you do it because of Brent?"

I sighed. "At first, I wanted to prove I wasn't the ice queen he accused me of being. But then I forgot about him completely. This guy was just so... melt-worthy."

"The look on your face has me convinced," Kat concluded, smiling. Leaning over, she tapped my knee. "So what's his name? When are you seeing him again?"

"I don't know his name, and he said he doesn't go here. So I probably won't see him again."

"You mean you just had incredible, amazing sex with some sexy man, and you didn't ask for his name or number?"

"No."

"Why?"

I shrugged.

"Unbelievable," she muttered.

Leaning my side into the cushions, I smiled. "You know, I was worried I couldn't feel like that, and now I know I can."

"I'm happy for you," Kat said sincerely. Then she smiled. "Clearly, you just have a type."

I laughed. "I guess so."

"Ooh!" Kat leaned forward to her laptop, which was open on the coffee table. "I was waiting for this part," she said, hitting the keys to turn up the volume on whatever she was watching when I came home.

I glanced at the screen, doing a double take. "You're watching the game?"

She turned sheepish. "I'm not watching for the football. I'm watching for him," she told me, pointing at the screen.

A photograph filled the screen, and my breath caught. Messy dark-blond hair, green eyes, strong jaws... lips that would match up perfectly with the giant hickey on my neck.

"Who is that?" I asked, voice strained.

Kat turned the volume even higher, the voice on the screen filling my ears.

...Lincoln U has a special guest on the field tonight, former Renegade, Noah Scott. Scott is one of the most recognizable tight ends in the NFL who sustained an ACL injury last season and is currently in recovery. When we caught up with Scott before to-

night's game, he told us he was starting to go a little stir-crazy off the field, and that's why he agreed to assist for a couple home games here at his alma mater. As you know, Scott was plucked right off Renegade turf by the NFL three years ago...

Insistent snapping went off in front of my face, and I blinked, staring at Kat's fingers.

Lashes still fluttering, I turned to face her. "Sorry, did you say something?"

"Why do you look like that?"

"Like what?" I parroted.

"Like you've seen a ghost."

"No ghost," I said, eyes straying back to the screen. The photo wasn't there anymore. Instead, they were playing footage of a bunch of people standing on the side of the field. The camera zeroed in on a face I'd only seen briefly but one I would never forget.

Noah Scott.

I tried the name out in my head. But it was thick on my tongue, so I didn't say it out loud. No. *No way.*

Likely following my stare, Kat turned back to the screen too. Her sigh was audible. "He's hot, right? I don't even like football, but I will watch that man walk around on the field any day."

I made a sound, part strangled, part squeak. All disbelief.

Kat grabbed my shoulder, giving me a light shake. "Meg?"

Still unable to tear my eyes away, I watched him push one ear of the headphones back and smile at someone beside him. My heart started to pound. "That's him," I said, hoarse.

"Him?" Kat repeated. "Who?"

I nodded, still staring. I couldn't not look. "That's who I hooked up with in the locker room."

A beat of silence.

Another.

Kat flung herself at the laptop, jamming her finger at the screen, poking the image of Noah Scott. "Him?"

I nodded.

"You're telling me that you had sex with Noah Scott? Noah Scott the NFL player?"

My mouth worked, but it took my voice a moment to catch up. Finally, I tore my eyes away from the laptop and looked at Kat. "I didn't know him. He was just a guy."

"Just a guy? How could you *not* know Noah Scott?"

"You know I hate football."

"So do I, but I still know who he is!"

I felt my cheeks flame. My eyes sought him out on the screen again, but he wasn't there. Instead, the cameras were focused on the game being played on the field.

I wrinkled my nose and turned back to my friend. "I didn't know."

"You're sure it was him?"

I nodded.

"Now I understand why you gave it up so easily," she mused.

My mouth dropped open, but then I started to laugh. Kat joined in, and we both fell into the cushions.

After a few minutes, we stopped laughing, and Kat grinned. "I'm jealous."

"I really didn't know."

Her eyes turned curious. "And now that you do?"

I shook my head. "It still doesn't matter. To me, he isn't Noah Scott, former student at our college and some big-time NFL player. To me, he's just..." I trailed off, remembering the way his lips felt against mine, the way my body stretched around his just right.

"He's just what?" Kat asked when I was lost in the memory too long.

"To me, he's just the guy who finally made me melt."

Kat sighed wistfully.

"But maybe let's keep this between us."

She nodded. "Girl, no one would believe you anyway."

I giggled. It didn't matter because I knew. And even if it was just a one-time hookup... it was one I would never forget.

Want to read more from Cambria Hebert? You can check out her library on her website, www.cambriahebert.com.

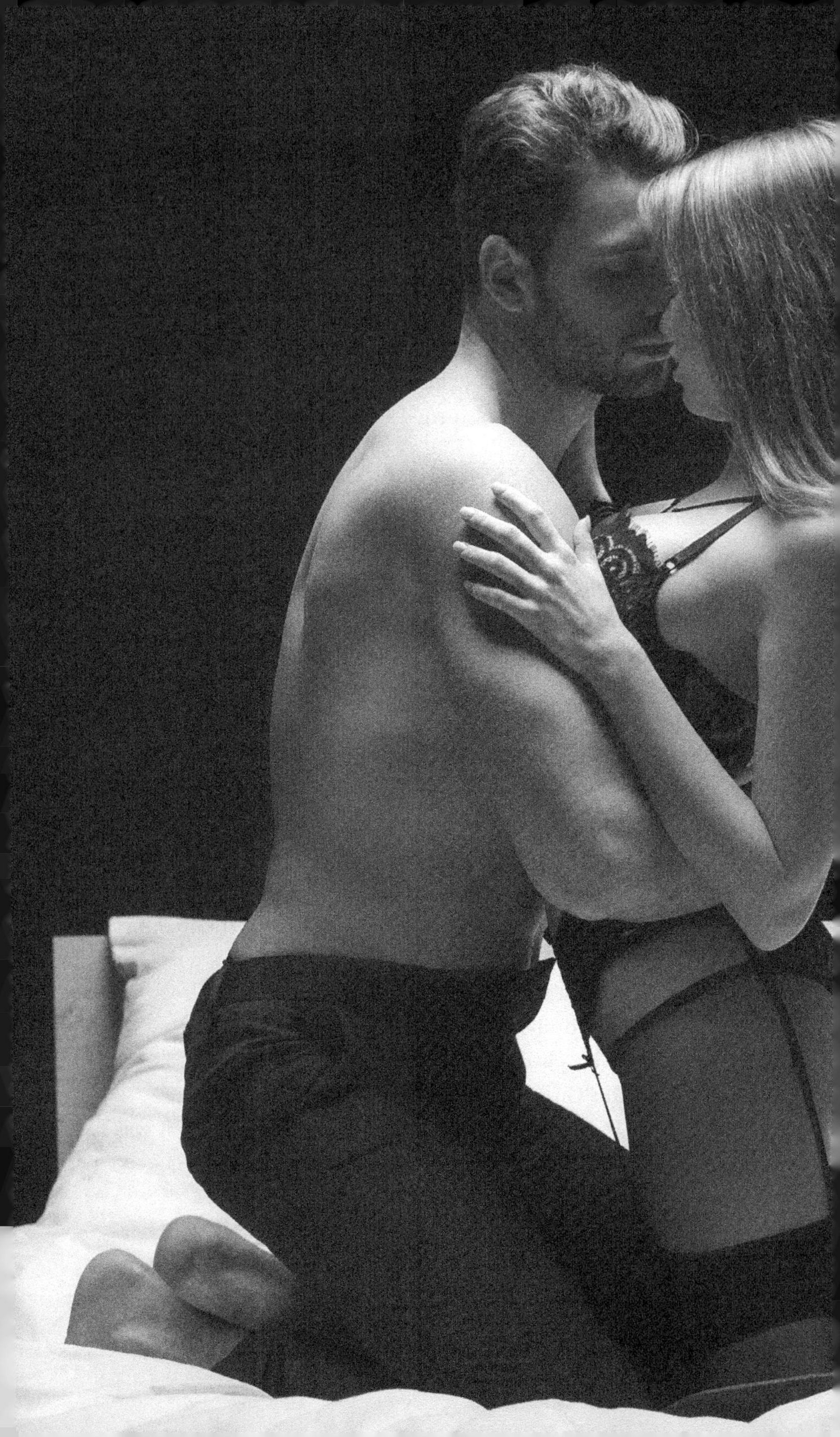

Perfect HOOKUP

CARY HART

Chapter ONE

Finley

"I still can't believe you're here." Charlee, my best friend who abandoned me for her insta-family, pulls me in for what feels like the millionth hug since I showed up at her house this morning.

"Well, believe it, because we're up next." I point to the line at the ice cream stand dying down.

"Oh yeah." She scans the park for Jillian, her husband's five-year-old stepdaughter she adopted on her wedding day. "Jilly!" Charlee calls out. "I scream."

Jillian stops what she's doing and spins around. "You scream." She takes off running toward us.

"We all scream..." Charlee laughs.

Jillian skids to a stop. "For ice cream!" she yells, practically out of breath.

"I love that you have this." I can't hide the smile plastered across my face.

"Me too!" Digging into her diaper bag, she pulls out a wet wipe and hands it over to Jillian before checking on Livie, her newborn daughter, who's been asleep in her stroller since our little walk through the park. "Being here is good for the soul." Charlee stands up straight, stretches her arms above her head, and flashes me a smile. "You know, you could always—"

"Don't even go there." I hold up my hand, stopping her before she gives me another lecture on my dating life. Ever since she moved to Mason Creek, she's tried to get the rest of us to follow.

"Just because you've found your perfect cowboy in Mason Creek doesn't mean the rest of us will."

"Look at Joey!" she defends. "She seems to be fitting in just fine."

She's not wrong. Joey, her younger sister, does seem to be happy, but our home back in Lavender Falls hasn't been kind to the Evans family. Any place would be better than there.

"I have responsibilities and..."

"Look who came to see me," a blue-haired lady behind the window interrupts. "My little Jillybean."

"Hattie!" Jillian runs up to the window and stands on her tippy toes, barely able to see over the counter. "I want a large cotton candy cone with sprinkles, please."

"Why don't we do a cup? That way you don't get so messy."

"But, Mommy, I like to lick it." Jillian frowns.

"I do too," a deep voice rumbles from behind me, thankfully out of earshot. I twist around to sneak a peek at the owner of the panty-melting voice and can't help but stare. He's tall, tan, and gorgeous. His deep blue eyes light with mischief, knowing I heard what he said. And the way his charming smile grows, I'm pretty sure he knows I'm thinking about his little comment. He looks like lemonade on a hot sunny day, guaranteed to be refreshing.

Charlee looks between me and the handsome stranger Charlee definitely needs to introduce me to. Like now.

"Oh—hey, Toby." Charlee reaches over and pinches my side.

"Hello," he greets her, his baby blues staying locked on mine.

"What about me?" Jillian squeezes between me and Charlee, standing at Toby's feet. "Gonna say hi to Jillybean?" She tilts her head all the way back, squinting from the sun beating down on us, batting her little lashes. *In a few years, her daddy will have to lock her away.*

He pauses, waiting for me to say something, but I stay silent. Can't say I've ever met a man who made me speechless. *But he's not talking either*, I tell myself, like it's supposed to be comforting. *Get it together.*

"Down here," Jillian pipes up, tugging on the bottom of his black t-shirt.

I owe this kid a bagful of her beloved suckers for breaking up our awkward silent stare off.

Toby clears his throat. "Hey, kiddo!" He squats down until they're eye to eye. "You know, if you get a cup, you'll be able to play and eat, but if you get a cone, you have to eat it before you go back to the playground."

"Did Mommy tell you to say that?" Jillian eyes her mom before glancing back up to Toby.

"Nope." He shakes his head back and forth. "And you know what else?" He boops her nose.

Jillian giggles. "What?"

"You get more sprinkles." Toby leans in, whispering loudly. "Hattie only does it for people she really, really likes."

"She does?" She looks back at her mom then to Hattie. "You do?"

"I sure do!" Hattie agrees, waving her over.

"Gimme a cup, please." Jillian goes back up to the window to watch. "With lots and lots and lots of sprinkles."

"Coming right up." Hattie pulls down a cup and begins to fill it.

"And can you put some gummy worms, Oreos, and lots of hot fudge on it?"

"Jilly, no." Charlee sighs, rushing up to the window, leaving me and this Toby guy all alone.

"She's cute." Toby stands, crossing his arms over his chest, and I can't help but watch the way the material stretches across his toned chest. I try not to like my lips as I imagine what's underneath.

"Yeah, so cute." My eyes dart up to his, and I mentally wipe the drool from my mouth.

How pathetic am I? Here I am standing in front of Twisted Sisters in the middle of a park, surrounded by kids, dreaming about licking the flavor of the day off every inch of his body.

Get a grip!

Say something else. Ask him if he's from here. What his favorite restaurant is. Anything to take the attention off me foaming at the mouth like a woman who hasn't gotten laid in weeks...okay, months.

"Finley, whatcha getting?" Charlee butts in, saving the day.

"Just whatever, but in a cup." I wave her off, ready to try to carry on a civilized conversation with Toby. Instead, the other window slides open.

"I can help the next person in line." Hazel, Hattie's twin, with fiery red hair and lips just as bright, peeks her head through the opening. A slow smile spreads across her face when she spots Toby. "Well, hello, dear! Come over here and let me see that handsome smile of yours."

As if we weren't having a conversation, Toby walks right past me, heading to talk to Hazel. I mean, technically he was talking and I was drooling, but still. We were in the middle of something.

Oh well!

I shrug it off and move to pay for the ice cream as Charlee maneuvers the stroller through the grass to a nearby picnic table where she can still watch Jillian while she plays.

"Do you take debit?" I pull out my card from the back of my phone.

"Put that away, sweetie." Hattie waves me off. "It's already been taken care of."

"You didn't have to—"

"I didn't," she cuts me off. "That handsome feller over there did."

I don't even have to look. I know exactly who she's talking about: Toby.

Picking up my cup, I lift it in the air and turn toward him, but I don't have to get his attention. He's already watching me. "Thank you," I mouth.

He nods.

I can't believe it. He bought us ice cream, I thank him, and he just nods. Who does that—especially after what just happened between us? Okay, maybe it was one-sided, but he could've at least said you're welcome.

Whatever.

I spin around to make my getaway and come face to face with the trashcan, almost knocking it over. Here I was trying to make a stealthy getaway and now all eyes are on me.

"Oops." I shrug, playing it off like it wasn't a big deal, and shove a big bite of huckleberry ice cream in my mouth. "So good." I point to the cup, talking with my mouth full, looking even more ridiculous.

"What was that about?" Charlee is sitting down on a bench rocking the stroller back and forth while she licks her cone.

"I don't even know." I plop down beside her. "I need to lay off the self-help books and podcasts and focus on my reality and how pathetic it is."

"You are far from pathetic," she tries to reassure me, but my attention is on Toby as he walks by, licking his ice cream cone.

"Ladies."

I'm all but fanning myself. "See? Pathetic."

"You know what you need?"

"I'm not moving here," I blurt out, knowing exactly where she's going with this. Move here, find a cowboy, fall in love, live the midwestern dream.

I can't.

I won't.

As much as I would like to be able to pick up and move, it's not for me. I have responsibilities. My parents need me. Either I step up and start taking an interest in wanting to run their business or they have to sell. They worked too hard to make all their dreams come true for their kids just to sell them off.

At the same time…their dreams aren't mine. And that's something that have to realize as well.

"You need to relax, and I can't believe I'm saying this, but…" She bites her lip as she shakes her head. "You need to find someone to hookup with. Release all that tension building up inside you." She nudges my shoulder.

"Oh wow!" I snort. "Channeling your inner Vanny, I see," I say, referring to our friend who gives zero fucks about anything in life. If she thinks it, you'll know it. It's why we love her.

"Maybe—"

"Definitely."

"Remember the podcast Vanny sent the group a few weeks ago?"

"Nope." I take a bite of my ice cream before it begins to melt. "She sends so many."

"It was the Hotline Hookup one where Dr. Feelgood talked about having the perfect hookup." Charlee's lip curve into a wicked smile.

I know exactly what podcast she's talking about—the one that made me sign up for the dating application. Except, instead of landing a booty call, I paired up with her brother, of all people. Thankfully, we were both able to laugh it off, but if I can't pull a hookup in the small town of Lavender Falls, Georgia, I'm sure as hell not going to find one here in Mason Creek.

"I'm guessing by those wheels turning up here—" Charlee taps the side of my head, "you know exactly what I'm talking about. The question is why haven't you tried it?"

"Who says I haven't?" I toss my cup into the nearest trashcan and watch Jillian as she goes down the slide for the millionth time.

"Want to talk about it?"

"Nope."

"Then let's all go out tonight."

I give her the side-eye knowing damn well she isn't going anywhere. That girl is a homebody, and Livie is barely three months old. She won't leave her.

"Okay," I drag out for dramatics.

"I'm serious. Who knows when the next time I'll have you, Joey and Vanny here at the same time. I'll pump and Grady can stay home with the kids."

I lean back to get a good look at my friend. She's saying one thing, sounding like she wants to go, but her body language is telling a different story. Of course, if I had a man like Grady Jackson to go home to, my body would be saying the same thing.

"Why don't we just order in pizza and have a slumber party at Joey and Cole's? Cole can hang with Grady and the kids." It seems like the more logical solution since Cole and Grady practically live next door.

"No way! We're going out and you are going to find someone to hookup with."

"Whoa!" I hold up my hands. "You had me at going out, but hooking up wasn't part of the plan."

"It totally is. It's *the* plan. The perfect one."

"Says who?"

"Dr. Feelgood."

"Gah!" I groan. "I don't even have anything nice to wear. I kind of packed on short notice. I mean, it's Montana."

"No excuses." Charlee stands.

"I'm not going to win this, am I?"

"Nope!" Charlee calls for Jillian who hugs each and every one of her friends before running toward us. "What, Mommy?"

"It's time to go, sweetie."

"How come?"

"We need to help Finley find something to wear."

Jillian scans me from head to toe before her eyes get as big as saucers. "Can I be the Fairy Godmother?"

"You sure can." Charlee hugs her daughter to her side.

"Mommy, you can be Gus and Vanny can be Jaq."

I laugh. "Who can I be?"

Jillian jumps onto the bench and stands behind me, gathering my hair and piling it onto my head. "You get to be the princess!"

"I do!" I turn around and tickle her sides, causing the sweetest little giggle to escape.

"But you have to find your prince before you come home...or your dress falls off."

Charlee leans in and whispers, "See? Even the kid knows."

"Shut your mouth." I playfully smack her arm.

"Let's go, guys! I have to go home and find my wand." Jillian hops down. "Bippity, bobbity, boo!" she repeats as she skips to Charlee's SUV.

"I guess we need to let the girls know the plans."

"Done and done." Charlee smirks.

"Great," I mumble. "What could possibly go wrong?"

"Nothing." Charlee looks over her shoulder, obviously having supersonic hearing.

"Or everything."

Perfect fairytale…perfect hookup. Same difference, right?

Chapter TWO

Toby

"Toby—earth to Toby." Max, a bartender at Pony Up I've been shadowing the past few weeks, snaps his fingers.

"What, man?"

"What's going on with you tonight?" He eyes me suspiciously.

"Not a damn thing, why?" I lie to us both.

"You've been staring out that window while wiping the same spot for the past fifteen minutes."

I glance down and notice he's not wrong. "Shit." I spin around and toss the rag into the sink.

I've been here for weeks, living, breathing, and learning the small-town life—all for a lead role as a bartender on a new small-town series, and yesterday, my agent broke the news that they decided to go with a bigger name to pull in viewers and up the ratings.

Which fucking sucks, but the silver lining—if you can call it that: there's a slim chance I might be up for a different role depending on the storyline. So, I decided to stay put. And after today, I'm glad I did.

Or I might not have met Finley. She's not from around here. That, I know because there is no way in hell I would have not remembered those hazel eyes and the way she was nervous and obviously bothered by me. The feeling's fuckin' mutual.

Lucky for me, Grady called up here letting us know Charlee's stopping in at some point tonight with her sister and friends. He gave me strict orders to give them whatever they want, but if I think they're getting out of control, to water down the drinks. It's something we normally do anyway, but my word gave him peace of mind. I get it.

"All right." Max clasps my shoulder. "I get it. You don't feel like talking, but if you ever do, I'm here." He stares at me for a moment before the bell chimes and his eyes fly up behind me. "Holy fuck." He pats my back. "Turn your ass around. The woman of my dreams just walked through the door."

I hang my head. I don't even have to turn around to know exactly who he's talking about. Charlee's friend, the sexy-as-sin brunette from Twisted Sisters.

"Cover me." Max tosses his towel and starts to walk off.

"Hold up." I grab his elbow.

"What the fuck, man?" Max growls, looking between my face and my hand. "You got three seconds—"

"She's mine," I clip back.

"Shut up." He eyes the girls as they find a table within bar view. "What's her name?"

"Finley." Charlee never introduced us, but as soon as she hollered out her name, I knew it was one I would never forget.

Max narrows his eyes. "Is she why you were watching the doors earlier?"

"Yep." I have no reason to lie. I grab a couple beers and head toward their table.

"And she's yours?"

I spin around, holding the longnecks up in one hand. "She will be." I wink.

Max mumbles something before he turns his attention back to the bar.

"Looky here!" Someone grabs the beers from behind me. "It's as if you read my mind, Tobes!"

"Cole," I grumble.

"Just put these on my cousin's tab."

"Which one? I see at least five possible contenders."

Cole shrugs. "Eeny, meeny, miny, moe it." Cole twists the top off and takes a swig. "Ahhh, now that's a what I call a Cole one."

He watches me as he takes another pull. "Seriously?" He drops his hands to the side. "Come on...cold one—Cole one. It's totally punny."

Normally, Cole's antics have me rolling, but this little pit stop makes me wonder if it's more of a cock block.

"Not laughing," I deadpan. He's like the monkeys at the zoo. If you don't engage, they'll stop showing off.

"Then you need this more than me." He shoves the beer back into my hand. "Drink up, buddy."

"I'm on the job."

"I won't tell." Cole winks as he walks back over to the pool tables, and one of the girls from Charlee's table heads my way.

"Hey, sexy bartender friend...can I get a word?" A sassy brunette tries wraps her arm around my shoulders, but since she's about a foot shorter than me, she fails miserably.

"It's Toby."

"I'm Vanny." She walks us over to the bar. "Now that we got the pleasantries out of the way, let's get down to business."

"What's that?"

"I'm going to ask you for drinks, hit on you, flirt with you from across the room, and I'm going to need you to play along."

"Why?"

She turns us around so I can see Finley and the rest of the girls at the table. "You see the girl with the same color hair as me?"

I've been watching her since she walked through the door.

"Yeah."

"Good..." She wiggles her finger for me to come closer. "I need you to fuck her."

If I had been drinking, I would have just spit it out everywhere.

"You what?" I ask again, not sure I heard her right.

"You heard me. Finley is an out-of-towner. She needs a no-strings attached night, if you know what I'm saying. I could explain why this would be beneficial for you as well, but the way you're watching her instead of listening to me, I feel like this won't be a problem for you."

"You want me to hookup with your friend, and that's it?"

"Yes!" She grabs ahold of my face with both hands and forces me to face her. "The girl needs to be sex-ed up. And Charlee—"

"What does Charlee have to do with this?" Was the married mom of two the mastermind behind this whole proposal?

"Nothing. Well...everything. She saw the way you and Finley threw sparks at each other. Actually, she said flames, but I didn't believe her until now." Vanny backs up a couple feet and cocks her head to the side. "You like her. Like really like her."

"I don't know her," I admit. It's the truth, even though something about her seems familiar.

"It's called chemistry, Toby. Can't fight it, and sure as hell can't deny it. Got it?" She walks right past me, grabbing my hand along the way. "Now, get me some tequila and lemons, bitch. I'm about to offer you Finley up on a silver platter."

"Enough." I tug away. "I don't fuck with drunk girls."

"Who says she's getting drunk? The tequila is for me—the jealousy is for her." Vanny winks while grabbing a bottle from behind the bar, much to Max's protest, and helping herself to the lemons. "Add this to Grady's tab and get ready to enjoy the show." She snags a tray off the counter and balances it better than most waitresses.

"Shit show," I call after her, running a hand through my hair. She flips me off.

Everything about this screams it's a bad idea, but if this fast-forwards my plans with Finley, I'll take it.

Chapter THREE

Finley

"Ladies...it's time to get *fucked* up!" Vanny carries a tray of shots and a bowl of lemons.

Shit. The last time I got fucked up with Vanny, I ended up naked in a hot spring, but maybe this time won't be so bad—especially since we have mama bear, aka Charlee, chaperoning and she's no drinking.

"What's this?" I take a glass, sniffing the contents.

"No way. I'll pass." Charlee pushes her glass toward Joey. "Pumping and the hangover isn't worth it."

Joey shrugs. "Whatever. More for me."

"Here." Vanny slides a glass toward Charlee. "Yours is lemonade."

"Bring it in." Vanny holds her shot out. "What do we say, ladies? When life gives you lemons..."

"Slice 'em up and drink tequila!" we all chant in unison.

"That's right!" Vanny laughs. "Cheers to our last night here!"

We all set our glasses down and get ready.

"On the count of three—lick, salt, shot, suck." Vanny looks around. "Got it?

I don't bother responding. I just give her the middle finger salute and prepare for what could literally be an unforgettable night.

"Three!" she yells.

I slam down my glass and wait for Joey to take her second.

"Go, Joey! Go, Joey! Go, Joey!"

Joey sucks the last lemon, sticks out her tongue, and shakes her head, scrunching up her face. "Whew!"

"What a way to start the night." Vanny stands, flips her chair around, and sits back down. "I can't even remember the last time all four of us got together."

Charlee looks between me and Joey, jabbing her thumb in Vanny's direction. "Is she being serious right now?" She swivels in her seat. "Was my wedding that forgettable?"

"Doesn't count." Vanny sucks on another lemon. "You were knocked up."

"Ohhh!" Joey and I nod in agreement.

"She isn't wrong," Joey points out.

"It was the hot springs and the blackberry gin." I point to Vanny. "Remember when Grady walked up and she was buck-ass naked?"

Charlee holds up her hand, pointing to her two-carat princess cut diamond. "He put a ring on it, didn't he?"

"No, no, no, no, no!" Joey shakes her head, waving her hands around.

"Beg your pardon?" Charlee sits back in her seat, daring her to say otherwise.

"No...not that. We all know you're Mrs. Sexy Cowboy." She waves her off. "What ya'll forgot was I didn't get to partake in your naked wilderness adventure." Joey slaps her sister's leg. "I was at home cleaning up the wedding aftermath. No thanks to Donovan."

"You know what?" Charlee leans forward. "I think we should thank Donovan."

"No way." Vanny stands. "I'm getting another round of shots—on Mr. Sexy Cowboy." She hollers at Toby, "Hey you! Hot bartender guy!" I want to slink down in my chair, but I don't. Because Toby's eyes dart up to our table and land straight on me... me! Not Vanny who continues to bark out orders. "Another round—make them doubles." She walks off to the bar and instead of watching my very sexy friend strut her way up. He watches me watch him.

Joey snaps in front of my face clearing me from my Toby induced fog, while her and Charlee carry on their debate.

"I'm serious, though," Charlee continues. "If I'd never walked in on him, I might have actually married him."

"Yeah, I don't want to picture that," I agree.

"Then I would have never found Mason Creek, Grady, or my babies." Charlee tears up. "Who I already miss, by the way."

Joey pats her hand. "Everything happens for a reason, sis."

I need to remember this. Everything does happen for a reason and maybe there is a reason for me to be here tonight and maybe that reason is Toby... Toby... *Shit!* I don't even know his last name.

"That it does," Charlee agrees. "So, what's this I hear about you signing up for a dating app?"

"Really?" I feign being shocked because there is no way in hell that I'm going to give up my experience for their entertainment.

"Don't even say another word *Looking for Lust*."

Busted!

"What?" My eyes are so wide I feel like they're about to pop out of my head. "How did you...?" I shake my head. "Never mind. Let's just pretend that didn't happen. Stuff it back in the closet, I say."

Joey smirks. "I think that closet's getting full, don't you?"

"She's got a walk-in." Charlee snorts.

"One day, you'll have to clean it out," Joey reminds me.

Not going to happen, but I'll play along.

"Until then, I'll continue to be a packrat of secrets."

"What's this about secrets?" Vanny carries half a bottle of tequila and a root beer in one hand, and a bowl of lemons in the other.

"Apparently nothing." Joey rolls her eyes, pointing to me.

"Gotcha." Vanny hands Charlee the root beer. "I thought you would like to play pretend." She nods to Charlee's boobs. "Can your milkers handle that?"

"Shut up." She takes the bottle and twists off the top. "Thanks."

Joey reaches for the bottle of liquid courage. "Are we drinking from the bottle now?"

"Nope!" Vanny smacks Joey's hand away. "I have plans for this. In the meantime, let's talk about you and your many dates."

The girls go on and on about all Joey's dates. Something about a momma's boy, being stood up and who knows what else. I'm not really paying attention because Toby and the other bartenders are talking to some gorgeous blonde in a sexy red dress who is obviously giving all the bartenders an eyeful by leaning her silicone inflated boobs on the counter. However, Toby surprises me. He takes a step back and his enchanting blue eyes land on me.

"Bullshit!" Joey shouts.

"What in the world...?" I mumble as Joey reaches across the table, snags the bottle of tequila out of Vanny's hands, and downs a shot...or maybe two.

"I'm going to need this if I'm going to deal with you three tonight." Joey takes the bottle with her as she plops back down in her seat.

"No need to get your panties in a wad." Vanny reaches over the table and yanks the bottle back. "We just think maybe there's a reason you haven't felt like sharing."

"Obviously," Joey eyes her sister, "I haven't found my perfect cowboy."

"Yet!" Charlee adds.

"What she said." I nod, feeling the weight of the alcohol kicking in.

"Yeah...who cares about that? I want to know if you touched some penises. Yes, that's plural." Vanny leans closer. "Have you been a naughty girl, Joey?"

I giggle and wait for the show to begin.

Joey scoots her chair back. "I think it's time for a potty break."

"Not a chance—spill the beans."

Joey scans the area before signaling for us to move in closer.

The sound of four chairs scooting against the concrete floor is like nails on a chalkboard. Joey waits for us all to gather around before she fills us in on the dating drama.

"Jimmy—super sweet, just not my type. Remi stood me up. Said he was nursing a hangover. Perry liked to talk about his BMW and his pet pig, Judy. That one was a hard pass for me. Then there was Nick. He was totally my type and ghosted me after our date.

No penises were involved. The most I've gotten is a kiss on the cheek."

"Lame." Vanny gathers our glasses and opens the bottle.

"Don't worry, Joey," I pat her leg, "the process works, but it can take a while."

Joey turns toward me, her mouth opening then quickly closing. She's dying to ask me about my profile she somehow found but fills me in on her next date instead.

"Well, there's this guy I'm seeing next week: Caden Cross. He's taking me to my first rodeo."

"That'll be fun!" Charlee smiles. "I remember when Grady took me to my first one." She gets that faraway look in her eyes.

Vanny yawns. "Here we go."

"Never date a bull rider!" I offer up some free advice.

"Why?" Joey cringes.

"Because they consider eight seconds a good ride." I burst out laughing, giving myself a mental pat on my own back.

"I'll drink to that." Vanny chuckles. "Okay, who wants to play blind shot?" Vanny pours us each a glass, minus Charlee.

I probably shouldn't agree to do this, but maybe it wouldn't be a bad thing. A little liquid courage never hurt anyone—especially someone looking for the perfect hookup.

I look over at Joey, and she shrugs. "Yeah, why not."

Vanny seems pleased with our answer.

"Okay, this is how it's going to work. You're going to take a shot then turn around and suck a lemon out of some random dude's mouth." Vanny claps. "Sounds fun, right?"

"Yeah, it does." I scan the room, knowing exactly who I'm going to pick. "Let's find me a cowboy." I know exactly who I'm going to pick. The sexy bartender pouring a row of rainbow shots.

"I'll be the guy finder." Charlee stands and runs to the bar.

"Where's she going?" Finley asks.

"I hope to grab Toby." Vanny winks, and jealousy rears its ugly head. "Have you seen that guy's ass?"

Yeah, that did it. I want to run up there and lick him just so I can claim him as mine.

What's wrong with me?

Charlee comes back, waving three handkerchiefs. "Put these on."

"Charlee..." Vanny stomps her foot, "why do you always have to be in charge? You're changing the rules."

Charlee tosses me one and mouths, "I got you."

God, I love that girl.

"Because I have a baby at home—and I'm sober. Enough said." She hands the other handkerchiefs out. "Like I was saying, put these on and grab your shot. I'll find you a guy and explain the rest when I get back." She leaves the table, going on her manhunt.

"Are we really trusting her to do this?" I watch Charlee make a beeline to the bar knowing she has my back.

"Who cares?" Vanny already has her blindfold on and shot in hand. "I'm ready."

"I mean...why not?" Joey picks up the cloth and ties it around her head.

"Fine. I guess it's not a big deal." I crane my neck to see where Charlee went. Toby is still behind the bar and she's nowhere in sight.

Sighing, I give in, cover my eyes with the red and white material, and wait. "This is crazy," I say to no one in general.

"I know! I like it," Vanny chimes in.

"Okay, ladies—are you ready?" Charlee is back, but none of us speak up.

"Gentlemen, like I said before, you're not allowed to speak. These ladies are a little toasted and one-hundred percent single. Hint, hint." Charlee giggles.

"I want to go first!" Vanny raises her hand.

Of course she does.

"Nope. Your game, my rules," Charlee orders. "You'll all go at the same time. I'll place the guy directly behind you and he'll reach around. You will lick his hand, he will salt it, you lick it, take a shot, then spin around and suck the lemon."

"That doesn't make sense," Vanny argues. "What if I suck his nose?"

"Point taken," Charlee agrees. "Guys, it will be up to you to guide them."

"Sounds good," a sexy familiar voice says from behind me.

"Toby!" Charlee whines.

"Wait? Toby's here." Vanny gets excited. "Dibs."

Not today, sister.

"My rules, Vanny," Charlee reminds her.

Yes they are!

"Okay, ladies! Ready, set, shot!"

Charlee is like our personal referee, barking out, "Lick, salt, suck, shot, suck." We follow her orders...maybe a little too well. The moment my mouth is on skin, I lick and taste something familiar. Maybe pineapple from those rainbow shots earlier. But before I can get another taste the hand is pulled away on a groan.

I pout puffing out my lips. "No fair."

The not so stranger chuckles.

Next comes the salt. I wait for the mystery hand to be placed back at my lips before I suck, swirling my tongue to get every last grain, not caring that I'm probably making a fool of myself making out with a stranger's hand.

Next comes the tequila. I throw it back, ignoring the burn as warm hands spin me around. They move from my waist to my face, guiding my mouth. I smell the lemon before I taste it. All my senses are on overload, and my guy is taking his sweet time, drawing out the mystery. Two can play this teasing game.

My tongue darts out as I lean in and run it along the edge of the lemon, tracing his lips. When he exhales sharply, I feel it on my tingling lips. Before I can suck the lemon, his mouth moves against mine as the lemon falls between us.

He moans.

I gasp.

The kiss was over... just a tease.

"I've been wanting to do that all night." Toby whispers as he pulls off my blinded and heads back to the bar after kissing me speechless.

Turning, I find Joey wiping her mouth and a blindfolded Vanny sucking face with a very shocked Jase, who finally gives in to the kiss.

What the hell was Charlee thinking?

"Charlee!" Joey shouts.

I don't know why she's acting so upset. Those two obviously are into each other. Plus, he's easy on the eyes. It's not the worst thing in the world to be kissing Cole Jackson.

"Sorry, Joey." Charlee fights back a laugh. "Call it the roommate experiment." She flashes Cole a smile before giving Joey a hug. "Grady's here. I've gotta go before Vanny comes up for air and kills me." She kisses Joey on the cheek and runs out the door.

"And you..." she whispers to me. "Two words: Bartender Toby."

"I don't know..."

"Maybe you don't, but I do. He's taking off in an hour and has graciously volunteered to take you home."

I should care that my best friend is pimping me out to a townie, but I don't. Especially after being kissed into orgasmic bliss just a few minutes ago.

"Charlee, what if—"

"You can thank me tomorrow." She blows me a kiss before turning on her heels and running straight for the door.

"Jase, hundred dollars says you can't hit the bullseye with one of those blindfolds on," Cole hollers to Grady's cousin, who is making out with Vanny.

Jase finally ends the kiss, pulling off Vanny's blindfold. I'm not the only one shocked. Her eyes are as wide as saucers. "Hey, Georgia." Jase's wicked smile earns him a death glare.

She reaches between them and shoves him back hard. "Asshole," she hisses, then turns around and downs another shot. He walks away without saying a word, and Cole just shrugs.

"Where's Charlee?" Vanny scans the room. "I'm going to kill her."

"Calm down, Fido." Cole picks up the bottle of tequila. "This party is moving to my house."

"Not so fast." Joey sets the bottle down. "We don't have enough room."

"You can have my bed. They can have yours."

"Where will you sleep?"

"On the couch." He winks, grabbing the bottle again and pulling Joey by her hand.

"Take me home, cowboy."

I knew it!

Roommates my ass.

"I think I'm going to stick around for awhile." I excuse myself.

"No can do, kiddo." Cole stops me. "We came together. We all leave together."

"Fine." I give in. It's not worth the fight. Plus, they're killing my buzz. "I just need to use the restroom and I'll meet you out front."

I need a minute to gather my thoughts and figure out how in the hell I'm going to tell Toby that whatever is happening between us is over before it started.

Chapter
FOUR

Finley

"What in the world do you think you're doing?" I ask my reflection as I stand in front of the mirror.

I have two choices: let Toby take me home or go home with Joey, Cole, and Vanny. I know what I need to do, but the urge to be wild and carefree for one night is exciting.

"Gah!" I grab a couple paper towels from the automatic machine and run cold water over them. I thought about splashing my face but couldn't remember if Charlee's mascara was waterproof or not, so I blot the back of my neck and take a couple deep breaths, trying to sober myself up.

"Finley, are you in here?" Joey opens the door and steps in. "You coming or what?"

What do I do?

It's now or never. I have to choose where I end up tonight.

"I-I...um..." I turn off the water and lean against the sink as I toss the paper towels into the trash.

"Joey...let's go," Vanny barges in. "We gotta go."

"I'm just waiting on Finley." Joey eyes her friend.

"She's good." Vanny winks. "Toby is taking her home."

"I don't think that is a good idea." Joey crosses her arms over her chest while I just stand here watching them debate on what they think I should do. I mean, I guess it's better than me arguing with myself. Maybe this way someone will actually decide for me.

"Of course it is. Have you seen Toby?" Vanny holds her arm out to the side, making a muscle. "Those biceps are made for wall-banging, and he can hang my picture any day."

I see red.

"Okay! That's enough." I take a step closer. "If anyone is going to get wall-banged, it's going to be me."

"Who's wall-banging." Cole peeks his head in. "I wanna join." Cole makes a fist, banging on the drywall.

We all turn to look at him. "Get out, Cole!"

"Dammmn!" Cole shrieks. "Change of plans. Finley gets the couch." He reaches for Joey's hand. "Now, let's get out of here."

"No can do, cowboy." Joey breaks free. "You got the couch or the party stops here."

Cole pouts and steps back out to where we can't see him. "Fine, but this cowboy is saddling up and riding out in ten minutes."

"We'll be right out," Joey promises.

"Yeah, what she said." Vanny smirks.

"Give us a minute." Joey hands her purse to Vanny. "I promise I'll be quick.

"Are you seriously kicking me out?" Vanny gasps.

"Yeah..." Joey twists her lips and shrugs. "I guess I am."

Vanny wiggles her finger. "I'll remember this." Then turns and walks out.

I'm not sure what's going on. I simply came in here to gather myself so I can figure out where I'm sleeping or not sleeping tonight. I never meant for it to turn into a huge ordeal.

"Fin...this is me being the realest of reals with you right now." Joey closes the distance between us, placing her hand on my arm. "I'm not letting Toby take you home."

"Why?" I find myself whining.

"Because all of us had too much to drink," Joey admits.

"Charlee doesn't think so." I fight back.

"My sister has been living in La-La Land since moving to Mason Creek. She's drinking the Kool-Aid, my friend."

"And you aren't?" I raise my brow, daring her to say different.

"No, I'm not. I'm dating and that's it."

"What if this leads to a date?" I can't believe the words come out of my mouth. It's everything Dr. Feelgood warned about. No date. No excuses. Just great sex and a memory for your spank bank. Nothing more, nothing less.

"You're leaving tomorrow. Unless there's something I don't know about?"

She's right. We have a car picking us up at eight tomorrow night so Vanny and I can catch the red-eye back to Georgia.

"You're right."

"Say that again?" Joey leans in, holding her hand to her ear.

"You're right." I roll my eyes.

"I know. Listen...come home with us, and if you still feel like you want to pull off the perfect hook-up, go over there tomorrow."

"Before I leave?"

"Yep. That way it's not awkward. You saw, you came, you conquered." Joey pauses before we both burst out laughing. "You know what I mean."

"I know *exactly* what you mean."

"Okay then, let's get out of here so you can let Toby down gently. That man has been slowly eye-fucking you all night."

"You think?" I ask, just to hear her say it again. I thought we had something going on, but I wasn't sure if it was Charlee putting thoughts into my head and I was seeing more than what was actually going on.

"Shut up." Joey grabs my hand and pulls me out of the bathroom. "Everyone with eyes in Pony Up could see what was going on between you two. Now, come on." She jerks me forward, and I come face to face with a wall.

"Ow!"

"You okay?" His deep voice vibrates through my body, his hands cupping my face as I look up into his baby blue eyes.

"I'll meet you outside." I hear Joey, but my eyes never leave his. I'm spellbound.

"Uh-huh."

"Fuck me." He runs a hand through his unruly brown hair.

"Is that an invite?" My eyes go wide realizing the question came from me.

Where in the hell did that come from?

"Shit." Toby's gaze lowers to my mouth, and the tip of his tongue darts out as he slowly licks his lips—or maybe I'm drunker than I thought and seeing things in slow motion. "I should have never let Vanny take that tequila."

"Maybe. Maybe not." I reach out and lay my hand against his rock-hard abs. "Maybe you should take me home and find out."

And there she is...horny, drunk Finley.

It's why Charlee set up the hookup. It's also why I was trying to sober myself up in the bathroom. Joey was right. Nothing good can come from this.

Toby lowers his face to mine, the warmth of his cinnamon breath tickling my nose. "Don't tempt me, Finley," he warns, making me wet and tingly. If he can do that just by looking and breathing in my direction, imagine what his touch would do.

"Nope." I over-emphasize the "p" with a pop. "I think you're the one tempting me." I run my finger down his abs, stopping right above his belt buckle. "You kissed me, or did you forget?"

Toby brushes his lips against mine. "You're making me lose control, darlin'."

I stick my tongue out, wanting a taste, but he's too quick and moves back.

"Tease."

"Far from it." He walks me backwards until I hit the wall. "That's the thing, Finley. You've been teasing me all fucking day."

"How?" My voice is barely a whisper.

"From the moment I saw you at Twisted Sisters, the way you licked that spoon, the sway of your ass, the way you made fun of yourself for running into the garbage can..." He presses his body against mine, showing me exactly how he reacts to me. "I can't get you out of my fucking head," he growls as he lowers his mouth to my neck, showing me how much he wants me with each lick, nip, and suck.

"Toby..." I moan, not caring who's around. "Take me home," I beg.

He stops as if I just doused him in ice water and steps back, his chest heaving, his eyes filled with desire.

"I can't do this." He takes another step back.

"W-Why not?" My bottom lip begins to tremble.

"Dammit." He is back on me. "Don't do that."

"Do what?" I can feel the tears pooling in my eyes, but not because I think he doesn't want me—he's been very clear on that—I'm just sad.

"Don't cry. This isn't what this is." He brushes a wild hair behind my ear, his fingertips caressing the side of my cheek, causing goosebumps to spread like a wildfire.

"I'm not crying. I'm sad."

"Why?"

"Because..." I take a step forward, closing any space he may have left. "I'm going to miss your kisses, your hands on my body, the weight of your body as you press into me. I'm going to miss everything I had and everything I wish I could've had. And that makes me sad."

"Fuck..." He tips his head back, taking a moment before he looks me in the eyes. "You can't say stuff like that to me and expect me not to lose control. It's taking everything in me not to rip every single piece of clothing from your body. I want to kiss every inch of you, touch every inch of you, feel the way your pussy pulsates around my cock while I give you the best orgasm you've had in your life, you'll be changing zip codes the next day. Do you understand me?"

Do I?

I understand, my body understands, and my soaked panties sure as hell understand. It's my mind that's wondering why in the hell isn't he making good on his word. Let's do this already.

"Then what are we waiting for?"

"For you to sober up, sweetness." Toby gently grabs my chin and forces my mouth closer to his for a kiss full of promises. I close my eyes and open my mouth to his sweet kisses, letting him devour me.

He smiles against my lips, and I open my eyes at the loss of him. "Well, I think that did it." I'm halfway serious. I could possibly pass a sobriety test if it meant hooking up with Toby.

"Not enough. Take the night. If you still feel this way in the morning, I'll take you out for an early dinner…" Toby's arms drop to my hips, and he pulls me closer, a cheesy grin plastered across his face. "And then I can have you for dessert. What do you say?"

"I can't." I wince. "I leave tomorrow."

"For real?" He twists his lips, as if contemplating changing his mind. Which I would totally be up for.

"Yeah, I take the red-eye out tomorrow night."

"Red-eye?" I can see the wheels turning.

"Then come over for breakfast. Spend the day with me until you have to leave."

I tap my finger to my lips, pretending to think about it. "I could do that—*or* I could just come over tonight."

"Finley!" Joey calls out. "We've got to go."

"Joey! Get your ass back here." Vanny chases a giggly Joey around the corner. She didn't seem that wasted earlier. Maybe we all are really drunk and my thoughts aren't as sober as I think they are.

Am I making a fool of myself?

"Who cares?"

"About what?" Toby asks.

"Yeah, about what?" Vanny and Joey stand there, waiting for me.

"One, I didn't know I said that out loud, and two, I was just having a conversation with my subconscious who apparently can't keep her mouth shut."

"You're soooo wasted." Joey grabs me by the arm.

"So are you." Vanny grabs her by the arm.

"All of you are." Toby holds out his arms, slowly moving us toward the door like a flock of sheep. "Let's get you *all* home safely."

"We're good. You can have Finley." Vanny is the first to stray when we reach the front door.

"Apparently Finley is only good for morning sex, not drunk sex," I mock.

"Sweet! You know morning wood is the largest of all the erections." Vanny eyes me. "Good for you, Fin. Go big then go home."

"An erection is an erection," Joey chimes in.

"Not according to Dr. Feelgood." Vanny wraps her arm around Joey's shoulders. "You really should subscribe to his podcast."

Toby lowers his mouth to my ear. "You know that's not what I said, right?"

"I know," I whisper. "Are you sure you want to see me and this isn't some lame attempt to quietly get rid of me?"

Toby's laugh vibrates against my back. This is when I notice he's hugging me. My back to his front. His arms wrapped around me, holding me up. "Give me your phone."

I could step away and get it for him, but then I'd have to leave, and the safety of his arms feels far too good.

"It's in my front left pocket." I tip my head up. "You get it."

And he does, but his fingers don't wander. He sadly does as he's told. "Look at the camera, darlin'." Toby holds the camera above my head so it will unlock it. "Say no more tequila." He snaps a selfie of us before he drops a pin into my maps. "This will get you to my house. Come over and I'll make you breakfast."

"You will?" I can't help but sound hopeful. I've never had a man cook for me besides my dad.

"I will."

"Ladies! Ladies! Ladies!" Cole appears, holding open the door. "Your chariot awaits."

I spin around in Toby's arms. "I guess this is goodbye."

"Not a chance." Toby gives me the sweetest hug. "It's see you in the morning. Now, go home, drink some water, eat something greasy, and take two ibuprofens."

"Yes, sir." I lean in for a kiss but Cole pulls me back.

"Gotta leave room for Jesus, kiddo."

"I'm not a kid." I huff.

"The sooner I get you home, the sooner you can start prayin' for the sins your about to make tomorrow." Cole guides me out the door. "Say goodbye, Tobes."

"Bye, Tobes."

"I think he meant me," Toby calls out. "Remember to check your maps! Cole knows where I'm staying."

"Do you?" I follow behind him as he walks us to his truck.

"Maybe. Depends."

"On what?"

"Whatcha talkin' about?" Joey skips over to us, but Cole puts his hand out, keeping her away. "I'm January, she's February, March your cute little ass out of here."

"Cole!" Joey whines, but Vanny challenges her to a race to see who can get to the truck the fastest and she takes off.

"So, what do you say? Are you willing to team up? You help me, and I'll help you get to your a.m. booty call."

"It's not a booty—"

Cole coughs. "Bullshit." Then coughs again.

"Okay, maybe it is, but what do you want from me?" I ask, curious as to what I have to offer.

"I'll drive you to Tobster's if you help me woo your friend tonight."

"Joey?" My head swings around. "So, you really are into her, aren't you?"

"I mean, I guess if into her means being madly in love with your best friend's sister slash new roomy named Joey, then I guess I kind of am."

"I knew it!" I jump up and down. "I knew it! I knew it! I knew it!"

"Calm down, Skippy. This has to stay between me and you. Got it?"

I make like I'm zipping my mouth shut and throw away the key, but Cole catches it.

"Is it a deal or not?" Cole asks, dangling the imaginary key in front of me.

I snatch it and free the words dying to get out. "It's a deal!"

The perfect arrangement.

Chapter FIVE

Finley

The door clicks shut with a thud, and my heart hammers in my chest. I barely know this guy. This isn't like me at all. I don't know what I'm doing here but from the moment his lips touched mine at the bar, I knew that couldn't be the last time.

So, here I am, predictable me being unpredictable. The one who always has a plan is going completely rogue to take what I want for once.

And what I want is Toby.

"Penny for your thoughts," he asks me.

"A quarter for yours," I counter.

"How about some coffee and waffles?" he asks, as if reading my mind. I haven't eaten since the food Cole fixed me last night and passed up breakfast hoping Toby really would cook for me.

"Sure." He grabs my hand and pulls us into the open kitchen area. Natural light pokes in through the open blinds.

His cabin is small but airy. Everything I thought it would be. Warm woods, rugged leather furniture. What I didn't expect is this kitchen. Stone and stainless steel. Where the rest of the cabin is dated, the kitchen is new.

Looking around, it's pretty tidy for a bachelor pad.

"Oh, thanks. I'm a bit of a neat freak." I realize I must've said that last part out loud. This time, I can't blame the tequila for the loose lips.

"So, have you lived here long?" I try for a little morning small talk to try to break the ice.

"Nope. I'm not sure how long I'm staying, but I'm enjoying myself while I am."

His words rush me to reality. This is only temporary. A simple hookup. Like Vanny said this morning. Whatever happens in Vegas, you leave in fucking Vegas—or, in this case, Mason Creek.

"Oh, so you're not a college boy paying your way through school pouring drinks?"

Toby holds his arms out. "Do I look like a college boy to you?"

I blush. The guy standing in front of me in a white tee that stretches across his chest and gray jogging pants that leave nothing to the imagination is all man. "Not in the slightest."

"That's what I thought." He winks. "So, what about you? What brought you to Mason Creek?"

This question I can handle...for the most part. "My friends. Charlee, Joey, Vanny, and I are from a small town in Georgia. Charlee moved here about a year ago and started a family, then Joey came to help but decided to stay. I'm just here visiting."

"Interesting." Toby turns around and hits the power button on the Keurig. "Coffee?"

"Please. And what's so interesting?"

"You said you were visiting friends. That means you'll be back."

Oh, great. Is this where he starts to have second thoughts about hooking up? "Yeah, I don't visit as much as Vanny, but I'm going to try to make it out here again in July."

"That's only a few months away." He hands me a cup of coffee. "Cream, sugar?"

"Black is fine." I blow for a second before taking a sip.

"Nice. I don't know too many women who drink their coffee black."

"I don't." I take another sip. "It's my hangover drink of choice."

"Okay then. If you weren't feeling the aftershocks of last night, how would you normally take your coffee?"

Why is he asking me this? It's not like I'm ever going to see him again. How I have my coffee shouldn't matter. "Two creams, one sweetener is my norm."

"And your not norm?"

"Well, if I'm going fancy, I usually like a latte with a double shot of espresso, two pumps of sugar-free cinnamon dolce, topped with whipped cream and sprinkled cinnamon sugar."

"Well, that's detailed." Toby chuckles as he brings the steaming mug to his lips forgoing any blowing. This man is just as hot as his coffee.

"I feel like we should cheers or something." I hold out my mug. Toby mimics my movements. "This is a first for me."

"To one-night stands." I say the words I don't want to mean. Being around Toby is comfortable. I don't want to forget this feeling.

"I'm not sure if I like that. Pick something else."

"It's all I've got." I shrug.

"To a day worth remembering." Toby clinks my mug and takes another sip. "Yeah, I think that fits us better."

Shake it off.

It's just a day. Nothing more, nothing less.

"I'll drink to that." I smile and set my cup down on the island. "So, where are these waffles you promised me?"

Toby steps around from the kitchen island and boxes me in one arm on either side.

"Waffles can wait." He kisses me hard then lifts me onto the counter, moving between my legs as they wrap around him.

On instinct, I tug at his shirt, then he returns the favor, leaving me in my bra He's practically climbing on the island laying on top of me. Hands in my hair, our bodies tangled, I don't know where I end and he begins. Then he abruptly pulls away and climbs down, pulling me with him, his erection very noticeable.

"Why are we stopping?" Kissing him has my body remembering last night. I know he was worried he would be taking advantage of me or I would forget, but there's nothing about Toby I *could* forget. You don't forget men like him. Not when they make you feel the way he made me feel last night. And just now.

"Because I promised you food." He spins around and starts opening cabinet doors. "Except we have a problem."

"What's that?"

Toby looks over his shoulder and winces. "I'm out of mix." He moves to the fridge. "How about some eggs?"

"Perfect."

Toby pulls out the carton, only to find one egg left. "It's yours if you want it."

"Really, it's okay." I try not to laugh.

"What about..." He opens the freezer. "Well...shit. I thought I had some frozen biscuits, but I don't." He stands there with the freezer door open, and I can feel the draft where I'm sitting. I shiver.

"Oh, sorry." He closes it as I reach for my shirt.

"Don't do that." He comes over to me and throws my shirt out of the way. "I like seeing you like this."

My hands go up to cover myself.

"Nope. Don't hide from me." Toby rubs his chest. "And I won't hide from you."

My lips twitch with a smile, and Toby heads back to the freezer. "I have one egg and bread, or I can run to the market unless you want ice cream for breakfast."

I perk up at the sound of ice cream. "It depends. What you got?"

"Only the best ice cream flavor ever."

"Peaches-n-cream?"

"That must be a southern thing." Toby shakes his head.

I laugh, rolling my eyes. "No, I'm pretty sure it's an everywhere thing."

"Well..." Toby pulls a brown carton out of the freezer. "I'll take your word for it, but me...I'm a chocolate guy."

I gasp. "That's it. We can't be friends."

Toby sets the carton down on the counter and settles between my legs where I'm still sitting on the island. "Oh? I thought we were about to be more than friends."

"You know what I mean." I laugh nervously as Toby peels back the carton lid.

"Chocolate is the greatest flavor in the whole wide world."

"What are you, ten?"

"Seriously? How could you deny that?"

"Chocolate is boring."

"Boring, huh? Is that a challenge?" Toby reaches around to grab a large spoon from the drawer behind him.

"I'm about to show you just how *boring* I am." He looks at me sitting here in my pink lace bra, joggers, and tousled hair.

"What?" I'm starting to feel insecure.

"This just feels right. You being here, seeing you like this, in my space nearly..." He shakes off the thought I wish he would finish.

"Is that so?" I challenge him.

He reaches for the band of my joggers. "May I?"

I nod.

I don't know what he plans to do but feeding me naked on his counter wasn't my first thought.

"Here," Toby lowers his gray joggers. "Let me level the playing field."

His baby blues lock on me as he moves back to where he was before. This time, my legs wrap around his bare skin, leaving goosebumps where we meet. He unclasps my bra and slides it off before tossing it on the pile of clothes.

"Looks like you're not that tidy after all."

"Just wait, darlin'. I'm about to get a whole lot messier." Toby warns as he reaches for the ice cream and dips the spoon into the frozen chocolate. "Time for breakfast, baby."

He stands between my legs, the spoon in one hand, and gently urges me back with the other. I slowly law back on the smooth granite, spread out before him in nothing but my pink lacey panties.

My getting lucky panties, as Charlee calls them.

His hand moves down my chest, between my breasts, teasing me, then over my stomach, coming to rest on my hip.

"Ready?" he asks. Before I can respond, I feel the coldness of the spoon making a trail back up the way his hand just left.

He traces up my torso to circle around my nipples. First one, then the other. I suck in a shallow breath as he moves the icy spoon and drops chocolate ice cream, making a messy circle with the sugary goodness.

He leans over me and puts a small amount on my lips then seals his mouth over mine, kissing and licking away every trace.

I buck my hips and moan into his mouth. "More."

"Good?" He opens his eyes and smiles down at me. "Told you."

"I think I need more to be sure." He's making me feel bold.

"Coming right up." He repeats the process a couple more times, until our lips are a tingling combination of hot and cold.

I'll never be able to eat chocolate ice cream again without remembering the feeling of falling apart under his heated touch with the taste of chocolate on our lips.

He gives me one more kiss, but this one isn't slow. Or soft. His mouth moves down my neck, then lower, nipping at my collarbone, the dripping spoon following close behind.

After he makes what feels like an intricate design on my bare skin, from knees to neck, he sets the spoon aside.

His tongue drags along my sticky skin, lapping up the melting chocolate tortuously slow.

He takes his time as he pushes my legs up and kisses up one inner thigh and down the other. My core aches from the near misses of his lips as he passes over the lacey pink fabric.

He moves back up my body, swirling his magic tongue as he goes, then stops and sucks my nipple into his greedy mouth with a gentle tug.

While his mouth stays on my breast, teasing me, his hands move to remove my panties.

"Chocolate covered panties. My favorite," he teases as he steps back to pull them down my bare legs and stands, tucking them into the waste of his briefs.

His eyes are on me, wild and hungry. I'm spread before him, covered in chocolate and kisses.

I push up on my elbows to watch him watch me.

"Like what you see?" Who is this brazen woman? She's not me. I'm not her. But something about him makes me more...everything.

"You know I do. Like what you taste?"

He puts his hands on my thighs and moves upwards. Reaching the apex of my thighs, he runs one finger up my center, and I nearly come off the island. "Oh God!"

"I'll take that as a yes."

I'm not above begging at this point.

He presses back into me then quickly withdraws his finger.

"Say chocolate is the best flavor ice cream in the whole world..."

"Chocolate is the— "He tucks two fingers back into me and curls them. "Best. Best. B-B-Best flavor ice cream in the whole—WORLD!"

"Told you so." He teases me with his words and hands at the same time.

"You aren't playing fair," I cry out, moving my hips against his cupped palm for more friction.

The anticipation builds, heightening all my senses. I've never ached for someone the way I do for Toby. But since ice cream is my love language, I should have known.

Love. This isn't love. This is lust. And sugar. And probably some residual tequila in my system. But I'm not worrying about tomorrow, I'm not thinking of forever. I'm thinking of this moment and how I'm craving his touch, desperate for a release.

He withdraws his hand once more and leans over, replacing his capable fingers with his magical tongue.

Kissing.

Nipping.

Rubbing.

His mouth is euphoric. I could easily get addicted to him and his touch. His kiss.

I can't help myself; I tangle my fingers in his hair and hold him while he eats me like a starving man.

When the first shockwave passes, I feel him moan against me, drinking and sucking and never stopping.

"Toby!" I cry out, releasing him, certain the invisible hold he just put on me will never fade.

He kisses his way back up my body as the aftershocks hold me still. When his mouth closes over mine, I taste myself on him. And *chocolate.*

"Looks like I found a new favorite flavor." He gently draws me up off the island and into his arms. "How about we clean up?"

"What about you?" I ask, suddenly feeling exposed. Like he didn't just make a meal of my body while I begged for more.

"We'll worry about me after I get you cleaned up." He puts the lid on the carton and shoves it back in the freezer. "We may need that later." He winks.

"Toby!" I blurt out. "I want you. And I want to please you,"

He stalks back over to me and kisses me senseless, leaving me feeling like I'm floating on a cloud. I'm so lost in the kiss, I don't realize that he picks me up, relocates to his bedroom, and lays me on his massive bed.

"Ask and you shall receive."

Then everything moves in fast forward and slow motion at the same time. We've both wanted this since last night, but today, in the broad daylight and fully sober—mostly sober—I still want him. In fact, I want him more than ever because of how he respected me, treated me, cared for me. But no more waiting. He stands to pull down his boxer briefs and opens the nightstand. "Shit. I'm out of condoms."

"I'm on birth control. Are you...?" I pull him back down, praying this is something he doesn't normally do. I don't know this man, but whatever he says, I'm willing to take his word for it.

"I'm clean. Are you sure?"

"Yes."

My need for him builds as he grips my hips and he drives into me. Looking for something to grab a hold of, I reach over my head and come up short.

My palms find his shoulders and pull him to me as he gives us both the ecstasy we've been dancing around since that first tequila-covered kiss at the bar.

Electricity burns its way through my veins as he picks up the pace. We chase down the crashing high together as it builds and builds, a tight coil in my belly threatening to snap. I need him closer. And then, the moment we come tumbling down, I feel the doubt seep in.

"I need to shower and get ready to leave," I lie. I just need to get away. My emotions are all over the place. Because of this... him. It's even more than I imagined. But we agreed only one night. Or, in this case, morning. But the push and pull being near him is something I've never felt before. How can this be a perfect hookup when he feels more like a perfect partner?

I sit up to go.

"Not yet." His blue eyes plead with me.

"Maybe a little while longer won't hurt." I let him pull me back down on the bed with him and get lost in his embrace.

Chapter Six

Finley

Eight weeks later...

It's funny how someone can come into your life and change everything. I always knew what I wanted before Toby. Like how I wasn't a country music girl until the slow dance in his cabin and peaches-n-cream was my go-to ice cream flavor.

Now, I'm standing in the grocery store looking the flavors like I don't even know who I am anymore. Maybe I'm being a little dramatic. I've just felt off the last couple weeks since I got home from Mason Creek

Lavender Falls has always been my home, my safe place where I was born. A lot of people can't wait to get away from the people who raise them or the town they grew up in, but I love my nostalgic small town.

It's the perfect place to raise a family and have a life if you're okay with everybody knowing your business. My friends found that in Mason Creek, and now I'm one of the few remaining in Lavender Falls, standing in front of the freezer full of ice cream, questioning all my life choices. My head tells me peaches-n-cream, but my heart tells me chocolate.

"Excuse me, honey, are you gonna stand there all day staring at the ice cream or are you gonna pick one? I'm running late for my church bingo."

I look over my shoulder to see Miss Martha, the church secretary, looking at me impatiently.

"Oh my goodness." I hold a hand over my chest. "I didn't even know anyone was behind me. What can I get you?"

"I just need a tub of vanilla to go on this peach cobbler *I* made."

I try not to smile. Miss Martha is known for special ordering baked goods from Slice of Pie and claiming them as her own. Granny, the sweet old lady who owns the bakery, just laughs it off. Everyone in Lavender Falls knows Slice of Pie when they taste it. There's no denying it.

"Let me get that for you." I swing open the door and reach in to grab her a party-size gallon of plain vanilla when an overwhelming dairy smell hits me, making my stomach roll. "Oh no!" I drop the carton in her cart and cover my mouth with my hand, feeling sick.

"Are you okay, dear?"

I need to get to the bathroom—now!

"I'm sorry I have to go." Abandoning my cart, I take off down the aisle and barrel through the double doors to the back room, barely making it to the bathroom before I throw up the entire contents of my breakfast into the toilet.

What in the hell?

I grab some tissue and wipe my mouth before flushing the toilet. I stand there for a minute, wondering if this is it or if another wave is going to hit me.

I don't know what's wrong with me. I went out last night with a couple ladies from work, but I didn't even drink. So that's not it.

Exiting the stall, I walk over to the sink and let the cold water cool my wrists before splashing some on my face. I examine myself in the mirror.

"What is wrong with you?"

I don't look well. Maybe I need to call Dr. Walters. Maybe I'm coming down with something. My parents asked me to cover for their manager at the Funky Chicken last week. Maybe I caught something when I was sanitizing the machines. I heard the stomach bug is going around.

I take a few more minutes to make sure I'm not gonna be sick again and head back to grab my shopping cart. I just need to check out and get home. Life stuff and decisions will have to wait for another day.

When I leave the bathroom, I step out into the pharmacy area, and I met with a wall of truth. An entire wall full of contraceptives and pregnancy tests. I feel like I'm gonna be sick again.

"Nooo..." I shake my head. "Could I be?"

Think.

Think.

Think.

When was the last time I had my period? I panic, mentally calculating in my head.

My eyes go wide, realization kicking in.

This can't be happening.

We were only together once—once! And I'm on the shot. Actually, I'm set for another one as soon as I start my period.

A million thoughts race through my head as I race out to my car.

I have to buy a pregnancy test. I just can't do it here. The thing about small towns? News travels fast, and I don't need anything to travel until I know what the news is myself.

***

I drove an hour away, two towns over, to go through a drive-thru pharmacy and pick up three pregnancy tests and laid them all out on the counter.

I wasn't sure if I should take them all at once or wait and see, but I wasn't sure if I had it in me to pee on three different sticks. So, I took them all.

I only had to wait a few minutes, but it seems like hours. Pacing back and forth, back and forth just waiting to see the outcome of these three stupid tests.

"Seriously...why is this taking so long?" I stare at the clock wondering if I had a superpower would I want to fast forward time or pause it.

You know what I really wish I had? Ice cream. Because I could really use some comfort food right about now.

My stomach starts to churn.

Shit!

I cover my mouth with my hand. This can't be happening.

I close my eyes, trying to forget about ice cream, the guy, and the timer that's ticking down.

I don't know anything yet. How I'm feeling right now might just be the flu or my nerves. I've been under a lot of stress lately with my parents hounding me about my future. All this could be a false alarm. There is no way I'm pregnant.

No. Freakin'. Way.

Beep! Beep! Beep!

The alarm sounds, and my eyes fly open.

It's now or never.

I step forward, fighting the urge to squeeze my eyes shut. I'm being ridiculously paranoid. Glancing down, I face my fears.

Two blue lines.

A pink plus sign.

Digital "pregnant."

I'm stunned, frozen in place, unable to fast forward. There is no way to get around this. I'm pregnant, and now I have to figure out how to tell my perfect hookup he just became my baby daddy.

To continue reading about
Toby and Finley's story one-click Sweetest Line.
If you fell in love with the Charlee, Joey, Vanny and even Cole, while reading Perfect Hookup, then check out my contributions to the Mason Creek Series now! And if you want
to find out if Dr. Feelgood finds love head
to my website and download UnLucky in Love.

https://authorcaryhart.com/books/unlucky-in-love/

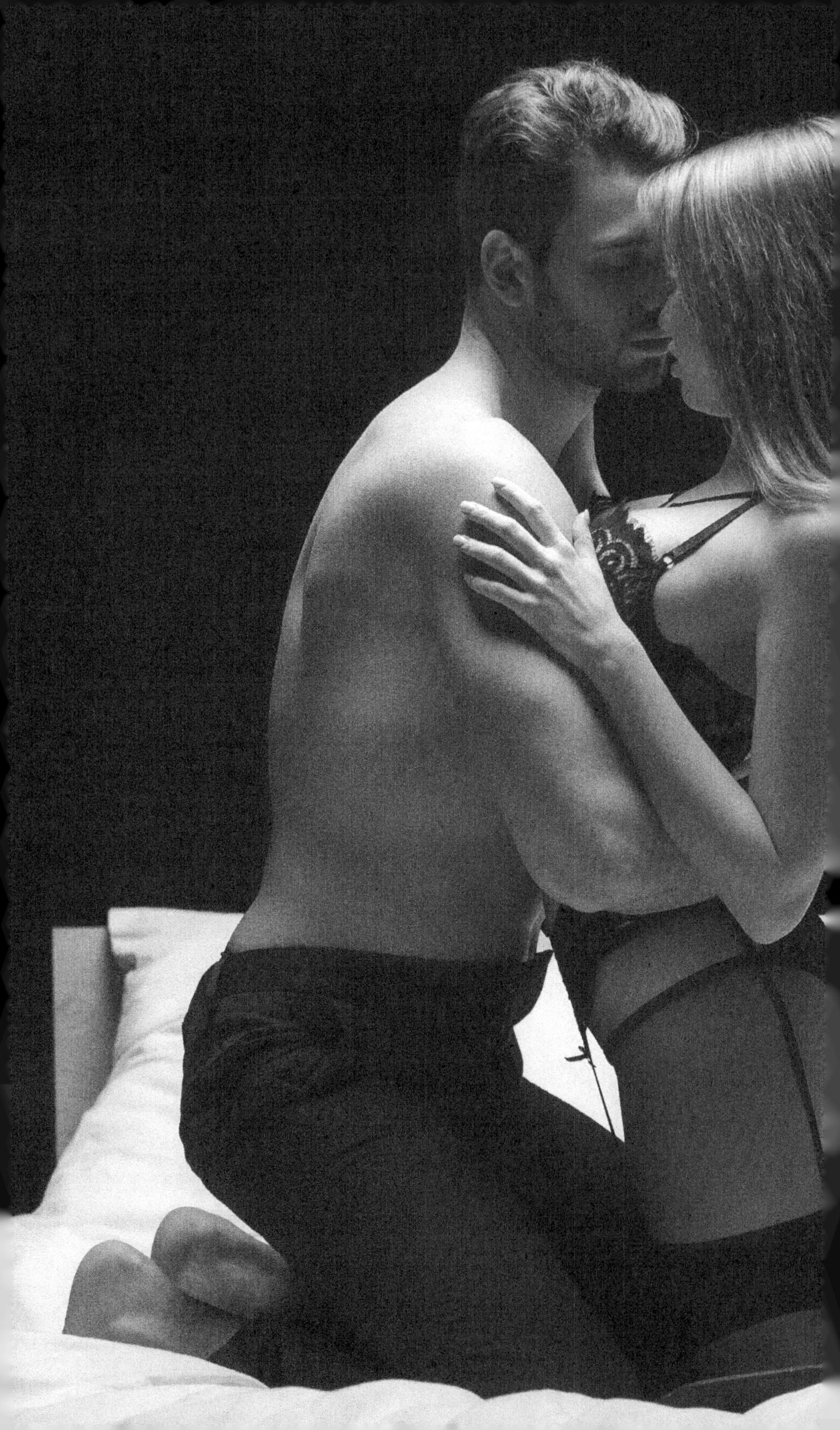

When the
MOOD STRIKES

HARLOE RAE

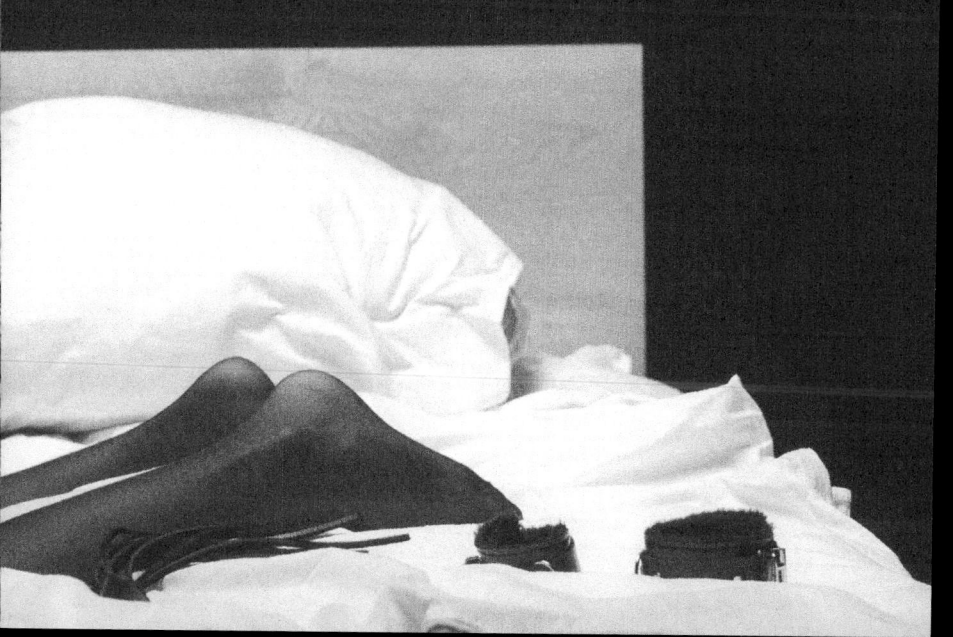

Chapter ONE

Joy

I stumble backward through the unzipped canvas flaps. My mouth remains firmly planted on Cole's even as we're blinded by darkness. His tongue lashes against mine while my fingers spear into his hair. Our combined hunger floods the small space with a heat I can feel in my lower belly.

This wanton behavior propels me into uncharted territory. Bold and brazen aren't typical traits for me. In fact, I've never had a one-night stand. But there's something irresistible about this man. When our eyes met across the grassy field during the final song of Country Fest, I was struck with an insatiable demand to meet him. That instant attraction led us here... along with just enough booze to lower my inhibitions.

Cole releases me only to reach an arm back to whip off his shirt. Then he hoists me against him with a firm grip on my ass. I wrap my legs around him, crossing my ankles snug at the base of his spine. He turns to drop onto the air mattress with me straddling his lap. The flimsy bed squeaks beneath our rushed desires. I barely notice our slight topple as Cole grinds us together.

His teeth flash in the nonexistent light when he smirks. "You're so fucking sexy."

I allow a giddy laugh to escape. The melodic sound slaps off the tent walls. "You're not so bad yourself."

Even perched astride him, he sits taller than me. My gaze is level with Cole's mouth. The impulse to lean in for a kiss comes naturally. His tongue automatically seeks mine as our lips slant together. I lift my arms to loop around his neck, drawing him impossibly closer. He bucks his hips in a preview of what's to come. This no-strings romp is going to deliver exactly what I crave.

A hiss escapes me at the thick length pressing between my thighs. Even through our clothes, I can tell he's equipped with more than enough inches to satisfy me. Desperation has me tugging on my skirt until the fabric is bunched around my waist. Cole rumbles in approval when his palms find my ass bared.

"Just a tiny scrap to protect you." His deep timbre skitters across the fluttering pulse in my neck.

I wiggle in his hold. "What will you do with it?"

He pinches the front of my thong, pulling until the silky material is taut between my pussy lips. The pressure on my clit is an exquisite pleasure. My pelvis rocks forward to ease the ache that only churns tighter. This emptiness needs to be filled. I want Cole to do the honors. Now.

The urge has me fumbling for the button of his shorts. He loosens his grip to make the task easier in our entwined position. I use the slack to grant me immediate access to his dick. My fist curls around his generous girth, offering a few trial pumps.

"Oh, shit. Just like that."

"I've never done this before," I blurt.

Cole goes still. "Are you a virgin?"

"Hardly." My grip on him tightens and he grunts. "But I've never had sex with a guy I just met an hour ago."

"Ah," he exhales. His relief hangs heavy between us. "Do you still want to?"

I stroke his arousal faster. "Very much so."

"Thank fuck for that."

His hand cups my center and I'm sure he can feel the warmth beckoning him to enter. He wrenches my wedged panties to the side, exposing me completely. Two fingers slide through my wetness.

"Damn, sugar. You're drenched."

"Yes. There," I wheeze when he nears my clit.

His fingers vanish before the flames can spread. "When you come, it's gonna be around my cock."

"What're you waiting for?"

"Condom," Cole grits when I roll my wrist with erotic precision.

I release him and hover in anticipation. He scrambles for the foil packet in his pocket. Several curses spill from his lips as he struggles in the dark. The air mattress shifts under our weight, nearly upending us. My fingers dig into his skin for balance as a laugh bubbles from me.

"Shit," he grumbles. "I'm normally not this clumsy."

"And I'm normally not this easy," I quip. "It just adds to the memory."

The reminder that this is a one-and-done threatens to spoil the mood. Then his mouth finds mine, chasing off everything other than the here and now.

"I'm gonna make this good for you," Cole assures.

"And I'm gonna let you."

Once the rubber is rolled on, he guides me to sink down on his cock. The stretch of him sliding into me has my breath hitching. I spread my legs wider to welcome him. We exhale in unison once he's buried to the hilt.

I use my grip on his shoulders to begin a measured tempo. Cole matches my rhythm, rocking his hips up to meet mine. The harmony is quick to steer our passion into a feverish rush.

We might be one step above strangers, but our bodies move with a familiarity reserved for rehearsed lovers. Friction builds with each thrust. I purr as tingles spread from my core. The hypnotic pace pulls me under a trance that shuts out everything other than his dick filling me to the brim.

Cole's hands drag upward along my sides, lifting my shirt with the motion. "Your skin is so soft."

I moan when he licks along my collarbone. "Your palms are so rough."

"Combustible combination," he rasps into my freshly exposed cleavage.

"Keep going," I urge.

His fingers unclasp my bra. "Try to stop me."

I wiggle free from the confines and toss the lace behind me. Cole's lips drift across my breasts. The gentle touch sparks a shiver, but not from cold. I'm burning up with him surrounding me. The humid air spurs a feverish need and I arch against him for more. His cock plunges deep while he latches onto my pebbled nipple.

"So good," I mewl.

Cole groans into my skin. His tongue drags over to love on the other side. Heat spirals outward from his lavish affections. I tighten my inner muscles around him, earning me a rasped grunt. With a fluid motion, he flips our position. My back hits the bed as he continues pumping at a relentless pace.

The new position strikes at just the right angle. I slap my hips against his to gain more friction. Tingles spread as relief dangles just beyond reach. Cole must hear the desperation in my breath. His thick length spears into me with the precision to shatter the barrier holding my orgasm hostage.

Spasms clench my core as I tip over the edge. Pleasure floods my veins and I surrender to the carnal bliss. My limbs are racked with pleasure while Cole slides in for a final thrust, joining me into the passionate abyss. His body trembles on top of mine as he gives me everything I've been begging for.

"Fuuuuuuuuck," he groans after the high subsides.

I drift my palm along the dampness coating his back. "Wow, I'm glad I chose you to pop my cherry."

Cole wrenches away from the nook of my neck to gape at me. "You better be joking."

A loose giggle flies from my lips. "Calm down, big boy. My one-night stand cherry. That was top notch."

The tension slips from his expression. "Still want to just leave it as that?"

"I think it's for the best." Even as regret tries to settle in my gut.

Chapter
TWO

Cole

Where it begins again after six months apart...
In their house during winter

I unlock the door and step inside the foyer. A savory aroma greets me, followed by an alluring hum. My feet carry me toward the sound to find my fiancée swaying her hips in front of the stove.

At the sound of my approach, Joy turns to grace me with a welcome smile. "Hello, Mr. Baker."

"And hello to you." I stride forward to wrap my arms around her, resting my palms on her swollen belly. "How long until you're officially Mrs. Baker?"

She taps her lips in thought, as if the exact number isn't memorized. "Ten months, two weeks, and four days."

My exaggerated groan is exhaled into the crook of her neck. "Why're you making me wait so long?"

"The best things take time." Her hand rests beside mine where our baby grows in her stomach.

"At least she arrives soon." I nuzzle against her like the lovesick fool I am. "Have I told you lately that I'm grateful we found each other against the odds?"

Joy sags into my embrace. Her ass rubs against me, rousing my lust that's never too far from reach. "You did this morning. Feel free to tell me again."

"How about I show you?" I drift my hand down to cup her pussy. Only a single layer conceals her from me, and I can feel her warmth begging me to stoke the flames.

"Dinner is almost ready." But that doesn't sound like a protest.

My lips pepper kisses across her shoulder while my fingers stroke her slit. "I just want a snack to tide me over."

"You'll spoil your appetite." Joy's voice is breathy with desire.

"Quite the opposite. You always leave me hungry for more." I spin her in my arms, moving us until she can prop against the counter for balance.

As I sink to my knees, she tugs the hem of her dress up. The fabric bunches around her hips and puts her lace-covered pussy on display. With a swoop, I bury my face in her center and pull in a deep breath. Spicy honey and addictive sugar fill my lungs.

"Fucking delectable," I groan against her.

Joy yanks at my hair. "Don't make me wait."

My woman is always on edge with these pregnancy hormones pumping through her veins. She can orgasm just from nipple play and I'm here for it. A few solid swipes to her pussy might get the job done tonight. The thrill of knowing I can please her that easily expands my chest to comical proportions.

I drag her panties down until she steps out of them. Then she drapes a leg over my shoulder. Her elbows rest on the granite surface behind her to offer balance. I flatten my tongue and sweep through her folds.

A rumble rolls off my chest as her unique flavor floods my mouth. Her tangy arousal spurs me into action, and I begin ravishing her. Joy rocks her hips, feeding me more. Her moans are the most gratifying tune. I dig my fingers into her ass while latching onto her clit. The suction makes her knees quake.

"Yes, yes, yes! Right there," she cries.

I follow the commands with expert precision. My lips form a tight seal and I give a harsh pull. Her trembles tell me that she's close. When I slide a finger into her tight center, she bucks against me.

"You're gonna make me—"

Joy's words cut off on a wail as spasms rack her limbs. I drink her down, groaning at the amount she gives me. She's such a generous lover. In return, I bury my face in her. My mouth and chin are soaked in her essence. To be bathed in this woman's passion is the greatest gift.

When I'm certain she's floating in the afterglow, I sit back on my heels. Joy's skin is flushed with pleasure and satisfaction. She smiles down at me, bending to touch my cheek. I lean into her caress and press a kiss to her inner wrist. My heart overflows with warmth.

"Love you," I murmur.

"I love you so freaking much, babe."

"Not sure what I did to deserve you, but I'm damn glad I did it."

"Ditto." Joy's grin spreads. "Now feed me, fiancé."

My brows wag. "Like actual food or...?"

She rolls her eyes, but can't hide the amusement that's shining through. "Let's start with the pasta and see where the night takes us."

Chapter
THREE

Joy

Where they get the green light after six weeks without...
In the car during spring

Cole slides behind the wheel and fastens his seatbelt. I'm chomping on my bottom lip and absently staring out the window when he glances over at me. He reaches for my restless fingers and threads them through his.

"We don't have to leave her," he murmurs against my knuckles. My smile wobbles as I glance over at him. "My parents shoved us out the door. There's no way we're getting Belle back without a fight. Plus, this will be good for us. We're due for a date night." "Are you sure?" I nod. "But let's go before I change my mind." He shifts the truck in reverse and asks, "Where to? I bet Roosters will serve us even if we're sniveling the entire meal." My scoff denies his suggestion. "We're not spending our first evening alone at my brother's bar. Try again, stocking stuffer."

Cole begins driving without a chosen destination. He's tugging his bottom lip between his teeth when I peek at him. I notice his gaze bouncing between the road and my boobs, which are almost popping out of my shirt. My focus lowers to check on the ladies. They're practically begging for attention. Maybe I should've pumped before we left. Or not. Breastfeeding definitely has it's perks, and Cole is getting a nice eyeful. I prop myself on the center console, leaning closer purely for his benefit. "See something you like?""Tease," he grinds out. My shoulders shimmy to add extra jiggle. "Oh, I'm sorry. Are you suffering, babe?"

Cole slams on the brakes when I rest a palm on his thigh. "What're you doing, sugar?" "Just a little preview," I purr.

My hand wanders up. His breathing turns labored. A thrill skitters along my spine at the tremble in his rigid muscles. I throw caution out the window, gripping him through his jeans. He groans a tortured sound.

"Fuck, Joy. You're playing with a loaded gun," he warns. I hum. "Doesn't it feel risky?"

My fingers make the task of unfastening his pants quick and simple. Cole grunts when I wrap my fist around his steely girth. I roll my wrist for a downward slide. His teeth clack together with a harsh exhale.

"I'd rather play it safe."

That slows my jerking motions. "Oh?"

"It's been too long, and I can't see straight." I stretch to kiss his clenched jaw. "Then find somewhere to stop for a bit, big boy. I wanna go for a ride."

Cole makes a few sharp turns that land us in a bank parking lot. "This should do. Nobody's gonna notice us on a Saturday night."

I glance at the deserted area. "Looks good to me."

He points to the back. "Ladies first."

My desperate need won't allow me to hesitate, even if I wanted to. Cole is right behind me and settles in the middle of the wide bench seat. I'm almost drooling in anticipation. His impatience rivals mine and doesn't leave me hanging long. He drags his jeans down in a fluid motion and pats his lap. I straddle him in a hurried motion that's reminiscent of our first time together.

Cole's palms shake as he touches my thighs. That desperation rattles within me as well. It's been too long since my fiancé has been buried deep and joined our bodies as one. We're about to be rid of this forced dry spell.

"This is gonna be quick and dirty," he says and tugs my panties to the side. "Good call on the skirt."

"I might've been hoping this would happen." Goosebumps pebble my skin as he licks along my throat. "Get inside me. Right now."

He plunges into my slick center and a loud moan welcomes him. I spread my legs wider, seating myself lower, and driving him deeper. It's no surprise I'm wet for him, but there's still a tug as I stretch around his length. The push and pull create a smooth rhythm, our bodies rocking together in rotating cycle. Our movements are fluid, connecting as one, as if we've done this a thousand times. It's a milestone to aim for.

Tingles spread from my core. The time apart makes relief bloom bright on the horizon. I bounce on him, chasing that promise of pleasure. Cole watches his dick enter me as I increase my tempo. Each slap of our hips meeting is a call home after too many nights away. His fingers dig into me, trying to slow the pace. I squirm in his hold.

"Harder, babe. I want all of you," my hitched exhale demands.

Cole never denies me. His movements become faster to strike deeper. Filthy nonsense begins spilling from my lips. He bucks into me as I grind down. My hair brushes his knees when I toss my head in pure bliss. Then his fingers delve between my legs, swirling around my clit. The pressure he applies is more than enough for me to see stars. Spasms begin to quake my limbs.

"Are you close?" Cole's lips brush across mine, his tongue licking along my bottom lip.

I nod against him. "Uh-huh. Just a bit more..."

He circles my clit to work me into a frenzy. That's the final shove I needed to tumble over the edge. Cole thrusts once more and follows me into oblivion. Pleasure floods in a fiery rush, causing me to suck in a sharp breath. Our simultaneous orgasms heighten the experience. I clench around him as the waves keep crashing against me.

"Holy fuck," he curses and slumps into the leather.

I press my cheek to his heaving chest. "Yep, this is much better than being parked on a stool at Roosters."

"You got a much better cock in this lot," Cole chuckles.

My inner muscles squeeze him. "Wanna make me cluck again?"

"Might as well, sugar. We already fogged up the windows."

I drag my finger through our love mist. "The panes can definitely use another coat."

"And we have all night," he reminds against my lips.

The post-coital glow is instantly replaced with a fresh surge of lust. "Then let's make it steam, Mr. Baker."

Chapter FOUR

Cole

Where the theater is dark and only two seats are occupied...
In the last row during summer

A sideways glance at Joy has me swallowing a curse. My fiancée is draped over the armrest with the popcorn bucket wedged between her tits. She doesn't bother to hide the hunger from her gaze. Her appetite must be craving something other than buttery fluff.

I blindly toss a popped kernel into my mouth. "Keep looking at me like that and we won't make it beyond the previews."

As predicted, Joy's palm rests on my thigh. "Where will we go instead?"

"Temptress," I mutter without malice.

"You love me," she croons in return.

I thread my fingers through hers and offer a gentle squeeze. "More than words can describe."

"Does that mean you'll let me... test the limits?"

The pause in her statement gives me a hesitation of my own. "Care to be more specific?"

"Gladly."

Joy lowers to the floor and kneels between my legs. I'm too stunned to move while her fingers unfasten my jeans. Normal brain functioning kicks in once she has my dick in her hand.

I still her jerking movements. "What're you doing?"

Her grin is smug. "Thought that was obvious."

"But here? What if we get caught?" Why I'm the voice of reason is beyond me.

"Then we leave. The risk is fun, right?" She bends until her lips are almost kissing my cock.

Joy's words have me relaxing in the cushioned chair. Since our sexcapades in the car several months back, we've become more adventurous. Our moments alone are rare and we take advantage whenever possible. That's why my fingers thread through her hair, inviting her to continue.

My fiancée smiles around my tip, sucking ever so slightly. My pulse gallops as I surrender to this talented vixen. She knows just how to get me off. We'll probably still catch the previews if she starts now.

Her mouth sinks down at a lazy pace. She's warm and wet and irresistible. I bite my knuckles to stifle a groan. My muffled pleasure spurs her into faster action. Joy begins bobbing on my length. Her suction gets more intense as she withdraws, but her warmth sizzles in my veins on the descent. I'm a fucking goner when she wraps her fist around my base. With that added pumping motion, my release barrels forward at dizzying speed.

"Fuck, fuck, fuck," I chant.

Joy hums in approval while increasing her motions. My balls tighten as tingles erupt from my cock. Then the blissful relief follows. I go rigid in my seat as I spill everything. She takes it, greedily gulping in audible slurps. I'd blush if I could hear beyond the ringing in my ears. Besides, there's nothing to be embarrassed about.

When she releases me from her clutches, I'm wrung out and slumped sideways. A satisfied grin paints her lips while she returns to her seat. She discreetly wipes at the corners of her lips while reaching for the popcorn. Her nonchalance gets me hard all over again.

I chuckle and feign a casual slouch. "Just wait until intermission, sugar. I'll be ready for a sweet treat."

Chapter FIVE

Joy

Where the wet bags aren't just for umbrellas...
At the bar during fall

Water sloshes at my ankles as we dash toward the bar entrance. We're only protected from the mid-afternoon rain shower by the umbrella in Cole's grip. He shakes out the drenched fabric once we get under the awning.

"I bet the floors are gonna be slick." My fiancé juts his chin at our destination just beyond the doors.

"Not a problem, babe. Roosters has wet bags." I stomp my soaked flip-flops on the concrete in a pitiful attempt to shake off some excess moisture.

"What the fuck is a wet bag?"

"You'll see." I wrench on the handle and step into the vestibule. "Garrett ordered some after traveling to Philadelphia and realized what we'd been missing."

But my excited boasting on my brother's behalf turns out to be premature. The only option available is a sorry sack left discarded in its own puddle.

I frown at the sad sight. "Well, damn."

Cole nudges the plastic heap with his shoe. "Sloppy seconds or go without?"

Our history suggests it doesn't matter. "Eh, let's not leave the poor bag behind. It still has a solid purpose."

Cole shoves our umbrella into the sloppy pouch. "Since we're already soaked, how about a trip to the bathroom?"

I blink at him innocently. "Will you dry me off?"

He palms my ass while steering me through the crowd. "Quite the opposite."

A thrill skitters through me. "My goodness, Mr. Baker. You're becoming very favorable to public sex."

His stride slams to a halt. "Who said anything about sex?"

My lips part with a stilted breath. "Um, I thought that's where we were headed."

He chuckles. "Yeah, sugar. I just need to fuck with you every once in a while."

"Keep the ribbing to condoms," I jest.

"Or wet bags," he counters while shaking our soggy sack.

The remaining distance to our destination passes in a blur. We slip into the restroom and lock the door. Anticipation clings to me while arousal pools in my lower belly. The space is small, but it will do the trick in a pinch. Cole shoves me against the wall, cradling my head at the last moment against the impact. I still wince at the abrupt movement.

His face nuzzles into my neck. "Relax, sugar."

"A little warning next time," I mumble against his stubbled jaw.

He inhales and groans. "You smell so fucking good."

My body arches into his. "I do? Like what?"

"Every filthy fantasy I've been having since puberty. Strawberries, chocolate, vanilla, and meant to be mine."

"Seems like you're hungry for a snack."

He licks the column of my throat. "I'm gonna gobble up all of your delectable decadence."

I shiver against him. "That sounds promising."

"Yeah, baby. I'm gonna eat everything you offer." He drifts his hands down my sides while lowering into a crouch.

"Wait. What're you doing?"

He presses a kiss to my lower belly. "I'm gonna make you feel really good."

"You don't have to do that. I thought we were gonna bang quick."

My chuckle is more of a gritty rasp. "I'm well aware, baby. But I want to give you an extra boost. Keep relaxing and enjoy."

Cole flips my skirt up and gets to work. My panties disappear before I can try to assist in lowering them. Then his tongue traces my slit from back to front, ending with a swirl around my clit. I tremble in his grip, resting my palms on his shoulders for balance. A path of goosebumps rise on my skin as he eats me like a buffet that closes in five minutes.

I swivel my hips to aid in the release process. Moans spill from me in a nonstop stream. He drapes my left leg over his shoulder, spreading my bared center wider for his taking. I grind into his face, faster with each twirl from his tongue. Cole dips a finger into my center. My inner muscles immediately clench around the intrusion. I whisper as tingles sprint through my muscles. Relief is already near.

"You know just how to touch me," I murmur.

He hums in approval against my slick flesh. I drag in a sharp breath when he adds more suction to my clit. I rock harder against, seeking more friction. I'm not afraid to chase my pleasure. When he wedges a second digit into my pussy, I begin to quiver uncontrollably.

"I—I'm gonna...oh my, yes, yes..."

With a final swipe through my core, Cole rockets me into ecstasy. I expel a long line of expletives while my body quakes against his. He doesn't stop, only lashing harder to send me into oblivion.

When the buzzing in my ears quiets to a dull roar, I slump across his kneeling form. "Wow, babe. That was unnecessary."

He grunts after kissing my inner thigh. "Your pleasure is a priority. I'll never cease to send you soaring."

"Damn," I exhale. "What did I do to deserve you?"

Cole rises to his feet and cups my cheek. "I ask myself the same question every single day."

"We shouldn't let our love go to waste." I'm reaching for his jeans before the buzz of my orgasm has worn off. The denim keeping him modest is no match for my seeking fingers. I rip at the button and zipper with gusto.

His chuckle tickles my ear. "Now who's being favorable to public sex?"

"Definitely me."

"You'll never hear me complain about having sex, sugar."

When I get his hard length in my hand, a loud moan spills from me. He's so long and thick and hard. After a quick maneuver, he has my legs wrapped around his waist and that solid length kissing my entrance. He grinds against me for a moment, sliding his hardness through my folds. I crane my neck backwards and get lost in the motions.

"I need you inside of me."

"So impatient," he murmurs against my cheek.

"For you, yes."

His harsh grip on my ass is a delicious bite. With the speed of a starving man, he drives himself deep inside of me with one solid thrust. I let my jaw hang open with a silent scream. The time for going slow is clearly over.

"You're so big," I whimper.

"Only because you're so tight."

I angle my hips and he manages to sink even further. "We fit so well together."

He pulls out, only to propel forward with a punishing thrust. "Fuck, yes. I never want to stop fucking you."

"Please don't." I paw at his shirt, lifting the hem to get a view of his abs as the muscles flex with his efforts. "Oh, oh...yes, that feels so fucking good."

"Want more?"

"You have more to give?" At this point, I'm confident I'd seen it all.

His smirk is dangerous, but I'm too lost in my lust to really fear anything. He presses his middle finger to my mouth. "Suck."

I don't hesitate, pulling him in with adequate suction. My tongue swirls around the thick digit and I moan at the flavor of his slightly salty skin. My mouth waters, making me gulp with a heavy swallow.

"Enough, or I'll come from your filthy sounds." He removes his finger with a pop. Before I can question his intentions, Cole sinks that naughty finger—wet with my salvia—into my ass.

"What are you—" But the protest dies on my parted lips. This foreign invasion feels good. Great, actually. I shift to adjust, and he wiggles that sinful touch deeper. "Ohhhh."

"That's right, sugar. You love me back here." He drags his digit out before pushing back in.

"It's strange, but good."

"We can play more later," he assures.

Cole's thrusts increase in pace while he fingers my ass. The combination of sensations quickly shoves me to the edge. I claw at his hair and arm while my climax engulfs me.

A burst of white heat explodes in my vision. "I'm coming! Oh, oh…yes, keep going. So, so hard."

He shudders in my grip and loses himself inside of me. We're a mass of twitching muscles and pure pleasure. The bathroom and public space vanishes. All that's left is this, us merging as one and rocketing to the stars.

When the aftershocks have worn off, he releases my thighs and I manage to stand. I'm sure I look thoroughly fucked. My fingers snag on several tangles in my hair.

Cole laughs at my grimace. "Good thing we got the wet bag."

"And why is that?"

Cole wags his brows. "The sloppy seconds can take the blame for your disheveled appearance."

I furrow my brow. "You don't appreciate the wet bag, do you?"

He taps my nose. "Doesn't matter. I love you, and your flexibility when the mood strikes."

Thanks for reading my dirty additions for Cole and Joy. I hope you enjoyed them! Don't forget to read Stocking Stuffer if you haven't already. It's a freebie novella you can get on my website –
www.harloerae.com
Happy reading!

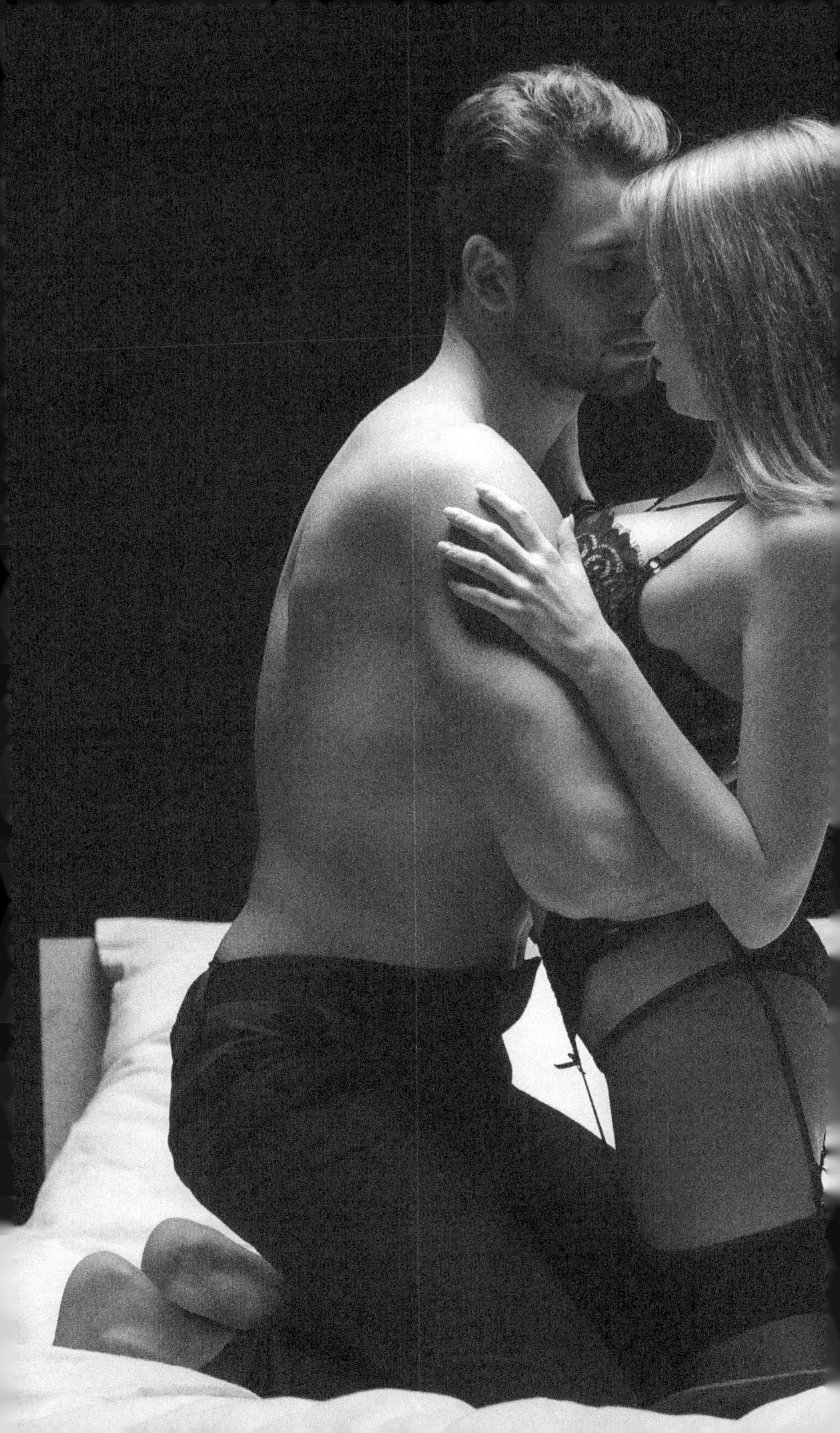

VOYEUR

HILARY STORM

Chapter ONE

Ariana

It's the blinding sun that has me stopping at the coffee shop, choosing to divert from the harsh rays in hope that a few minutes will make the difference for remainder of my walk home. I take this same path every day but this isn't a usual problem of mine. I tend to work late so the sun has usually set before I even step out of my office.

Being a workaholic is just one of the characteristics I picked up on being the daughter of a single father for most of my life. I say most... because I was four when my mother packed a bag and left us both, never looking back. Even my attempts to locate her when I was twenty failed, but I knew they would. She wants nothing to do with me and at this point in my life the feeling is mutual even though I can't fully say that about my past. Nevertheless, I refuse to let my childhood define me, but to say it didn't mold me would be a bold-faced lie.

"Black with sweet cream, please." I order even though I know this cup of caffeine will have me up most of the night. I'll be up anyway... so I may as well embrace it.

I'm digging deep into my satchel for my cash when I'm bumped from behind. The *bump* was more like a shove that sends me up against the counter and into a display of travel mugs that crash to the floor. Clatter and chaos take over the room and before I can balance myself again, my satchel is stripped from shoulder and yanked out of my hand. *What the hell?*

I move toward the door in a haste, trailing the guy wearing a beanie with my bag gripped tight in his right hand. My instincts weren't near quick enough because he's out the door and halfway down the block before I step out on the sidewalk. "Shit." *This day just keeps getting better.*

Sensing the attention of everyone in the coffee shop, I turn around and exhale. "I've called the police for you. I'm sorry that just happened. Come have a seat and I'll get that coffee you ordered." One of the baristas meet me at the door to hold it for me and for the first time today, someone is being nice. Which only takes me back to the real reason I'm even at this place at this exact time. *Fucking Steven.*

"Your coffee is on the house today." A girl that looks like she's barely eighteen sets my cup in front of me and with a pity smile, she leaves me to hustle back to the register to pick up the mess that was just made. It takes about four minutes for the shop to go back to normal but my heart is still racing as my adrenaline spikes up in frustration.

My computer. My phone. My cash. All of my cards. My freaking keys. Everything in that bag was important and just the thought of trying to replace it all is overwhelming.

A young cop opens the door to the coffee shop and looks my way almost immediately. I must look like a damsel in distress or something... or maybe he can just feel the rage seeping through my skin the longer I sit here. "You'd like to file a police report? Tell me what's going on." I start talking and before I can finish, he's sliding a piece of paper across the table for me to fill out.

I'm almost done writing all of the details on his form when I feel the air around me shift. *Someone is watching me.* I turn my head to find a man in a sitting on the back wall, peering in my direction as if he's curious about what I'm writing. "What's your problem?" My sass is prominent, but who can blame me?

He shakes his head slightly, giving me a smirk in the process and no doubt finding something about my situation amusing. With my irritation spiked to a new high, I continue filling out the report, knowing it's most likely all for nothing. What are the odds I'll get my stuff back? *Probably zero.*

Once the police officer gets everything from me that he needs, I finally take the first sip of my coffee. I can still feel the weight of someone watching me and sure enough when I look up, Mr. Suit is leaned back in his chair with his head tilted back just slightly. He's watching me through hooded eyes and with a dark sultry look on his face. I can practically see his mind running through ideas... or maybe it's memories? Maybe I remind him of someone. Who knows.

What I do know is he's making me uncomfortable and after this shitastic day, I can't handle another guy further complicating my life.

Without another glance in the suit's direction, I leave the coffee shop I should've never entered. The sound of my heels clicking on the sidewalk start to echo when I turn down the alley. Even I'm aware of the many reasons I should not be walking through here after the kind of day I've had but this is the last block before I get to my place and the urgency to get there only grows with each step.

I'm almost to the clearing when I hear the screech of tires that freeze me mid-step. It only takes a second for all the hairs on my body to rise with awareness. The fully blacked out SUV parked in the middle of the alley is one giant red flag. But the beefed-up guy in a suit walking my direction is an even bigger one. I almost run. Run for my fucking life. And the urge to scream is there... I'm just silenced and paralyzed by fear.

This would be the way I die. I can practically hear the newsflash now. 'A twenty-five-year-old female was dumb and died in an alley on her way home from work today. This was after she was mugged at a local coffee shop. It's a wild one out there guys... make good decisions. Stay safe.'

"Ma'am... is this your bag?" He raises his hand, my satchel in his grasp while my mind is all over the place trying to comprehend this guy. *Who is he? Where did he come from? How does he know this bag is mine?*

I manage a tiny nod, which encourages him to step closer. "I'll just set it down here and let you get it. Everything should be there." He places it on the ground about ten feet in front of me before he turns to walk back toward his SUV.

"Wait. How did you get this?" He doesn't respond.

He doesn't stop or look back. He doesn't even look my way when he crosses over to get back into the driver's seat and I can't see through the tinted windows to know if he's watching me now... but my intuition says he is. That weight is back, and that usually means I'm being watched.

I move to reach for my bag and after a quick scan to confirm that everything is still inside, I look up to see the SUV hasn't moved.

Having so many unanswered questions doesn't bode well with me, so of course, I walk toward the SUV and reach for the passenger handle. I'm not surprised when that door doesn't open, but I am startled when the back door does. I see his designer dress shoe under the door before *he* steps into my full view.

"It's you," I say on an exhale while I manage to back step a few feet to put some distance between us. That same sultry stare from the coffee shop begins to stir my insides once again. "What's your deal? Did you have me mugged so you could play hero?" His laughter interrupts me and the sight of this distinguished man holding his chest in full on amusement isn't lost on me.

"No. But I did call my security to nab the filth who mugged you. He made it two blocks before they laid him on his ass." I clutch my bag against my stomach as the urge to keep it secure finally hits me. Jesus, I need to be more aware of my surroundings.

"Uhh. Thank you." I say unsure of how to react or how to pay him back.

"You're welcome." His confidence is powerful. His eyes are dangerous. He was blessed with the kind of eyes that can pierce straight through the soul of any woman. *Soul-snatching eyes.* And don't get me started on his dark hair and perfectly trimmed facial hair. Or the fact that he stands about a foot taller than me and is obviously ridiculously important or he wouldn't have his own security team.

"What are you some sort of drug lord?"

"If I told you, I'd have to kill you." His demeanor is flirtatious even though his words are not.

"Okay. Well, thank you for... this." I stutter and raise my bag as words fail me. It's not that he scares me. He intrigues me and I can feel myself slipping into his little game of being dark and mysterious. I can just tell he likes to play games and with my recent track record, I'm due for something different. I'm due for a something real and easy.

"Let me take you to dinner."

"Uhh..." He doesn't let me continue to stall.

"You're trying to come up with a good reason to say no. Well, there's not one. I find you attractive. You can't take your eyes off of me... so we should have dinner and see where it goes." I lift my brows at his blunt offer and before I can get a counter response out of my mouth he's talking again. "Unless you want to skip dinner and come home with me."

"No. Dinner will be fine." My guard is so far up after this day that I can't even appreciate this guy asking me on a date. I feel obligated and not the slightest bit in the mood for a night out.

Neither of us speak for a few seconds and it's not until he reaches for a strand of my hair that I relax just a little. "Your hair..." He releases a breathy whisper but stops himself this time even though he's still thinking about whatever it was he was about to say while still twirling my hair between his fingers.

"I can meet you somewhere later, if that works for you?" I decide it's time to put some distance between myself and this guy. His little sexy advances are far too risky for a girl that hasn't had sex in months.

"What's your name?" He finally lets the strand of hair fall to my shoulder.

"Ariana... my friends call me Ari."

"Ariana." *That sexy exhale of his again.* Like he's in the middle of getting a blow job and can barely hold it together. "Here, put your number in my phone and I'll call you so you'll have mine." He hands me his phone and I briefly consider giving him a bogus number but choose to listen to the devil on my shoulder instead of the logic and experience telling me to run far away from this man.

He hits the call button when I hand him back his phone. Mine rings from my bag and he smiles. "My name is Lucas. Call me when you're ready for that dinner date."

He watches me as I back away with a slight smile on my own face. This guy is good. Freaking really good. I mean another minute here and I'd be climbing in that SUV of his just to see what he'd say next.

I'm not surprised to see him still watching me when I glance back before turning out of the alley. I knew he was watching me. *I could feel it.*

Chapter TWO

"You're a piece of work, Steven. You know this is wrong."

"Aria... this is not personal. It's just business and right now you're not showing me numbers." The urge to retch everything I've eaten this week is hovering over me as I listen to this snake pretend he's justified in firing me.

"You know Michael has been undermining me and stealing my accounts. Since when do associates from the same firm compete?"

"Since I challenged each of you to bring your best. If the accounts think that Michael is a better fit for them, I can't stop that." Bring our best? Michael wine and dines the clients at the local strip clubs. That's not something I will ever do to keep a client loyal to me. I guess it goes to show that even men with billions in the bank are complete scum balls.

"So, everything I've worked for is just gone?"

"You should look at it as you've gained experience here that you can't get anywhere else. Take that with you and grow from here." He says all of this knowing I signed a non-compete contract when I started and can't do the same type of work for two full years.

"Eat a dick, Steven. I'm going to fight this." The civil part of me is long gone and now I'm livid. I'm not sure how I will take on a big accounting firm, but I will find a way and when I do, I'm going straight for Steven's jugular. His spineless leadership is the cause of this.

I hang up the phone and toss it to the couch in frustration. "God, this day sucks." My voice no doubt being heard downstairs, but that not stopping me from further ranting. "I should've just stayed home this morning." The sound of footsteps pounding toward my front door distract me only long enough to open the door. I already know who it is.

"Helen... it's crap. He just fired me because *I'm not showing him numbers*. It's horse shit. How can I compete with a guy who takes his clients out for sex and booze. Unless I start opening my legs for every Tom, Dick and Harry... I'm doomed."

"Honey. Calm down. You knew they were up to no good. And Karma will take care of those who wrong you. Just watch."

"In the meanwhile, I'm fired. I'll have no money. I'll be out on the streets."

"Stop that. As long as there's still breath in my lungs you will not be on the streets." Her kindness stops me in my tracks. I don't know what I did to deserve an angel on this earth as sweet as Helen, but I'm so thankful for her right now.

"Thank you, Helen. You mean so much to me."

"And you mean the world to me... but I'm not gonna have you up here screaming away all of my customers. A woman has to sell booze for a living even if she isn't willing to sell the sex part." I can't help but feel bad about my choice of words while ranting to my landlord who owns and runs the bar downstairs. She was nice enough to rent me the top floor for a great rate and I hate that I came across as anything but grateful for everything she's done for me. "I know, I know... you didn't mean it like that. Now come downstairs and help an old lady out since you're now jobless."

I can't even argue with her, not that I have the energy left to try. "Let me change and I'll be down." She leaves my door open so I can hear the roar of the music and laugher when she opens the door at the bottom. *Great, it sounds packed.* I guess one good thing about working for Helen tonight... is that time will pass quickly and that means less time that I will think about wanting to choke my old boss.

Once I've pulled my hair into a messy bun and replaced my work attire with short jean shorts, a tank top and comfortable shoes, I dig my phone out from between the couch cushions.

I'm not surprised when I see a text from Lucas,

Lucas: What time should I pick you up tonight?

Me: Sorry... I have to help out a friend. Raincheck?

Lucas: I can do a late dinner.

I decide not to respond right away because his directness puts me off a bit. This guy is persistent almost to the point of annoyance and I'm just not sure I'm in the right mood to be near a guy that determined to get his way. I slide my phone in my back pocket and take the steps two at a time until I'm behind the bar, moving alongside Helen to fill orders.

The night goes by extremely fast. So fast that I don't even take a break until well after last call is over. Helen meets me against the bar with two beers in her hand and I find myself in one of those cherished moments I know will forever be a favorite memory of mine. Helen is like the mother I never had and I can't help but want to have some special instants with her.

"You know you need to find you a man. Fuck some of that stress out of ya." I almost choke on my first sip as Helen's advice slaps me in the face.

"Yeah. Well, I haven't seen you with any man in tow." I counter thinking she'll leave me alone if I remind her she's the pot calling the kettle black with all that nonsense.

"Just because I don't let 'em linger, doesn't mean I don't get mine. Trust me now. There's only one reason us strong females need a man. You buy your own shit... but you can still enjoy that dick." She takes back the remainder of her beer and walks around the bar to start wiping everything down.

Before I can stop myself, I'm spilling secrets I had no intention of sharing. "I had a guy ask me on a date tonight."

"And instead, you're here... with me." She shakes her head like she can't believe I'm this hard to teach life's great lesson.

"Exactly."

"Go call him and skip that dinner. Go straight for dessert and then if you're not feeling it... don't see him again."

"That simple." She's crazy.

I roll my eyes while she goes on and on about me needing to be laid. "Yes, it's that simple. That's what men do. Nothing says we can't do that too. Go in with the expectations of just getting fucked and then walk away when you get what you want instead of sulking away with disappointment because you had your expectations too high."

My screen is lit up with a few text messages when I glance down. And I'm not even going to pretend it doesn't make me smile seeing them.

Lucas: Ariana... I'm a patient man when I want something. But the longer you make me wait... the more I'll make you beg for it.

He sent that almost four hours ago. I type a response and contemplate sending for a few seconds before I actually do it.

Me: Is that so?

Something tells me challenging this man will only increase how determined he is. But there's something to say about a guy who is straight up about what he wants. He hasn't mislead me about his intentions and it's very clear that he wants to have sex with me. He's hot. So, why not.

Lucas: You asking for that dinner, now?

Me: I'm thinking of going straight for dessert.

Lucas: Where are you. I'll pick you up.

Me: 1817 Maine St.

Lucas: I'll be there in twenty minutes.

My heart begins to race and Helen picks up on my changed expressions.

"So, who's the lucky one to receive that text?"

"The guy who asked me out earlier." I shrug and move to clean some of the bar tops.

"Get out of here. I can finish this up."

"He won't be here for twenty minutes; I can help until then." I'm purposely not going upstairs to change my clothes. He might very well show up in a suit and that'll be alright. With any luck we'll both be naked within a few minutes so what we wear won't be important.

Chapter
THREE

Nerves have me flattening out the wrinkle on the stomach of my tank top when I'm taking the last few steps to his car. He was just down the block when he texted that he was almost here. He also said I would know which car was his. *He wasn't lying. Holy crap.*

The door slides up to open but he's walking around the car to guide me in before I can manage to do it myself. Chivalry isn't dead. *Or at least it's alive before they get to sink into your pussy.*

He's still wearing his suit but takes off the jacket when he sees how I'm dressed. He's now donning slacks, a nice button-up shirt and a tie, looking like a millionaire and I can't help but regret my decision to look like a bar waitress from Hooters. He doesn't seem to bat an eye or act like it concerns him, so I continue to go along with this crazy plan. As Helen put it... *Get fucked and then walk away.*

The roar of his car echoes through the streets and into the darkness when we reach the edge of town. His focus on the road is sexy as hell while the speed we're going only intensifies my desire to let loose with this man. He's chaotic. And powerful. And unpredictable. And all of that excites me.

When we hit the open road, he rolls down the window and allows the wind to take over the madness. My breath almost stollen from me each time he shifts the car into another gear. "Touch yourself." His voice is hard to hear through the noise of the world rushing around me, so I look at him in question.

He nods as if he knows I heard him, but I'm still not sure I heard him right. "What?" He reads my lips before he pushes the buttons to close the windows once again.

"I said. Touch yourself." *Oh. I did hear him correct.* I'm just not sure I have that in me.

I shake my head in quick short motions before I search for the words to divert him away from this demand.

"I promise... you won't regret it. Touch yourself. Let go and just let me take you over the top." Oh shit. He's serious. And even though this sounds exactly like what I came here to do... I allow my insecurities to take control for a few seconds. This is absolute insanity. Have I lost my mind?

Well, in a day where I lost my job and had my stuff stolen... I could easily plead insanity as my reasoning for this one-night fling. And besides this *is exactly* what I came here to do.

With a new boost of confidence and outright craziness flowing through my head, I finger the button open on my shorts. My skin tingles as my hand slides down the front of my shorts, beneath my panties and between my legs. I'm sensitive to even my own touch. It's been far too long for me and the way my body is reacting is only further proof of that.

I arch my back in the seat, my head falling against the head rest as my eyes roll upward in pleasure the second I dip my index finger inside of my warmth. "Oh, fuck," His words come through a growl.

He's watching my every move. I can feel him... the heat of his stare driving me to burn even hotter for him and that encourages me to be bold and vocal.

I use the tip of my finger to put pressure on my clit, rotating circles and edging myself closer and closer to the high I so desperately crave. Hunger blinding me from anything other than this man watching me, empowering me to be selfish and wild.

Feeling adventurous, I slide my free hand up my tank top and palm my breast. My bra gets in the way, so I unfasten the center clasp and moan when my naked breasts are exposed to the cool air. "I want you naked." I don't hesitate with his newest demand. Giving him what he wants has somehow became a win for me. I crave his attention and it turns me on when he pushes me to do more.

I do a slow tease and remove my clothes as provocatively as I know how. I'm not saying it's the sexiest thing he's ever seen, but it's for sure the sexiest I've ever tried to be. In attempt to push the limits, I perch on my knees and lean over the console to draw him into a kiss. Along the way, I change my plan and go for his tie instead, slipping it off his neck and onto mine.

"Fuck, that's sexy." He shifts in his seat this time and that makes me proud. I'm actually pulling off this sexy torment thing. Knowing how to knot a tie comes in handy and I swear his eyes darken six shades watching the tie dangle between my tits. I'd know for sure if it wasn't dark, but the shift in his stare definitely turned, exciting me like crazy. I glance at the odometer and see that we're only slightly speeding now, his focus has shifted to me instead of the road. He likes what he sees and that feeds me even further.

My fingers slip around my neck and I cock my head back to make sure he's looking into my eyes when I squeeze implying that I like it rough. He smirks and slides his hand over mine, taking over the grip when I slide my fingers south.

I toy with my nipples letting him watch what it looks like when my middle finger circles my clit. He knows what I'm doing. And so do I when I let my tongue swipe over the wrist of the hand that's holding my neck in place.

"I knew you'd be fun to watch. You're gonna be my dirty girl. My fuck doll when I decide to play." He's making plans in his head and I'm just here for the shock and wow of a good fuck. I don't want to kill the mood I'm in, so I decide not to put him in his place about his grand plan. Besides... no one should ever be held accountable for the decisions they make when they're horny. That's just bad practice. "Touch yourself again. Sink those pretty little fingers into that tight pussy." Our eyes are locked for far longer than they should be while he's driving down the road, but in this moment I don't care. Maybe it's the danger of it all that has me squirming and ramped up so high that I'd come undone if he dared to touch me himself.

My touch takes me close though. A little bit of torture for us both while the road passes by in a flash around us. I slip my finger inside once again, this time deeper drawing a moan from between my lips. The sound of my voice has him sliding a thumb over my bottom lip, his full attention on the way it pulls down with his move. "I want to hear it all."

God, the way this man can pin all of his attention to a single body part of mine and light it on fucking fire. I burn for his approval.

I dip two fingers in, eliciting an even louder whimper until I adjust. Slipping them both to my clit, I massage circles over and over until I'm writing in his passenger seat. My nipples are tight and so so sensitive. "I want to watch you come. Come for me Ariana." He says my name like he's said it his entire life. And I listen to him like he's the one in charge. With a furious pace, I massage until I'm too sensitive to take it another second and I sail over the top into the best orgasm I've ever had. Sex has never had me spinning like this and I've never been one to do this solo in the past. *That may change after today.*

His grip tightens on my neck, inevitably drawing out my orgasm longer. I'm drenched by the time he loosens his hold and my body is quivering at the thought of him trying to touch me, even though a tiny part of me really craves it.

He draws me toward him until we're both face to face, tips his head up in a quick nod while the tip of his tongue flicks over my lips. "So fucking beautiful. I will never get enough of you."

Little did I know those two sentences would change my life forever.

Chapter FOUR

"He just watched you do all of that and then took you home?" My best friend can't believe the story and frankly... I feel like it might've been a dream. You know, the good kind. A sexy, hot and sticky dream. "He didn't expect you to suck him off or anything?"

"Nothing. He stopped the car and watched me while I put my clothes back on and then he palmed my thigh as he asked me when he could see me again."

"And did you tell him today?"

"No. I left it in the air." I kick the covers off and finally put my feet to the floor. I haven't really had a good reason to get out of bed yet. Now that it's noon, I should probably at least pretend to be alive today.

"Good lord. You wouldn't know a good thing if it slapped you in the face. Of course, you'll see him today and then every day for the rest of your life if he can promise you that kind of outcome."

"Kara... you know that's not realistic." My phone vibrates on the counter allowing her to hear it as well. Damn speaker phone.

Lucas: I'm picking you up at 7 tonight. Wear your sexiest dress.

I respond to his message with a simple thumbs up. I mean I'd be an idiot to say no to him... but I'm not dumb enough to think he wants anything more than me to simply comply to his wishes. If he plans to make me feel like he did last night... I'm definitely in for another round. *Or seven.*

"He's picking me up tonight. So, calm down. You can live vicariously through me yet another day."

"Funny. Talk to me when you've been married for three years and the only thing that sucks on your nipple is a teething baby." The sound of that pain has me cringing and considering never having children. "There's your weekly dose of birth control, brought to you by yours truly."

"What would I do without you?"

"Good thing you'll never have to find out. Alright, now go out tonight. Have lots of amazing mind-blowing sex and then call me to tell me about it tomorrow. Bryce is almost home for lunch."

"Okay. Talk to you tomorrow." I hang up with Kara and decide to make a day of cleaning up. The anticipation of seeing Lucas tonight gives me something to do with my time, which is fortunate since I'm currently unemployed. I've already sent my resume to three accounting firms that're hiring this morning, so with any luck one of them will email me back.

***

After shaving and moisturizing all the things, I slip the sexy black number over my head and shimmy it into place. I'm going braless tonight, but that's not even the best part. I'm not wearing panties either. I might just be good at this tease and tempt game he likes to play.

I blush when the bar erupts in whistles and catcalls when I step through the door. This would be one of those moments that I wish there was a privacy wall that allowed me to slip in and out without being seen.

"Holy hell. You took my advice. I can tell by that glow on your face." Helen yells over the bar while she's filling two beer glasses with precision.

"I did. And I'm doing it again tonight."

"No. No. No darlin'. That wasn't the advice. One and done. Beat them at their own game."

"We're gonna go for two and done with this one." I can feel the smile on my face fall as the bar goes silent and my words echo through the entire place. The heavy feeling of Lucas sweeps over me and it only takes a second to know that he chose to come in to get me over my suggestion of allowing me to meet him at the car.

He's in another suit. This one has to be designer the way it was literally made to fit *his* body. His stare slices me open, making me vulnerable and wanting to please him once again. "You look beautiful." He takes my hand and twirls me around while the entire bar continues to watch our every move.

He runs his finger down my bare back until his hand rests on my lower back and he's guiding me out the door. I look to him to gauge his reaction to the fact that I live above a bar and feel relief when he doesn't seem to care. If he disapproves, it's not obvious on his face. Although, I can imagine a guy like him having a killer poker face.

We're almost to the alley when he breaks the silence. "Bare back. No panty lines." He pulls me back against his chest and speaks into my neck before we reach the SUV. My eyes lock with the driver waiting to open the door for us once we're closer. He diverts his eyes in a rush, but I keep looking at him while Lucas slides one palm down my arm and his other hand splays open over my mid-section. His wandering fingers find their way over my chest and then back down until he's palming my pussy from underneath the dress. "Do you want him to watch you?"

My head falls back against his chest as I take in the rush and barely bring myself to shaking my head in response. His fingers being so close, yet so damn far away is a distraction and I can't concentrate on two things at once when he's this close.

I don't want the driver to watch me. *Do I?* It was amazing when Lucas watched… but I'm not out here trying to have a full audience witnessing me have orgasms.

"Do you like to dance?" He begins to sway in place with me, his erection grinding into my back. This time I nod. I haven't danced in forever... but I used to love it. Kara and I'd get lost in the music and have so much fun back in the day. "I'm taking you dancing." He takes a step forward, inevitably moving us both toward the SUV and snapping me out of my stupor.

The ghost of his touch is still lingering over my skin, leaving me just as sensitive as I was last night in his car. I've been with this man for less than five minutes and I'd literally climb him like a tree and fuck him senseless if we didn't have an audience. How does he get me so riled up in such a short amount of time?

I slide across the back seat and watch him follow in behind me. Darkness surrounds us the second the door is closed and even more so when the privacy window is raised between us and the driver. His fingers roam over my thigh the entire drive, but he doesn't slide my dress any higher... no matter how much I will him to.

The club is packed. If his goal was to make me crazy starved for his touch and then release me into the wild... mission accomplished. Every brush of a body against mine or the image of a couple gyrating to the sultry music has me nearly begging for the same attention. I want him all over me. I want people to see that *he* is with *me*.

I lost him in the crowd when I first took the dance floor, but eventually found him leaned against a bar on the second level watching me over the railing. Sliding my palms down my legs I sway my hips and relish the way my dress edges upward. So close to exposing me to the entire club. He shifts his stance and I know then and there that he's wanting me to push the limits tonight. For him. For myself.

I continue to dance for him while the club chaos swarms around me. My focus entirely on Lucas and his on me. I don't even turn my eyes from his when a girl slides in behind me and starts mimicking my movements, grinding her tits against my back and her hips into my ass. I even keep our connection when I turn my head to kiss her. Full on tongue action between nips and nibbles on my neck.

God, this feels so good. Her hands start to slide over my body and I don't miss his grip on the railing get tighter. He's not glowering at me like he's jealous… he's begging me to give him more. *He loves this.* He wants to watch me. He gets off on watching.

He holds up two fingers before curling a single one, giving me the signal for both of us to go to him.

I take the hand of the female I haven't even bothered to take a look at and lead her up the stairs to meet my voyeur. Excitement runs through my veins while I contemplate the possibilities of this newly realized information.

"My dirty girl. Feel what you do to me." He takes one of my hands and places it over his bulging cock. His eyes roll shut at my grip and through a breathy grumble he continues, "I want to watch you two together. I want you to fuck that girl for me, Ariana."

Chapter FIVE

I've never kissed a girl before tonight. It's not that I'm against it... I've just never felt the connection with a female enough to venture out of my comfort zone. And it's not even that I find this girl sexually appealing. I'm attracted to the way Lucas looks at me when I push the limits. It's intoxicating, like the best drug I've ever experienced in my life.

"Are you up to give this guy a show? He likes to watch." I whisper in the girl's ear and my stomach rolls when she nods a quick response.

"Where are we doing this?" My question has Lucas pulling me by the hand, through a few doors and down a long hallway until we step in front of an elevator. Lucas uses a key card revealing a little piece of his life to me in the process.

The three of us step inside and stand in silence until we reach the sixth floor. The doors open to a full apartment that's crisp and clean with everything in its place... as if a perfectionist lives here. *Or as if no one lives here.* Maybe this is just one of many of his places he goes to get his thrills.

I grab Lucas' tie and lead him to the bedroom. The extra-large king bed was obvious from the elevator but I'm even happier when I see the chair in the corner. I don't miss that the chair is positioned to have a perfect view of the bed. And I also don't let myself think about how many others he's brought here. I lead him until he's standing in front of the chair and then use an index finger to his chest to make him sit.

He lets out an exhale as he sits back and I give him a little show. His eyes never leave mine as I sway my hips and touch his thighs. Part of me wanting him to change his mind about the girl and for him to tell me how much he wants to fuck me. But he doesn't.

He does slide his hand up my leg and give me a little squeeze of encouragement. With a slight smile, I turn for the girl and slide my straps off my shoulders. She follows my lead and does the same with her own before we both send our dresses to the floor. I don't even know this girl's name but I lean down and kiss her breast. I watch Lucas over her shoulder and reposition us so that he can see better. I repeat my movement and give him the dramatic view of my tongue flicking over her nipple before she goes to her knees at my feet.

We're still close enough to Lucas that I can prop one heel between his legs, giving him an even better view. The girl's tongue swipes over my clit and I can feel my entire world shifting in that very moment. She draws it out, slowly... purposely dragging my sensations to the tip of my clit so she can nibble and torment me even further. "Ah god." I quiver and shiver as feelings I've never felt before crash through my body.

My eyes go from his to hers... back to his. Two of the sexiest images of my life are right in front of me and I can't decide which is better. The darkness in his stare as he takes everything in or the gaze in her eyes as she looks up at me for encouragement and praise. Both begging me for me anything I'm willing to give like I'm the queen of the damn world.

Lucas shifts and palms his cock through his pants. The bulge is obviously mean and in need of attention but I can't help but want him to let me take care of it. I drop my leg and sit on his lap, purposely grinding my ass over his rock-hard erection at the same time opening myself up for the girl on her knees in front of me.

I lay back on his chest, my head falling to his shoulder when she runs her tongue back and forth on my clit. She slides a finger inside me while she continues to lick and nibble her way into the forefront of my focus... and for a moment, I almost forget Lucas is behind me. Until he moans. "God, yes."

He palms one of my breasts and she reaches up to palm the other. Her finger slides in and out of me with a curl and pressure that again draws every sensation forward, leaving me breathless and squirming while she focuses on my clit.

She fucks me with her mouth and I writhe on his dick until I'm a mess of screams and sensations, bucking and moaning through the insanity of all the attention. Can it really be like this every time I'm with this man. Yes, it was her tongue and fingers doing the work... but it was his presence that sent me to the entirely new level of euphoria.

"You can leave." I try to say it nicely, but I'm not sure it's possible to be nice and kick someone out in the middle of sex.

I slide to my knees in front of Lucas and begin unzipping his pants before she has the chance to grab her dress and leave. "I know you wanted me to have sex with her... but right now I want you." I pull out his cock and lick the underside from base to tip. He lifts his hips to lower his pants and I take him to the back of my throat before I gag and then lick him again. "You like to watch... so you can watch me do things to you."

His smirk during a pressed grind to the back of my throat is one of the best images I've ever seen. Maybe I'm a voyeur too, because seeing him respond to what I do is as intoxicating as letting him watch me.

"I'm going to watch you do so many things, my precious dirty girl. But don't mistake my love of voyeurism as some sort of celibacy promise. I will be fucking you every chance I get."

His words have me climbing into his lap and straddling him while he slides inside of me. *The girl's foreplay made this easier for sure.*

He fills me up completely and maybe it's the wild ride up to this point that has me so riled up but when he grips my neck and uses it as leverage to fuck me senseless, I know right then and there... I'm a goner. Lucas has that devil dick that I will forever crave. He'll have me messed up for life trying to get this again if we ever decide to go our separate ways.

And that makes him very dangerous. Too dangerous to allow this to happen again.

If you'd like to stay in touch with me, check out: www.hilarystormwrites.com.

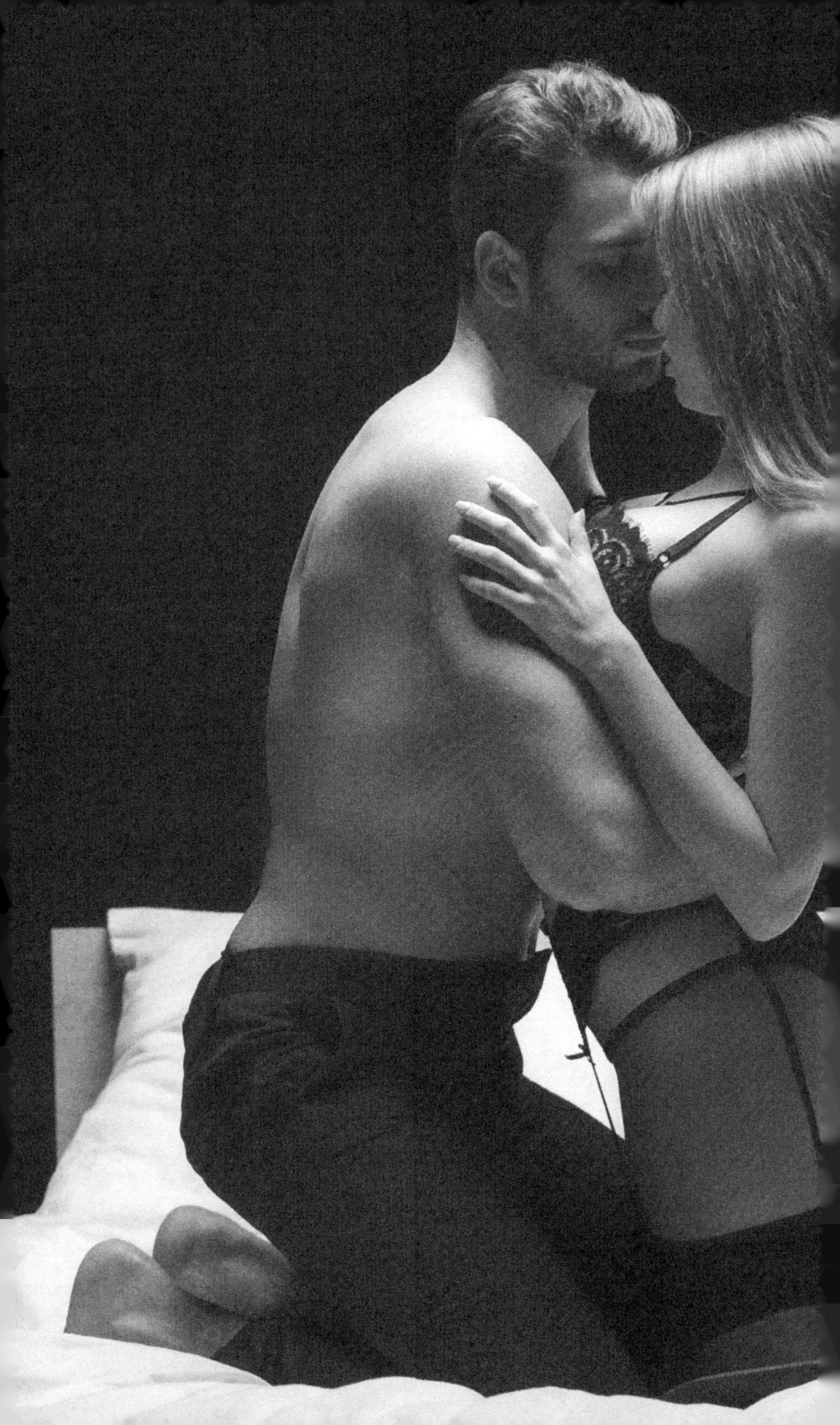

Forbidden Nights
WITH THE ROCKSTAR

J. SAMAN

Chapter ONE

Fallon

He doesn't know I'm here. From the moment I bought the tickets to the moment I got on the airplane to the moment I swiped my ticket at the arena tonight I debated letting him know. I've also debated not seeing him at all. But even as those last thoughts crossed my mind—the practical ones that permanently live in my head—I knew that wasn't going to happen.

I knew from the second I saw the tickets for Greyson Monroe's show go on sale that I would purchase them. I would fly to wherever I had to, and I would see him.

And more than likely fuck his brains out.

It's been a year and a half since I saw him last. A year and a half of college and studying and exams and very little Grey. A year and a half where we'd text and occasionally call, and I'd try not to worry about my best friend. A year and a half since Suzie, Central Square's manager, and Grey's brother Zax's girlfriend died and Grey's band and world fell apart.

The lead singer for Central Square no more, Grey is a solo artist with a chart-topping album. And I couldn't be prouder of him. This was always meant to be him. His fate. I just never quite knew where I fit into all that.

I was the girl next door. His best friend and he was mine.

But that didn't stop me from asking him to take my virginity. Or from sneaking out my window and crawling into his so I could sleep beside him. He made me feel wild and dangerous and beautiful and smart and *seen*. All of which no one else had ever done before.

Or since for that matter.

It's why I couldn't let him go when he left at sixteen with Central Square. It was the same with him. I think both of us needed that comfort. That lifeline and trust and connection we have in each other. Over the years it's been our bedrock.

I met Greyson when I was fourteen. He was my neighbor, a ridiculously hot teenager who would sit on his roof and strum on his guitar and sing. That's what lured me to him. How fearless and brave he was when I was anything but.

Still, I should have told him I was coming.

What if he has plans after the show? What if he has a harem of groupies waiting for him to service them one after the other?

I'm being reckless. I left Yale—missed my Friday afternoon class—and flew from JFK straight to LA for this and I have exactly two nights before I have to return. My parents can never know about my friendship with him. They hate him and they hate his family for so many reasons. The man is forbidden to me and not simply because he's not the type of man they'd ever want their perfect princess to be with.

Never in my life have I truly gone against my parents. It's impossible. My family's expectations run high and are impossible to live up to. So me getting involved with a hot, bad-boy rock star? Pfft. Please. They'd never allow that to happen. It's certainly not in my plans either. I have to finish college and then it's medical school and then residency.

My life is all set before me and unchangeable.

I shake all that off. Whatever. I'm here and I don't regret it. Besides, it's only been sex and friendship between Greyson and me and nothing more. Only a fool of a girl would expect or imagine anything more with Greyson Monroe and I am not a fool.

The stadium is dark, growing edgy, waiting for Greyson to return to the stage for his encore. Fans are clapping and shouting, cheering, unable to contain themselves as the tension builds and builds with each second of his absence.

My heart picks up the rhythm as the drummer begins striking a heavy beat. *Boom, boom, boom.* Swirling white and red lights zigzag across the stage. The arena booms, the floor vibrates beneath my feet, and cheers pour out from every direction as Greyson comes running back on. He drags a hand through his damp hair and gives everybody an impish grin that has my heart pinching in my chest.

His dark eyes glimmer against the lights, his white T-shirt clinging to every muscle of his chest and abs.

Bringing the microphone back up to his mouth he says, "Hey! Are you having a good time tonight?"

Everyone starts screaming, myself included, jumping up and down as if it's the beginning of the night and not the end. In moments like these, it's so easy to get lost. To be a total fan girl and swoon over the sexy, insanely hot rock god on the stage.

He makes my heart palpitate. He makes my panties wet. He makes my skin buzz.

Every time I see my guy perform, I become a totally obsessed groupie.

How could I not?

I'm so proud. So freaking proud of him. I mean, damn. Look where he is!

It warms my heart endlessly to see how many people love him. How far he's coming from the kid sitting on his rooftop singing words in his head and strumming chords from his heart.

I scream again, jumping up and down and clapping like a mindless fool, totally swept up in the moment because he did it. He turned losing Suzie and the end of his band into a new beginning instead of the end. Everything inside me swells until I'm an emotional wreck. It's almost silly how much my emotions overflow but I don't care enough to stop the tears.

That's my best friend up there on that stage making everyone in this room fall helplessly in love with him.

"As you all know this last year and a half has been rough for me." He laughs sarcastically. "Rough is a bullshit euphemism falling apart. I miss my Suzie. She was our heart. Our foundation. Our light. She was the big sister I never had, and I'll never stop missing her." He clears his throat. "Hey, I didn't mean to get emotional like this, but we lost Susie and with that, I know you lost Central Square. I know what that did to you. And I am so grateful to you for sticking with me. For continuing to support me and my music. I love you." He punctuates that last part with a smile and damn.

So many whistles and ovations and sighs from everyone here.

"It's always the bleakest darkness before the most beautiful dawn and that's what this has been for me. I want to thank you all for being here and continuing my dream of being a musician. This is a song I wrote for you Suzie. Miss you, girl."

Grey launches into a ballad. One of the biggest hits from his first solo album. It's so sweet and heartfelt. Not something that Greyson Monroe normally does as his music tends to be more upbeat and vivacious. The sort that gets your bones rattling and your feet moving.

But I can't help as more tears drip down my cheeks as I watch him sing this song for Suzie, the girl who was so full of light. She had a stroke in the shower at the age of twenty-two. Unbelievable. Heartbreaking doesn't even begin to cover it.

The song comes to an end, and then he immediately launches into another one, the anthem of his album. I dance and sing along with it, having listened to this album more times than I can even count. Listening to Grey's voice has gotten me through some of the hardest moments of my life.

As the song starts to come to an end, I slip on my VIP backstage badge and meander my way through the crowds over toward the fence line that separates the backstage from the main arena. There's a line of people, mostly women, and no one looks happy. A few are even screaming at the security guards though I can't quite make out what they're saying.

I scoot around them, going over to the side where there's another burly guy standing vigilant. I plaster on my sweetest smile and hold up my badge that I paid some serious scratch for after-market. "Hi. Is this where I enter?"

"No groupies tonight," the security guy barks, his stern voice.

I wave the badge at him again. "Not a groupie. I have a badge."

"No badges were sold for this event. No one is allowed backstage tonight. Mr. Monroe's orders."

Frustration slams through. I don't even care about the lost money or that I bought something fake. I should have called Grey from the start because I was hesitant and unsure but now all I want is to see him. I have to tell him how proud I am of him.

"Please, I'm his friend. You have to let him know I'm here."

The guy gives me a bored look that suggests he hears that at least ten times a night.

"No, I mean it," I persist. "Please just let him know that Fallon Lark is here. He'll come for me," I promise the security guy. I could call Grey, but he never has his phone on him after shows. He always leaves it on his bus or in his hotel room. He likes to unwind and let go after shows and disconnecting is part of that.

The concert ends, Grey waves goodbye, and then everything goes black. Floor lights turn on and people start filing out, but I don't budge. My hands land on the metal railing and I take a step closer until I'm practically pressed into it.

"Please. Just tell him. Fallon Lark. That's all I ask."

The security gives me another look, staring, straight into my eyes, and grunts in resignation. He presses a button on his earpiece. "I have a Fallon Lark here to see Mr. Monroe. She claims she's his friend."

I don't roll my eyes at the way he says *claims* with a sardonic tone. Instead, I thank him and hope the message gets relayed.

Seconds and minutes tick by. I'm not even sure how long I stand here, the arena growing emptier and emptier. It feels like an eternity and with each second that passes my heartbeat grows faster and faster, worried that he won't come this time. Worried that he is too busy to see me or that he never got the message because the security guys think I'm a liar.

But just as my hopes begin to dwindle, the security guy touches his earpiece, and then suddenly he moves the gate and waves me in. "Up the stairs. Someone will take you to him."

"Great! Thank you so much!"

I scoot past the metal partition and up the stairs and then suddenly I'm backstage in the dark with no clue where to go. No one is here to greet me. No one so much as stops to notice me as roadies clear the stage, moving back and forth with large, heavy equipment.

Tonight is Grey's last show in LA.

I make my way down a corridor, wandering around aimlessly only to be suddenly scooped up off my feet and spun around in a circle. A squeal catapults from my lungs, laughter along with it. His smell, the feel of his arms, I'd know him anywhere.

"You're here? I can't believe you're here." His smile rubs across my cheek, and instantly I loop my arms around his sweaty neck.

"I'm here," I breathe, relief mixed with something warm and delicious swirling through my chest. I've missed him. I've missed him so much.

His face lands on my neck and for a moment all he does is hold me like this. Bride style with his face buried in my neck and mine in his as we cling to each other unable to form words.

He starts walking, carrying me through the back of the stage.

"You can put me down." My voice is light, unable to hide my amusement only Grey isn't being playful.

"No," he says, his voice serious, so unlike him. "I want to carry you. I want to hold you so that after you're gone again, I'll remember what it feels like. I've fucking *missed* you, Fall Girl."

My eyes close and my breath stutters in my chest.

"I've missed you too. So much." I squeeze him tighter, resting my head on the top of his chest as he carries me. After going so long without each other, neither of us wants the connection to be severed.

"How long do I have you for?"

"Two nights. I have to be back at school on Sunday."

"I like how you said nights."

I smirk, pulling back slightly so I can catch his eyes. I quirk an eyebrow. "I didn't say you were getting lucky."

He grins devilishly. "You didn't say I wasn't."

Chapter TWO

Greyson

I set her down when we reach the green room. I was tempted to just keep going. To race out back and hop in my car and drive her straight to my place. But I have stuff here and I'm sweaty as fuck. Two nights. With my girl.

I can hardly contain myself and I know she can feel that.

It's been a year and a half since I saw her last. Since Suzie died and Fall Girl came to hold my hand as my entire world fell apart. I have my brother and my former bandmates who are still my closest friends, but Fallon Lark has always been different to me.

My high school best friend's twin sister. At least until an accident made us enemies. Fallon was completely forbidden to me. I was the bad boy, and she was the good girl. I was the kid with big rock star dreams, and she was the princess with her entire life planned out for her. Even now, she's not supposed to be here. No one knows we've kept in touch over the years.

And no one knows the way I secretly burn for her. Not even her.

We're friends first. Friends who do occasionally fuck, but that was never the primary focus of our relationship.

Fall Girl skips over to the black couch along the wall and drops down, helping herself to come cheese and crackers, and fuck, do I love this girl. I can't stop staring at her, making sure this isn't a dream. That she's actually here with me and I get her for two nights.

"Do you want a drink?" I offer and she pauses. Cracker loaded with brie in hand, her violet eyes cast up to mine.

"Is it lame if I say I haven't had a drink in months?"

"You mean lame because you're in college and supposed to be going to frat parties and getting trashed."

Her head bobs and then she snickers. "Yale frats are so awful. Rich, entitled douchebags who use money and daddy to bail them out of everything."

"Should I ask the obvious question?"

I go over to the counter and pull off my sweat-soaked shirt, tossing it on top of my duffle and using the cold, wet towels they have in here to wipe down. I'll shower at home, but I need a change of clothes first.

Her lids lower and her gaze turns heated as she stares at my chest and abs for a long beat, admiring the ink on my arms before she clears her throat and pops the cracker in her mouth, looking away as a touch of rose flushes her cheeks.

"Yes, I hooked up with one of them. At the beginning of the year. He was terrible." She snorts again, shakes her head incredulously, and then grabs a piece of cheddar.

I hate hearing that. I know she doesn't know this. I'm her friend and she's talking to me as one, but I fucking *hate* hearing about her with other guys. Yes, I hook up too and I realize it's a double standard, but if it were ever possible for her to be mine for real, I'd never look at another woman again.

I go into my duffle and pull out a clean shirt, throwing it on to hide the frown I can't erase from my face.

"Should I kick his ass?" I quip. Please say yes. I'll fly out to Connecticut right now.

"Not worth it. Definitely not worth it." She chews as she talks, covering her mouth with her hand as she does. "Anyway, I don't go to a lot of parties. I study and I do my good girl Lark thing. I had to get ready for med school applications and things."

"Did you get accepted?"

She lowers her lids and smiles softly. "I did."

"Where?"

"Everywhere I applied. I have to talk to my parents more about it. I know they have a lot of opinions on where I go. I'd be happy with any of them."

Of course, she would be. Fallon Lark is only happy if she's making her family happy.

"What about you?" she parries, shifting on the sofa. "The new album is doing tremendous things."

I walk over to her with my bag on my shoulder and take her hand to help her to stand. "It's doing incredible things," I confirm. "Things I'm beyond grateful for. Things I wasn't sure it would do." Central Square hit it big when Suzie posted a YouTube video of us. I was sixteen. Zax was twenty. The other guys were somewhere in between. Overnight we landed a record contract and a fifteen-month tour schedule and that was it. We left Boston and I never looked back.

With the exception of Fallon.

Then Suzie died and it all fell apart. Or maybe it was falling apart before that, and I was trying too hard to hold on. I don't know now. I just know that the last fifteen months of my life have been hell. Filled with panic attacks and no sleep and holding my brother up since Suzie was his girl. I didn't think I'd find any success on my own and I didn't know what I was going to do if that was the case.

I lead us out into the mild California night. It's about midnight now, but I'm not the least bit tired. I'm shocked Fall isn't out on her feet given the time change. I nod to the security guys and open the passenger side of my car, and within minutes we're racing out in the direction of my place. A penthouse I rarely use. Most of my time I spend back home in Boston.

It's where Zax and Callan are.

Asher is finishing up his last year at Alabama, hoping to make it to the NFL though he was only a starter this year. Lenox is in Maine where he's been hiding pretty much for the last year and a half since Suzie died. She was his twin.

We pull into my building, and I hold her hand the entire way. Then something dawns on me. "Where's your stuff?"

She shifts her weight as we ride up the elevator. "I um. I wasn't sure if I was going to stay or not when I flew out here and I didn't want to have a bag with me at the concert."

"Why weren't you sure if you were going to stay?"

She gives me an evasive half-shrug, but I jerk on her hand, forcing her to look at me. "You know why. I'm not supposed to be here. I'm not supposed to be with you. But I missed you and I haven't seen you in so long." A deep breath. "So I came."

"I'll have my assistant get you some stuff since I assume you don't want to go shopping?"

She gnaws on her lip and shakes her head.

I slip my phone out of my back pocket and shoot off a text, telling him some basics that she'll need. He replies instantly that he'll have them sent over first thing.

"You'll have stuff by the morning," I tell her with a sly smirk.

She makes a displeased noise in the back of her throat, likely because I'm being highhanded and didn't ask her first, but I don't care. She's here with me.

I pivot us until I have her pressed into the wall of the elevator. We have a connection. We always have. More than friendship, she refuses to acknowledge it and most of the time we're together or talking on the phone, I pretend it isn't there.

But the truth is, I've been in love with her since I first laid eyes on her.

I hate it as much as I love it. She'll never be mine and loving her is futile and frankly a little self-destructive. I've debated letting her go and sometimes I even play at it. I don't chase her. I don't go to see her. I can't. This love is pain, and I don't do so well with that.

It's why I understand her uncertainty.

Still, that won't stop me from being with her until the last second I can be and then I'll lick my wounds and force myself to keep going as I always do when she leaves me.

Panic-tinted desperation rushes over me at the thought of her going and the second the doors of the elevator open, I swivel her around and press her into my foyer wall. I don't give her time to move. Time to look around my place or explore. A gasp flees her lungs as I lean in, and before she can say anything, my mouth is on hers. My hands get lost in her long, inky hair as I twist my head to the side and plunder deeper.

Her fists take hold of my shirt as if she's not quite sure what to do, pull me closer or push me away. Her inner dilemma doesn't stop her from opening for me though and granting my tongue access.

"Shower with me," I breathe into her mouth, lifting her up in my arms and wrapping her legs around my waist. Before she can answer, I'm carrying her across my apartment, my mouth feasting on hers the entire time. My cock swells between us and she moans, grinding against it. I press us into the wall beside my bedroom and kiss her, my mouth climbing down the column of her neck. My nose glides along her soft skin and I inhale, my eyes rolling back in my head.

Her smell.

Motherfuck she smells *so* good. So good I almost don't want her to shower, but the idea of her naked body wet and slick against mine...

I groan, grinding up and into her, making her gasp and her head fall back against the wall.

"I didn't come here for this."

I grin. "No? What did you come here for then?"

"You. Your show."

"You have me, and you saw the show." I pull back, meeting her lust-drunk eyes. "Do you want me, Fall Girl?"

She blinks, swallows, and then nods shakily.

"It's okay to want me." My hand cups her face, my thumb dragging on her swollen bottom lip. "I'm still your Grey. I'm still your friend. I always will be. But we can do this too. We can be this too for each other."

Her legs lower and she slips out of my grasp, and for one awful moment, I think she's about to leave. But she doesn't. She takes me completely by surprise as she walks into my bedroom, her back to me she slowly peels her shirt up and over her head, tossing it in the direction of a chair I have in the corner.

My cock jerks in my jeans, already leaking for her. Her jeans are next and then she's standing there, in the middle of my bedroom only wearing her bra and panties. I rub myself over the denim, unable to stop my need.

She's so sexy. So unbelievably sexy. Gorgeous curves and luscious ass.

But I can't see her tits and I have to change that now.

I enter my bedroom, go over to my dresser, and pull a few things out. I set them on top and then turn to her, watching as she does the same with me. Now we're facing each other, our breathing noisy, her heavy tits rising and falling in her thin bra. A bra I know she wore for me even though I know she likes sexy underthings.

"What now?" she asks softly, her voice silk.

"Crawl to me."

Her eyes flash at the request. Usually we rabidly tear each other's clothes off and fuck with heat and urgency as distance and time and passion get the better of us.

"Crawl to you." It's not a question. More of a mental declaration of her own limits. She licks her lips and then sucks her bottom one into her mouth, chewing on it. On a heavy breath, she lowers herself to her knees and I just about lose it right here. "Now what?"

"Come suck me off."

With a coy smirk, she removes her bra and then puts herself on all fours and I'm dead. So fucking dead. She is erotic and stunning, easily the sexiest thing I've ever seen. She crawls towards me able to see exactly what she's doing to me as she does. This isn't demeaning. She has all the power here and she knows it.

I'm hers. Her captive. Her slave.

I'd do *anything* for this woman right now.

Her tits sway, her pretty rose-colored nipples hard, her long hair frames her face and drapes over her shoulders. When she reaches me, she sits back on her heels, staring straight up at me as she goes for my button and zipper.

"God, you're perfect." My fingers capture a strand of her hair, her eyes glowing at me. "So irresistibly perfect I can hardly stand it."

My pants and boxer briefs hit the ground and then she's stroking my cock, squeezing it, and stars burst behind my eyes.

"Fuck that feels good." "If you think that does, just wait." She pumps my cock straight into her wet, eager mouth and my hand automatically fists her hair. The urge to fuck her face is brutal, but I let her lead, loving how she's loving this. Fall Girl gets in her head a lot. But when she allows herself to relax and let go, she's an absolutely fierce vixen.

Pleasure sizzles up my spine as she bottoms out, gags, swallows, and then goes at it again. She did this to me the last time I saw her. I was in bed, not having slept in who knows how long, and she climbed under the covers and sucked me straight down her throat. She blew my mind and then slept in my arms that night and I don't want her to leave.

Not ever.

I'd give anything, do anything for her to be mine.

But that's not our reality. It never will be, and I've had to learn to manage in her absence and breathe when she walks out my door. Two nights with her. That's all this will be until the next time she finds me and ruins me.

"That's it," I praise. "So good, Fall. That feels so good."

"Mmmm," she hums against me making my balls draw up. She continues to fist my cock, driving it into her mouth as she bobs and licks and swallows my dick. But then she moans again, and it takes me a second to realize that she's fingering herself. Her panties are pushed to the side and her finger is rubbing her clit.

I drag her hair up into a ponytail and twist my neck so I can see her hand better. "Fuck. I can smell you. Your pretty cunt smells so good. You need to be fucked. Don't you?"

A blush rises up her face and I smirk because my dirty, crude words never fail to both push her limits and make her even wetter.

I growl at the thought. "I can't wait to taste you. To lick all the cum from inside you as I make you come again."

She keeps going and now my hand in her hair is helping her along. I'm not going to come down her throat, but I want her to come on her fingers first and then around my cock in the shower.

And just as I tell her that, her hips grind harder into her hand and the moans on my cock grow louder and she's coming.

It feels incredible. Her moans and vibrating whimpers nearly tip me over the edge, but I watch her face and I watch her hand as she orgasms on it. The moment she starts to sag, I pull my angry dick from her lips and then haul her up by her hair straight into me. My lips crash against hers and I pick her up again, unable to stop myself because distance feels impossible.

We go into my bathroom, and I turn on the shower for us. I set her down on the counter and grin at how adorable she is with her legs crossed, perched on marble all the while she watches my hand with rapt fascination. I grab a condom and then once I'm naked, I lift her again, putting her on her feet so I can slide her panties off her.

"You're so beautiful." My forehead meets hers, our eyes locked. "I've missed you, Fall Girl."

"Missed you."

I take us into the shower, get us both wet, and then drop to my knees. "My turn."

Chapter THREE

Fallon

Greyson is on his knees before me, staring up at me, his eyes glinting with raw, masculine desire. He's so hot like this that it makes my head spin. With his eyes locked on me, his tongue darts out, flicking my clit.

My lips part and a breathy moan slips out.

"More?"

I nod, gnawing on the corner of my lip. My fingers glide through the wet strands of his hair. I've messed around a bit with boys at school, but that's what they've all been.

Boys.

None of them could hold a candle to Greyson Monroe. Not the rock star version of him. Not the best friend version of him. And certainly not the lover version of him.

I get a wicked grin and then he's pulling one of my knees over his shoulders, opening me up fully to him. He squeezes my hip, gliding his hand back to my ass, and then he's pushing my pelvis toward him as his mouth dives in.

I writhe and squeal as his mouth assaults me, licking a trail from my ass all the way up to my clit before thrusting deep inside of me. His thumb spreads my lips open and then he's using the pad of his thumb to rub my clit as his tongue pushes in and out of me, fucking me, swirling all around, licking and tasting every part of me he can.

My hand tangles in his hair, my pussy rocks into his face, and I nearly black out at how good this feels. His stubble on my inner thighs and smooth mound. His fingers playing with me, gripping at me. His mouth feasts on me, taking no prisoners as he groans and grunts at the taste of me. I hold him closer, pressing him in even deeper as his lips capture my clit, sucking it into his mouth.

"You want my fingers too? Or just my mouth?"

Jesus. The way he talks. I've forgotten about how dirty his mouth can be.

His finger starts rimming my opening as he stares up at me. He's not letting me get off the hook with this and I can already feel a blush rising up my face.

"Tell me," he demands, and after I crawled across the floor to suck him off and now have him on his knees with my pussy open to him, I have no idea why I'm shy about anything.

"Both. I want your fingers inside me and your mouth eating me."

His eyes smolder. I don't even get a smirk or a grin. He's too worked up. All fire.

His fingers plunge inside, quirking and rubbing on my spot as he gives me a long, dirty lick. My back arches and my eyes close. Especially when I feel the sharp sting of his teeth on my clit only to have him soothe it with the flat of his tongue. He starts flicking me, fucking me, eating me like he'll never have the chance again.

I grind against him, fucking his face, chasing my orgasm until it explodes within me. I come. I come so hard and for so long and the steam of the shower makes it harder for me to catch my breath.

Grey keeps going. Licking and rubbing and pushing in and out and I can't think. My thighs tremble with the effort to hold myself up and I know I'll have bruises from his grip on my ass.

I'm warm and tingly and wet and it's noisy.

He's noisy.

Slowly I blink my eyes open and watch as he stands, his lips glistening with the evidence of my orgasm. In a mindless rush, I grab the back of his head and slam his lips to mine. I want to taste myself on him. I want to prove to myself that this is real. That when

I return to Yale and graduate this spring and go to medical school and live that life that I didn't imagine this.

That I didn't imagine him.

Never am I more real than when I'm with him.

It's a piece of myself I miss more than anything. A piece I long for and dream about and get myself off to. What would be if he wasn't so forbidden to me? If my family didn't hate him? If there was ever a possibility?

There isn't and I know there isn't. It's the sex endorphins talking, and I need to push them away. Grey still hasn't come, and his cock is as hard as I've ever seen it, but instead of lifting me and pushing inside me as I expect, he starts washing my hair instead.

I go to touch him, but he pushes me away, shaking his head no.

"No as in you don't want to come?"

He smirks. "Oh no, I plan on coming. A lot. A few times tonight at least. I just want to take my time with you and the shower isn't the best for that."

"Then let's finish up."

He starts nibbling on my neck. "Impatient?"

Yes! "I just feel bad. He looks... painful."

"He is a bit. But it'll also make coming inside you even better."

We finish washing up and then Grey wraps me in a large, fluffy white towel before doing the same with himself. We dry off and I brush my hair, but that's all I get before I'm whisked into the living room of the suite. Grey sits down on the chair and holds my hands as I straddle him.

"Ride me. Ride me hard."

He rolls a condom on and then I position myself over him before sinking down. My eyes flutter closed, and I throw my head back as I grip the arms of the chair. Holy hell. Full. The man fills me up and then some, nearly to the point of pain.

His hands capture my breasts, lifting their heavy weight in his hands and squeezing them. I moan, rocking forward, digging my clit against him.

"Fuck, you're teasing me now."

I grin and roll my hips again, undulating in a slow rhythm that holds him inside me, exactly where he is.

"Fall Girl."

"Yes, Mr. Monroe?"

His hands cup my face, forcing my eyes open. "Do you feel how deep inside you I am?"

My breath catches. "Yes."

"Baby, I only want to be deeper. Take me deeper."

Holy fuck.

His hands go to my hips, and I follow his motion, using my knees as leverage to push up, sliding along his slippery cock until he almost falls out of me. His carnal gaze holds mine and then he slams me down just as he thrusts up. I cry out and that cry turns into a long, loud moan as he continues to pump up into me.

Over and over. Faster and faster. Harder and harder.

It's exquisite. It's earth-shattering. It's everything and all I can do is grip the arms of the chair and hold on as he takes me, uses me, fucks me how he wants me. He watches me, he watches my skin flush and my tits bounce. A drunk, dizzy look on his beautiful face.

He exhales a ragged grunt, wrapping his arms around me and dragging me closer to his chest as he sits up straighter.

Somehow that manages to pull me tighter, to force his cock in deeper.

"Oh!"

He grins, biting at my breasts, swirling his tongue around my nipples. "Again?"

"Yes. Please. Again."

He does it again, plunging up and angling himself in at the same time, hitting my front wall and smashing my clit against him at the same time. I'm delirious with it. Lost in him. As it always is. This is why I wasn't going to tell him I was here and yet why in the end I couldn't stay away.

He eats at me. Absorbs me. Consumes me until I'm flayed open and all that's left of me is his.

His arms band around me, crushing me to him, and then he half stands, pumping tirelessly into me, slamming into me until all I feel is him. The heat of my orgasm comes at me, a brush fire I wasn't fully prepared for. With a scream I clutch at his back, scraping my nails along his skin. He roars, face smothered in my neck, teeth scraping at my skin as he pounds me, shooting himself and filling the condom.

Then he collapses. On his back. On the floor. Dragging me down on top of him.

I giggle lightly at how we're positioned. Both naked, stranded at an awkward angle in between the chair and the coffee table. He laughs too, his dark eyes light and content.

It's late. Somewhere in the wee hours of the morning and even later for me since I'm used to east coast time.

Still, I don't care.

Even as I yawn and lay my ear against his chest, listening to his steady, strong heartbeat as he plays with the wet, sex-snarled strands of my hair.

"Come with me," he says but then lifts me up and takes me with him, carrying me into the bedroom. He sets me down and pulls the white comforter back. Exhausted, he tugs me down and covers us both, cocooning me in all things him. "Tomorrow I want to take you around. Show you LA."

My chest pinches at that. I swallow as I whisper, "I'm not sure that's the best idea." If only he weren't so famous, so recognizable. If only. If only.

He nods against me, holding me tighter. "I know. I just..."

"Me too. Having a famous best friend I'm not allowed to be friends with kind of sucks."

"But at least the sex is good, right?"

I giggle lightly. "You think I'd be here if it wasn't," I quip and he pinches my ribs, rubbing the spot away with his thumb and kissing the crook of my neck.

We grow quiet after that and just as I begin to drift, he murmurs something into the skin of my neck. Something I can't hear. He snuggles me closer to him and I breathe out an even breath, too exhausted to question or fight anything.

After all, my time with him is already passing quicker than I'd like it to.

Chapter FOUR

Greyson

In all the years of my life, with all the crimes and tragedies, I've never woken at dawn. I've never seen the sunrise. Not even when we were in foreign countries and time changes take over. So it startles me when I feel a hand on my face and a whisper in my ear.

"Come on, Grey. Come watch the sunrise with me."

I'm a zombie, but I move. I am hapless and helpless and forever her slave, so I amble out of bed, listless and zonked. She's wearing my T-shirt and nothing else except her panties and it's sexy my exhausted cock instantly stirs.

The stairs that lead up and out of my apartment to the roof are heavy and treacherous. I drag along, clutching to her tiny shorts and loving how they dance along the creamy skin of her upper thighs.

A sunrise isn't high on my priority list, but she is and if she wants to watch that ball of flames soar across the LA sky in the wee hours of daytime, I should at least get to hold her in my arms as we do. I tell her that much and she laughs, thinking I'm partially kidding when I'm anything but.

My hands find her hips from behind and I trickle kisses along her neck, up to her ear, and then back down.

I love you.

They're words without purpose. Words that have led me to the edge and thrust me over the cliff straight to my downfall. Words I can pretend away and make believe aren't mine when they are in fact a living legacy and tribute to my heart.

They're the words of a high school boy.

The words of a worthless hero. One who never figured out how to win the goddess of his dreams. The words of a man who will never possess his heroine.

But she smells like heaven and feels like sin and molds into my chest as if she was born to be there. That's what gets me. That's what's always gotten me.

How perfect she is for me and yet how forbidden.

I hold her and I breathe in the scent of her hair. She sighs and I follow. The sky is painted gold and bright pink.

"It's all about the sunsets here," I whisper.

"Sunrises in Boston and sunsets in LA."

"I still prefer Boston. Even if I never wake for the sunrises when I'm home."

"I have an eight a.m. class Monday mornings. I'm used to being up early."

I whistle through my teeth. "Why on earth did you do that to yourself?"

She hitches up a shoulder against me. "I don't mind. School is what I do. It's what I'm good at and believe it or not, enjoy." She giggles. "Sometimes I forget just how opposite we are."

She spins around and catches my conflict. The conflict that's immediately chased by desire when I see her pretty face. Her hands climb up into my hair, cupping the back of my head. "Have you ever had another friend like this?"

I frown, not understanding her meaning.

"A friend that you hook up with, but it never goes anywhere else."

Now I frown for a completely different reason. "No," I tell her honestly.

"But you don't have girlfriends."

It's a statement and not a question so I don't answer her immediately. "It's not that I wouldn't want a girlfriend. It just has to be the right girl."

Hint, hint, nudge, nudge.

"And groupies aren't the right girl?" she surmises.

"Groupies are groupies and don't care about anything beyond the moment and any bragging rights that come with it. They're easy and convenient, and as long as you're careful, don't linger or cause issues. But the truth is, I'm not with them that often and I rarely allow them backstage anymore."

She smirks up at me, her violet eyes filled with mirth. "Don't I know it. It was nearly impossible to get backstage and surprise you. I bought a fake pass and everything."

"You don't ever have to buy anything, Fall. You just have to ask and anything you want is yours."

"I was worried about seeing you."

My forehead falls to hers. "I know. And now?"

"Now we're like this and I'm not so worried anymore."

"Because you know it's only this?" My chest pinches, but I don't even need her to answer. I know that's why.

She twirls the ends of my hair in her fingers. "If you weren't you and I wasn't me, we'd be perfect together. But that's not our reality."

"You mean if your family didn't already have your entire life planned out for you and didn't hate me?"

"Yes. All of that. But we're also worlds apart. And friends. I love our friendship. It's everything to me." Her head falls to my chest, and we grow silent. As much as I'd love to argue this with her, she's not wrong. She's brutally accurate with our situation. And I don't blame her for it either. In a way, I appreciate it. I'm grateful for it.

"Let's go eat," I say after a few moments watching as the sun continues rising up in the eastern sky and I'm too antsy to stand here. I take her back downstairs, and since Fallon does not like typical breakfast food, I make us grilled cheese and we eat it in front of the television. She's snuggled into my side as we watch whatever movie she's making me watch.

I don't care enough about it to notice. I haven't stopped staring at her as she watches it. As she laughs and smiles and her eyes sparkle at whatever romance is happening on screen.

The alarm rings on my phone, signaling someone is disarming it and entering the apartment. "Your stuff is here. My assistant is leaving it by the front door."

"But I like your shirt."

"I like you in my shirt."

Her eyes are still on the screen and mine are still on her, only my rapt focus shifts when I hear moaning coming from the surround sound.

My gaze flickers up watching as the couple starts to go at it. Heavy kissing and a lot of touching and I smirk.

"Boring," I quip.

Her eyebrows hit her hairline as her gaze turns challenging. Playful. Heated. "Oh yeah? You think you can do better?"

A wicked grip curls the corners of my lips. "Oh, Fall Girl. I know I can."

With my eyes locked on hers, I roll her onto her back and slide down her body. She makes a tiny little whimper as I lift her shirt and tickle the skin of her belly.

"Let's get you naked."

"You first."

I chuckle. "Yes, ma'am."

Reaching behind my head I drag my shirt off and then undo the button and zipper on my jeans. I get distracted though when she sits up and pulls her shirt off. I attack her panties, ripping them off her.

In a flash, I have her spread out and then I suck her sweet pussy into my mouth, playing with her pulsing little nub that is begging for my undivided attention. Her back arches immediately. Her head thrown back along with it.

She tastes so sweet. So naughty and forbidden, my cock pulses with the thought.

I can't touch this woman, and yet I am.

In a flash, I move us so that I have her straddling my face. And with her like this, I lick her dripping pussy that is so hungry, she can't help but grind against my mouth. And I want it. All of it. I want to watch as she loses her mind over me. Her hands up in her hair. Caressing her perfect tits. Pinching her rose-colored nipples. Her inhibitions are gone, and her desire is taking over.

And fuck.

How I dream of these moments with her. Every time I close my eyes and take my hard cock in hand, it's her I'm picturing. Doing all the dirty things I'm doing to her now. All of it and yet, she is so lovely she puts every fantasy to shame. Her eyes. Those pretty eyes are on me. As my tongue and lips and mouth eat at her.

She's not embarrassed. Especially when her hands run through my hair while she grinds herself against me. Seeking a pleasure I'm crazy to give her.

"That's it," I tell her softly, my hands groping the globes of her ass. Pushing her deeper into my face. Splitting her ass cheeks apart. Finding all the ways to give her pleasure. "Do you want to come like this?"

"Yes." More mindless grinding, her hands now back on her breasts. Fall has never been much of a talker during sex, but I know she loves it when I do.

I blow cool air on her, and she moans.

"Right after you come all over my face and I'm done licking your pussy clean, I'm going to lower you down my body and slam you down on me. Straight onto my cock. Then I'm going to fuck you till you scream."

A hiss and a gasp as my lips suck her in, my tongue flicking at her clit as my fingers slide inside her, pumping in and out.

"Ah. Grey," she cries, getting so close her body is trembling and she's having trouble staying upright.

"I'm going to watch your pretty tits bounce as I fuck you. I'm going to take you hard at first. Pound into you. All week when you're back at school, you're going to be sore, thinking about how good I gave it to you every time you move."

"Oh fuck, *yes!*"

A few more grinds while my fingers find her G-spot and she's coming. Hard. Wet. Delicious. Her hands rip at my hair while she mindlessly rocks along my face, and I continue to lick her, dragging every ounce of her orgasm out of her. But the second she starts to slow, the second she starts to whimper and sag, I yank down my pants, roll a condom on, pick her up by her hips, drag her down my body, and slam her down on my cock.

Just as I said I would.

"Yes," I hiss. A cry. A plea. And the feel of her. My god, the feel of her.

I am home. Inside her, this is where I am meant to be. Always. With my hands on her hips, I lift her again and drive her down on me just as my hips thrust up. Over and over, I fuck her like this. Hard. Rough. So deep I'm buried to the hilt. Our bodies pumping, seeking, destroying as one.

I fuck her the ways I've been needing to fuck her. Her pussy drinks my cock in, sucking it deep and holding on for dear life. She's tight. And hot. And fucking wet. And Christ, she feels like a heaven I never dared imagine.

"More. More. More." It's a rhythmic pattern as she bounces on me. Digs forward so her clit can slide against my pelvic bone. Her dark hair is everywhere. Her violet eyes on mine. My hands all over her tits and it's like fuck *yesss*! Yes!

My hand plants into her spine and I'm flipping her over so she's on her back and I'm above her. She wants more and I intend to deliver. Taking her hands in mine, I pin them above her head and then I unleash myself in her. Without restraint. Wild and unbridled. Skin slaps against skin. Loud and lewd in the otherwise quiet of my house.

And she's loving it.

Her tits bounce everywhere. Her lips are parted with moans and cries and pleas escaping. Her clit a home base for my fingers while my dick slides against her G-spot. And when I find it? When I start to hit her just right?

Fireworks. Explosions.

Her pussy clenches my cock like a fist and she starts to come all over me, coating me in wet pleasure that has me bellowing out. I collapse on top of her, panting for my life in thick gasps. I lick the sweaty crevice of her shoulder, my cock already pleading for another round.

If it were endless, I'd do all the things to her. Fill her every hole. Test her every limit. Watch her boundless pleasure.

But I don't and it sucks. The clock is already ticking down.

Chapter FIVE

Fallon

The waves of the pacific are choppy, the wind whipping salt up into the air and my hair about my face. Grey convinced me to venture out onto the beach in Malibu, promising that the beach is both private and exclusive. Meaning we won't be photographed and even if we're seen together, the patronage is discrete.

My flight is set to leave this afternoon and both Grey and I are dragging. Two nights together was a gift. A gift I'm not ready to let go of. I don't know when I'll be able to see him next. I graduate in May and then it's off to med school in the fall and I already know Grey has another few months left on his tour and then he tells me he's back in the studio to record his next album.

It's impossible.

Everything with us is.

We're eating an early lunch of tacos and sipping on margaritas because why not while watching surfers attempt to tackle the waves.

"I get the appeal," I tell Grey, taking everything around us in. "The sun, the waves. Do you ever consider moving out here permanently?"

"Nah. LA has its appeal, but there are paparazzi everywhere you go in the city and the traffic is unbearable. Plus," he glances over at me, "and I know this sounds crazy, "I like the seasons. I like the cold and the snow."

"I get it. I feel like Boston is home too."

"But that's not where you'll be living."

"Nope. Med school and then who knows with residency."

He nods, staring out at the waves, his knees bent and his hands resting between them. "Take a walk with me before we have to get you to the airport?" He stands, wiping off sand from the butt of his shorts and then reaches his hand out to me. I take it, allowing him to pull me up and after tossing away our trash, we stroll, sandals in one hand, drink in my other.

We're silent. Lost in our own introspection, the heaviness of what comes next settling between us.

"I wish you didn't have to go. And I'm not saying this because of the sex. I'm saying this because I wish you didn't have to go. Or at least I wish we didn't have to go so long in between visits."

"Me too." I fall into him, my head on his upper arm and I loop my pinky through his. "Maybe one day though, right?" I peer up at him through my lashes. "Maybe one day the stars will align and we'll both be in the same place at the same time. You'll be stuck with me then. I'll be that clingy groupie friend who refers to herself as your entourage when really what I'm doing is mooching off concert tickets and cool after parties."

"I like you as my groupie."

"Then one day, right?"

He peers down at me, something tragic in his eyes. "One day."

We leave for the airport after that. Grey insists on driving me though I tell him I'm fine taking a cab or an Uber. Truth, I think it would almost be easier that way. A goodbye at his place instead of at the airport.

The last time I saw him was when Suzie had died and this time everything between us feels heavy. Different heavy, but still heavy. Like unspoken words and longing and what-ifs. It's not us. Not our standard and I'm anxious to bring us back to that. I can't leave Grey wondering. Wondering will get me nowhere with him.

He's Greyson Monroe.

He doesn't do real or serious and it's impossible for us anyway so why even contemplate it.

Sex is what blurs us. It's what has us straddling lines we shouldn't be straddling.

"When do you get a break?" he asks as we sit in stop-and-go traffic on the way to LAX.

"This summer. What about you?"

"This summer. We should make something work somewhere. Something intentional. Something I know about ahead of time and can plan around." He tosses me a rogue smirk.

"Let's do it then. Let's plan for this summer. I'll know more once I get back to school and decide on where I'm going next."

"Good. Okay." Another quick look. "You good?"

"I'm good. You good?"

"Definitely. These last two nights were the best. They were everything. I just wish they didn't always end like this with so long in between."

"I know."

It's all I can say as we're pulling into the airport, wading through the line of cars before he can pull up to the gate.

"You can just drop me."

"Are you that worried about someone catching us together?"

The answer isn't so easy. There are a lot of layers baked into it. A lot of things between us that lead to different paths I can't take without consequences.

I lean across the console and wrap my arms around him, hugging him fiercely to me. I don't want to let go, and he doesn't either and for several minutes this is all we do. We don't kiss again. We never do when we reach this point. We're not lovers. We're not romantic. We're Fall Girl and Grey and Fall Girl and Grey cannot be either of those things.

Hell, we can't even be friends.

So with my heart in my throat and my eyes wet, I kiss his cheek goodbye and climb out of the car. His car doesn't move and because the windows of his SUV are tinted, I can't see him, but I can feel him watching me go. I throw a backward wave and then head through the mechanical doors into the cool, crowded airport.

That's when the tears start to fall, rolling down my cheeks in an endless river.

Once again I'm leaving the best part of myself behind with him. And there is nothing I can do to change that.

Thank you for supporting this incredible charity.
You can learn more about this story and my others at http://jsamanbooks.com.

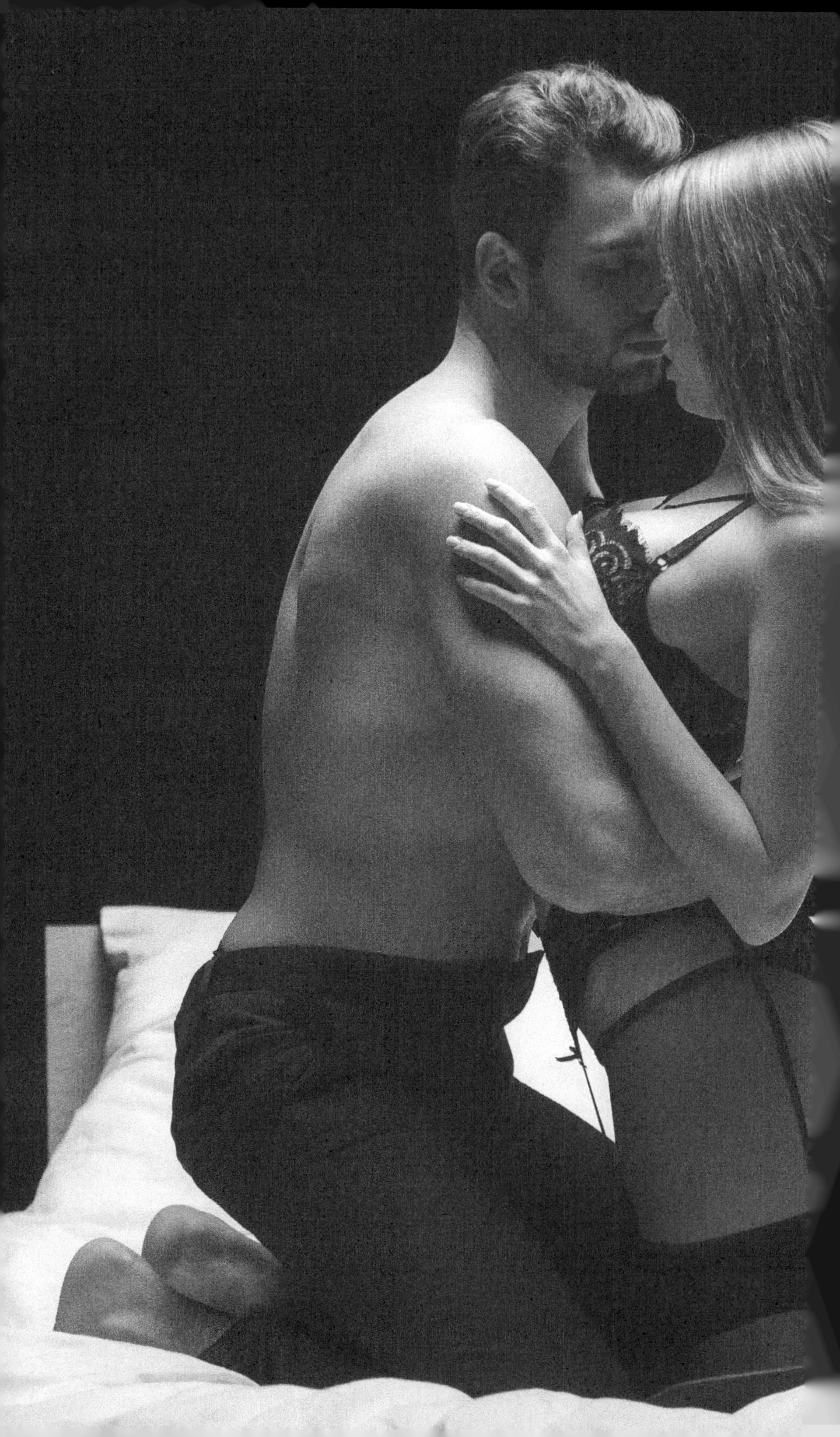

My Boyfriend's DADDY

J.D. HOLLYFIELD

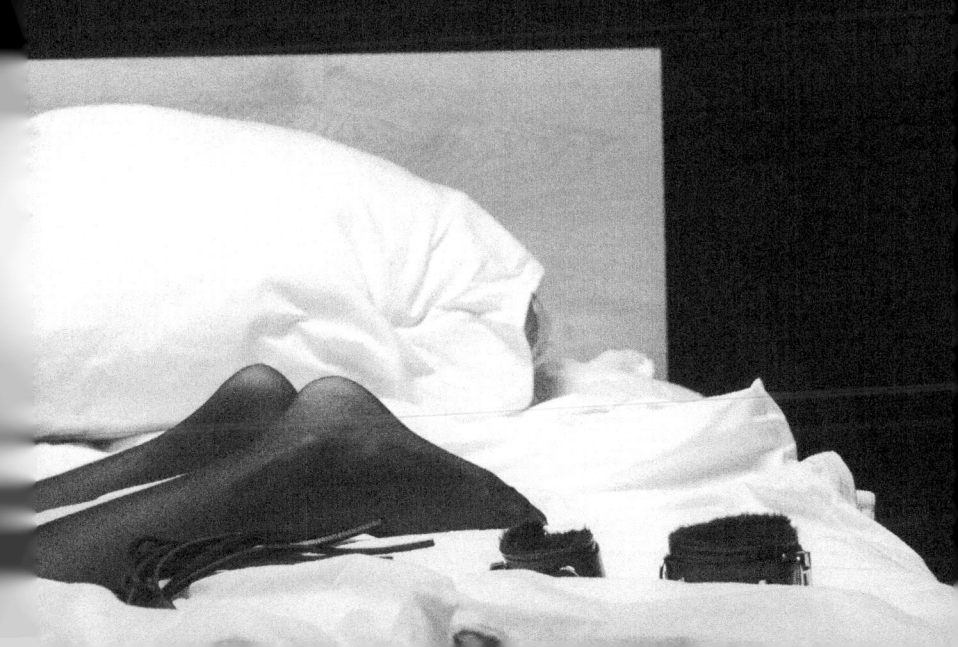

Chapter ONE

Georgia

I sit across the kitchen table from Noah in his father's home, watching as he takes down another beer.

"Are we going to talk about this?"

He opens a new beer before answering me. "What do you want to talk about? You said you don't want to be with me."

"I said, I think we need a break."

"Same fucking thing." He slams the beer onto the counter and pushes out of his chair. Gripping the back of his neck he walks away. I knew this was a bad idea. I never should have come home with him, paid internship or not. I know what I should have done. But since I don't have a backbone and thought we could make it work, I agreed to come.

Noah and I met during our freshman year of college. He was everything a girl could ask for in a boyfriend: athletic, smart, had a sense of humor, and, most importantly, hot. Too hot for his own good if you ask me. And we hit it off right away, which, in college terms, meant we slept together within five hours of meeting. Yep, welcome to college. I'd never done anything so spontaneous before, but I'd also never drunk as much. Thankfully, my walk of shame after a guy I barely knew turned into a full-blown relationship.

It was really lust at first sight. We couldn't keep our hands off each other. Our entire freshman year consisted of us constantly pawing at each other. It was hot. Crazy. And nothing I'd ever experienced.

But outside of the sex, Noah and I were very different. I struggled to be on the same page as him as far as our beliefs and moral values. He came from a rich family, whereas I was from a small town, and my family barely got by. It's not that money made us different. It just made it harder for us to find common ground. Soon, his cocky attitude began to outweigh the attraction. Without that as part of the equation, I realized that we didn't have much more than sex in common. Not to mention, I was over his aggressive side when things didn't go his way.

A few months back, Noah's father offered him a paid internship at his company. Since we were still inseparable then, he couldn't fathom going home and not being together all break. And because I was horny and free for the summer, not to mention I could use the money, I agreed when his father made me an offer as well.

I just wish I had been smarter and not made decisions with my libido instead of my head.

And now, I'm stuck in an unfamiliar town, about to start a job for a man I don't know, with a boyfriend I just suggested be my ex. Great. Good work, Georgia.

"You know what, fuck this. I'm going to bed. You can come with me or sleep wherever you want. There're a million rooms in the house."

"Noah. . . Are you serious?" Noah snags another beer out of the fridge, and leaves me sitting at the gigantic kitchen island. I want to go after him, but I stop myself. What is there left to say? I meant what I said. We need time apart. Sex can't fix our problems. I know that now. He's controlling and manipulative. And when he doesn't get his way, he gets ugly.

Noah didn't start off that way. In the beginning, he was this gentle giant. But the more I got to know him, the more comfortable he felt around me. He slowly began to let his mask slip. Show me the real him. And that Noah had a lot of demons. He was still funny and sweet at times. Amazing in bed. But he was also damaged, like he'd been hurt in a way he would never admit. It was too beneath him to show his scars. He was a Blake, as he would say. Men like him were never anywhere but on top.

On the outside he had it all. Money, popularity. But on the inside, something tormented him. Maybe it was his insecurities of being left. Not loved the way he needed to be. We both suffered from the loss of a parent at a young age. Maybe that's why we craved each other so badly. Two damaged kids trying to fill the emptiness.

I stare at his back as he disappears down the hallway and up the stairs. I debate following him, knowing it's what I should do or just find a spare room. Sleeping alone with my thoughts sounds like the better idea. I'm not ready to lay next to him and allow him to convince me that what I want is wrong. Because I know this is for the best. I do love him. In some way. But I don't know if I have it in me to give him what he truly wants.

I walk to the fridge and grab a bottle of water. Maybe it's not too late to go home. My mom would understand. *Bill would be thrilled to have the object of his obsession back under the same roof.* My mom's husband was a real winner. A heartless asshole who thought it was okay to hit a woman. Reminding myself of the real reason I left home without looking back, I grab my bag and head upstairs to find a spare room. The house is gigantic. I'm not sure why his father needs such a big house for one person. But then again, money equals power. And they sure seem to have a lot of it.

I walk down a long hallway. Music blares from a closed door and I assume it's Noah's. I continue, needing as much space as possible from him right now. When I finally stop at the last room on the right, I open it to an enormous bedroom. The instant scent of cologne hits my nostrils. I don't know what comes over me, but I move inside. Admiring the décor, my eyes land on a huge king-size bed. The silver sheets look luxurious, and I'm tempted to brush my fingers across them to know how they feel. I walk in further, taking in a tall dresser and lounge chair in the corner. The door to the en suite bathroom is cracked open, and I'm able to see a large glass—

"Are you lost, or is this my lucky night?"

I startle at the voice and twist around, almost losing my balance. A large hand grabs my arm to steady me. Instantly, a wave of tingles shoots down my arm. My eyes take in the man holding me, and even in the dim lighting, I can see that he's gorgeous.

"No, I'm sorry. I was just looking—"

"And you thought whatever you were looking for would be in my bedroom?"

His lips press firmly together while his eyes roam down my body. My breasts have suddenly come to life, pebbling under my lace bra.

His bedroom.

Noah's father.

A burst of heat coils in my core. He's still holding my arm, and my skin prickles. His gaze finally works its way back up and pauses on my lips. He steps closer, and I can smell the faint hint of booze on his breath.

"What's your name?"

"Georgia," I answer, a slight quiver in my voice.

"Georgia. . . like the peach." His thumb begins to rub circles on my skin. "So, what is it, *Peach*? Have you found what you're looking for?" His warm breath tickles my cheeks, and nervousness skitters through me as I try to find the words to answer him. He must sense my discomfort because he lets out a dark chuckle. "Well, well. . . Not sure how you got in here, but I'm willing to venture you're here to fuck?"

He leans in, his lips mere inches from mine. My heart thrashes against my chest. His fingers dig into my arm, and my eyelids feel heavy. I'm going to let him kiss me. Noah's father. I'm going to let him—

"I'm Georgia." I finally find my voice. "Noah's girlfriend," I rush out.

His body stiffens, his grip causing a slight pain. He drops it like it's on fire and steps back. "I thought you were—what the hell are you doing in my bedroom?"

"I—I was. . ." How am I supposed to admit I was looking for a spare room since I royally pissed off his son? "I got lost. The house is so big."

He backs away more and brushes his hand over his mouth. "Get out."

My tongue is lodged in my throat. "I'm sorry, I. . ." I hurry past him.

I'm almost at his door when he calls my name. I turn. "None of my son's guests are allowed in this part of the house. Do you understand me?"

"Yes." I nod and make a quick exit.

***

I finally find a room to take shelter in. I undress and climb into bed, but there's no chance in hell of falling asleep. My entire body is buzzing with nerves and confusion. Arousal. I can still feel the spot on my arm where he held me. My cheeks warm, remembering the closeness of his breath and how he looked at me. Like I've never seen a man look at a woman before.

Oh, shut up, Georgia. You're nineteen.

But for a moment, he didn't know that. I wasn't his son's guest. I was someone he thought was waiting for him. Ready to fuck.

I bite my lip and untuck the blankets over my legs. What would have happened if I didn't confess who I was? Would he have gone through with his reasoning for why I was in his room?

The way he said fuck lit a fire inside me. The thought of him towering over me. His experienced hands all over me, working me in ways I've never felt before. Stretching me to fit him. I reach for a spare pillow, tucking it between my thighs. I squeeze the material, needing to release some pressure.

What is it, Peach? His voice was dark and arousing. My hand slithers down my belly into my panties, and I work my fingers over my wet slit. The look in his eyes and his voice replay in my head. Every word he spoke repeats as my orgasm builds. I add two greedy fingers to the mix, sliding in and out, imagining they're his.

Suddenly wishing that Noah's father was finger fucking me while his son slept down the hall.

"Fuck," I whisper, already close to my peak. I bite down on my lip and cup my breast with my free hand. *I'm willing to venture you're here to fuck.* "Yes," I work faster, adding a third, needing to feel more. I'm so wet that the faint sounds of my masturbating fill the air. I turn my head and bite the pillow to silence my moans. My legs start to quiver, and my walls grip my hand. "Fuck, yes. Fuck me. *Fuck me. . .*" I moan out the last of my fantasy as an intense orgasm blasts through me.

It takes a few minutes for my heart rate to come down. The exhaustion of the day suddenly catches up to me. I remove my hand, reach for a tissue, and wipe off the remnants of my orgasm. I snuggle under the sheets and fall asleep, shamelessly dreaming of my boyfriend's hot, mysterious father.

Chapter TWO

Georgia

A shift in the bed arouses me, and I open my eyes to Noah climbing into the bed. I quickly sit up. "Noah, what are you doing?"

"Relax, Georgia. It's just a bed. We've slept together a billion times. Just let me sleep here. I'm not going to pull anything."

Even if I disagreed, he's already managed to disappear under the covers. I debate on changing rooms. Obviously, this isn't a good idea. There's no way he's not going to try something. Putting us together in a bed, sex is bound to happen. And I don't want to confuse him. But when I look over, he's asleep.

Go figure.

I slide back down, resting my head on the pillow. My post-orgasm high knocked me out, but guilt quickly sets in now that I'm awake. I totally masturbated to Noah's father. What the heck is wrong with me? I have some serious issues. There's no denying it was hot. And damn it, I would do it all over again if I was alone. I give Noah my back and close my eyes, trying to think of anything that isn't a tall, dark, forbidden man who has quickly embedded himself in my sexual fantasies.

***

Pounding on the bedroom door jolts me awake. I try to move out from under the heavy blankets that I realize are Noah's leg and arm.

The banging sounds again.

"Jesus, stop," Noah gripes.

"I'll stop when you get up. We had a deal."

My breath catches in my throat. That voice. *I'm willing to venture you're here to fuck.* My cheeks burn with embarrassment.

"We're just sleeping, Dad. Not a big deal." Noah maneuvers off me and sits up. I follow, only to remember I'm wearing an oversized T-shirt. I look over at Noah, who's in nothing but boxer briefs. More shame blasts across my face.

"Is that so?"

At his question, I make the mistake of looking at him. His eyes are trained directly at me. Like last night, they blaze with a fire that causes my thighs to quiver. Not caring that his son is beside me, he does exactly what he did last night, allowing his eyes to rake over me. I sit motionless, wanting to cover my shirt where my nipples have pebbled.

Noah's hand lands on my bare thigh, and I jump.

"Relax, he's all bark, no bite. Dad, it's fine."

I'm not so sure about that.

He finally releases his hold on me and addresses Noah. "My house, my rules. Separate room. Now, get up and get dressed. I don't appreciate tardiness on your first day of work." And then he's gone.

I don't realize I was holding my breath until he's gone. Noah, remembering our fight, climbs out of bed, his cold demeanor back in full effect. "Gonna get ready. Meet you downstairs." And then he disappears down the hall.

Chapter THREE

Jackson

"Thanks, Jim. Get me the financials by lunch. Great." I hang up and take a large sip of coffee. My meeting went to shit yesterday, so instead of going home and preparing for my son to arrive, I went to Exquisite and drowned myself in bourbon. What I didn't expect was to get home and find a young woman in my bedroom. Was I surprised? Yeah. Was it completely unheard of? No. I've had my fair share of sexual partners, even those instructed to enter my home with a provided code and wait for me naked, and ready.

I'm a man with distinctive taste. I have no shame in wanting to bind and gag a beautiful woman. The little purrs they make when they're tied up, then spanked and fucked are always music to my ears. The feel of my fingers digging into plush fresh creating pleasurable pain. Just thinking about it wakes my dick up.

It's why I find myself at the private gentlemen's club most nights. The desire to have a woman on her knees and watch the intensity in her greedy eyes as I gag her with my big cock. Fuck her while pretty little tears stream down her face. And most importantly, the dominant satisfaction of my cum coating her throat.

I'm a ruthless asshole. I don't deny that. But I'm a man who knows what he wants and has no shame in taking it. This brings me back to the little surprise I found waiting for me last night.

Georgia, like the peach. Noah's fucking girlfriend.

I thought I had set up a playdate, and since I'd been over-served somehow forgot. When I walked into my room and saw her, even from the back, my cock sprung to life. Unlike the usual women I hire, she was dressed in black yoga pants and a short, tight shirt that exposed her lower back. Her hair fell to her shoulders. I could tell without even touching it that it would feel like silk between my fingers as I tugged and pulled on it.

The little thing jumped when I spoke. She was nervous, and it only made me even more hard. I enjoy a woman who knows what she wants. But the ones who need to be taught are a rare breed. This one reeked of innocence, and I wanted nothing more than to ruin her. I'd start by tasting with her full lips and work my way down, teasing her tits. They were plump, and I knew my cock would be in between them at some point in the night.

I stepped up to her, ready to push her to her knees because those pretty pink lips needed to be around me, but before I could demand she drop like a good little girl, she opened her mouth and ruined it all.

She wasn't there to fuck. My cock was more pissed than I was to find out why she was there. Invading my private space. Noah knows better than to ever come in here, let alone allow any of his guests. And there she was, inviting herself into my bedroom to snoop around.

I wonder how far she got. Did she open any of the drawers? See any of my toys? If so, did she like them? Did they intrigue her or scare her? I shouldn't have made her leave so quickly. I should have given her more of a scare so she knew never to trespass again. But, fuck, after she left, I can't deny I didn't fantasize about her in my bed. Her innocent mouth. My fingers shoved up her so deep she thrashed and begged for more.

Thankfully I passed out. But when I woke this morning, I knew I needed to shut the whole insane fantasy down. For Christ's sake, I wanted my son's girlfriend to blow me.

I'm a sick man, and I have no problem crossing moral lines with a fucking smile. But this one. . . This especially can't fucking happen. Noah and I are hardly on speaking terms these days. I don't need to jeopardize our barely existing relationship over a girl. *His* girl. Because that's exactly what she is.

I take another sip of coffee when Noah walks into the kitchen. "Morning," I greet him.

He grunts, barely acknowledging me before heading to the coffee machine.

"Welcome home. Sorry I wasn't here when you two arrived."

"Didn't expect you to be."

I deserved that one. I won't deny I've been a shit father. I've put my business before my family. It's why his mother left me, and it's why he resents me. But he also doesn't seem to mind all the perks of being rich. "I had business to take care of."

"Sure, you did."

His smart mouth pisses me off. Shitty parenting or not, he's not going to disrespect me. Even if I've been fantasying about his sexy little girlfriend. "You better watch—"

"Hey, babe. Morning."

Noah cuts me off. My head turns to where he's looking. Georgia, like the peach. She's standing in the doorway, her fingers linked together. She's nervous. Hmm. . . I wonder why. "Georgia, this is my dad, Jackson. Dad, Georgia."

It's at the tip of my tongue to say we've already met, but she jumps to it before I say a word.

"Hi, nice to meet you." She walks up to me and sticks her hand out. So, this is how we're going to play this. I smirk.

I reach out, and slide my fingers along her palm, noticing how her small hand is engulfed by mine. I drop my smile, replacing it with a bored look, even though my dick jerks at the softness of her skin. Ever so gently, I rub my thumb against her pulse point. "Nice to meet you, *Georgia*." I add more emphasis to her name, loving how her hand trembles. She tries to pull away, but I hold on a second longer and then release her. "Grab breakfast. We're leaving shortly." I stand, giving Noah a hard stare, and walk out of the room, but not before catching Georgia's eyes and winking.

I'm going to hell.

Chapter FOUR

Georgia

The drive to work is torturous. The silence between Noah and me is unbearable. He's barely said two words to me since last night besides introducing me to his father.

"Are you just going to ignore me all summer?"

"Not ignoring you, George, just have nothin' to say."

I throw my arms out in frustration. "That's my point! You never want to talk about things unless it's easy. You never want to talk about the hard stuff. I poured my heart out to you yesterday, and the only response you had for me was that I was on my own finding a place to sleep."

"That's bullshit. I told you you could sleep in my room. You chose not to."

"And apparently, it was the right decision. Does your dad not approve of me being here?"

He scoffs. "Who cares what he thinks—"

"I do. I want to make sure we're following his rules. I don't want to disrespect him. He seemed pretty mad when he saw us in bed this morning."

His hands clench around the steering wheel. "He can fuck off. He has no say in what I do."

"And me? Am I just supposed to rebel like you seem to want to?"

Noah exhales. "Georgia, it doesn't matter. He's just trying to be controlling. Act like he's a parent all of a sudden. To me, he's just a guy who pays my tuition. And what does it matter to you? After this is over, we go back to school and go our separate ways."

The hurt in his tone makes me feel guilty. But he's not innocent in all this. My choices aren't selfish. I had to do what was right for me. And maybe for him as well in the end.

"Noah, I know you're mad at me."

"Mad? Why the fuck would I be mad that my girl broke up with me? You couldn't do this before we committed to a whole summer together? You gonna pretend you don't still want me when I find some nice summer pussy to keep my bed warm since you're too busy being a selfish bitch?"

I hiss at his words. Here we go. The true version of Noah Blake. "You know what? Fuck you."

"Can't do that anymore, babe. You're not my girlfriend."

I jump out as soon as his car settles in a parking spot. I inhale the fresh air, needing to calm down, but the summer heat only makes it worse.

"Georgia, where are you going?"

"Away from you," I say, walking down the sidewalk.

"Well, you're going the wrong way. The office is right here."

Shoot. I stop, and because I have no other choice, I turn around and follow Noah into the building.

Jackson Blake is the CEO of Wellman-Blake Supply, a mass distributor for essential raw materials. For the summer, we'll be runners for anyone and everyone while growing business experience in the industry.

Noah pushes through the large glass doors and waves at the receptionist. "Welcome home, Noah. Heard you're with us for the next three months."

"Sure am, Rachel. If you're lucky, I'll make some time for you, and you can treat me to lunch." He winks at her as if I'm not standing right next to him. She smiles, then notices me.

"And you must be Miss Price." I nod, sparing her my bright smile. "Well, your father is waiting for you both, so just head back."

"Thanks, Rach." Noah walks off, not bothering to wait for me. I follow him since I have no idea where I'm going. We stop at a large office, and Noah sticks his head in. "He's on a call. We can go in and wait." Noah walks in and flops onto the leather couch. Throwing a dismissive glare at me, I walk past him and take the empty chair in front of Mr. Blake's desk. He's in an intense conversation. His brows are furrowed, and he continuously taps his pen against the top of his large mahogany desk. I feel a bit misplaced. Maybe I should have sucked it up and set next to Noah.

I look over my shoulder and see Noah with his head dipped, scrolling through his phone. When I turn back, I find his father staring directly at me. It immediately creates a layer goosebumps down my arms. His eyes drop, and I follow them, realizing that my skirt hiked up my thighs when I sat down. I bring my hands to the hem and slowly cross my leg, exposing a sliver of my inner thigh. The tapping stops, and his hand is frozen, clenching the pen tightly. His gaze burns hot as he blatantly focuses on my legs. I figured last night was a mishap. Even wondered if he would remember finding me in his room. But the way he drank me in when I stepped into the kitchen. That wink. And now...

You're playing with fire, Georgia.

What am I doing? I'm mad at Noah. This isn't the way to get back at him for hurting me. Even though the temptation is becoming harder to resist. I pull at my skirt. I must be losing my mind. Hitting on his *father*? Jesus, Georgia, get it together. I quickly stand and excuse myself, telling Noah I have to use the bathroom. Once safely inside, I turn the faucet on cold and run my wrists under the cool water to calm my nerves. When I feel more like myself, I head back to the office. Noah and Mr. Blake are quietly arguing.

"Georgia, sit."

"Yes, sir." I nod and sit next to Noah.

"As you know, this is an internship. An opportunity for you to learn and add to your resumé after college. I expect you to treat this as a real job, so no fucking around." His gaze locks on Noah. "It will be paid. Normally we don't do paid internships, but I'm making an exception. You'll both start in sales department. I've set up trainings for you to participate in. Tomorrow, I'll have you both shadowing on cold calls."

J.D. HOLLYFIELD | My Boyfriend's DADDY

"Exactly what is it we're selling?" I ask.

Mr. Blake's attention turns to me. "Yourself. It takes a skilled salesman to land a deal. I need you to prove to me you can handle this job. I have a long list of college students wanting to be where you are."

"I want to be here. I need this job," I rush out.

He nods. "Good. So, I'll expect you to catch on quickly. Learn fast, and you'll excel."

"When's lunch?" Noah asks, and his father's demeanor changes. "We do get lunch, don't we?"

"You know you get lunch. You get an hour. Don't abuse it."

"Great." Noah stands. "Let's go," he says to me.

I slowly stand, but his father's voice stops me.

"Noah, go find Lewis. He'll get you set up. I'm keeping Georgia with me."

"Why?" he asks, annoyed.

"Because you know you're way around and what to do. She doesn't."

An older man pops his head into Mr. Blake's office. "Noah, you ready?"

Noah shakes his head and mumbles 'fuck it' under his breath. "Yep. Let's do this."

I'm still until Noah disappears from sight. Slowly I lift my eyes to Mr. Blake. He leans back in his chair. "So, Georgia. Tell me about yourself."

It's a harmless question, yet it causes my heart to race. I wipe my palms down my skirt. "What would you like to know?"

"Everything. Where are you from? What brings you to Chicago? Why were you really in my bedroom?"

His last question causes me to jerk in my chair. "What—I—"

"I won't have you pulling anything in my home, Miss Price. You aren't the first of Noah's girlfriends to find themselves 'lost.' Don't think for a second, you're the exception."

His words hurt and quite honest, are insulting. "Respectfully, as I said last night, I was lost. And I don't appreciate the judgement you've already come to about me. It's downright insulting."

He gazes at me, amused. "Is that so?"

"Yes. First of all, I'm not like his other girlfriends, so you don't have to worry about me falling into whatever trap you leave for them." I watch as an eyebrow raises. "And not that it matters, but Noah and I broke up last night."

He straightens and leans forward, linking his fingers on the desk. "Broke up?"

"Yes. . ." Maybe I shouldn't have admitted that. If I'm not dating his son, I risk losing this job. And I can't go home. "It's complicated." Dammit. I messed this up. I should have kept my mouth shut.

"What happens between you and my son is your business. What happens in my home and my company is mine." He pushes his chair back and stands. "Now, I'll give you a tour so you know your way around." He walks to the front of his desk and waits for me to stand. I do so, remembering at the last minute how much taller he is than me. How imposing he is up close. "After you, *Peach*." Once again, he catches me off guard, and I can't help but stare up at him. My eyes fall shamelessly to his full lips. The same ones that were almost against mine only hours ago.

"Yeah. Sure." I nod, turning on my heel, and feel his palm press against my lower back. I'm stunned by his touch and stumble.

His hand wraps around my waist to steady me. "Easy there. We don't want you to injure yourself on the first day." My body screams at me to beg for more. My brain screams to knock off this ridiculous idea that something is going to happen.

I straighten, and he slowly releases me. "This way." He escorts me out of his office and down a long hall. He introduces me at each door we pass. It takes some time for my brain to kick in and ignore the crazy idea that he may be flirting with me. He's Noah's father, for heaven's sake. A grown man. Why would he be interested in someone like me? His persistent touch on my lower back snaps me out of my hysteria as we enter another office.

"Hank, I'd like you to meet Georgia. She's interning with us for the summer."

The man stands and extends his hand. "Hey, Georgia. Nice to meet you. What do they have you on?"

I open my mouth to say sales, which I still haven't figured out, but Mr. Blake replies first.

"She's going to shadow me this summer."

I turn, gaping up at him. "I thought—"

"She's impressed me. I think learning from the best will be worth her while."

"That's awesome. Great opportunity, Georgia. I remember when he mentored me when I first came on board. He was hard as hell, and I had a few choice words for him when he wasn't listening. Hope he takes it easy on you."

Mr. Blake looks down at me, his smile unnerving. "Oh, I don't plan to."

We say our goodbyes and continue down the hall. A million questions and emotions are running through my head. What does he mean he won't go easy on me? Why am I suddenly working with him? Why do I feel this insanely powerful attraction to him?

Instead of asking, I focus on steadying my heartbeat. I blindly follow him until I realize we're back at his office. "Take a seat." I'm not sure if I can. "I'm good standing, actually."

"Sit down, Georgia."

His voice is stern. It's the voice of a man who isn't told no. I take my place in a chair across from him as he sits behind his desk. "If I didn't press, would you have withheld the details that you were no longer dating my son?"

Damn it, not this again. "I'm a hard worker. Reliant. Trustworthy. I hold all the qualifications required for this position. I don't think it matters."

"And this morning? You two looked cozy. Far from broken up."

"It's—He. . . he came in my room sometime during the night. Just to sleep. We were together for ten months. Habit, I guess."

He doesn't immediately react. He's observing me, which makes me jittery in my chair. "My intentions weren't to hurt your son. It's just best this way. If you think it's best that I not work here, I understand—"

"Did I say anything about firing you?"

"No, it's just—"

"I don't plan on firing you. Just the opposite. You're mine for the next three months. You say you hold all the requirements for this job? Prove it. Starting with your compliance. Can you do that for me, Georgia?"

A flood of desire shoots to my core. Ashamed that I can't erase the fantasy his words create, I cross my legs to relieve some pressure. I'm hot, my panties are wet, and I've obviously completely lost my mind. I want to tell him I'm willing to comply with anything he demands.

But I need to stop this inappropriate behavior. The last time I got wrapped up in a man almost twice my age, he was fired, and I almost got expelled. But damn it, I know what I want. Between my thighs throb at the forbidden thoughts of him. Him licking at my sex and talking filthy to me. My nipples pebble. Maybe I should just make a move. I was bold last time, and it paid off.

Stop this.

This is only happening because I need sex. I stopped sleeping with Noah weeks ago. I needed to separate my emotions from my physical needs.

Whatever the excuse, my mind won't stop. My imagination has me sprawled over his desk while his tongue slips past my slick heat, fucking me with his—

"I said, can you do that for me, Georgia?"

"Huh?" I snap out of my haze. Jesus, Georgia. "I—yes. I can. Anything you want."

His smile rivals the Devil's, delightfully sinister and filled with determination. "I'm sorry. If you'll excuse me, I need to use the ladies' room."

He nods. "Of course. Do what you need to do. Come back refreshed." My eyes whip to his. Does he—can he sense that I'm turned on? If so, why is he being so subtle about it? I could run and tell Noah his father made passes at me. But did he? Or is it all in my head?

I nod and stand, praying I haven't left a wet spot on my skirt. I tuck my hair behind my ear and race out of his office.

Chapter Five

Jackson

I walk into Exquisite No, I storm in there like a man on a mission—get a half bottle of bourbon in me and find a girl. Young, brunette, and willing to let me destroy her.

"Good evening, Mr. Blake. Your regular table?"

"Bring a bottle of Pappy Van Winkle I want a guest in my lap in fifteen minutes." That should give me enough time to consume enough alcohol and erase the image of her from my mind.

I pull at my tie and throw myself into the velour lounge chair. A waitress sets a bottle on the table, and my hands twitch as she pours it around the large cube of ice. "Is there anything else you need—"

"No." I dismiss her and take a large pull of the drink, not stopping until I empty the glass. I have no idea who that was today. It certainly wasn't me. It *shouldn't* be me. That little girl was tempting me. Did she know how easily she was making me break? How much I want her? Those creamy thighs taunted me. And her lips... Fuck! I pour myself another glass, and it's gone just as fast.

Is Noah behind this? Is he setting me up? See if I take the bait?

The worst thing is, I took it. Hook, line and sinker. She was a little temptress without even realizing it.

Here at the club, I can fulfill any desire I can imagine. And I've been damn close to doing everything. So why am I willing to risk it all for her? My son's girlfriend.

I almost dragged her over my desk when she confessed they weren't dating. It was a relief that I wasn't about to cross a line and fuck my son's girlfriend. But it had to be a trap. His way of proving himself right about what happened two years ago.

I wasn't lying. My part of the house is forbidden to all guests. And for a damn good reason. Noah hates me for so many reasons I've started to lose count. But I refuse to take the blame for being the reason he cut me out of his life.

I saw Tricia for what she was the second Noah brought her home. On the outside, she appeared to be a sweet kid. Shy. Polite. Had all the right answers to any question. But she also had ulterior motives. And I smelled that deceitful shit the moment she looked at me, looked away, and fucking blushed.

I've always warned Noah about people taking advantage of him because he came from money. People will befriend you just to get their greedy hands on what you have. And people sure as fuck did. But he didn't care. They were his friends. He let them all feed of his cushioned lifestyle. But she was the worst. The ringleader. And when Noah wasn't looking, she targeted me. She would make the smallest of advances and say harmless comments that appeared innocent to Noah.

But having the experience I did, I knew exactly what she was doing. She'd been baiting me for months. Even after I told her to stay the fuck away from me and threatened to tell my son what a scheming bitch his girlfriend was. Yeah, she was hot, and in different circumstances, I would have let her suck my cock. But I wasn't touching that shit with a ten-foot pole.

The problem was she didn't take my rejection well. When I came home after telling her off, she was naked in my room. She'd thrown herself at me before I could comprehend what was happening. And, of course, Noah walked in seconds later. The lies she spewed made me furious to the point of murder.

But it didn't matter what I did. The damage was done. My son thought I tried to seduce his girlfriend, and since it was her word against mine, I did.

It wasn't too long after that he left for school, and our relationship has been strained ever since. It's why I have strict rules about visitors. Anytime he's home and throws ridiculous parties, my bedroom is forbidden.

So when I found Georgia there, looking like a lamb come to the slaughter, I thought I had arranged for a girl to be waiting. I was so drunk I forgot that Noah was home, let alone that it could have been his girlfriend. And it was a damn shame it was because the moment I saw her, I had plans to ruin her.

I pour myself another drink as a girl walks up to my chair. "Good evening, Mr. Blake." She smiles sweetly and perches on my lap when I sit back. I need the relief more than the bourbon, so I discard my glass and tug her higher up my lap. "What's your name, sweetheart?"

"Gail, baby."

"Gail, huh?" I want to like it, but it feels sour on my tongue. *Georgia, like the peach.* I need to get her out of my head. I grab Gail's hair and tug, exposing her neckline. "So, Gail. Tell me a little bit about yourself?" Fuck, am I seriously trying to roleplay my day today?

"I'm just a small-town girl, looking for someone to—"

I don't let her finish and set her off me.

"Is it something I—"

"You're dismissed." I reach for my glass, my anger building.

Moments later, a club host walks up. "I'm so sorry, Mr. Blake. Was there something wrong with Gail? She's been one of our most popular—"

"No." She's just not *her*. "It's fine. Get me a room. I want the Exquisite Gold Level." Because I need to expel that little temptress from my system. Knowing she's living under my roof, and I have to be around her when I leave here will take a lot of whipping and fucking to erase her from my mind.

"Yes, Of course. Do you have any girl in mind?"

"A brunette. Petite."

"As you wish, Mr. Blake."

J.D. HOLLYFIELD | *My Boyfriend's* DADDY

I slam my drink and make my way to the private rooms. If fucking her out of my system doesn't do the trick, I'm fucked.

And so is she...

Chapter SIX

Georgia

Hands are all over me.

I try to distinguish who they belong to, but they're too fast. Too strong. My breasts are squeezed, and my throat is grabbed. My hair is clenched between fists and tugged back until I can feel the brush of warm lips against mine. There are soft whispers, but I'm unable to identify the voice. Hands slither down my belly, disappearing between the soaked folds of my sex. His fingers aren't gentle, far from it. He doesn't work me up, just shoves four fingers inside me—

The sound of my alarm pulls me from my dream. A very vivid dream. I reach for my phone to shut the sound off when I realize I'm not alone. An arm wraps around me, pulling me back into bed.

It *was* a dream. Right?

"Relax. I know you love to press snooze at least seven times."

Noah.

It's Noah.

I don't mean to, but I lean into him, relief washing over me.

"Curious what you're dreaming about, though. You were practically panting in your sleep."

I shove him off me and get out of bed. "Dreaming about chasing you down and stabbing you."

"Wow. Savage. You'd think *I* was the one who broke up with *you.*"

I turn around, giving him a nasty look. "No, more like the way you've been treating me."

Noah hops out of bed. "Oh, so wait. . . I'm the bad guy here? I'm not the one who pulled this bullshit about breaking up."

"No, you're an asshole who has no idea how to have a relationship—"

Noah is on me, backing me up against the dresser. "You keep saying that. And I keep telling you—"

"What's going on in here?"

Noah backs up at the sound of his father's deep voice. "Nothing."

"Doesn't look like nothing." I'm holding my breath. I hate any time Noah gets like this. Aggressive. Mean. He's never physically hurt me, but I've seen it in his eyes. He wants to.

"We're fine. Don't you have morning calls to make or something?" Noah turns to his father, and I swear they look like they're about to square off.

"Get ready for work," his father says, turning on his heel to leave, but not before he catches my eye.

When he's gone, Noah turns to me. "I'm sick of you acting like I'm the bad guy here. You don't want to be with me? Fine. But stop making me out to be the only fucked up one. 'Cause baby, you're right there with me." Then he disappears down the hall.

***

Noah and I remain silent the entire way to work. If he thinks I'm going to apologize for anything, he's wrong. I hate that he called me out. Called us out. Because the fact of the matter is he's right. I'm no less fucked up than he is. He may come from a rich family, but that doesn't mean he also can't be all sorts of messed up.

Unlike Noah, who has his financial future paved for him, I'm drowning in loans. Ones my mother swore she would help me with. Loans I wouldn't even need if she hadn't married Bill and allowed him access to my college fund. My dad was the breadwinner. He had the great job, with great benefits. It allowed our family to take vacations. Live in a decent home. And it allowed my parents to put aside money for my little sister and our futures. When my dad died when I was ten, that all changed. My mom was lost. Heartbroken. She'd been with my dad her whole life. Being alone was so unknown to her, it scared her. It's why she linked herself to the first man who showed her attention. A man who fed her lies. Wore this cape, hiding all his faults. They married within a year of my dad's death.

Lettie was too young to understand. She couldn't see what a bad man Bill was. Or maybe it was because he never laid a hand on her. He was a drunk. He had no money, no desires and was in and out of work. He also convinced my mom to allow him access to my college fund. From the fights I could hear, he'd gambled my entire future away. Everything my parents saved… it was gone.

I despised my mom. For her poor decisions. Not putting her children before her desperation. And worst of all, I missed my dad so damn much. He was my hero. He took care of me. He was supposed to teach me how to ride a bike. Threaten my first boyfriend about getting home before curfew. He was supposed to walk me down the aisle at my wedding. And when he left me, so did any affection I'd been shown. Mom was so wrapped up in her own emotions, she never thought to worry if her children were okay. Feeling loved. It makes sense the dark path I took afterward. I just wanted someone to love me. Notice me. And that's exactly what Mr. Bishop did.

Henry Bishop. Julian Valley High's favorite teacher.

He saw me for me. His smile was so genuine when he sat and listened to me vent. I thought he cared about me. Before I knew it, we were having sex in the back of his car late one night after the parking lot had emptied.

I shake off the memory.

Gotta love daddy issues.

When Noah finds a parking spot, I get out. Since I know where I'm going this time, I don't wait for him and take the elevator to the tenth floor. Forgetting Noah, I try and reroute my thoughts. What does Mr. Blake have in store for me today? He wants me compliant. I'm not great at selling, so sales calls will probably be a challenge.

"Where are you going? The call center is this way." I turn back to Noah, who's sporting a frown.

"To your father's office. I'm working with him today."

His brows shoot up. "What? No, you're not." He storms my way. I prepare for whatever fight he has in store, but he blows past me and disappears into his father's office. I hurry after and catch the start of their argument.

"What the fuck?"

"Morning to you too, son."

"Georgia's in the call center."

Mr. Blake sits behind his desk, looking less than pleased at his son's outburst. "She's with me today."

"No." Noah shakes his head. "I don't think so. She's at the—"

Mr. Blake stands, pressing his palms firmly against the top of his desk. "This is business, Noah. And I will not have you coming into my office and showing me disrespect."

"Business, huh?" Noah shakes his head again. "Whatever you say." He turns and says to me, "Watch yourself with him." And then he walks out.

I stare at his back until he disappears out of sight.

"Sorry about that."

I turn to Mr. Blake. "What was that about?"

"As you know, my son can be a bit difficult sometimes. Let's get started." He shuts down any more questions. What did Noah mean by watching out for him? He stands and gestures for me to sit at the conference table in the corner of his office. "As you know, or as I hope you know because you've done some research, we're the leading global distribution company of raw materials. Our biggest material is plastic. Our clients' needs are across the board, from industrial and automotive to packaging materials, anything functional. We tap into several markets, which allow us to do all this. This location mainly houses our sales, customer service, and logistics teams. It's important that we develop strong relationships with our clients and continue to keep them happy and coming back."

"So, will I be working in customer service? Or sales?"

"Neither. I have a gut feeling that you have a bit more ambition than my son does. As mentioned, you'll shadow me. I plan on showing you how to invest in your career. Do you want to work behind a desk and take calls, Georgia, or do you want to be the one running the company?"

"I. . . I want to be the one running it."

He smiles. "Good girl."

The intercom on his desk buzzes. "Mr. Blake, Wayne is on line one. There's an issue with one of the warehouses."

"Excuse me." He gets up and takes the call. "When? Did you check the systems? And? Okay. I'm coming to oversee it myself. Thank you. See you soon." He hangs up.

"Everything okay?"

"Let's go."

"Where are we going?" I stand.

"Field trip. Our closest warehouse is about thirty minutes from here, and they're having a system issue. We're going to go and see what the problem is." His hand dips to the small of my back and directs me out of his office.

"But shouldn't—"

"Shouldn't what, Georgia? I'm the boss. I make the rules."

I was going for more like, shouldn't someone else go with him? This seems inappropriate. But also exciting and illicit. "Okay, *boss*. Let's go."

His smile is what sex fantasies are built off of. He tells the receptionist we're heading into the field and won't return until after lunch. The lunch bit brings my thoughts to Noah. Not that he sought me out yesterday for lunch, but what if he does today? *Watch out for him.*

"Everything okay?" Mr. Blake asks.

I snap out of my stupid thoughts. "Yeah, of course."

Chapter SEVEN

Jackson

After telling Rachel we're headed out for a field call, we leave the office. I don't normally volunteer to visit my sites since I have employees to do it for me. And there is absolutely no reason I should be taking Georgia with me. But when an opportunity arises, I take it. The thought of being alone and breaking her down was a no-brainer.

I text Vince, my private driver, on the ride to the lobby because I want all my attention on her.

"Mr. Blake." Vince nods and opens the car door as we step out of the building.

"Thanks, Vince. After you," I say to Georgia, and press my palm to her lower back. Her body trembles under my touch, and I love it. I'm tempted to brush my hand down her ass. *Look but don't touch, Blake.* As much as my cock wants me to bury it deep inside her, my damn conscience is right. She belongs to Noah. Broken up or not, I see the way he looks at her. The same way I would if she were mine. I'm half tempted to ask what went south for them. Are they still fucking? Damn it, why am I thinking about my son's sex life? *Because the girl he's having sex with is the same little toy you want to play with.*

After this, I need to set some boundaries. I can't trust myself around her. Noah is right to call me a ruthless bastard. I've always taken what I want, consequences be dammed. It's why I'm fucking rich. Why my company is thriving. The problem is, Georgia is no different. Wrong. Off-limits. My *son's* girlfriend. Those red flags mean nothing to me. Because if I want her bound and sucking my cock, I'll have it. It just depends on what repercussions I'm willing to accept because of it.

***

The ride over is pleasant. She has yet to relax around me, and I love that every question I ask makes her skittish.

"So, you've asked all these questions about me. Why don't you tell me about you?"

I love the slight shake in her voice. It makes me want to suck her bottom lip into my mouth. Nibble on it and bite, causing her the slightest amount of pain. "What is it you want to know? Did you not find everything you wanted to know in my bedroom?"

My cock twitches at her intake of breath. Naughty little trespasser.

"I really wish you would stop bringing that up. I wasn't snooping. I told you, I was lost."

"Well, good thing I found you before you got into any more trouble." Trouble as in her falling onto my cock. She swallows, and my mind goes to an even darker place. It's a shame we get to the warehouse when we do because I'm tempted to test the waters. Would she allow me to touch her? Stop me if I slid my hand up her skirt? Refuse if my fingers slid inside her perfect, tight cunt? The way her cheeks change color tells me she wouldn't think twice about stopping me.

"Here we are," I say.

She blinks and breaks away from the hold our gazes are locked in. Looking out the window, she says, "You own this?"

I chuckle. "Yes. I own seventeen of them."

"Wow, Mr. Blake, that's—"

I rest my hand on her thigh. "Call me Jackson." Yep. I'm going to hell.

Her lips part, and my dick springs to life. *Don't even think about it.* My grip on her tightens, then I quickly release her. "Now, let me show you around." The door opens, and I climb out, waiting for Georgia to do the same.

"This is our one hundred and eleven thousand square-foot, full-service production facility. You'll find state-of-the-art machinery equipped with cutting-edge technology. This location is mainly for our plastic distribution." I open the door to the warehouse and gesture for her to enter. "We offer a full line of thermoplastic, which is most efficient, and thermoset profiles in and standard a client desires. Sheet, rod, rube, you name it, we can supply it."

We turn down the main hallway, and I stop at the row of hard hats hanging on the wall. I grab one and turn to Georgia. "Safety protocol," I say and lift it up to gently place it on her head, tucking a loose strand of hair behind her ear. "There."

Her chest rises and falls. I see Wayne in my peripheral and grab my hat. "Morning, Mr. Blake. I'm sorry you had to make the trip out here."

I shake his hand. "Not a problem. I just want to make sure we get ahead of this. Let's walk and talk."

"Sure thing. This way." He leads us down the hallway that opens to the manufacturing facility. Wayne's call this morning was to inform me that a production machine went down. "The systems ran as usual this morning. Then Greg noticed an operating error. When I went and checked the log, it seems that the preventive maintenance wasn't logged in this month."

"Is that normal for it to be skipped?"

"Never."

We take a left and walk down a narrow aisle. "How the hell does this get overlooked?" All it takes is a union inspector to be called in and see that our equipment isn't up to date on maintenance and shut us down.

"I'm not sure. This has never happened before. Someone would have had to skip it."

Who the fuck would do that? "Like someone purposely sabotaged the log?"

"That's my guess."

"Let me see the log. I want to know every single employee who's touched it and who was supposed to oversee—"

"Shit! Look out!"

Instantly, I grab Georgia, pressing her to my chest and taking us both to the floor. Within seconds of us hitting the ground, a steel pipe crashes into the forklift next to us, and I cover her face as sparks shoot off in all directions.

"We got it. We got it." Greg shouts.

I quickly turn Georgia in my arms. My eyes search hers. She looks freaked. "Are you okay?" She doesn't answer, and it worries me. "Are you hurt? Did you hit your head?" My hands start to graze down her body. "Georgia, answer me—"

"Good thing for these hard hats."

I bring my eyes back to hers. Her lips slowly curl up into the sexiest smile, and I can't help it, but my dick jerks. It's then we both realize our close proximity. Her taut little body is tucked under mine, and there's no denying she most definitely can feel the hardness of my cock. "Glad you find humor in this, *Peach*."

There go those lips again. Parting and teasing me.

"Mr. Black, are you okay? Either of you hurt?" At the sound of Wayne's voice, I release Georgia and stand, helping her up.

"I think so."

Wayne looks at Georgia, and she replies, "Yeah, I'm okay."

Hearing those words allows me to take my worry off her. My anger kicks in. Something could have happened to her. I turn to Wayne. "What the fuck was that?"

"I don't know."

Gary runs up. "The system failed again."

"What do you mean, again?"

"Same with the machine. It just glitched and shut down."

"How is that possible?" Both men look as stunned as I am. The likelihood of this happening is almost impossible. "Someone better fucking answer me—"

"I don't know. The system should be flawless. There's no way this would—"

"But it did." I'm shaking to the brink of exploding. "I want all production halted immediately. Wayne, get everyone who has access to the operations room in your office *now*!"

Georgia jumps at my side. I grab my phone and text Vince with instructions, then turn to Georgia. "I'm sorry. We're going to have to cut this field trip short. Vince is going to drive you back to the office."

She nods. "Yeah. Of course."

"Gary will walk you out." As much as I want to kiss the disappointment off her face, this needs my attention. I break away and turn to Wayne. "Let's go."

Chapter EIGHT

Georgia

I thank Vince for the ride and make my way into the building. My phone buzzes as I get into the elevator, and I pull it out of my purse.

> **Noah: Where the fuck are you?**

Great.

> **Me: At work. And you?**

> **Noah: Bullshit. Rachel said you left with my dad. You serious?**

I roll my eyes. I don't bother replying. The elevator dings, and I walk out, right into Noah and his furious gaze. "What the hell were you doing at the warehouse with my dad?"

"Are you stalking me now?" I try to walk past him, but he doesn't allow it.

"No, I'm looking out for you. Stay away from my dad."

"Are you kidding me? I work for him." I make another attempt to move past him, but he grabs my arm, pulling me into him.

"What else are you gonna do for him?"

"Fuck you."

"Don't tempt me, baby. I'll never turn down a good fuck with you—"

I raise my hand to slap him, but the large glass entrance doors open, and Rachel sticks her head out. "Excuse me. Sorry to interrupt." Noah drops my arm along with his nasty snarl.

"No problem." He gives me one last glare, then slaps a smile on and turns to Rachel. "What's up, Rach?"

"Your father called. He wanted to make sure that Miss Price made it back okay."

Noah turns to me, an accusing scowl on his face, and replies, "Tell him his teacher's pet made it back in one piece." He walks past me, shoving his shoulder into mine, throws open the door to the stairwell, and disappears.

***

"Asshole," I cuss under my breath. Noah's car is gone. He left work, leaving me to fend for a ride home. I shake my head and pull out my phone, searching for my ride app. I text Noah while I wait.

Me: You're a real prick. Just makes me happier that I made the right decision.

Three little dots come across my screen, but after a beat, they disappear. "Ugh!" How did I never see what a dick he truly was? *Because good sex clouded your vision?* Well, no more.

I call my sister on the ride home.

"Hey! How's it going?"

I miss hearing my baby sister's voice. The only reason I was torn about taking the internship was leaving her alone all summer. But the second she finishes high school, I'm forcing her to a university, far far away from him. That's if Bill doesn't get his hands on her college funds first.

"It's good," I lie. The last thing I need is for her to worry about me. I'm the older sister. I should be the one worrying. "I really like the job so far."

"And Noah? You two good?"

I should have never let on that I was unhappy with him. "Yeah. We're fine. The same stuff."

"George, you don't have to stay there if you don't want to."

I do. Because I refuse to be near Bill. And I hate that my sister has to. "I know. It'll be fine. With the money I'll make over the summer, I'll be able to pay off a huge chunk of my loans and not feel so stressed out."

"Ugh, I hate that Mom's not helping you. I told you, you can have the money Mom put away for my—"

"Not a chance. That money is for you."

"But George—"

"No buts. You're going to college, Lettie." My car pulls up to the Blake estate. "Hey. I gotta go. Call you over the weekend?"

"Yeah. Love you, Georgie."

"Love you too, Lettie."

I hang up. Our call was supposed to make me feel better. Instead, it made me feel worse. Bill never dared lay a hand on Lettie like he did my mom, or even me. But if I ever got wind that he touched a single hair on her body, I would kill him myself.

I get out and walk past Noah's car. I briefly imagine keying it, but shake off that intrusive thought and enter the house. It's quiet. The last thing I want is to run into Noah, so I hurry up the stairs and shut myself in my room. I peel off my clothes and crawl into bed.

I have yet to process what happened today with Mr—Jackson. At every touch and glance, he stokes this fire inside me. He's started a need within me that I don't know how to sort out. I'm a sexual person—I always have been—which has been a blessing and a curse. I'll be the first to admit I've made some horrible decisions in my life. Mr. Bishop was an itch I needed to scratch. He was older and off-limits. A game I wanted to play and win. He was attentive and knew exactly what I needed. We fucked; made love. It was wrong and thrilling. And when it ended, I was devastated. Either because it was over or we got caught, I don't know. My need to play in dangerous territory cost him everything. His job. Reputation.

I was able to finish the school year, but then Mom transferred me. Not that that made a difference. It only allowed me a new selection of people to play with. Maybe if my dad had never died, I wouldn't try so hard to fill the empty space he left. Man after man, I allowed them to have me, chasing the need to feel full. Whole.

My mother called me a slut. Bill's disgusting gaze looked at me with lust.

I shake off the memory.

A splashing sound reaches my bedroom window. I get up and pull back the blinds. Jackson is in the pool. *Go to bed, Georgia.* I watch him, each stroke accentuating his muscles. God, he is beautiful. *Don't do it. Don't even think about it.* "Since when do I do the right thing?" I say to myself.

I grab my white bikini out of my suitcase, change, and head downstairs.

The sound of the sliding glass door grabs his attention, and he spots me as I walk out. "Mind if I join you?"

The lights from the pool glow against his glistening chest. He lifts his arms, brushing his fingers through his wet hair, enticing me more.

"Sure that's a good idea?"

He's giving me a chance to make the right decision. Noah is inside. *Watch out for him.* "I think it's a great idea. Unless you want me to—"

"Get in the fuckin' pool, Peach."

I can't hold back my smile and dive into the pool. When I emerge, Jackson is mere inches from me. I run my hands through my hair, asking for trouble when my chest juts out.

"You know how this looks. If Noah walks out."

"That two people are having an innocent swim?" I ask, sucking in my bottom lip.

He swims around me. "And is this innocent, Peach?"

"I'm not sure."

My heart rate jacks up a notch. He's behind me. I can feel the heat of his body with him so close. Heat coils between my thighs. His warm breath grazes over my earlobe. "What exactly do you think is going to happen?"

He's baiting me. He wants me to confess what I want. I gasp when his hand loops across my belly, tugging me against him. He's hard everywhere. His erection presses between my ass cheeks.

"What do you think—"

The sound of the sliding glass door resonates through the backyard. Jackson releases me. When I twist around, he's already on the other side of the pool.

"Are you fucking kidding me?" Noah walks up, looking from me to his father. "Wow, you two didn't take long."

"Noah, knock it off."

"No, fuck that. Seriously? Can't you get your own pussy? Oh, wait. You can't, so you have to go after—"

"I said knock it off," Jackson snaps.

Noah turns his anger on me. "And you. Why am I not surprised? Should have seen what a fucking slut you were the first day I met you."

"Noah! That's enough."

"You're right; it is enough. Makes me not feel so bad that I'm going out tonight to get my dick wet since you won't do it. Enjoy my sloppy seconds, *Dad.*" Before I can respond, he's gone.

Jackson swims to the ledge and climbs out. He grabs my towel. "Swim time's over."

I tread through the water and lift myself out of the pool. Stopping in front of him, I look up, as he slowly wraps the towel around me, his fingers grazing the side of my breasts in the process. I'm in limbo, waiting for him to make the next move. But he doesn't.

"Enjoy the rest of your night," he says, leaving me standing there as he walks into the house. My entire body is on fire. Lust surges through me. My nipples pebble, and I know what I need to do.

I go back inside. Looking out the front window, I see Noah's car is gone. I head upstairs and down the hall, passing Noah's, then my bedroom. Jackson's door is closed. I debate knocking. I don't want to give him the opportunity to send me away, so I twist the knob and walk in. My heart is hammering against my chest. "Jackson?"

The sound of the shower grabs my attention. I move toward the partially closed door and open it. I suck in a staggered breath at the sight of him standing under the spray with his hand wrapped around his large cock. My subtle gasp gets his attention, and he lifts his head. I'm frozen in place. Even with my interruption, he continues to stroke himself. I can't look away. He drags his fist up and down his shaft, watching me. "What do you think is going to happen here, Peach?"

He continues to stroke himself, and it's turning me on to no end. My sex throbs with need. So many fantasies rush through my mind, and I struggle to form an answer.

"You want my cock in that pretty mouth of yours, Peach?"

A gush of arousal soaks my suit bottoms. I nod. "Yes."

He pumps into his hand harder, faster. "Come here."

I can't take it anymore. I want him in my mouth. I undo the ties of my top and slide out of my bottoms. His eyes roam my body, and he squeezes his cock. I open the door and step into his space. I think I've forgotten how to breathe. I hold his gaze and, with deliberate slowness, drop to my knees.

"Open up, Peach. Show me how hungry you are."

For more books by J.D. Hollyfield check out her website!
https://authorjdhollyfield.com/

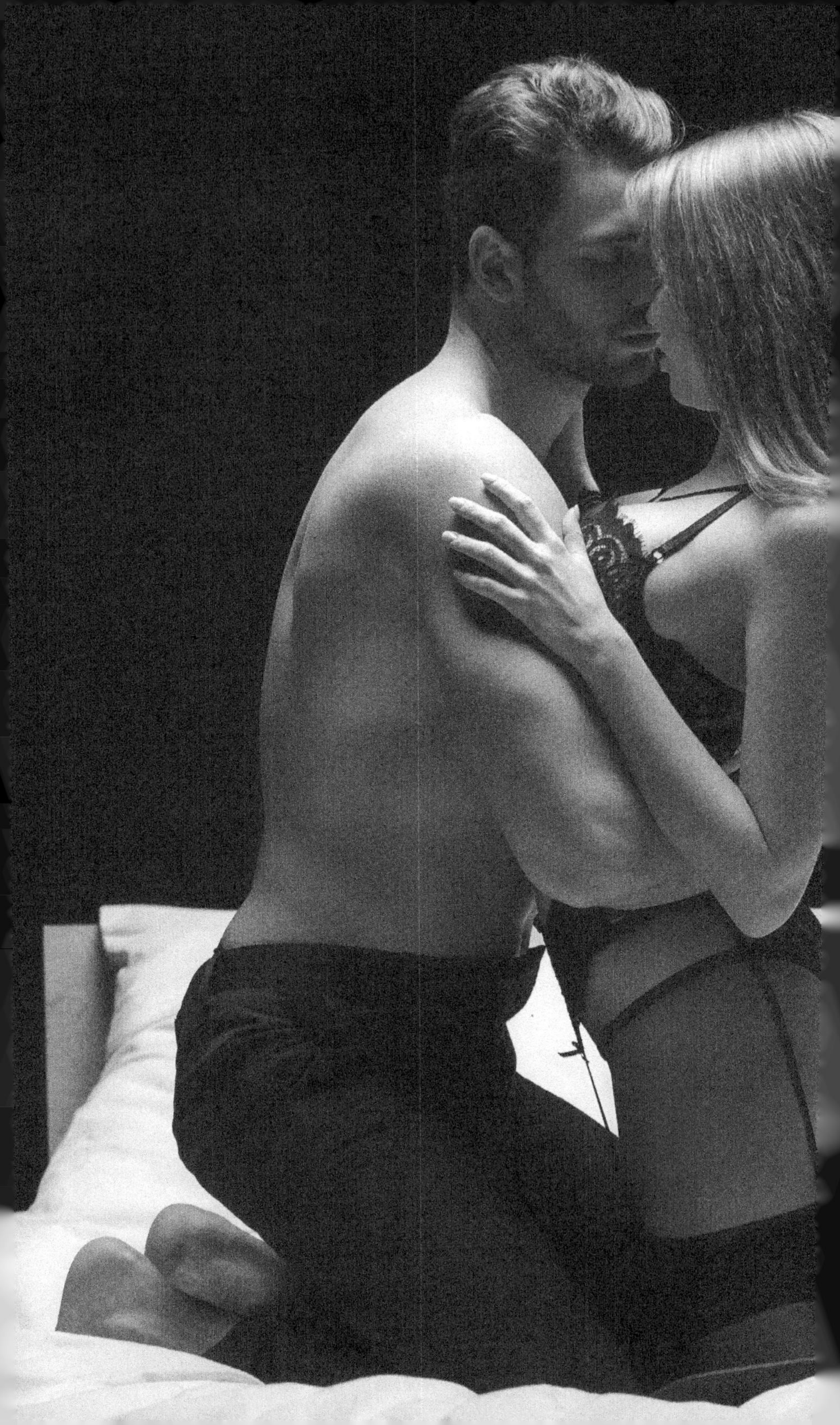

Corium
EVER AFTER

C. HALLMAN & J.L. BECK

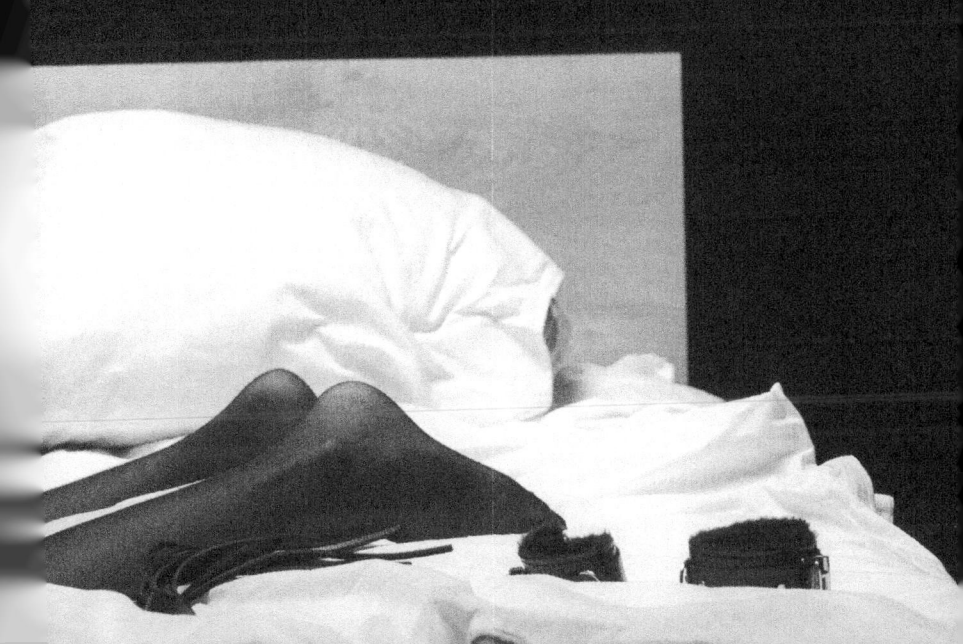

Chapter ONE

Quinton

My favorite part of each morning is waking up before Aspen does. It's been over two years since we got married, and I've still not grown tired of it. If anything, my obsession with my wife has only grown. Aspen invades every part of my mind, every fiber of my being, and there isn't a moment of the day I'm not thinking of her. Even when she is close, I want her closer. When she is happy, I want her to be happier. And on the off-chance something made her sad, I want to burn down the world and kill everyone and everything that made her frown.

Even in the dim light coming from the bathroom, I can make out her beautiful features. Normally, they are relaxed and soft, but today frown lines are covering her forehead and her jaw is tight as if she is grinding her teeth together. She must be having a bad dream.

Propping myself up on my elbow, I gently run my index finger over her forehead, trying to flatten out the creases. When I run my finger down her jaw, her lips part, and she sucks in a deep breath. Her eyes move behind her eyelids, but she doesn't open them. I swipe my thumb over her full lips, and she parts her lips further, inviting me into her mouth.

Taking the invite, I press my thumbs into her waiting mouth, massaging her warm tongue. She closes her lips around me and sucks softly.

"Naughty girl," I whisper, my voice raspy.

Aspen traps my thumb between her teeth and bites down gently before a grin tugs on the corner of her mouth. Her eyes finally open, and I see the mischief brewing in the depth of her baby blues.

I pull my thumb from her mouth so I can kiss her plump lips. She immediately leans into me, snaking her arms around my neck and pulling me closer. I'm more than happy to oblige, covering her body with mine until there is no space between us.

My leg wedges between her thighs, and I feel her hot cunt on my skin. My cock is already hard, and I would love to fuck her until she can't walk, but I have other plans today.

I break the kiss. Both of us breathing heavily, eager to tear off the little clothes we are wearing. "As much as I would love to have a morning quickie, we actually have somewhere to be in an hour, and I want you to eat breakfast before."

Aspen yawns, using the back of her hand to rub her eyes. "It's Saturday; we don't have any classes."

"I know. I have a surprise for you."

"Surprise?" Aspen perks up right away, the sleep disappears from her eyes, and excitement replaces it.

"Yes, and if you want to see it, you better get this sexy ass out of bed before I lose all restrain." My idle threat has her moving quickly. She ducks under my arm and rolls out of bed, leaving me cold and yearning for her touch.

"What kind of surprise is it?" She questions as she starts pulling things out of the dresser, her gaze on me. I prefer this side of her compared to the many other sides of my wife that I've seen. The things she's gone through—that I put her through. I'll never forgive myself, which is why I spend every single day reminding her of our love, of how much she means to me.

"Well, a surprise only works if you keep it a secret, right?" I make the gesture of my lips being sealed, and she rolls her eyes.

"I could always beg..." She bats her long lashes, her eyes doing that thing that makes my cock instantly hard. Fuck, she's a temptation, but she's going to ruin my plans if I don't get her back on track.

"Later, baby. You can beg me all you want when we get back, and if you're good and behave, I'll make you come on my cock."

She snorts. "You'll do that anyway."

I watch as she gets dressed, and it takes more self-will than I care to admit not to try and fuck her. *Think of the surprise.* Since I'm an early riser, I'm already dressed for the day. Even after everything that happened with my leg and being pushed down the stairs, I still go to the gym daily.

Aspen interrupts my thoughts as she skirts by me, her yoga pants accenting her ass perfectly. I shove out of bed and follow behind her.

She makes a pit stop in the bathroom and starts running a brush through her hair. Our gazes collide in the mirror as I watch, completely obsessed and blinded by her beauty. I can see the wheels in her head turning. Sometimes she gets anxious, and it's best to just remind her everything is okay.

"I guess I should've asked if I needed to dress up, but I assumed..." I take her gently by the chin and lean into her, cutting off whatever tirade she was going to go off on. Worry gives way to desire that shines bright in her eyes.

I'll never get enough of her.

"Shhh, stop worrying. There is no need to dress up. We aren't even leaving Corium." I drop that little nugget of info to get her thinking more.

Her pink lips part. "So the surprise is here? At Corium."

I nod and release my grasp on her chin, placing a soft kiss at the corner of her mouth. Mine. Forever. For always.

"Hmmm, there aren't many options for surprises here, but you're Quinton Rossi, so anything is possible."

"Exactly, now let's go get some breakfast and coffee. I'm hungry and what I wanted to eat for breakfast isn't available." I grin.

"Why're you so obsessed with me?" she taunts and rushes toward the door. I give chase because no matter how much I love her and how much we have been through, there is one part of me I can never shut off, and that's the need to dominate her, to keep her in my arms. She is my prey, and I am her dark wolf.

"I'll forever be obsessed with you, Aspen Rossi. My wife, my everything." I growl into her ear as she rushes out of the bedroom, me hot on her heels. Today's going to be a good day. I can feel it.

Chapter TWO

Aspen

I trust Quinton with my life. I know he would never put me in any danger or cause me any pain. Yet, as he leads me to the dorms of Corium, my heart beats irregularly fast, my palms are sweaty, and fear is swirling around my gut to the point of nausea.

"You okay?" Q asks, reaching for my hand to interlace his fingers with mine.

"Yeah, just antsy to see this surprise."

"Well, that's good, because we are here." Quinton comes to a halt, and I follow suit.

Looking around, I don't see anything besides the empty hallway. I'm about to ask what the hell he is talking about when Quinton turns sideways, lifts his arm, and knocks at one of the dorm rooms.

I've never been to this part of the dorms, so I have no idea what to expect, which is probably the reason the uneasy feeling won't leave my gut. Quinton must pick up on my anxiety. He squeezes my hand gently.

"Don't worry, I think you're going to like this, and if not, you don't have to do it," he assures me, and a little bit of tension disappears.

The door opens, and a guy—I've only ever seen in passing before—greets us. "Hey, guys, come in. I'm all set up." He addresses us both but keeps his eyes trained on Quinton.

I'm not sure if people automatically do this or if Q threatened everyone with torture if they look at me too long.

Both scenarios are very possible.

Clinging onto Quinton's hand like it's my life raft, I follow them inside the dorm room. Scanning the open space, I immediately notice how much smaller this is than the apartment we are staying in, but still bigger than the room I had when I first came to Corium.

He must live here by himself since there is only one bed in the corner. The walls are covered in hand-drawn art, which is really the only thing that gives this room some life. The little furniture that's in here is bland and colorless.

My eyes land on a weird-looking chair wrapped in clear foil. The table beside it is also wrapped in foil, with some kind of tools on top.

"I came up with three designs, but, of course, I can change anything or even go a completely different way," the guy I don't know explains.

Still not completely sure what's going on here, I glance over to Quinton for an explanation.

"This is Billy." Q offers, "He is the one who did my tattoo, and if you want, he'll tattoo your back today."

"Oh..." My mouth stays in an open O shape long after the word has fallen from my lips. Realization settles in, and my whole body relaxes.

"Like I said, you don't have to do this," Quinton repeats.

"I want to," I blurt out. "I'm just surprised, that's all."

"Why don't you look at what Billy came up with, and we go from there?"

"So I came up with this." Billy points to three drawings laid out on the coffee table.

Never letting go of Quinton's hand, I take a few steps closer until my thighs bump against the edge of the table. My eyes go wide as I take in the drawings. All three are absolutely stunning.

The first one is a lotus that looks so realistic it's coming right off the page. The second is a serpent winding itself around a rose.

It's drawn in an edging style that looks both interesting and artful. The last one is an intricate fine-line mandala that has so many little details it's hard to look away.

I take all three in, trying to figure out how the hell I'm going to choose. "They are all stunning. Honestly, I don't know how to pick one. I love everything."

"Could you somehow combine the three ideas?" Quinton questions before I can voice the same idea.

"Absolutely." Billy doesn't hesitate. He actually seems pretty excited about the idea. "Give me a few more minutes to draw up the stencils." He gathers his papers and pencils, sitting down at a small desk next to his bed, where he starts drawing.

"Do you really like it?" Quinton asks softly. "I thought you could use it to cover up the scar you hate."

The reminder of the scar feels like a jab with a knife. I have become good at hiding my pain every time I remember what happened to me that night, but I'll never be good enough to hide from Quinton.

My husband wraps his arms around me, pulling me into his strong chest. "I'm sorry," he whispers into my hair. I've told him a million times to stop apologizing. It wasn't his fault, yet he blames himself.

I bury my nose in his shirt, letting his unique scent calm me through the dark thoughts. They always linger in the back of my mind, but times like these have them trying to claw their way to the front until my head is consumed with dread, fear, and grief.

Q holds me, drawing small circles over my back until Billy finishes drawing my tattoo.

"Here it is," he announces, bursting with pride. One look at the drawing tells me why. It's stunning. "If you want anything changed, let me know. Quinton told me the most important thing is to cover up the scar. I can definitely hide it in the petals of the lotus. You won't even see that it was there at all."

I stare at the beautiful drawing. He really did combine all the ideas, leaving the fine lines of the mandala in the background. The lotus is the center, and below, the snake is going to line up with my spine like it's slithering up my back. It's both feminine and badass." "I love it!"

"Perfect. I need you to take off your shirt." As soon as the words leave Billy's mouth, both he and Quinton go stiff. Billy's eyes go wide as he realizes what he just said. "I mean just to tattoo... obviously. Nothing more. I'll go to the bathroom while you get changed. You can lay down on the chair; I've already disinfected everything." He scurries away into the bathroom, and I give Quinton a knowing look.

"You knew I had to take my shirt off for this."

"Knowing and actually doing it are two different things. The thought of someone else seeing your bare skin, even if it's just your back, is driving me insane."

"Good thing we'll only have to do this once." I grab the hem of my shirt and pull it up over my head.

Quinton's gaze lowers to my boobs immediately, like two magnets pulling his eyeballs toward me. The thin fabric of my bra is still between us, but that doesn't stop my nipples from hardening and tingling with excitement.

"Maybe we should have had that quickie after all." Quinton circles around me, dragging his finger over the tender skin on my stomach, ribs, and lower back until he is standing right behind me. His skillful fingers unclasp my bra, and I let the straps slide down my shoulders slowly. Cool air washes over my already heated skin.

"I can't believe you let me get naked in someone else's room," I tease, making Quinton growl angrily behind me.

Reaching around, he cups my breasts in his large palms. His touch is urgent and rough as he pulls me against his chest.

"I know what you are doing." Quinton pinches my nipples, and I let my head fall back against his shoulder with a moan.

"Me?" I ask innocently.

Of course, he knows exactly what I'm doing. I'm egging him on, making him a little jealous. It's no secret that I love my husband's dark side just as much as I love his soft side. Maybe even more so.

"Lie down on the chair before I bend you over the couch and fuck you raw." Heat blooms in my core, and I have to force my legs to move before I bend myself over the couch. Teasing my husband has become one of my favorite pastimes, and we don't have time for that right now.

The chair smells like disinfectant, reminding me of a hospital. My mood darkens in an instant. I straddle the reclined chair and press my chest to the back, letting my arms dangle to the side.

Quinton walks around me, making sure Billy won't get a glimpse of side boob. When he is somewhat satisfied, he straightens up and yells, "You can come in now."

The bathroom door opens, and Billy pops his head through the opening as if he is still not sure if it's safe to come out. When he realizes I'm situated on the chair, he opens the door further and steps into the room, still a little apprehensive.

Quinton is standing next to me, his arms folded across his puffed-out chest. His eyes are set into an angry glare, and his foot is tapping against the floor impatiently. He didn't think this through. He didn't foresee what it would do to him, having another guy touch me, no matter the circumstance. Somehow, I find this a little funny.

"Okay, so I'm going to clean her skin and put a stencil on," Billy explains with a shaky voice while putting on a pair of latex gloves.

A moment later, I feel a cold rag being rubbed over my back. Then he carefully centers the stencil and transfers it onto my skin. "We'll hide the scar right under here." I feel his fingers run over what I assume is going to be the lotus. "Do you want me to leave again so you can look at it?"

I'm not sure if he is asking Quinton or me since I'm not used to having people talk to me when I'm with my husband. Nevertheless, I answer. "I don't need to see it. I trust Quinton's judgment."

More importantly, I hate looking at the scar, the last physical reminder of what happened that night, of what Matteo did to me... what he took from us.

Normally, thinking of that night fills me with dread, and though I'm not feeling great thinking of it now, I also feel a huge relief knowing that I never have to look at it again. Once I have the tattoo, at least I will be more comfortable in my own skin. The bad will be washed away and replaced with something beautiful.

Chapter THREE

Quinton

I really didn't think this through.

Aspen is sprawled out shirtless on the tattoo chair. Billy can't see anything besides her back, but even that seems too much. Even worse, he is touching her. I try to tell myself this is how it has to be. He can't tattoo her without touching her. Unfortunately, the primal part inside of me doesn't care.

For the last few years, I have spent every minute of the day keeping Aspen safe. I don't let anyone touch her, talk to her, or even look at her. So this goes against everything I'm used to.

"Quinton? Is it okay?" Aspen cranes her neck to look up at me while the rest of her stays still, and I would swear Billy's starting to sweat. He'd better. He better know how to behave himself with her.

Is it okay? No, none of this is okay, but that isn't the question she's asking, and we both know it.

I stand beside him to examine the placement of the stencil, and I have to admit his design is brilliant. It will perfectly conceal her scar to where nobody would ever know it exists. "Yes. The placement looks good."

A careful choice of words. "I'm pleased so far." I make a point of glaring down at Billy when I say it, and although his eyes are carefully trained on her back, I'd bet anything he gets my meaning.

"Great. I'll get to work now." He sounds relieved. I'm sure the sooner this is done, the better for him.

"Come sit over here." Aspen gestures to the wheeled chair near where she's waiting to get inked. "Come talk to me. I want to be able to see you."

I know what she really means, what she's driving at. She has to sense what this is doing to me and wants me to calm down. She's asking for the impossible. How can I calm down when another man has his hands on what's mine?

There's a twinkle in her eyes, that little gleam I saw earlier. "You're enjoying this, aren't you?" I mutter once I'm seated, speaking to her but staring at Billy. He'd better hope his hands stay where they need to be.

"Getting tattooed?" Suddenly, she gasps, reaching for me, and I take her hand. "At the moment, not particularly." Yes, because he's getting started, and the way she winces tells me how she's feeling.

I take her hand gently despite the dangerous heat that's beginning to boil my blood. At least he keeps his eyes on his work, but of course, he'll be in close contact with her throughout the process. My eyes are glued to him, following the direction of his gaze, even the way he breathes when he has to lean in especially close as he works on the intricate mandala.

"That's not what I was talking about," I mutter, briefly meeting her gaze before my eyes dart back to Billy.

Chuckling softly, she gestures for me to lean in closer. "You know, this is kind of a permanent thing."

"I know."

"So maybe don't intimidate the poor guy so much he makes a mistake." Her smile is loving, and that, plus the pressure from her fingers around my hand, manages to loosen the worst of my tension. She's right. I don't want him marring her perfection because I couldn't handle myself.

Still, I'm keeping an eye on this guy.

The only thing that keeps me going is reminding myself this is for her. She needs this; she deserves it. Something beautiful to cover up the ugliness. Since I played a part in how that ugliness came to be, I think I can suck it up and grit my teeth through watching a man touch her. I can do anything, as long as it's for her.

She winces, and I stroke her cheek, offering a sympathetic smile. "You'll get used to it."

"I usually have a higher threshold for pain," she grits out.

Yes, because she's brave and strong, stronger than me. In so many ways, she's like the lotus currently being placed on her back. She's been through unfathomable shit but has come out even more beautiful on the other side. She never let it break her, none of it. Even when I made it my mission in life to break her down, she refused.

That's how I know she can get through this.

"I can't wait for everybody to see it." The excitement in her voice makes me smile, even if she'd better hope she doesn't intend on flashing her bare back to everyone we know. "I bet Scar will love it."

"Don't go giving her any ideas," I warn, and she laughs gently. If I focus on keeping her laughing, I won't be so concerned about leaving her on display like this. There will never come a time when I'm comfortable with letting others see and touch her. She's too precious for me to allow that.

"Right. I'm sure your dad would freak."

That gets me snorting because I can see it in my head. How he'd blow his stack if he thought I influenced my sister into having her back inked, even if the work was good. We Rossi men tend to be overprotective of our women.

"How does it look so far?" she asks. "Do you like it?"

"I think it's a beautiful design." I might want to tear Billy's hands off for touching my wife, but I can admit he exceeded my expectations with how he combined his three concepts.

"So long as you don't go around showing it off," I warn with a growl. I'm only half joking, something I'm sure she's aware of. "Very few people will ever know this exists."

"Anybody who sees me in a bathing suit will."

Jealousy rears up in me at the idea. "Then we'll only go swimming on private beaches or when I take you out on a boat."

"What if I'm wearing a dress that's cut low in the back?"

Now she's deliberately throwing out scenarios intended to make me lose control—and she likes it. It gets her off to see me lose my shit over her. "What if you always wear dresses that cover your back instead?"

She rolls her eyes, giggling softly. "If you say so."

It might not take as long as it seems for Billy to finish since, as far as I'm concerned, time is crawling. Every moment that passes ratchets up my tension a little more. Occasionally, he'll glance up at me, and each time it's to find me watching him like a hawk. His hand shakes, but he steadies it before returning to the work. I catch Aspen watching me with a knowing gleam in her eyes, but she doesn't understand. She never will.

"Wow, and Lucas went through this for every piece he's had done?" she asks out of nowhere. Her father's skin is a canvas that reflects the winding path his life has taken. "I can't imagine him sitting still for this long."

With a sigh of obvious relief Billy turns off his equipment. He stretches, rolling his head slowly like he's easing the tension in his muscles. "All done. Do you want to take a look at the finished product?"

"I'll show her when we get back to the room." Because he's not going to spend another moment around my topless wife now that he's finished. He steps aside when I take his place, looking down at his work.

I have to admit, it's beautiful. And it suits her perfectly. "You look great," I tell her since I notice the anxiety on her features when she tries to look over her shoulder to gauge my reaction.

"It's really sore," she admits. "How long will it be sore?"

Billy opens his mouth like he's going to explain, but I cut him off. "A few days, maybe a week. It depends on how careful you are not to lie on your back at first. I'll take good care of you."

Then I turn to Billy. "I'll be cleaning her up. I know what to do." I head straight for the bathroom while he gathers his equipment and wash my hands thoroughly before he takes my place without saying a word.

Smart guy. I don't like having to explain myself.

"Stay there," I tell my wife when it looks like she's about to get up. "I have to wash you off. You'll need to do this twice a day until you're all healed up."

"For how long?"

"Since when do you mind your husband touching your back?"

"That's not how I meant it."

I know, but she's been teasing me all day. It only seems right for me to give a little bit of that back to her. "I might decide to make a habit out of washing you from now on. What do you think about that?"

She snorts, then hisses in pain when I begin to clean the fresh tattoo. "I think you're looking for an excuse to touch me."

"Since when do I need one?" It doesn't take long before I couldn't care less about teasing her. Not when the act of caring for her gets me heated. I don't know what it is about her. It takes nothing to awaken the hunger I always feel when she's involved. The touch of her skin—I've spent years memorizing its softness and smoothness. Exactly how to caress it to make goosebumps cover the surface. She's a work of art created just for me, and it's my duty to protect this perfection.

Once she's clean, I apply ointment with a gentle touch, then cover the piece with plastic wrap. "It won't be like this forever," I remind her, helping her out of the chair. Her bra might be a little much for now, so I tuck it into my back pocket. The sight of her body stretching, her muscles flexing, and her breasts lifting stirs my hunger again, and this time it translates into the beginnings of an erection. I need this woman like I need oxygen.

"Let's get you into this." With one eye on the closed bathroom door, I help her into her shirt. She winces but shakes her head when I look at her in concern. Stubborn thing. Part of me wonders if she plays down the discomfort to ease my mind.

"Thank you for this. I would never have thought of it." She leans against me, gazing up into my eyes with nothing but pure love in hers. To this day, I don't fully believe I deserve it. How could she see me and love me like she does? Yet another piece of proof that she is truly meant for me.

I press a kiss against her forehead and take a deep breath, soaking in her unique scent. "Anything for you." I mean it with every part of me. I would move heaven and earth for her and not think twice.

There's another story happening below my waist, and of course, she feels it. The light in her eyes changes to something deeper, and she bites her lip. "Even this turns you on?" she whispers, wrapping her arms around my back and pressing herself tight against me. Her nipples are hard, brushing my chest now that she's braless.

"Everything about you does," I growl. "Let's get out of here and get you back to our place before I have no choice but to take you here and now."

Chapter FOUR

Aspen

I don't think I've ever walked the halls this fast—almost at a jog—when there's no emergency. Q is in that much of a hurry to get me alone again.

It's not that I can't relate. I want him, too, just as badly. Even with my back as sore as it is, that does nothing to cool the heat in my core, to soothe the ache between my thighs. All it takes is the slightest touch, and I'm like Pavlov's dog, slobbering for its next treat. In this case, the treat is my husband. His hands, his tongue, his dick, and what they do to me.

And it's more than that. It's the feeling of connection. Every time we're together like this, our bond grows. It might seem like all we're doing is giving in to lust—and we are—but something bigger is at work. Something deeper.

And when he practically flings our apartment door open and hurries me inside, I know we're going to strengthen our bond one more time.

The door's barely closed when his hands are on me, sliding up over my hips, under my shirt to cup my boobs. "Watching me get tattooed turned you on this much?" I barely get the question out before moaning at the way he thumbs my nipples. They were already hard, thanks to my anticipation, and now every flick sends signals straight down to my throbbing clit.

"Everything you do turns me on." He breathes into my mouth before claiming it with his. As always, I give myself over gladly because I know I'm safe. He's my home; he is my life. We're so close, we may as well be one person. One soul.

Every brush of his lips and sweep of his tongue undoes me a little more as he backs me across the room, my arms around his neck, moaning into his mouth before we bump up against the sofa.

An animal growl rumbles in his chest, and my knees go weak at the sound of his need for me. Right away, he hooks his fingers around the waistband of my pants and pulls them down in one swift motion before dropping to his knees.

I run my fingers through his thick hair, gazing down at him with love and want, fighting to see which will win out. I'll never get tired of seeing him like this, so strong and commanding but also weak for me. Knowing I can bring him to his knees without trying. All I have to do is exist.

"You have no idea," he growls against my skin, sending shivers up my spine. "Having to watch him touch you. Knowing his breath warmed your skin. It almost broke me."

"I know," I whisper, my voice shaky, legs trembling as he works his way closer to the place where I'm hot and dripping for him.

"Because I'm the only man who gets to see you like that. Right?" He looks up at me, and our eyes meet. The light flashing behind his would take my breath away on its own, but paired with his skillful touch, I'm left fighting for every sip of air.

"Yes," I manage to croak before he continues lapping at my sensitive skin, holding my legs in place. His fingers bite into my flesh, rough and demanding, leaving me walking the line between pain and pleasure.

He needs this. Needs to claim what's his. I know him and love him enough to understand, just as I know there was never any question of who I belong to.

I'll always be his. We were meant for each other, and all the pain and fear and even trauma we've been through together has brought us closer. Brought us to this moment.

With a grunt, he pulls aside the crotch of my thong. It's wet, soaked through, and now he laps away what's left on my smooth, swollen lips. "Quinton!" I gasp when the tip of his tongue parts my lips and delves deeper, fluttering through my folds. This is hardly the first time he's eaten me, but that sudden, electric thrill never changes. It's like the first time every time.

My nails scrape along his scalp before I grab the back of his head and hold it close. He wants me. He's so hungry for me he couldn't wait until he reached the bedroom. Just the sight of another man touching me drives him wild. All of this goes through my head, along with so many other thoughts and feelings, and before I know it, I'm grinding my hips, bearing down on him. Eager, desperate for relief from the unbearable heat burning me from the inside out.

And all he does is grunt and growl, not bothering to hide how my taste affects him. When he adds two digits, pumping them in and out of my pussy, I go wild, bucking against him, the pressure in my core building and growing as he massages me inside while closing his lips around my clit and sucking.

Fireworks explode behind my eyelids in the split second before it all breaks, and I cry out helplessly, shaking from the force of an orgasm so intense there's a moment when all that exists is the rippling bliss racing through me from head to toe. I almost collapse with weakness, but he stands and lets me lean against him while he pulls his shirt over his head. I take mine off, too, and let the thong drop to the floor.

The sight of his naked torso lights my fire again—maybe it never went out. Maybe it's always burning in the background, ready to be stoked again. And it is by the feeling of his rippling abs, broad chest, and shoulders under my nails as he kisses me again, claiming every inch of my skin with his hands. And I give it to him gladly, all of me, knowing I'll always be safe. I will always end up melting in the heat between us.

His erection is between us, and I move against it, savoring his helpless grunts. He grabs my thigh and lifts it, opening me up so he can drag his head through my wetness. I move with him, teasing him even while I'm teasing myself. Dragging it out, heightening the tension, knowing it will be so much better when we finally let go.

He groans into my mouth, fingers digging into my ass cheeks, his body trembling the way mine is as he turns me in place and bends me over the back of the sofa. "Lucky me," he grunts, scraping his short nails down my sides while I squirm and moan. "I get to look at this every single time I take you this way. I get to watch it move when you do."

Before I can say anything, he's dragging himself through my slit again, and this time when he reaches my entrance, he pushes inside, driving deep, pushing me forward. "Oh, fuck!" I shout, and he responds with a low chuckle before taking me by the hips and rutting me, forgetting everything about pace and rhythm in favor of taking. Fucking.

And I love it. This is what I crave. Letting go of everything, forgetting everything around us, and going wild with abandon. Pushing back against him, claiming him as he is claiming me. It doesn't matter what's going on anywhere else in this massive structure. Right now, it's just this. Our bodies connecting, the insane friction from his thick cock as it moves in and out of me until the air is full of the wet, sloppy sound of our bodies crashing together. Both of us breathing harder and faster, his fingers so tight against my flesh I know he'll bruise me.

"Who do you belong to?" he demands, moving fast enough that my boobs bounce hard enough to hurt. He takes them in his hands, gripping tight while he pumps into me like a jackhammer.

"You!" I howl, so close again. "Only you! Oh, my god!"

"That's right. That's who I am. Your god." Yes, and I'm his to use the way he's using me now, the way he's asserting control after hours spent feeling like he had to give some of it away. Reminding himself who I really belong to, heart and soul.

I welcome it, all of it, because it's right. That's how it's always been for us.

The feel of his hands on me, his cock inside me, all builds up until an explosion in my core sends shock waves of pure bliss radiating through me. "Quinton! Yes!" I sob, wracked with tremors, tears filling my eyes. "I'm coming!" Though I'm sure he feels it now that my muscles have tightened around him, increasing the pressure.

"Mine." I hear him over my ecstatic cries, his voice getting louder with every breath he takes. "Mine, mine."

He crashes against me one last time before I'm filled with the heat of his cum. He holds me in place, his thighs against my ass while he empties himself deep, his hot breath fanning across my shoulder. He's careful not to touch my tattoo, I notice, and even in the wild, shaking haze, my heart swells with love. Even now, he's so careful with me. It's one thing to fuck like animals, but at the core of it, there's nothing but love and tenderness in him.

At least when it comes to me.

This time, when he growls, I hear the difference. He's satisfied. He's calmed the beast in him, at least for now. "I will never get tired of you," he murmurs with love in his voice as he pulls away from me, and right away, I feel an inexplicable sense of loss. I want him back, even though I know it's impossible. He can't be inside me all the time, but that's when I feel whole.

"I hope not," I whisper, giggling. "Because we're kind of married. So you're stuck with me."

"I wouldn't call it stuck." When I turn around, he pulls me into his arms, careful not to hurt me. "Stuck isn't the word for it."

With my ear against his chest, the drumbeat of his heart fills my awareness. The scent of his skin, his cologne now mixing with perspiration. His gentle, tender touch. I'm in heaven. That's the only word I can think to describe it.

"What word would you use?" I ask, running my fingers up and down his back while his heartbeat begins to slow as he relaxes.

"Lucky. I'm the luckiest man alive." His breath stirs my hair before he kisses the top of my head. "Only this is the kind of luck I have to keep earning day by day. Because you are not a woman to take for granted, Aspen Rossi. Every day, I plan on earning you. And if that's all I ever do with my life, from now until the day I die, I'll consider myself successful. Just to know I earned your presence and your love."

My heart is too full for words, my throat tightening with emotion while tears sting behind my eyes. If I could speak, I'd tell him he doesn't have to earn anything. That I'm his and will always be his, forever. He's got me.

For now, it's enough to hold him and let myself be held. Some things can't be said in words, anyway.

Chapter FIVE

Aspen

Where the fuck are these stupid tests? This is a school filled with people in their late teens and early twenties. Lauren must have some tests flying around here somewhere. I dig my hand through the metal drawer, pushing boxes of gloves and gauze aside.

I knew I was in trouble when my period didn't arrive two weeks ago. I thought maybe give it another week, then I'll test. I wanted to be sure, but my period never came, so here I am.

I brush the long strands of hair from my face and peer around the room. I've looked everywhere, and still nothing. I huff out an angry breath and press my forehead against the cabinet. Tears prick at my eyes. Great, now I'm gonna cry again. This is a fucking nightmare. It's not like I can just drive to CVS and get one. We're in the fucking tundra of Alaska.

"Can I help you find something?" Lauren's voice catches me off guard. I slam the drawer shut and spin around to face her. She is casually leaning against the doorframe, her arms folded in front of her chest.

"Oh, hi..."

"Don't *hi* me. Tell me what you are looking for." Dr. Lauren doesn't seem mad, more annoyed than anything. I guess that's a perk of being the headmaster's daughter. "Aspen, come on. You know, all you have to do is ask."

"Of course, I know. It's just... I wanted to be sure before telling anyone."

"Tell anyone?" She blinks, a silent question hanging in the air between us.

I force a shuddering breath from my lungs. Here goes nothing.

"My period is late, and I'm pretty regular, so I needed to take a pregnancy test to make sure my assumption was right."

A smile splits Lauren's face. "Oh, all you had to do was ask." She walks in the direction of the medicine cabinet, which I know is locked with a fingerprint code and password. Seems like a lot of security for a pregnancy test, but if I've discovered anything at this university, it's that nothing is over the top. There is always a reason for a rule or stipulation.

Still, I find myself talking before I can stop. "You keep the tests in here?"

Lauren types her passcode in and then places her finger on the little screen.

"Yes. It's really surprising how often students have to come and ask for a test or Plan B. Unprotected sex is on the rise, and as you know, this is a school for the offspring of criminals." She pauses and opens the door to the cabinet. "It's better to know the things your enemies are up to and develop any type of blackmail you can." Turning, she places the white box in my hand.

Did she say what I think she did?

"Blackmail? Why would you blackmail them?"

"I wouldn't. But I do take note of who comes to me and for what. All that info is passed on to the higher-up people. If they see anything that might be discrediting or useful to them, then it's at their discretion to use that information."

All I can do is shake my head. I'm not really surprised, but at the same time, I am. So many laws are being broken here the government would have a field day in this place.

"So what you mean to tell me is that none of my information is secure or private?"

Lauren lets out a laugh. "Don't act so surprised. You know as well as I do that nothing said or done in this place is *private*."

That makes the anxious bubble in my belly bigger and the box in my hand heavier. I don't want anyone else to know until Q and I are ready to tell them. "Would it be okay to keep this between us? At least until we're ready to tell everyone?"

I know I'm asking her to do the opposite of what she's supposed to do, but Lauren is trustworthy. Plus, she can always report the test later.

"Of course. That's no problem, and if you'd like, you can go into the bathroom and take the test. I can help with the results if need be."

I step from foot to foot nervously. I'm terrified that I might be wrong but also excited at the possibility. I didn't know I was pregnant the last time, and things ended horrifically.

I know the same won't happen now, but it's just the fact that the past did happen, and letting go of it is something I haven't fully mastered yet. Not that I'll ever forget what happened or what I lost. It'll forever impact me, but it doesn't have to control me.

I nod my head, and she guides me toward the one-stall bathroom. My throat tightens. The stall door closes, and I force a ragged breath out of my lungs as I open the test. I've never had to take one of these before, so I read the directions.

It seems easy enough. I do my business and pee on the end of the stick before placing the blue cap on the end of the test.

All I can think about is Quinton's reaction. I'm certain of the test results already, but I wanted to be sure. Now I have to think of a way to break the news to him.

***

He should be back from his workout any minute now. I've paced our apartment ever since I got back from Lauren's office, clutching the test almost like a weapon I didn't want anyone to discover.

Q said he had some things to discuss with Lucas before he got started in the gym, leaving me with nothing to do but pace like a caged animal. I'm not sure if I want time to speed up or slow down.

What's he going to think? I mean, we don't use birth control, so this was bound to happen.

Still, it's one thing to know you want something and another to actually have it happen. We've only been married two years and are still so young. What if he wanted to take more time for us? What if...

That's just it. I won't know until I find out. Otherwise, I could drive myself mental by asking all these questions.

I'm not going to tell him right away. Maybe I'll bring up the subject of children and family. Like I'm joking or something, speaking vaguely about what might happen in the future. Now that we are going to be leaving Corium, it only makes sense to talk about the future. He doesn't need to know exactly why I'm choosing to bring it up at this very minute.

I just have to play it cool until I'm sure he feels like this is the right time.

And if he doesn't. If he seems sort of negative about the idea, I know I have to approach it differently. Maybe I could remind him of how the best things in life can't be predicted or planned. Like the way we met, the process of becoming part of each other's lives. I could never have imagined back in the beginning how we would end up in this place. Married, happy, and on the verge of starting our family.

A baby. Our baby. No, it can't make up for the loss of that first baby, but this might be where we begin to heal from that. It's not like the pain is at the forefront of my life anymore, but there's still that faint sense of something missing.

Finally, we'll be whole again.

That is if he sees things the way I do.

I'm still wearing out the floor next to our bed when he enters the apartment. This is it. I have to play it cool. He is so good at seeing through me, after all. Sometimes, I swear he can read my mind.

"Here you are. What, are you all ready for me?" he asks with a wolfish grin. Because while it seems like he's always horny, he's never hornier than when he's fresh off a workout. I guess it's all the blood flowing and his heart pumping.

I look at him, and suddenly, everything I planned goes out the window. "I'm pregnant."

So much for playing it cool and feeling him out.

He goes still, staring at me without blinking. "What did you say?"

"Pregnant. I'm pregnant." I go straight to the nightstand and pull out the test, holding it up for him to examine. "I just took it today. I hope you're not upset. We didn't really talk about when we wanted to start trying for a family, and I know it's still really early in the marriage and whatever, but sometimes things happen when they do for a reason, right? I mean, I guess that's always the case—"

He takes my face between his hands, and I would swear there's light glowing from under his skin. "You're having a baby. Our baby. My baby." Like he's still not sure he can believe it.

Somehow, I'm able to speak even with my throat closed to the size of a pinpoint and my heart thudding against my ribs. "I am. At least according to the test. Are you okay with it?"

If I had any lingering doubts, they dissolve when he smiles from ear to ear. "How could I be anything but fucking thrilled?"

"You are?" I ask with a laugh of pure relief.

"Aspen! This is all I want! That one final piece that's been missing. You're giving it to me."

"You kind of gave it to me," I point out, laughing through my happy tears.

"We gave it to each other." He pulls me in for a hug, wrapping me in his happiness and his love. "Thank you. Thank you."

There are tears on my cheeks when he touches my face again, tears that transfer to his skin when we kiss. In that kiss is the promise of so much. Future, family, love. So much love.

There's a wicked gleam in his eyes when he pulls back. "Come on." He tugs my hand, pulling me toward the shower. "Let's practice for when it comes time to make this little one a brother or sister."

***

Thank you for reading Corium Ever After! If you haven't read Quinton and Aspen's story you can find it in King of Corium. Go to https://www.bleedingheartromance.com/ to find links and more!

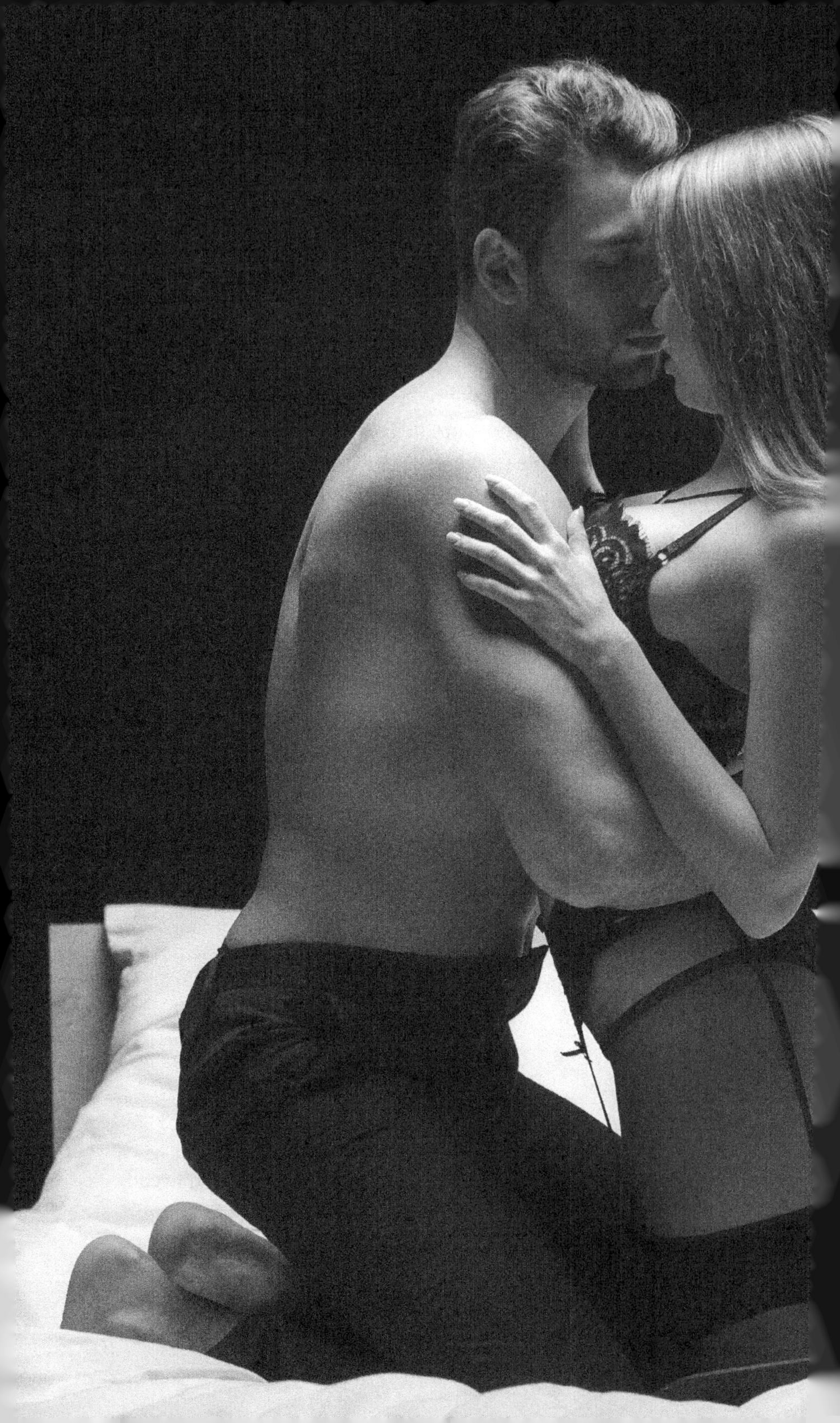

Love
STINKS

JENNA GALICKI

Chapter ONE

Russell

Love stinks. You love her. But she loves him. You just can't win. It was as if the lyrics to the eighties hit were written just for Russell. He didn't know which was worse—being trapped in a marriage to someone he didn't love or forced to watch the woman he loved love another.

Sitting next to his wife, pretending that his heart wasn't painstakingly longing for the woman across the yard, playfully splashing in the pool with her boyfriend, was killing him. But he couldn't look away.

Christopher was a decent guy. He made Layla happy, and he adored her. It was a hard twist to the knife in Russell's aching heart. To make matters worse, Chris integrated into their little group of friends with ease, and he was quickly becoming one of the guys. Just. Fucking. Great.

"Want some potato salad?"

Russell jumped at Donna's voice, forgetting that he'd been lusting after Layla while his unsuspecting wife sat next to him. It only took one look at her to know that "unsuspecting" couldn't be further from the truth. He was kidding himself if he thought Donna didn't know he had feelings for Layla, even if they never spoke about it.

"What?" he asked, as innocently as possible, even though her question was obvious by the way she held a serving spoon full of potato salad in the air.

"Potato salad," she snapped, whacking the spoon against his plate with a hard slap.

"Sorry," he mumbled, embarrassed at his behavior. "I was just watching Layla and Chris." At least he was being honest, as if that somehow made it any better.

"I know," Donna replied, glaring at him with an annoyed smirk as she chucked the spoon into the bowl.

"They're having fun. Do you want to go in the pool and join them in a game of volleyball?" he asked, trying to make an effort with his wife.

"No. I don't," she answered, curtly. "We're eating."

"We'll be done in 10 minutes. We can go in the pool after we eat."

Ryan, today's host and one of Russel's best friends since college, overheard as he set down a tray of freshly grilled burgers. "He's right," Ryan told Donna. "I never bought into that whole thing about waiting an hour after you eat to go swimming. If you're planning on swimming across the Atlantic, maybe, but not to go in the pool. Eat, then go for a dip."

"Thanks," Donna said. "But I'll pass."

Maybe if she'd ever shown interest in anything Russel suggested, his heart wouldn't have drifted. After all, he did love Donna once—a long time ago. He sighed, regretting his past decisions and questioning why he didn't fall in love with Layla first. He'd known her long before he met Donna. They were friends. Why hadn't his feelings for her bloomed sooner? Why did he have to be married to Donna, and Layla have to be in a serious relationship with Chris, before Russell realized he loved her? Why was fate so fucking cruel?

Because love stinks.

But he never gave up hope. All he needed was a chance. His heart ached to tell her how much he loved her—to tell anyone—but it was something he couldn't even tell his best friends. And as long as Layla was happy with Chris, he was forced to suffer the anguish and heartache of loving her from afar. He had no idea how he made it through the day sometimes because he thought about her constantly, and not being with her ate at his soul.

He concentrated on his burger and the conversation around the table. Suzanne was giving Dan a hard time about the amount of red meat on his plate and suggested he eat more chicken. Dan was appeasing his wife by simply adding a grilled chicken breast to his mile-high burger. Donna was asking Ryan about his secret sauce, but their host was taking the recipe to his grave.

Noise brought Russell's attention back to the pool. Layla and Chris had just stepped out of the water, and Layla was drying herself off with a towel. The mere sight of her took Russell's breath away, and, as hard as he tried, he couldn't divert his attention away from her dripping-wet body. His eyes washed over her tanned breasts, small waist, the curve of her hips, and all the way down her long legs. The emerald green bikini picked up the color in her hazel eyes, and her skin glistened from the reflection of the late summer sun. He couldn't remember when she looked more beautiful, and his chest hurt from wanting to be with her.

He watched as Chris playfully whipped his shoulder-length hair at Layla, and she laughed when water splashed across her face. She snapped her towel at him, but he caught it before the end made contact with his leg, and he tugged her to him. She crashed into his chest, and the breath she sucked in was clearly visible from across the yard. It was a gut punch to Russel's already weakened state, but he continued to watch the chemistry they shared, wishing it were him instead of Chris who put that loving look in Layla's eyes.

Layla continued to gaze at Chris, her beautiful rosy lips slightly parted and waiting for a kiss. Chris leaned in, but when his mouth was an inch away from hers, instead of kissing her, he picked her up and ran full speed toward the inground pool and jumped in. She screamed and kicked her legs on the way, but the enjoyment in her laugh eased the ache in Russell's core. He couldn't deny that he loved to see her happy, even if it was Chris who made her feel that way. He wasn't jealous of Chris. He envied the guy. He would do anything to trade places with him.

The cannonball caused a huge splash that sent water droplets across the table. Everyone jumped, but Russell didn't flinch. He was too engrossed in the scene in front of him, pretending he was the man play fighting with Layla in the pool. While the others complained, he remained focused on Layla as she climbed out of the water and threw a beach ball at Chris. The wet bikini hugged her body as she reached up to squeeze the water out of her sandy blonde hair, displaying all of her assets. She was perfect. Absolutely perfect. Like a vision come to life.

Russell's physical arousal forced him to avert his attention to his plate, thankful to be shielded by the patio table. He began to wonder how long he'd been staring at Layla and if anyone had noticed. He glanced around the table. Dan was loading his plate with sausage while Suzanne now moved on to harassing him about his cholesterol. Ryan, always the host, refilled the ice bucket with fresh bottles of beer from a nearby cooler. Russell's eyes stopped on Donna. She glared at him with eyes narrowed into sharp slits and her lips pressed into a thin straight line. Even though she was seething with humiliation, he knew she would never dare make a scene in public. As if he didn't feel bad enough about watching Layla with Chris, guilt knocked him over the head.

Donna deserved someone who loved her, and that person wasn't him. He'd been thinking about it for months and finally accepted that he needed to do right by her.

***

After several hours of yelling and tears, Russell returned to Ryan's condo, bag in hand.

"What are you doing here?" Ryan asked as soon as he opened the door. "It's after midnight." His eyes dropped to the duffel at Russell's side and his shoulders fell. "Oh, shit. What happened?"

Russell slowly looked up at his friend. "I left Donna. Can I crash here tonight?"

"Of course." Ryan stepped aside. "Come inside."

Russell dropped his bag near the door and sat on the leather couch. He leaned forward, rested his elbows on his knees, and stared at the floor without saying anything.

Ryan automatically filled two glasses with Jack Daniels, placed one on a coaster in front of Russell, and sat next to him. "Tell me what happened, bro."

Russell was quiet for a long time while he reflected on the events of not just tonight, but on his life. "I'm so tired," he finally said, letting out a long sigh. "Tired of it all." He was emotionally drained, and it was reflected in his voice. "I'm tired of pretending. Tired of going through the motions. I don't know why I didn't leave Donna a long time ago. I feel like such a fucking prick. I know you guys don't really like her, but I'm the one at fault here. She didn't deserve this. She deserves better. Someone who loves her."

"You don't love Donna?" Ryan asked with soft surprise.

"I haven't been in love with her for a long time."

"I knew things weren't great between you two, but I thought it was just a rough patch. I never thought you didn't love her anymore. Why didn't you say anything? Talk to me or Dan? We're always here for you, Russ."

He wished he could have confessed his feelings. He wanted to tell Ryan right now how much he loved Layla—spill the tirade of emotions that were clawing at his insides to be set free—but he wouldn't let himself. He trusted his friend, but he couldn't take the chance of the news getting back to Layla. If and when—and he prayed there was a when—he revealed his true feelings, he needed to be the one to tell her.

Exasperated, he looked down at the floor and wanted to cry. Just cry and let out the years of pent-up frustration and never-ending pain in his heart because they were too much to bear. "I'm so fucking tired of not being able to say how I feel. Pretending I'm happy when I'm really miserable." He slowly met Ryan's eyes, clutched his chest and scrunched up his face from the internal pain that had a hold on him. "Did you ever want something so bad that your heart aches? Real physical pain for something that you know you can't have? Something you'll probably never have? And it just *devours* you." He took a long drink of his Jack Daniels and leaned back on the couch, trying to read the invisible writing on the ceiling. "I married the wrong person. I don't know what to do. I don't know what the fuck to do."

Ryan refilled their glasses, stealing questioning glances at Russell, then took a sip of the bourbon. He contemplated something for a bit, squinting one eye and cocking his head to the side. "What's going on, Russ? Are you cheating on Donna?"

Russell grunted, about to say, I wish, but caught himself. "No. I never cheated on Donna. You know I'm not like that."

"I know, but . . ." Ryan shook his head. "There's more going on here, bro. What aren't you telling me? More importantly, *why* aren't you telling me? We don't keep secrets."

Russell slowly turned his head and stared at Ryan for a long time without saying anything because it was true. They didn't keep secrets from one another.

Ryan broke their gaze and took a long swig of his drink. "I guess some things are private, but they shouldn't be. Not between me and you and Dan. We should be able to tell each other anything."

"I know." Russell squeezed his friend's knee. He was lucky to have best friends that were like brothers to him. Few people could say that. But he couldn't confess. Not this. It was too big. Too important. Too detrimental. The night took a toll on his mind and body, and he had zero energy left. "I got so much shit on my mind right now. I feel like my head is going to explode. Is it OK if I just crash on the couch?"

Ryan gave Russell a warm and reassuring smile. "I got three bedrooms. You can have your pick. You don't have to take the couch. And don't worry about anything. Whatever you need. I'm here for you. You can stay as long as you want."

Chapter TWO

Russell

About a week after he left Donna, Russell called her to apologize, and they had a long conversation that didn't turn into an argument or involve yelling, pointing fingers, or laying of blame. She admitted that she was just as guilty for not moving on, neither having an explanation as to why they stayed married so long after it was obviously over. The call provided much-needed closure, and the heaviness that always weighed Russell down began to disappear. He never realized how oppressed and trapped he felt stuck in a marriage with a woman he didn't love. He also never knew how laden with guilt he'd been at stringing Donna along.

Now that his marriage was over, he felt free and ready to move forward with his life. It still gutted him whenever he saw Layla with Chris, but without Donna around, the shame and self-reproach were gone.

Things were finally starting to look up, and the two-bedroom unit that became available in Ryan's condominium complex proved his life was going in the right direction. Living with his friend had been a blast, but Russell was ready to move into his own place. He thought the cherry on top was that he was only two floors away from his friend, but it was that Layla was helping him move in. It didn't matter that all his friends were also helping. Layla was here without Chris, and these were the moments that made his heart soar.

While Ryan and Dan returned to the truck to get the last of the boxes, Layla, Suzanne, and Russell headed to the kitchen to put things away. He lifted a box from the floor and put it on top of the kitchen island. "Thanks, girls. I really appreciate your help."

"Are you kidding?" Layla replied, tilting her head to the side and causing her silky hair to spill over her shoulder. "You don't have to thank us, Russ." She rubbed his upper arm with affection. "We'd do anything for you."

His heart ballooned, and a tingle spread across his chest. Her touch, although friendly and amicable, set his body on fire, and he couldn't suppress the larger-than-life grin on his face.

She looked around the generously sized kitchen. "I love this apartment."

"I told Ryan I didn't need anything this fancy," he said with gratitude for his friend. "He found me this great apartment, he found a buyer for my house, and he won't take a commission from me. Plus, he let me stay with him these last few weeks."

"Ryan's a wonderful friend," Suzanne said. She opened the refrigerator and pointed to an aluminum tray. "I made lasagna, so you have something to eat until you go shopping. Put it in the oven at 350 degrees for about an hour."

"Thanks, Suzanne." He didn't want her to go to any trouble, but that was Suzanne—always taking care of everyone. "You didn't have to. I'm happy with just grabbing a burger or a taco."

"Oh, no," she replied. "I'm not letting you turn into one of those bachelors that eat nothing but fast food. You're going to learn how to take care of yourself if I have to teach you how to cook myself."

"And you need a set of dishes," Layla said, rifling through the box on the island. "Is this all you have?" She held up two plates and a handful of cutlery.

"It's just me. That's all I need."

Layla smiled and rolled her eyes. "Do you have pots and pans, at least?"

He shook his head, smiling warmly, enjoying the concern she showed for him.

"What about a coffeemaker? You need coffee."

He shrugged. "There's a coffee shop in the strip mall ten minutes away."

Her brows skyrocketed. "Ten minutes away? You can't wake up and drive to get coffee. You need a coffeemaker."

"He needs a lot more than a coffeemaker," Suzanne added, holding open the doors to his empty kitchen cabinets. "There's nothing else to put away."

Layla let out a short laugh. "Where's your kitchen stuff?"

"That's all I have. I don't know how to cook," he replied. "So, I didn't take anything."

"You're hilarious." Layla nudged him with her shoulder. "A stereotypical bachelor already. I think we need to take you shopping."

"That's for sure," Suzanne added.

He loved the idea because it meant one-on-one time with Layla, even if Suzanne would be joining them, and as hard as he tried, he couldn't tone down the silly grin on his face today.

"You're enjoying this. Aren't you?" Layla teased.

"Enjoying what?"

"All this attention. That's what."

"So, what if I am?" he replied, gingerly. "Seriously, girls, you're being too good to me. You don't have to do all this."

"We want to make sure you're OK," Layla said.

She touched his arm, and his eyes rested on her hand. He lifted his gaze to her face and saw concern there. *She cares about me*, he thought. *Maybe not in the same way I care about her, but she cares.* He nodded. "Thanks. I'm OK."

"I know things may seem unfair sometimes," she said, her voice and facial expression filled with empathy. "But I really think that everything happens for a reason. We just have to trust that, somehow, life is going to lead us down the right path."

Life *was* unfair. At least his life was. All he wanted was to be with Layla. It was his dream. But so much always stood in the way. He never had the courage to tell her how he felt, because he knew she only thought of him as a friend, and her friendship meant too much to him to risk losing it. But as she stood there, with her hand still on his arm and her face full of worry and concern for him, he had a shred of hope that maybe, one day, destiny would bring them together. "Thanks, Layla. It means a lot to me that you care."

Layla looked confused by his statement. She put her arm around his shoulder and gave him a small squeeze. "Of course, I care, Russell. You're one of my best friends."

Layla

"I feel so bad for him." Layla leaned her elbows on the shopping cart and watched Russell stare absently at a selection of comforters.

"Me too," Suzanne agreed. "But he'll be fine."

The three of them had arrived at South Coast Plaza earlier this morning and spent the last two hours at Macy's getting Russell everything he needed for his new apartment. He followed Layla and Suzanne, not giving much input on the things they picked out for him.

Layla wished she could do something to lift his spirits. The poor guy looked lost as he stood there and scanned the wall of bedding, as if his mind was a million miles away. She couldn't stand the forlorn look on his face. Russell was a good guy who deserved to be happy, and it was killing her to see him hurting. She went to him and placed a comforting hand on his shoulder. "Need some help?" she asked, trying to sound upbeat.

"I don't know what size bed I have," he confessed.

"It's a queen."

"How do you know that?"

"Because I saw it when it was delivered."

He gave her a quizzical look. "You could tell it was a queen just by looking at it?"

"Yes." She pulled a solid navy bed-in-a-bag set from the shelf. "This is a neutral color. What do you think? Masculine enough?"

He nodded once. "I like blue."

She tossed it in the cart, which was practically full. Suzanne hung back to pick up an extra set of sheets, while Layla led Russell to the towel section. "Do you have a preference?" she asked.

"Just regular bath towels. I don't need those giant ones Ryan has for the pool."

"I meant color," Layla explained. "What color do you want to introduce into your bathroom? It's all white which leaves it open to any color combo."

He thought about it for a few seconds. "What's your favorite color?"

"Red. But I don't think you want a red and white bathroom."

"Bad luck?"

"Not really, but it might give off a Bates Motel vibe."

He chuckled and then paused to smile at her. "You're so much fun to be around, Layla. Normally, I'd hate this—shopping and buying things I really don't care about. But you made this a nice day out."

He was so handsome when he smiled. It lit up his honey-colored eyes and highlighted the strength in his angular jaw. The sadness on his face and the torment in his eyes these last few weeks made her chest hurt for her friend. She'd do anything to see that beautiful smile on his face all the time.

There was always something a little melancholy about him, and she'd often wondered why. She'd known he and Donna weren't getting along the last couple of years, and Donna was never the loving wife—at least not from what Layla and the others had witnessed. She wanted him to be happy. He was always the first one to offer a hand and go the extra mile to help someone.

The divorce meant he was free to find his one true love, and she delighted in the idea. But during this transition from married man to single guy, the loneliness he felt was palpable. He was clearly struggling with adapting to his new life and being on his own, as would anyone going through a divorce.

So, the smile on his face right now hugged her heart. She pulled a few red towels off the shelf, feeling goofy. "Let's get an assortment. You can put the red towels out if you're trying to scare off a date."

"He quirked an eyebrow at her. "What if she thinks it's romantic?"

An idea popped into her head, happy that he was playing along. She snapped her fingers. "I'm going to order you one of those white bathmats that turns red when it gets wet. You can splash water on it, so it looks like blood splatter before she uses the bathroom."

He laughed, deep and hearty, swaying back and forth a little.

She had so much affection for this man. She laughed with him, enjoying the reprieve from the heaviness and worry that weighed him down lately.

"You two look like you're having fun," Suzanne said, holding an armful of bathroom accessories. She had a shower caddy, soap dispenser, toilet bowl brush set, and a wastepaper basket. "Is black OK?" she asked Russ. "Black and white is timeless. Plus, it'll go with any color towels." She glanced at the bright red linens in the cart. "You might want to get a different color. Red towels like that need to be washed separately. They'll bleed like crazy."

Russell and Layla both burst out laughing.

Suzanne eyed them suspiciously as she added the items to the cart. "I'll be right back. I forgot to get the extra set of sheets."

Now that they were alone again, Russell quietly stared at Layla, a tiny smile still curling the ends of his lips. "The real reason I hated the idea of doing this—going shopping to fill my apartment with things I'll probably never use," he motioned to the food processor in the cart, "is because it reminds me that I'll be alone. That I don't have someone to do the everyday things with like everyone else does. I know it's stupid because I'd rather be alone than stuck in a miserable marriage. I guess, buying all this stuff reinforced the fact that I don't have anyone. It's sounds like my life is going to be very lonely."

Layla's spirits wilted a little more with each word, and her heart landed on the floor with the last sentence. How could he think he was alone? She'd never let that happen. None of them would. "You're not alone, Russ. If you ever need anything, I'm here." A warm feeling enveloped her because she saw the way her words touched him. She reached out and hugged him tightly, and he returned the hug as if he'd never been hugged in his life, and it made a lump of emotion clog her throat for this kindhearted man.

Chapter THREE

Layla

Barely able to catch her breath and heaving so hard her chest hurt, Layla stumbled from the car, ran to Suzanne's house, and fell into the front door. She openly sobbed as she pressed the bell nonstop.

The lantern on the front porch flashed with light a few seconds before the door swung open.

"Layla, what's wrong?" Suzanne, filled with panic, pulled Layla into the house, shut the door, and called for Dan.

A garbled, incoherent array of syllables left Layla's mouth and ended on a sob.

"Calm down," Suzanne said. "I can't understand you. Take a deep breath." She placed a motherly arm over Layla's shoulder and brought her into the kitchen. "Sit down. I'll get you some water."

Dan came into the kitchen, his eyes widening with concern when he saw her. "Are you all right?"

Layla shook her head and tried to get control of her emotions. She had no idea how she drove the thirty minutes from her apartment to Suzanne and Dan's. The entire night was a blur. A nightmare she couldn't wake from.

"Drink this, sweetie. You'll feel better." Suzanne tried to hand her a bottle of water, but Dan scoffed.

"She needs something stronger than that. Get the Jack Daniels."

The alcohol was exactly what Layla needed. She'd never been a big drinker, but she downed half of it in two long gulps, and the burn sobered her. "Chris cheated on me," she managed to blurt out before another sob cut off her voice.

"What?" Dan and Suzanne said at the same time, shock prevalent in their voices.

Layla grabbed the neck of the bottle and refilled her glass. Another swig of alcohol gave her the jolt she needed to continue. "He fucking cheated on me!" Anger and gut-wrenching pain alternated control over her emotions, and, right now, she was seething. "I was in San Francisco for five days for work, and Chris got piss drunk with his buddies and slept with some bar slut." Although the tears didn't fall, her lips and chin trembled from the excruciating ache in her heart. Her world was shattered, and it felt as if a bull had just kicked her in the chest.

Suzanne shook her head as if she couldn't possibly have heard correctly. "Chris? That's not like him."

It reminded Layla how much his out-of-character behavior knocked her over the head and ripped her insides out, and a sob left her lungs. "I know. That's why it hurts so much. I never thought he could do that to me. To us. He threw everything away like it didn't mean anything. For some stranger. Because he was drunk."

Suzanne's eyes filled with tears, and she knelt next to Layla's chair to rub her knee. "I'm so sorry, honey. I can't believe it."

"That fucking son of a bitch," Dan snapped, his fist raised in the air. "I'm gonna go put my foot in his ass. Right now."

"Danny . . ." Suzanne warned, jumping to her feet and catching him by the arm before he could leave. "Don't go anywhere. Do you think that's what Layla wants?"

"Yeah. I think that's exactly what she wants. He deserves a clock in the head for being so stupid. Right, Layla?"

Obviously, she didn't want Dan to get physical with Chris, but knowing that he wanted to defend her put a drop of warmth back in her ice-cold body. "Yeah. He deserves a lot more than a clock in the head," she agreed, her face deathly serious. "But I don't want you to go over there, Dan. I left him. And I think his heart is almost as broken as mine. So, that's good enough."

Suzanne stood and hugged Layla over the back of the chair. "I can't imagine what you're going through. You can stay here until you figure out what you're going to do."

Layla nodded. She had no plan. After she came home from the airport and Chris confessed his infidelity, she'd screamed and cried, told him she never wanted to see him again, and ran out of their apartment. She didn't even pack a bag. She only took her handbag and landed on her best friend's doorstep, a broken mess.

***

Gut-searing pain obliterated Layla the moment her body regained consciousness. Having cried for most of the night, she didn't remember falling asleep, but exhaustion must have quieted her spinning mind. She couldn't stop envisioning Chris with another woman. She'd tortured herself by asking him a million questions and demanding specific details, but he wouldn't give her any. If he had, she wouldn't be creating endless scenarios, each more horrific to endure than the last.

The tears came once again as her mind entertained yet another faceless woman seducing Chris in the bar. She curled into a fetal position and hugged her knees to her chest in an attempt to shrink into a tiny ball and hopefully disappear. Her insides were torn to pieces with the uncertainty of the future, and she wondered how long it would be before her heart healed. She wished she could teleport into the future to a time when her body wasn't pulverized with betrayal. Her only other choice was to stay in bed and cry.

By some miracle, after several hours of intermittent sobbing, an inner voice gave her the strength to shower and dress. Her reflection startled her. Swollen eyes with dark circles stared back at her in the mirror, and grief distorted her features into someone unrecognizable. There was no pretending she was OK, because she was an absolute fucking wreck.

She thought about going back to bed, but despite the cement brick in her stomach, she was hungry, and she needed coffee. And a bottle of aspirin.

As she descended the stairs, the morning sun filtering through the living room windows surprised her. She'd shut off her phone and hadn't touched it since last night, so she had no idea of the time. She thought she'd slept the day away and wished she had. It would mean less hours to be awake and deal with the pain.

Noise brought her into the kitchen where she found Suzanne loading the dishwasher.

"How are you doing today, sweetie?" Suzanne asked.

Awful. Devastated. Inconsolable. She shrugged without making eye contact.

"Do you want breakfast? There's leftover bacon on the table. I can make you some eggs if you want."

She bit into a slice of bacon and her stomach revolted. "I'll just have coffee."

The sound of the front door opening, followed by footsteps and voices, caused Layla to strain her ear in the direction of the living room. Panic and humiliation made her face flush red hot. "What's Ryan doing here?"

Suzanne turned toward Layla, empathy covering her expression. "Russell's here too. The guys play basketball on Saturdays. And I have a shift at the hospital today. Are you going to be OK here by yourself?"

Nervous about facing Russell and Ryan, the palms of Layla's hands began to sweat. "Do they know?"

"I didn't say anything. I don't think Danny did either." Suzanne studied Layla for a moment. "Do you want me to get rid of them?"

"No." Layla sighed. "I guess I have to get use to telling people." She just didn't expect it to be so soon. Not even 24 hours had passed, and she was spilling her sorrows to all of her closest friends. She made herself a cup of coffee and took it into the living room, ready to get this nightmare over with.

"What are you doing here so early?" Russell asked, surprised to see her. He was at her side in an instant once he saw the expression on her face, worry making his eyes widen. "What's wrong?"

"I broke up with Chris," she answered in a low voice, gaze on her coffee cup. "I'm staying here while he gets his things out of the apartment."

Russell's jaw dropped open—a look Layla was getting used to. "What happened?" he asked.

She furrowed her brow and closed her eyes for several seconds, mentally preparing herself to say the words out loud. "He cheated on me."

Ryan moved closer, so he stood on the opposite side of her. "I'm so sorry, Layla."

"I can't believe it," Russell said. "Are you alright?"

She hated the endless questions about her wellbeing. Wasn't it obvious? Why did she have to verbalize that her world was turned upside down and her heart had been shattered? "No. I'm not. I'm devastated." Layla's eyes filled with tears, and her voice quivered. "I can't believe it either. But I guess that's what happens when you get piss drunk and don't know what the fuck you're doing."

"That's no excuse," Russell said.

"I know." She fingered her coffee cup as tears silently rolled down her cheeks.

Russell attempted to console her by taking the cup from her, placing it on the table, and giving her a warm hug. She was thankful for his compassion and clenched onto him.

"I was gone five days. Five fucking days." She pressed her lips together, holding in a sob.

Russell held her tighter. "It'll be OK. You just need time."

She appreciated his concern and his gentle words of assurance, which brought a small amount of solace to her battered heart and emotionally beaten body. Her head found its way onto his shoulder, and she rested it there, finding comfort in his embrace.

The swinging door to the kitchen opened with a whoosh, and Suzanne strolled into the living room with her handbag dangling off her elbow. "I'm off." She turned to Layla. "I'll be home late, but

Danny'll be here if you need anything." Her shoulders drooped, and she frowned. "Are you going to be OK here alone for a few hours while the guys play ball?"

Layla's stance weakened, and her knees almost buckled at the idea of being alone with her overactive black thoughts. Russell noticed and held her in a side hug.

"I'll be fine," she lied, her feeble voice giving way to the truth.

"No," Russell stated. "You shouldn't be alone." He jutted his chin toward Dan and Ryan. You guys go. I'll skip the game and stay here with Layla."

She looked up at him, surprise making her stand taller. "Russ. You don't have to do that. I'll be OK. Really."

He shook his head. "Not happening. Suzanne's going to work. They're going to the court, and I'm staying here to keep you company. We can binge watch something, or play cards, or go someplace if you want. But you're not going to be by yourself right now. I won't hear of it."

Her eyes immediately filled with tears, but happy ones this time, and she managed a tiny smile. "Thank you."

"OK," Suzanne said, on an exhale. "I feel better about going to work now. Thanks, Russ. Layla," Suzanne placed her hands on Layla's shoulders and looked her directly in the eyes. "You're strong, and you're smart. You're going to get through this." She hugged Layla, kissed Dan, and waved over her shoulder as she left for work.

Layla's lips quivered with love for her best friend. She didn't know what she'd do without Suzanne or any of the people in this room right now, who were like family. A tear slipped from the corner of her eye, and she wiped it away.

"Hey," Russell said, softly. "It's OK."

Nothing was OK. "I'm just overwhelmed by everything."

"You sure, hon?" Dan asked. "Do you want us to stay too?"

"No." She waved for him and Ryan to go. "I got Russell. I'm good."

"OK," Ryan answered, reluctantly. "Call if you need anything or if you want us to come back here."

Layla nodded and glanced at Russell, whose arm had returned to her shoulder. "Thanks, but I'm in good hands."

After Dan and Ryan left, she turned to Russell and wrapped her arms around his waist. "Thank you for being such a good friend. I don't know what I'd do without you guys."

He squeezed her tightly and buried his nose in her shoulder. She felt him breathing heavily, as if he were the one who needed comforting. She tried to pull back to look at him, but he didn't loosen his embrace. After a moment, she gently called his name. "Russ?" This time, he let her step back, but his arms never left her.

There were tears in his eyes, his mouth was pressed together in a tight line, and his face was pink. Then she realized that he'd been through the same thing not that long ago, and her break up with Chris must have brought back all the pain of his divorce, and she felt horrible. "I'm sorry. I know you just went through this with Donna, and it's still fresh. Don't be upset."

He shook his head. "It's not the same. At all. I wasn't in love with Donna anymore. You loved Chris, and he hurt you. In the worst possible way. It guts me to know that he did that to you. My heart is broken. For you."

His reaction, and the compassion pouring out of him, brought a tsunami of tears to her eyes, and they fell down her cheeks in droves.

"I'm so sorry." He hugged her to his chest and kissed the top of her head while she clutched onto the back of his shirt with all the strength in her fists. "I didn't mean to make you cry," he said, his voice cracking as he clearly tried to hold back his own tears. "I care about you Layla. I . . . I . . ."

He didn't finish his sentence. Instead, he hugged her tighter.

Her face was smashed against his shoulder as she sobbed softly for everything they had both lost: family; love; security; the future. They were kindred spirits grieving for the same things right now, and she never felt closer to him. She wished Chris were half the man Russell was. This man was loyal. Trustworthy. Loved with all his heart and had more compassion than anyone she'd ever met.

"Don't cry." He kissed her hair again. "You don't deserve this." He kissed her cheek, by her ear. "I wish I could make all the pain go away." Another kiss—this time on the side of her face. "I want to make you feel better. Forget all the hurt."

The flow of tears suddenly dried up, and she contemplated the man in her arms. New and unfamiliar feelings for Russell washed over her like a candle coming a flame. She pulled back to read his eyes and saw the same desire in them. They stared at one another in a way they had never looked at each other before. An inferno of heat and yearning ran through her like a flash fire, and she wanted this man who had been one of her best friends for years. She craved him. Needed him like she needed oxygen.

Their mouths smashed together with frantic want. He took control of the kiss, moving in purposeful circles. His hands snaked through her hair then fell to her lower back and held her against his body with possession, as if he were claiming her or as if she'd always been his. The strong embrace, the heat of his body, and the sweet taste of his lips made her yearn for more. Every part of her burned with hunger as she clawed at his shirt. He pulled it over his head and her eyes immediately dropped to his sculpted torso. She'd admired it from a distance in the past, but it never sent a surge of adrenaline through her the way it did at this moment.

She reached for him, ready to run her hands over every part of him and needing to know what his body felt like, but he surprised her by taking hold of the hem of her shirt, stripping it off, and throwing it to the floor in one swift motion. Her bra followed in the blink of an eye. His gaze immediately went to her breasts, and a lustful hunger covered his face as he stared at her with so much silent passion that it took her breath away. Feeling brazen and confident by the way he devoured her with his eyes filled her with wanton confidence and she teased him by slowly running her fingers across her collarbone.

A husky breath escaped him as he cupped her breasts and pushed them together. His touch made her tingle, and when his lips landed on her flesh, she shuddered. While his tongue fucked her cleavage with short, quick strides, his thumbs circled her nipples until they were hard as granite. Sensations shot through her like an electrical current, causing her breathing to come in heavy gasps, inflating and deflating her chest. She couldn't do more than roll her head back and pant while she clutched onto his shoulders. "Russ," she sighed. "Oh my God, Russ."

He took one nipple into his mouth and sucked on it while his tongue lapped at the hard nub. A heady fog made her blink several times, as her vision became obscured by cloudy white light. She clutched his hair and cried out as tingles traveled over her torso and landed at the sweet spot between her legs. Aching for contact, she tilted her pelvis toward him and whimpered when she couldn't reach him. She wanted to call his name again—tell him she needed him inside her—but she could barely catch her breath. It was as if a lifetime of suppressed passion had finally been released, like a pressure cooker blowing its top.

His lips moved to her mouth, and he kissed her, hard and unrelenting, as if he were suffocating and it contained the substance he needed to survive. With enough freedom to maneuver, her pelvis finally made contact with his rock-hard erection, and she groaned loudly. Begging for release, she jumped into his arms, wrapped her legs around his waist, and gyrated against him. Overcome by the multitude of stimuli coursing through every part of her body, she grunted loudly. Continually.

His breathing and ferocity overshadowed her moans, and she wondered where the hell it came from. Or maybe she was just witnessing Russell's normal tempo and libido at work.

Holding her by her buttocks and kissing her feverishly, he lowered their bodies to the floor. He broke the kiss to pull her jeans and panties down to her knees, tugged off her shoes, and pulled her clothing free. A second later, he stood over her, totally naked and covering his impressive length with a condom.

With her legs spread invitingly, she raised herself onto the palms of her hands and sucked in a breath as she admired his naked lower half. He suddenly dropped to his knees and flattened her to the floor with a kiss. His cock pressed into her inner thigh, and she wiggled so it touched her in the right spot, whimpering for more.

He pushed inside her, hot and deep, grunting as he did so. There was no pause in his momentum, no time to adjust to his size, which was both surprising and all-consuming, filling her completely. He pumped his hips wildly, causing thunderbolts of pleasure to reverberate throughout her body. She jerked and moaned, locking her ankles behind his back and hanging onto his shoulders. The hard floor beneath her, the deep, penetrating thrusts, and the heavy breaths leaving her lungs, filled her with an erotic charge. She let go of all thoughts, her mind a total blank, freeing herself to think about nothing except the exquisite sensations ricocheting inside her, and she just reveled in this moment.

Through the jerking motions of her body, she saw raw sexual energy mirrored back at her in Russell's eyes. He focused long enough to make eye contact with her and sighed her name in a sexy whisper. "Layla." Then his momentum picked up speed, pushing in and out of her body, hitting every nerve ending and delivering pulsating intense waves that rocked her to her core. She thrashed underneath him and let out a series of gasps. It was carnal. Rough. And un-fucking-believable.

Something went off inside her like a nuclear explosion, and she came with a loud animalistic cry. She held onto him and let the euphoria claim her, while he peaked and shot inside her with several pounding thrusts. He shuddered, and a huge smile spread across his lips as he breathed heavily. Dazed and exhausted, she smiled up at him, letting her arms and legs fall to the floor.

Adoration shone from his eyes as he leaned down and kissed her languidly. Then he rolled to the side and lay spread out on the floor next to her.

They stayed like that for several seconds, still trying to catch their breath, smiling up at the ceiling, until the flurry of passion slowly evaporated, and she was shocked back to reality. Grabbing her clothing, she quickly got to her feet. "I'm going to use the bathroom," she said over her shoulder, without lifting her gaze. She darted into the downstairs bathroom and leaned against the closed door, her heart still beating like crazy. What the fuck just happened? It was absurd! Russell was one of her best friends. A surprised laugh fell from her mouth, and she tried to hide it behind her hand. "Oh my God. What the fuck is wrong with me?" she whispered, moving her hand to cover her face. She wasn't sure if the heat on her cheeks was from the sexual encounter—which was hot as fuck, thank you very much—or the embarrassment from what they'd done. In Suzanne and Dan's living room. Where Dan and Ryan could have walked in and caught them at any moment.

She pulled on her clothes, washed her face, and studied her reflection in the mirror. She still looked awful, but she no longer looked grief stricken, and her heart hurt a little less. A lot less, actually. For the moment. And that's what she needed to focus on right now.

She realized she'd been in the bathroom for a long time, and she needed to go back in the living room and face Russell, but she had no idea what the hell she was going to say to him. "You fucking idiot," she told her reflection.

The bathroom door creaked as she slowly opened it. Walking lightly, almost tiptoeing into the living room, she found herself pressing her lips firmly together in order to hide a smile.

Russell was sitting on the couch, fully dressed, with his back to her. As soon as he heard her, he spun around. When they made eye contact, her smile burst through, followed by a small, embarrassed laugh.

He smiled back and chuckled softly. Sexily.

She circled the couch and fell into the spot next to him.

"Are we good?" he asked, casually, but there was so much more behind his eyes.

She felt way better than she did thirty minutes ago. That's for sure. She nodded, and they were quiet for a moment. "Russ . . . I'm sorry. I don't know what got into me." She covered her face with her hands to hide her flushed cheeks and groaned. "I don't want things to be weird between us now."

He put his arm over her shoulder and leaned closer to her.

"I'm sorry, Layla. I feel like I took advantage of you. You're in a vulnerable state right now, and I—"

"You did no such thing," she cut him off. "I was a willing participant. *Very* willing. We just . . . I don't know. I have no idea what that was about," she admitted, honestly, and realized that it wasn't awkward. They were talking about it just like they talked about everything else. "Let's just forget this ever happened. And please don't tell Dan or Ryan. I don't want Suzanne to know we just . . ." She flung her hand at the spot where they just had hot-as-fuck sex, preferring not to say the words out loud. "On her living room floor."

Russell's face went blank. "Neither do I. I won't say anything."

"Thank you." She sighed and leaned back on the couch, with Russell's arm still around her, and rested her head on his shoulder. They were both quiet for a long time, and her thoughts went back to the rollercoaster of the last 24 hours.

"You're quiet," Russell said. "Are you sure you're OK?"

"No. But I will be. I guess I'm starting to accept that my life is going to be different now without Chris." She sighed. "It doesn't hurt as much." Her heart lurched, just to remind her that it was still pulverized.

Russell cupped her shoulder a little tighter. "It'll get better. I promise. Remember when you told me about this big master plan and how everything happens for a reason?"

She nodded.

"Well, I think you were right. It may not be clear right now, but one day, hopefully, you'll look back on what happened and understand that it was for the better. He wasn't the one. You deserve so much better than him. Someone's out there for you, Layla. And he's going to worship you. Treat you like the queen that you are."

Emotion clogged her throat and made her mouth twitch. This man knew exactly what to say to make her feel better. "I hope so. And I hope I find him soon."

He gave her a small squeeze. "Me too. Me too."

They stayed on the couch, sitting closely and leaning into one another, and watched TV without saying much. It wasn't an awkward silence, because they were comfortable just being in each other's company without the need to make conversation. Layla was thankful for the quiet time because a tornado of thoughts and emotions swirled inside her head as she pretended to pay attention to the movie on the flatscreen, but her mind was all over the place. She kept going back and forth to the scene last night with Chris that drastically changed the course of her life, and that she just had sex—very hot sex—with Russell. She probably should regret the latter, but she didn't because it gave her something else to focus on. And reminisce over.

A key jiggled in the lock to the front door indicating that Dan and Ryan were back. Automatically, Layla and Russell moved a few inches apart to create space between them. As the guys entered the entry foyer, the sound of a basketball bouncing on the hardwood echoed into the living room. Layla and Russell exchanged a glance and smiled, clearly having the same thought.

"How many times does Suzanne have to tell you not to bring the ball in the house?" Layla called toward Dan.

The ball immediately stopped bouncing, and a few seconds later, Dan and Ryan appeared in the living room. They both stopped and looked at her. Guilt immediately washed over Layla, and she fidgeted in her seat. Her gaze darted around the floor, over the couch and end tables for any telltale signs that something happened in the room, other than two friends sitting together in front of the TV. She didn't see anything out of place and relaxed. Then a thought hit her like a slap in the face. The condom. What the hell did Russell do with the condom? She imagined it sitting in the kitchen trash and either Dan or Suzanne finding it. Her heart raced out of control while panic ran rampant, but she quickly realized that Russell was smarter than that. Either he wrapped it tightly in paper towels and hid it in the bottom of the pail, or he stuffed it in his pocket. She tried not to laugh as she imagined a used condom in Russ' jeans pocket right now.

"You look a little better," Dan told Layla, the basketball now tucked under his arm.

"We brought you soup." Ryan placed a small brown paper bag on the coffee table and gave her a lopsided smile.

She gave her dear friend adoring eyes. "Ryan, you are absolutely the sweetest guy I've ever met." She placed the bag in her lap, opened it, and the soothing aroma of chicken soup hit her nostrils. The instant cure-all didn't take away her woe, but it shrouded her in a layer of comfort like a warm blanket, and she realized that she hadn't fought back tears for a few hours.

With the guys back home, the conversation turned to basketball and sports, and Layla retreated to the guest bedroom.

***

It took a week for Chris to move his things out of the apartment. When he called to let Layla know, they had a civil conversation. Although, she did cry into her pillow for almost 15 minutes after they spoke.

She asked Suzanne to swing by the apartment to make sure all signs of Chris were gone and arrange for the bed to get hauled out to the trash. Layla couldn't look at it, no less sleep in it, ever again. She ordered a new one with floral bedding, and Suzanne took care of accepting the delivery and setting it up. The woman was a Godsend.

Her stay with Suzanne and Dan was much longer than expected, but she was finally ready to return home and resume her life.

She opened the door to the apartment with apprehension and felt the void as soon as she entered. She swept through the living and dining rooms and the kitchen, even checking the refrigerator, which she quickly regretted. All signs of Chris were gone, as if he never existed. Good. She wanted him erased from her life. She went into the bedroom feeling a little unsure, but the sight of the beautiful new bed immediately lifted her spirits. It was feminine and pretty, and it didn't contain any memories.

The bathroom also proved to be a safe zone, so she decided to shower, then fluffed up and positioned the pillows on the bed and climbed into the center. There were no left or right sides. The entire bed belonged to her. Content, she clicked on the TV and watched re-runs of Friends for a couple of hours.

Her phone dinged, and she reached for it, expecting it to be Suzanne. But it was Russell. "Hey, Russ."

"Hi, Layla. I was just thinking about you and wanted to check in. See if you needed anything or just wanted to talk for a while."

He'd been so sweet, and she was grateful for his friendship. "Thanks. I'm OK. I'd be better if Suzanne had cleaned out my refrigerator, though. There was milk in there that expired two weeks ago."

He chuckled. "I can't believe she didn't."

"I know. Right?"

"I'm gonna miss seeing you over there all the time."

She'd seen him almost every day at Dan and Suzanne's and wondered if he visited so much before she became their houseguest, or if he'd come by specifically to check on her. "You can always visit me here. That milk isn't going to walk itself out to the trash."

"You didn't throw it out?"

"I'm contemplating throwing out the whole refrigerator. There was also a container of yogurt that popped its lid, and blue cheese that I don't think started out that color."

"You eat too much dairy."

"After the whiff I got when I opened the refrigerator door earlier, I don't think I'll be eating any dairy for a long time."

He laughed softly. "I'm glad you're happy again. I like hearing the smile in your voice."

"Thanks, Russell. I appreciate the call. In case I don't say it often enough, you've been a really good friend to me."

"You've been a really good friend to me too."

They were quiet for a moment, and then he said. "Have a good night. I'll talk to you tomorrow."

"Tomorrow?"

"Yeah. I'll check in again. The first few days alone can be hard."

Ironically, he was the one she leaned on during the most difficult time in her life, not Suzanne. It was unexpected but welcome. "Thank you."

"Good night, Layla."
"Good night, Russ."

Chapter FOUR

Russell

Was it possible to teeter on the precipice of euphoria and despair? Like the slightest breath would either push you in one direction, where all your dreams would come true. Or it would push you in the opposite direction, where everything you hoped and prayed for would be erased. Extinguished. Gone for good. Because that's exactly how Russell felt.

On the one hand, sleeping with Layla fulfilled a fantasy that he'd been daydreaming about for years. It overshadowed anything he had ever imagined and filled him with so much joy he felt intoxicated. On the other hand, it may have friend-zoned him for life. How could she gloss over what happened so easily, as if it didn't mean anything? Hadn't it stirred anything inside of her? Woken up some kind of feelings for him?

The moans and panting, the gyrations, and the velocity of their lovemaking certainly proved there was a ton of passion between them. But was it just a rebound fuck? That's what he feared the most and the thought that constantly ate away at him. It feasted on his doubt like a carnivorous parasite, whittling away at the promise of a future together. It made him a nervous wreck and kept him awake at night.

But then there was the shining light that always brightened his darkest thoughts with a sliver of hope. The incident could have easily ended their friendship, but it didn't. It brought them closer. They talked on a more intimate level. They shared a secret, probably the only secret that existed between their close group of friends—other than the secret that he was in love with Layla.

While all this was going through his head, he watched Layla at the dining room table with Suzanne, working on a jigsaw puzzle. He leaned into the couch pillow, gazing at the woman he loved, picturing a different life. A fairytale world where every wish came true.

The cushion moved as Ryan sat down next to him, two beers in hand, and passed one to Russell.

"Thanks, bro." Russel took the beer, barely taking his eyes off Layla, but he saw Ryan follow his gaze across the room.

"You're so worried about her," Ryan said. "But I think she's good."

"I know. It's just . . ." He pressed his lips together and shook his head. "I'll never forget how upset she was when that asshole broke her heart. To see her cry like that just gutted me."

"I hear ya. But it's been a while now. I think she's moving on."

That beam of light in the back of Russell's mind brightened at the idea, and he felt as if his feet were planted a little more firmly on the right side of that precipice.

Ryan shifted on the couch so he could look directly at Russell. "Can you answer a question? Honestly?"

"Of course, bro. Anything."

"What is it with you and Layla?"

"Nothing," he answered, a little too defensively, nerves making his heart race.

"It's me, Russell. I know you. I see the way you look at her."

Russell heaved a heavy sigh, feeling like he expelled the weight of the world in one breath. Overwhelmed with emotion and so damn tired of the struggle inside him, he finally spoke the words aloud. "I love her, man." He put his hand to his chest. "With every piece of my heart and with my entire soul, I love her."

"Well then go tell her." Ryan extended his arm in Layla's direction. "What are you waiting for?"

The idea of putting his heart on the line scared the hell out of Russell, but he was smiling so wide his cheeks hurt. He suddenly wanted to tell Layla how he felt. The fear fled in an instant, replaced by assured confidence. He was finally ready.

Each moment that passed had Russell's blood surging in his chest with a mixture of impatience and anxiety. He couldn't take his eyes off Layla. When Dan came in from the yard and called everyone outside to sit around the firepit, Russell took Layla's elbow and walked with her to the circle of chairs. He grabbed the last blanket from the pile, handed it to her, and took the seat to her right.

"Thanks, Russ." She gave him an appreciative head tilt. "Where's yours? Aren't you cold?"

"Nah. I'm fine."

"Are you sure?" She looked at the depleted pile. "I can go inside and get another blanket."

Had she always been this sweet to him? Or was this new? And her smile seemed extra warm. He realized that he was just staring at her, smiling like a loon. "I'm good," he finally said.

"Who wants marshmallows?" Suzanne asked, handing out skewers and presenting a huge bag of the treats.

Russell took one and placed it on Layla's skewer, then took one for himself. They put their marshmallows in the fire and let them toast, the scent of char filling the night air.

"Suzanne," Dan called as he exited the house with a box of graham crackers and chocolate bars. "You forgot the best part. How are we supposed to make smores without these?"

Suzanne huffed at her husband. "Aren't the marshmallows sweet enough, Danny? How much sugar are you going to have?"

He held up the goodies in his hands. "This much."

Suzanne rolled her eyes and conceded. "Fine. Smores for everyone."

The temperature dropped after a while and the thin hoodie Russell wore did little to keep him warm from the cool night air, so he scooted his chair closer to the fire.

"You're cold," Layla said. "Move back so we can share." She held up the corner of the blanket, invitingly.

His eyes sparkled at her in disbelief. Was she flirting with him, or was it just his imagination?

She smiled and motioned to the blanket with her chin.

He moved his chair so it aligned with hers, took the end of the blanket and placed it over his lap.

"Aw," Suzanne cooed. "You two look cozy."

His eyes darted to Suzanne. Did she know how he felt about Layla? Or maybe Layla confided some newfound feelings she had for him to her best friend. It was crazy and surreal, but all the signs were there.

The subtle flirting between Russell and Layla continued over the next couple of hours as they all talked around the fire. Ryan was the first to leave, and, after a few more minutes, Layla stood up.

"I better go too," she said.

There was no way Russell was letting this night end. Filled with courage and confidence, he made his move. "Can we go someplace and talk?" he whispered to Layla.

"Sure. What's up?"

"I need to tell you something. Something I've wanted to tell you for a long time. And it can't wait."

She paused, clearly trying to figure out what he needed to say, and nodded. "Do you want to come back to my place? It's kind of late to go to a diner."

It was perfect.

They said their goodbyes without letting on that they had plans to meet up after they left, and, hopefully, Dan and Suzanne weren't suspicious that Russell followed Layla out the door. On the drive to her apartment, he rehearsed what he'd say to her. In every scenario, she fell into his arms and admitted that she loved him too. But what if she didn't? What if she said she loved him, but only as a friend? What if it ruined their relationship? Just because they got past sleeping together didn't mean they could get past an unreciprocated "I love you."

Sweat beaded on Russell's brow and he began to think this wasn't the best idea. But the little voice in his head pushed him on. What the fuck was he waiting for? If he wasn't going to tell her now, when the hell was he going to? She had to at least suspect that he had feelings for her. She had to.

There wasn't any more time to think about it because they were in front of Layla's apartment. He pulled into the spot across the street, and when he got out of the car, she was waiting for him on the curb.

"Hurry up. It's cold." She looped her arm through his and snuggled close as she pulled him to the front door and quickly let them inside. Once she locked the door behind them, she said, "I think the temperature dropped ten degrees since we left Dan and Suzanne's. Do you want coffee?"

"No." He just wanted to blurt out the truth. Or run out the door. His nerves were getting the better of him as the moment transcended. He started to pace, then stopped and looked at Layla. The second he locked eyes with her, all his nerves disappeared. This seemed so natural. So right. He didn't even have to think about what he was going to say. It all poured out of him.

"I've wanted to tell you this for so long," he began. "I thought it was going to be hard, but it's not." He hugged her and whispered softly into her ear. "I love you, Layla. I love you with all my heart and with every breath in my body." He pulled back a little and gazed deep into her eyes, his arms still encircling her. "I think about you night and day. Not a moment goes by that you're not in my thoughts." He took her hands and held them to his chest, and he felt his heart pounding. "I love you so much. You're like the air I breathe. You're the blood that runs through my veins. I've wanted to tell you so many times, but I needed to wait. Wait until the time was right. Until you were ready to move on. Until I thought I could actually have a chance."

She stared back at him with wide eyes and her mouth slightly ajar, clearly not expecting his admission. "How long have you felt this way?"

"I've loved you forever. You have no idea how hard it's been. I've wanted to take you in my arms and tell you how much I love you. Kiss you. Touch you. For so, so long." He caressed her cheek with the back of his hand. "I can make you happy, Layla. I know I can. Please, give me a chance."

She was quiet, and it worried him because he didn't know what was going through her head. "Don't tell me you don't have any feelings for me," he continued, before she could reject him. "I know you do. I've seen it in your eyes. I've felt it in your touch. I've heard it in your voice."

She looked down, then lifted her gaze to meet his. "I would be lying if I said I didn't feel anything for you, Russell. I do. I know there's been something going on between us since that day we were together, but I didn't know you felt this strongly. I don't want to hurt you. I could never live with myself if that happened." She ran her fingers through her hair and let out a deep breath. "This is all very overwhelming. I don't know what to say."

"Just think about it. That's all I ask. Please."

"I will. But this isn't something I'm going to take lightly. I'm going to have to seriously think about this. I don't want to jump into anything. I'm going to need time."

"Take as much time as you need. I'm always here for you, no matter what you decide. You know that."

He was apprehensive and unsure about her reaction, but it wasn't a rejection, and it left him hopeful. He felt higher than he'd ever felt in his life at openly expressing his love for her. He felt reincarnated and reveled in the freedom of letting his love pour from his heart. He held Layla in his arms for a long time and let his love envelop her, resting his cheek against hers. Before he left, he placed a delicate kiss on her lips.

He ended up at McBride's instead of going home because he needed a drink to calm his nerves. The initial exhilaration he felt began to wane, and now he was a basket case of mixed emotions. He was terrified that Layla would reject him. The ensuing awkwardness would compromise their relationship, and he would lose her as a friend. A knot tightened in his stomach and made him nauseous. One part of him almost wished he didn't say anything, but another part of him, a larger, stronger part, knew that he had no choice. It was the right thing to do. He needed to tell her how he felt because he couldn't spend the rest of his life wondering, what if? And if he ever had a chance with her, it was now.

For a moment, he let himself fantasize about the possibility of life with Layla, and he saw the world in a whole new light. A world filled with love and elation. A world where his one and only dream came true.

Chapter FIVE

Layla

She stared at the closed door after Russell left, utterly flabbergasted. She knew he had feelings for her, but she had no idea that he was in love with her, nor did she expect the devotion that poured from his heart. As overwhelming as it was, it thrilled her. She wanted to fall into his arms and let him love her, take care of her, and make her happy again, but she was unsure if she could trust her heart. She needed to listen to her head and not make a rash decision. Sure, she was attracted to him. Who wouldn't be? Underneath his strong, handsome features and rugged exterior he had a heart of gold, and he wasn't afraid to show his sensitive side. Which is exactly why she needed to proceed very cautiously. She would never forgive herself if she broke his heart.

Logic told her that her feelings for him were only infatuation. That she was just enamored with the romanticism of how he confessed his undying love. That she wasn't ready to make that kind of commitment so soon after her heart had been smashed. In the end, it wouldn't work out. She would break Russell's heart, and they couldn't recover. They'd end up growing apart, and it would ruin their entire circle of friendship. She didn't know if that was a risk she was willing to take.

***

It had been four days since Russell told Layla he loved her. Since her relationship with Chris ended, Russ hadn't gone more than one day without checking on her. Anxiety made her chest hurt whenever she thought about it, which was all the time. But that would all change tonight because they were having their usual Saturday night dinner at Dan and Suzanne's. She still didn't know if she was ready to see Russell, but she had no choice because she couldn't put it off any longer.

"I need a drink." She barged into the kitchen and went straight to the liquor cabinet.

Suzanne closed the oven door and turned toward Layla. "Why? What happened now?"

"Nothing yet." Layla splashed some Jack Daniels into a coffee cup and tossed it back. It tasted like lighter fluid, and she coughed and looked at the cup in her hand to scrutinize the remnants of the alcohol. "How the hell do the guys drink this stuff?"

Suzanne took the cup and placed it on the counter. "I hate to see you like this. Russell really fucked up your head."

She'd told Suzanne about the conversation with Russell the day after it happened, who wasn't exactly surprised. Apparently, Suzanne had "seen all the signs," while Layla had been oblivious. Dan and Ryan had walked into the room and overheard. Dan had been enlightened by his wife's suspicions a while ago, and Ryan admitted that he knew Russell was going to tell her he loved her. Word travels around fast in this group.

"It's not his fault my head's all fucked up," Layla said, feeling defensive. "He was honest. I'm the one having trouble handling it."

"Why are you having trouble handling it?"

"Because I don't know what to do."

"What's your heart telling you?"

Layla paused and let the tension and worrisome thoughts slip away so she could listen to her inner voice. She heard the words loud and clear. "I think Russell's sweet and romantic, and it was like a fairy tale the way he told me he loved me. I care about him, Suzanne. I really do. I'm just unsure."

"I gotta give the guy credit. It takes a lot of guts to put your heart on the line like that. Maybe you owe it to him, and to yourself, to see what happens."

"You really think so?" Hope sprung into Layla's voice.

"It's better than spending the rest of your life wondering what might have happened."

The doorbell rang, and Layla stiffened. It could have easily been Ryan, but, somehow, she knew it was Russell. The sound of his voice, as he greeted Dan from the other room, confirmed it.

"Wish me luck," she told Suzanne, then exited the kitchen.

Russell was right there in the dining room, staring at her, when she passed through the swinging door, and she stopped short. Words escaped her, and her feet refused to move.

He flashed a winning smile, filled with confidence and reassurance. "Hi, Layla."

Those two little words put her totally at ease, and she smiled back at him. "Hi." Her eyes drifted to Dan, who was standing a few feet away watching and listening to their conversation.

"A little privacy, please," she said to him.

"It's my house," he replied, annoyed.

She glared at him.

"Fine." Defeated, he threw his hands up and walked into the kitchen.

"I can't believe everyone knows." She felt her cheeks blush.

"They're our friends," Russell replied, undisturbed that their personal information didn't remain between the two of them.

"I know, but I'm the one who's going to look like the bad guy here, no matter what happens. If I say, 'thanks but I don't want to ruin our friendship', I'm a cold-hearted bitch. If I say, 'OK, let's give it a try' and it doesn't work out, I'm the bitch who broke your heart."

Russell's smile widened. "What if we end up living happily ever after?"

"I guess it would be a perfect world then. Wouldn't it?"

"That's one of the things I love about you, Layla. You always make everything right."

She stared at him for a long time, and her face grew serious. "I've been thinking a lot about the other night." She paused, trying to find the right words, but there wasn't any other way to say how she felt. "I don't want to jump into anything foolishly. I'm afraid I'm just infatuated with everything you said to me. Nothing's a bigger turn on than someone expressing how much they love you. I don't want to confuse that with genuine feelings."

His eyes brightened, even though she really didn't give him encouraging news. "Do you mean I have a chance?" he asked, hope making his pitch rise.

"I'm not saying anything yet," she cautioned. "Let's just take it slow and see what happens."

"Can I take you to dinner? Like a date?"

A laugh fell from her mouth. "That's what you call taking it slow?"

"Yeah. If I was moving fast, I'd wrap my arms around you, pull you against my body, and kiss the hell outta you. Right here in Dan and Suzanne's dining room."

She sucked in a breath, suddenly overheated at the reminder of what took place in their living room a few weeks ago. "I think I'd like to go on that date now."

"Right now?" he asked, surprised.

She laughed. "No. Not—" She reconsidered. "Yes. Right now."

They picked up their jackets and took off without bothering to tell Suzanne and Dan that they were leaving.

"What do you want to eat?" he asked when they were driving away.

"Where do you usually take girls on a first date?"

He glanced at her for a second, and then returned his eyes to the road. "I don't take girls anywhere. I haven't dated, Layla. You're the one who owns my heart. I wouldn't give it to anyone else. Not even for one night."

She stared at his profile while she processed what he just said and the intensity of his words. Her heart slowly melted at the sweet sentiment, and she covered his hand with hers as he rested it on the shifter.

His eyes shot to hers for a quick second, and his throat bobbed. After a moment, he asked, "Seafood OK?"

She nodded. "I'm happy with anything, Russ. I'm just glad we're spending this night together. Just the two of us."

His eyes glazed over, and he brought her hand to his lips to impart a soft kiss.

The gentle touch and the intimate show of affection made her sigh. She gazed out the window as they traveled down PCH, completely absorbed in the magical moment that had taken her by complete surprise. Her life had changed so much in such a short time. In a little over a month, her world had been turned upside down and her heart crushed to pieces, just to have it do a 360-degree flip where she was on top of the world, happier than ever and ready to let love in with huge hopes for a future filled with everything she ever wanted in a man.

The car pulled into the surface parking area in front of an upscale restaurant in Newport Beach overlooking the water, and she peered out the window. "Fancy," she said. "You really know how to impress a girl."

His eyes danced with light, and he flashed her a smile. "Nothing's too good for you, babe. This is just the beginning. I hope."

She sucked in a breath, enamored with these new feelings and the way his words affected her.

They entered the restaurant, and the hostess seated them at an intimate table for two in a corner with a direct view of the Pacific Ocean. The dimly lit restaurant, with candles on the table, screamed romance, and she felt like a teenager on her first date. Butterflies fluttered in her belly, a rush of blood pumped through her chest, and she felt giddy. A thousand thoughts were running through her head, and she had to fight an overwhelming urge to reach across the table and kiss this amazing man.

As he perused the menu, she looked at him with new eyes. She knew he was good looking, but had he always been this sexy? He wore a plain T-shirt that strained across the muscles in his chest. The short sleeves landed at the indent above his biceps, accentuating the curves in his arms. His light brown hair was beachy—messy but in a way that made him look carefree and athletic. A small amount of stubble showed off his strong jawline and perfect smile. His honey-colored eyes suddenly darted up to meet hers, and she sucked in a breath at their beauty.

"It's a special occasion," he said. "How about a bottle of champagne?"

"Champagne?" She glanced out the window at the serene ocean. "First this romantic restaurant and now champagne? You're going to spoil me."

"I intend to."

She locked eyes with him for a moment, taken back by the sincerity in his statement. She could feel herself blushing and picked up her menu to hide behind it. "What are you having? Everything looks amazing." In reality, she hadn't read a single item.

Russell scanned the menu. "I'm gonna have the shrimp scampi."

Her gaze dropped to her go-to entre. "I'm going to have the chicken—"

"Marsala." He completed her sentence.

"How did you know that?" she exclaimed with surprise.

"You always order chicken." He folded his menu and placed it on the table. "If piccata isn't on the menu, you order the marsala. Never the francese, but if they have cacciatore, well, then that trumps them both."

She was astounded that he paid so much attention to what she ordered. She stared at him in disbelief, her mouth slightly ajar. *Can Russell be for real? Can he really be this romantic and attentive? So genuine?*

"I've been doing a lot of thinking about us on the ride here," she said, slowly, unaware that she was about to say the next sentence. "I think we could have something really special, Russ. I want to give this a try—you and me. I don't want to take it slow. I want to dive in headfirst."

"Are you sure?" His eyes ballooned, and his smile spread to epic proportions.

"Yes. I'm sure."

The candlelight picked up a soft sheen covering his eyes, and he pressed his lips together as if trying to hold in his emotion. "You'll never regret this, Layla. I promise. I'm devoted to you. You have my whole heart, and they'll never be another. You've just made me the happiest guy in the world." He moved his chair closer to her and cupped her cheek in his hand.

Every fiber in her body tingled as she watched his lips draw nearer. Their mouths met with the softest of kisses, causing goosebumps to run down her arms and up her spine. The kiss deepened, and a warm rush of adrenaline hit her in the center of her chest and traveled through her body like a bolt of lightning.

When their lips parted, a hazy hue covered his eyes, showcasing the deep emotion that resided inside this wonderful, sensitive man. He hugged her and nuzzled his face into the crook of her neck. They stayed with their arms around one another, secluded in their little corner of paradise, for a long time, just savoring the other. It fulfilled every want and need she ever craved, and nothing felt more right than being in his arms. Lost in a serene state of bliss, she didn't know why she never thought about Russell as more than just a friend before. It made her wonder how differently their lives would have turned out if he never married Donna and she never met Chris. For whatever reason, fate brought them down different paths and brought them together after taking harrowing journeys. It didn't matter because this felt right. This is where she was meant to be.

***

As soon as Layla closed the apartment door behind her, Russell pulled her into his arms and kissed her. It wasn't filled with impatience or insatiable desire. The kiss was slow and languorous, and she savored every moment of it. Eventually, their lips parted, and he gazed at her with half-closed eyes that reflected pure love. "I've been waiting all night to kiss you again," he whispered.

Their touch was so new, yet she felt comfortable in his arms, like they'd been together their entire lives. His hands rested on her lower back, holding her body against his, comfortable and confident in his touch. As he continued to kiss her, she remained wildly lost in this man's embrace, as if caught in a spell, until the pressure of his arousal pressed firmly against her pelvis, and a tingle shot through her.

Impatient and brandishing a seductive smile, she took him by the hand and led him to the bedroom. He stopped in front of the bed and pressed his lips to hers again, soft and pillowy. Her body responded with wetness and enormous yearning, and she rubbed her pelvis against him for friction. She knew he wanted to go slowly, because their first time was rushed and frantic, but she wanted him.

She pulled at his shirt and slipped it over his head. Her eyes dropped to his magnificent abs, and she took in his physique with allure. Their last foray was a frenzied quest for instant gratification. A heyday of tangled arms and legs. It didn't offer time to explore.

She ran her hands over his chest and glided them lower, reveling in each indent and hard muscle under her fingertips while she planted soft, wet kisses across his shoulder. His skin was warm and taught, tanned, smooth, and unblemished. She licked a trail up the side of his neck and felt his throat bob and the gentle influx of his pulse under her lips.

He slowly turned his head and caught her mouth in a plentiful kiss. Mounting hunger for this man made her breathe heavily as his hand slid under her shirt, burning her flesh with his touch. She broke their kiss to pull her top over her head, and his eyes dropped to her breasts and stayed there. She felt beautiful and desirable as he stared at her, savoring the ego boost it gave her. She reached behind her back to remove her bra, but he stopped her.

"Let me do it," he whispered.

His strong hands slid behind her back, delicately unhooked her bra, and slowly peeled it away to expose her flesh. When her bare breasts came into view, a soft moan escaped him. He gently massaged one of her nipples with the pad of his thumb, sending a shockwave straight down between her legs.

Unable to withstand this man a second longer, she shed her remaining clothing and stood before him completely naked. His gaze washed over her from head to toe and back up again before he pushed down his jeans and fumbled with his sneakers, never removing his eyes from her body. When he was finally free of his clothing, he rushed to her. Kissing her lightly, he picked her up and placed her on the bed.

Sexual energy bounced between them as he lay down next to her and took a minute to search her face. He didn't speak the words aloud, but she knew exactly what he was thinking because she knew him so well. Or, maybe, because she was thinking the same thing. Even though they made love before, this moment initiated the start of something big. Something new and strong between them. They were moving from friends to lovers. Toward a future together. Maybe a lifetime.

So many feelings cascaded through her body and her head. She couldn't entertain them all, so she let her body take the lead, and she straddled him. With her lips and mouth, she licked and nipped at his flesh. When her lips touched his length and she slowly lapped at the tip with her tongue, he let out a long moan. She toyed with him, running her tongue up and down his cock, but purposely avoiding the most sensitive spot just to drive him crazy. By the way he fisted his hair and rolled his head from side to side while he groaned, she knew it was working.

Suddenly, he reached down and grabbed her by the wrists and pulled her up so they were face to face. "You little tease," he moaned, his voice cracking.

She smiled, coyly.

"Now it's my turn." He rolled her onto her back and propped himself up on one elbow. His lips brushed her shoulder while his hand ghosted over her flesh, barely touching her.

A shudder ran down the length of her body and made her toes wiggle. Every part of her shimmied with the need for more physical contact and release, but he took his time.

He lifted her hand and imprinted her palm with a kiss. His tongue slowly traced a fiery path up her forearm, lingering in the delicate area inside the bend of her elbow. His lips glided over her upper arm and the curve of her shoulder, making her pant. She let out a deep sigh and rolled her head to the side, allowing him full access to the sensual stimuli located on the softest part of her neck.

His hand traveled across her stomach, over her hip and the silky-soft skin of her inner leg, until he reached the wetness between her thighs. He didn't push inside, only cupped her aching pussy. Silently, she begged for a more invasive touch, but her movements weren't as subtle. She jutted her hips forward several times and moaned, begging for more. She felt his lips form a tiny smile against her neck before a finger finally entered her. Her body immediately clenched around it, milking it for maximum friction, and she groaned loudly. "More," she begged. "More."

He slid another finger inside her and whispered, "I want you so much."

"Then hurry and take me," she pleaded.

He retrieved protection from his wallet, covered himself, then crawled on top of her until his lips landed on hers with a delicate but heated kiss. He stopped to look at her before they went any further, and they shared an intimate connection that she felt in her soul. She had completely fallen for this amazing man.

The warmth of his hard length pushed into her, and her back automatically arched to its maximum extent, groaning at the exquisite fullness invading her body. She wanted it fast and hard, but he made love to her slowly, sighing with every thrust of his hips, and she found an unhurried pleasure in his leisurely pace, so different than last time.

Without warning, his momentum increased exponentially, and she gasped at the sudden undulations that hit her sweet spot every time he pounded into her. A multitude of sensations caused her to shake and shimmy underneath him. Her muscles were limp as she succumbed to the rush of endorphins that had control over her body. Her moans grew stronger, louder, more frequent.

He started thrusting himself deeper, harder, faster, until it pushed her over the edge, and she let go. She was floating high on a cloud of ecstasy where nothing ever felt so wonderful, and she stayed in that inebriated state for an indeterminate amount of time. When she finally came down and regained control of her senses, Russell was grunting, and his chin jutted up toward the ceiling. She watched the cords of muscles in his neck flex and move with every deep gust of breath that left his lungs until he stiffened, held his breath for several seconds, then a shudder started at the top of his shoulders, quaked over his torso, through his hips and straight down to his knees. He let out a deep, satiated breath, then gently lowered himself on top of her.

He wrapped his arms around her neck and quietly hid his face in her shoulder. She listened to his breathing slowly regulate, then he lifted himself up on one elbow and pressed his lips against hers. Without saying anything, he rolled to the side of the bed and wiped himself clean, then lay back on the pillow. He opened his arm so she could snuggle into him and rest her head on his chest, where she listened to his heart gently beating.

With one hand lazily behind his head, he delicately stroked her shoulder, and it felt wonderful, as if she belonged nestled in the crook of his arm forever. After a while, she glanced up at him because she thought he may have fallen asleep. His eyes were glazed over and far away, a soft smile on his lips.

"What are you thinking about?" she asked.

He sighed, happily. "I was just thinking about the events of the last few months that led up to this moment. A moment that, only a couple of years ago, I thought would never become a reality. I've fantasized about this a million times, Layla. But I never imagined I'd be this happy."

She looked up at him with a smile, her chin planted firmly on his chest. "I'm happy too." She returned her cheek to his shoulder and snuggled into his body and traced small circles on his chest with her finger.

He brought her hand to his lips and kissed her palm, then softly kissed the tip of each finger. He folded his hand over hers and placed it on his heart. "I've always wanted to do that," he said, closing his eyes. "I love you, Layla," he whispered, his voice heavy with sleep. He repeated the words, this time softer. "I love you." A third time, now barely audible. "I love you."

She sighed with contentment. "I love you too, Russ."

Visit www.jennagalicki.com to learn more about the author's books, including the Radical Rock Stars series, the Bulletproof series, Radical Rock Stars Next Gen Duet, and several stand-alone novels.

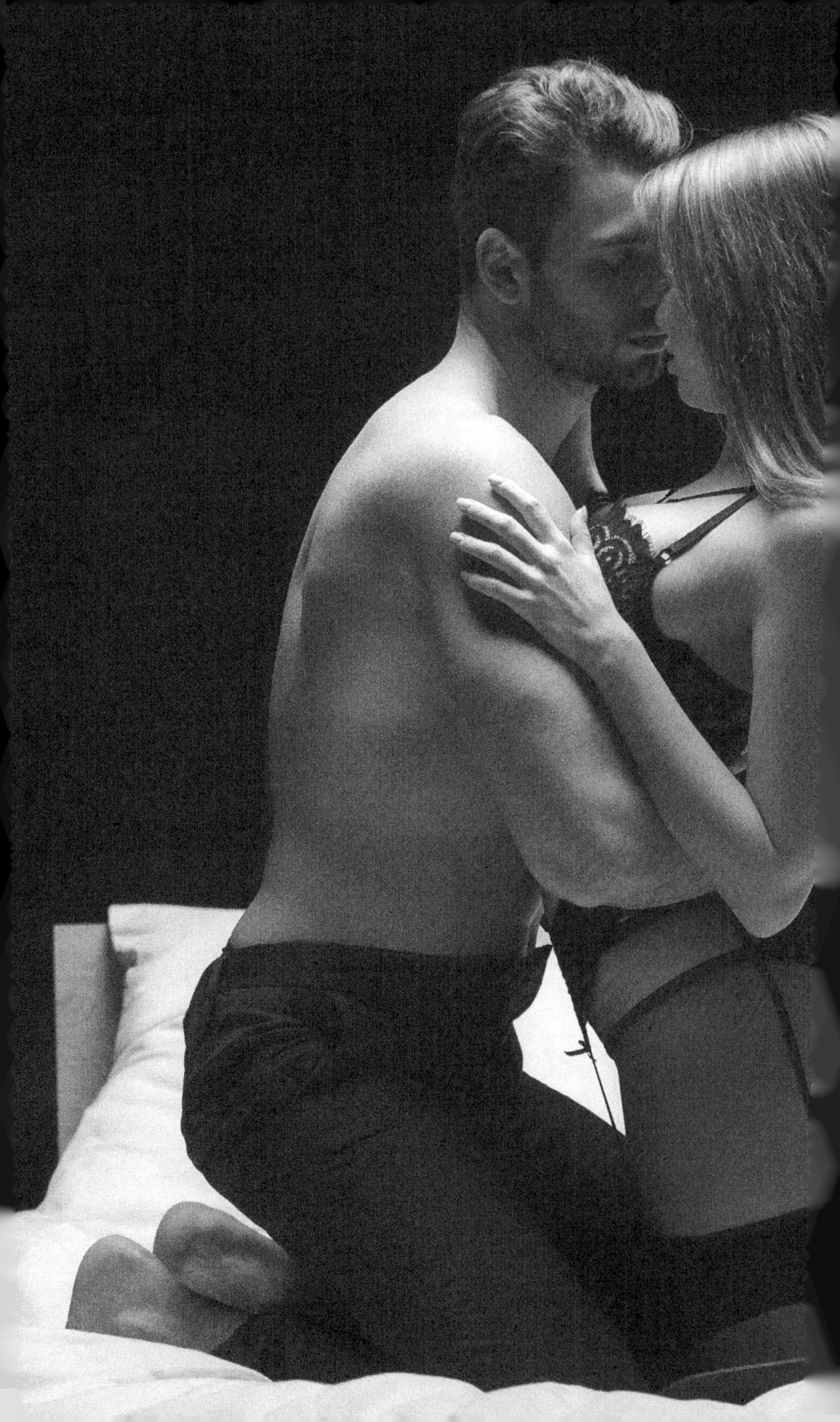

All
KEYED UP

JENNIFER HARTMANN

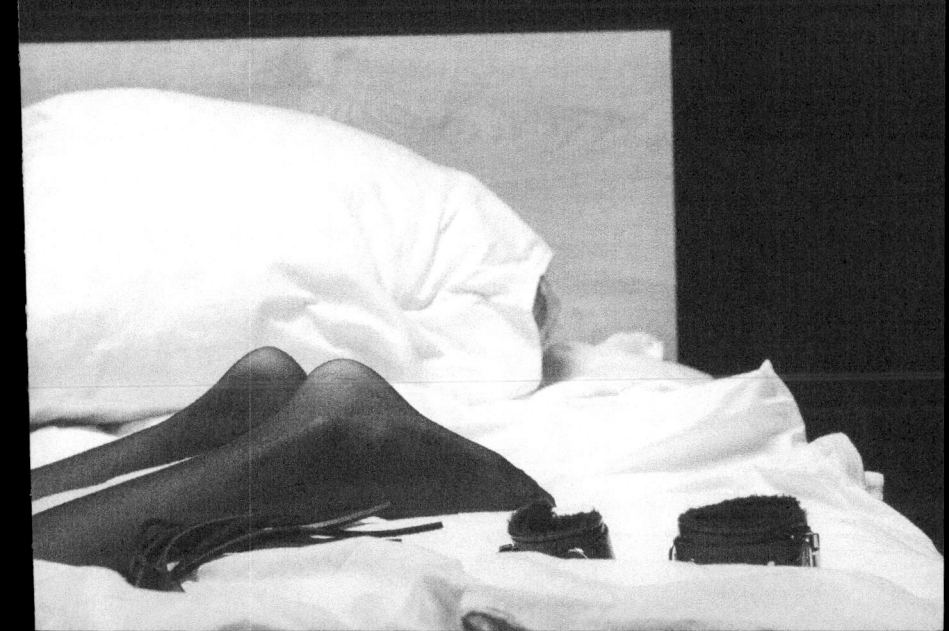

Chapter ONE

Alyssa

I thought it was supposed to be a tea party.

"It's a tea party, but for singles," is what Vanessa said to me as we breezed out of the office doors of Wilshire, our marketing firm, earlier today. "Are you in?"

I was distracted. My best friend, Lucy, had sent me a string of chaotic text messages, telling me she found a collection of field mice in her basement, a treasure trove courtesy of her rascally kitten.

Lucy: *SOS!!!!!*

Lucy: *Emergency!*

Lucy: *ALYSSA*

Lucy: **mice emojis**

Me: *Hi!*

Me: *Uh, you found a mouse?*

Lucy: *Seven. Seven mice. In the basement. All mutilated to varying degrees. Are they gifts? Are they meant for me?*

Me: *Yes. It's like Christmas morning. Cricket knows you* love Christmas.

Lucy: *This is The Nightmare Before Christmas.*

Me: *It's better than the impossible work deadlines gifted to me today. Let's trade! Karaoke next week? :)*

Lucy: *Necessary! *heart emojis**

So yeah, I was distracted.
Maybe I should have questioned why a bunch of twenty-somethings would be having a tea party, but I figured it was some kind of slang term I wasn't privy to.
An adult tea party.
Tea laced with alcohol.
Or...maybe it was a gossip party where everyone "spills the tea."
I didn't know, but I had no plans, so I smiled through my consent.
"Yep. Sounds great. Text me your address," I said while my heels clicked along the pavement as we wound toward our respective cars. "See you tonight!"
I've been here for a half an hour now, and so far, there has been no tea. Just the usual gathering of men and women, all mingling with alcoholic beverages and chatting in small groups around Vanessa's condo. I don't recognize anyone and wonder if I should have brought a friend or two.
Vanessa spears me with devious eyes as she holds up her car keys and jangles them in front of my face. "Who do you think you'll get?"
I'm so lost. A man sweeps past me, his gaze raking over me from head to toe as I fiddle with the hemline of my cherry-red party dress. He gives me a nod of approval as he sips from a tumbler and disappears into the kitchen.
"What are you talking about?" My nose crinkles as I glance at her keys. Apparently, the keys mean something. "Who will I get for what?"

"You know, to go home with. Has anyone caught your eye? Any hopefuls? We're still missing one of the guys, but he said he's running late." She shoves the keys back into her purse and tosses it on the sofa.

I rub two fingers to my temple, then sweep my hair over to one side until it's resting in a side part. "Please speak to me like I'm in second grade."

"Keys. Men. Sex."

"Sex?"

"Good Lord, Alyssa, I told you this was a key party—you know, but for singles. It's not a swinger thing. You're still single, right?"

My eyes round to giant saucers, my heart kicking up speed.

Key party.

Not *tea* party.

What the hell is a key party?

I pull my cell phone out of my clutch and furiously open Google.

"Oh my God, you didn't know?"

Pulse revving, I skim over the brief summary that pops up.

"*A phenomenon among swinging couples where guests would pick a random set of car keys out of a bowl and go home with whoever's keys they chose."*

I blanch a little.

"I'm so sorry," Vanessa continues, grabbing my forearm to keep me from conking out on her living room floor. "I thought you knew."

"Sure. Right. Okay." I reread the Google description a dozen times before browsing through an assortment of unsavory Reddit threads. "I mean, I don't really think this is for me, so—"

"Yo, Nessa," a voice calls from behind me. "Sorry I'm late. Diesel got loose and tried to woo the Doberman next door. She told him to fuck off, so I had to play vet."

The voice sounds familiar.

The name Diesel rings a bell.

No way.

I whip around, my hair catching on my lip gloss as my jaw unhinges. "You."

Dante Zucca stops in his tracks, neck craning back slightly. Mossy-green eyes glitter with recognition as they trail over me in a slow pull, top to bottom. A smirk curls on his lips. "Bugs."

"Ugh. Why do you have to call me that?"

Vanessa cuts in, finger flicking between us. "You two know each other?"

"No," I say.

"Yes," he says.

I scoff at him. "We matched on Tinder earlier in the year, but he stood me up." My eyes narrow with lingering disdain. "Then we saw each other at my friend's birthday party, and he made a regrettable impression."

"I knew you regretted not calling me."

Smug.

Smug and infuriating.

I cross my arms over my breasts as Vanessa is called away by one of her friends, leaving me and my failed Tinder match standing face-to-face in the center of her living room. He stuffs both hands into black denim, the ghost of a smile never leaving his lips.

It's been a solid eight months since I've seen him, after a coincidental run-in at Lucy's twenty-third birthday party. As fate would have it, he's a mechanic at the auto repair shop she works at.

Small world.

It's true he ditched out on our first date after we'd been chatting back and forth on Tinder for weeks, a spark climbing. There was chemistry there, I was certain of it.

But then he left me stranded at an upscale restaurant with no text or phone call, forced to simmer in my embarrassment as I guzzled down three glasses of wine to counter the shame.

Dante doesn't look apologetic as he stands in front of me now, glancing at my cleavage before swinging his eyes back up.

In fact, he looks delighted.

Jerk.

"How's the job going?" he asks, an attempt at conversation. "You preach about girly skin care stuff, right?"

I squint at him through mascara-coated lashes. "I'm an event marketing manager and coordinator for a popular skin care line."

"Right. Impressive."

"Impressive or intimidating?" I tilt my head to the left. "You did stand me up."

"Told you, something personal came up."

"I did take it personally, yes."

He sniffs. "I tried to apologize and explain. You blocked me."

"Life's too short to dole out second chances," I shrug, not sure if I actually believe that. Doesn't matter, though. When it comes to random guys on Tinder, it's legit.

Dante takes a step forward, his nautical cologne acting as a cloud of masculinity and sex appeal that I absolutely do not appreciate. I straighten my spine and shift my gaze to my red-tipped toes before glancing back up.

His smile softens as he extends a hand. "I request a do-over, Bugs. I think your stance on second chances is a tad jaded. Maybe I can change your mind."

"Not likely," I murmur, my voice losing its edge. I clear my throat and accept the handshake anyway because I'm not entirely stone-cold. "Have a nice time tonight. I'm going to mingle."

Ignoring the flicker of disappointment in his eyes, I spin around and stroll away, determined to hit it off with anyone other than him. Vanessa advised us to try and make connections and get to know the other guests, since we don't know who we'll be "going home with," but I'm feeling unnaturally nervous as I take an empty seat on the couch and cross one leg over the other.

The concept of this key party sounds absurd and depraved, and yet I'm still here.

As I glance around the room to check out the other men, a familiar gait floats into my peripheral vision five minutes later with two cocktails in hand. When he inches closer, my eyes pan up and catch sight of his coal-black hair, easy smile, and white Henley that looks striking against olive skin and inky tattoos.

Looking away, I inch my dress farther down my thighs.

"Got you a drink."

I grab it with gusto, groaning with dismay as he saunters up to me. "There are eleven other women here, you know. I'm the only one who doesn't like you." I bring the glass to my lips, blinking over the rim to drive the point home.

Dante grins at me. Instead of being put off by my attitude, he chooses to get comfortable on the couch beside me and takes a swig from his glass. "Presumptuous." He cocks his head in an arrogant sort of way, and his eyes gleam with something playful. "Also, false. You definitely like me."

"God, you're full of yourself."

"I prefer perceptive. Besides, I like this seat."

I scowl, my head swinging back and forth as the rum-infused soda glides across my tongue, caressing my throat with heat. "Please leave."

"I was invited."

"Occupied space."

He drums his fingers along his thigh as he stares at me. The amused grin lights up his face like a Christmas tree.

I never really liked Christmas.

My sister, Mallory, used to tell me that Santa was actually a wanted felon—he only knew when we were sleeping and when we were awake because he was a skilled stalker and child abductor.

Holiday light shows and jingle bells never had the same effect after that.

"Rough day?" Dante inquires, giving me a onceover and smelling obnoxiously good as he leans into the couch cushions. "You seem edgy."

"Now who's the presumptuous one?"

"I'm just saying, I can spot a worthy drinking partner from a mile away."

"I'm so impressed with your super-sonic vision."

He presses his lips together in a thin line, as if he's trying to get a read on me.

It should be pretty obvious: *bye*.

"I think we got off on the wrong foot," he tries.

I don't miss a beat. "I have chlamydia."

That's a lie. Maybe if I weren't so career-driven and promotion-hungry lately, I'd actually have the opportunity to contract a STI. But the truth is, it's been a minute. Almost a whole year. I've hardly had time to open up my dating apps, let alone go on dates, so my ovaries have basically shriveled up and died at this point.

Grimacing at the outburst, I hide behind my cocktail glass.

Dante stifles a laugh as he sips his own drink, long fingers curling around the middle of it. "Who hurt you?"

My eyes cut to him. "It all started in the third grade," I begin, my tone thick with an air of theatrics. "Little Tommy Parker. Ours was an unrequited love. He only had eyes for Suzie with the polka-dotted sweater vest." I feign some pretty realistic tears, but it's actually just heartburn from the heavy-handed rum.

He shakes his head through another chuckle and drapes an arm over the back of the couch. "Funny."

"You should go attempt to charm someone else."

A hint of a grin still touches his lips as molten-green eyes spear me with something heavier than amusement. Something earnest. I can't help but hold his gaze as a knot forms in my throat.

He offers the tiniest of shrugs. "I already told you, I like this seat."

"It's no different from the other seats." My skin feels hot. I blame it on the blazing chandelier lights above me.

Dante taps a short fingernail against his glass. "It's the closest one to you."

I inhale sharply, fidgeting on the cushion. I decide to ignore the line, even though it sounded mildly sincere. Pivoting, I tuck a piece of straw-blond hair behind my ear and release a sigh. "So, a key party is your idea of a good time? Prospects must be slim lately."

"Hm. Is that why you're here?"

"Actually, I had no idea what a key party was until I got here, so no, this isn't my typical outlet for Friday night fun."

"But you're still here."

We glance at each other at the same time and a reply dissolves on my tongue. I don't really have an argument for that.

Why am I still here?

I look away and chug my drink.

Chumbawamba's one-hit wonder "Tubthumping" blares from a nearby speaker as guests laugh and zip around the spacious condo, a blur of black cocktail dresses, flashy heels, and men in crisp dress shirts and colorful ties. A big glass bowl brimful of car keys sits like an ominous focal point in the middle of the kitchen island, the centerpiece among an assortment of different liquors and party snacks. I'm honestly not sure why I'm here—maybe loneliness, maybe curiosity.

My social life lately has mainly consisted of third-wheel dates with Lucy and her boyfriend, Cal, and I spend most Friday nights at a local wine bar watching my best friend live her dream as a well-loved acoustic performer. I'm proud of her. So proud. But it has also made me realize that I've put my own passions and dreams on hold as I try to climb the corporate ladder for a company that has never really appreciated me.

I like my job. I'm good at my job.

But it's not where my heart truly lies.

I've always wanted to be a journalist; telling stories, smiling behind the camera, educating and entertaining. I secured an entry-level position at my marketing firm while studying journalism at the local community college, and as I continued to move up within the company—and the hourly pay increased—it became that much harder to leave.

My dreams were put on hold, and the notion has been niggling at me lately.

Lost to my thoughts, I don't notice right away that another female has commandeered the empty couch space on Dante's left, while also commandeering his attention. The brunette in a slate-gray skirt and pinstripe blouse flips her hair back as she giggles, already captivated by something he said.

That's my cue.

Filling my cheeks with air, I blow out a breath and rise to my feet as the empty drink glass dangles from my hand. I step toward the kitchen for a refill, glancing once over my shoulder.

To my surprise, Dante stares back at me with that same earnest look in his eyes.

Chapter TWO

Dante

Another hour rolls by, and I haven't been able to keep my sights off of her.

Red dress, ivory legs, and an unreadable look in her magnetic brown eyes that I'm itching to crack. She's all mixed signals and smart mouth, but there's an invisible pull I'm dead certain she feels, too.

Meanwhile, the nameless brunette drones on beside me.

"So then he says, 'Oh my God,' and I say, 'Oh my God,' and we both could not stop laughing," she giggles, letting out a sigh as she smacks my knee.

I stare blankly into my non-alcoholic Coke, wishing it would morph into a double shot of scotch with the laser beams I'm desperately trying to conjure up with my eyes. "Incredible."

"No, it was terrible," she corrects me.

"That's what I said."

Alyssa's laughter floats over to me as she chats with my cousin's best friend, Vanessa, and some guy who isn't me. I glare at him. He looks like a typical frat boy with his cream-colored turtleneck and highlighted hair, the curls slicked back with pretty-boy styling gel. His hand moves to her lower back as he leans in, probably whispering something about epic touchdowns and his glory days as a star quarterback into her ear.

I stand, dismissing the brunette. "Nice meeting you, Riley."

"It's Rory."

"That's what I said."

Not looking back, I trudge toward the kitchen where Alyssa noticeably spares me a quick look. She's as aware of me as I am of her. I paint a smile on my mouth as I insert myself into the uninspiring conversation and set my half-empty glass of soda onto the counter. "Miss me?" I send her a wink and watch her fluster as she spins her cocktail between both hands.

"As much as I miss my two-week stint with mono in the seventh grade."

"Must've been some excellent mono."

Her eyes roll up.

Touchdown Dude glides his hand lower on her back until it's resting in the slender arch just above her ass. Alyssa squirms a little, folding her lips between her teeth before she sips her drink. While Vanessa blathers on about the party—who's connecting with who, and who she thinks should go home together—another female strides up to us, her eyes shimmering with interest as she glances my way.

"Hey, I'm Tulip," she says, popping the *P* with berry-stained lips.

"Dante." We shake hands.

The moment Touchdown Dude drops his hand, I lift mine and place it in the same spot on Alyssa's lower back, my touch featherlight, fingertips gently grazing. Leaning down, I murmur into her ear, "You're the prettiest girl here. By a fucking landslide. You know that, right?"

Her breath snags, muscles locking. I swear her balance teeters, her hip brushing up along my denim-clad thigh as she involuntarily inches toward me.

"Are you two an item?" Tulip asks curiously, a dark eyebrow arcing.

"Yes," I say.

Alyssa balks, taking a giant step away from me. Sweeping ruby-tipped fingers through her hair, she flusters for a split second before regrouping. "He's my brother," she quips with the hint of a smirk.

I smirk right back, quick on my feet. "Stepbrother. Not blood-related, so it's fine." I hold back a laugh at the mortified look on her face. "Forbidden, scandalous. Totally hot."

"Oh my God," Alyssa groans.

The woman strains a smile. "Cool. And you are…?" She bobs her head at Touchdown Dude.

I jump in quickly. "Her real brother."

A hand curls around my wrist and starts dragging me away from the four-person pow-wow. It's Alyssa, completely unamused by my antics. My grin widens. "Are we forgoing the key thing and jumping straight to the inevitable?"

"You're the worst. The *worst*. I'm not picking your keys. I'm not picking you for anything, aside from the only person in the world I never want to see again." She pulls me to a quieter corner of the room, her cheeks as red as her fingernails.

I fold my arms across my chest, catching the way her gaze skims the onyx tattoos rippling along my biceps that bulge beneath my short sleeves. "Brother? Really?"

We look nothing alike.

My father is Italian, my mom Puerto Rican, so my skin is a rich bronze, my hair jet black. Alyssa looks like a Barbie doll. Shoulder-length bob spun with sunshine, skin creamy and light.

Her eyes narrow with distaste as she pivots her attention away from my tattoos.

"C'mon, Bugs, you know you like me."

"Nobody likes you."

"Lucy does."

"Lucy doesn't count because she likes everyone. And stop calling me 'Bugs.' That's the most unsexy nickname ever." She shivers, like a family of carpenter ants started crawling up her leg.

"You set yourself up for that with your Tinder bio. Can't blame me."

She scoffs, pinching the bridge of her nose. "I did not. I said I hated bugs."

Her bio read something like: **"Hates bugs but would kiss a spider for some Pad Thai."**

A stretch, maybe, but it's a cute nickname.

And the fact that it ruffles her feathers and makes her cheekbones flush a charming shade of pink is just an added bonus. "Whatever," I sigh. "I have proof that you like me." Unfolding my arms, I sift through my pocket for my cell phone, then take a minute to pull up our Tinder conversations from a year ago. "See?"

Me: *You like me, don't you? ;)*

Alyssa: *Yes :)*

Alyssa blinks, swinging her head back and forth. "I liked you until you stood me up, and then I liked you even less once I met you."

"Well—"

Our banter is interrupted when Vanessa makes an announcement from the other side of the room, leaning over the kitchen island and waving a hand in the air. "Attention, please!" she calls out over the song "My Type" by Saint Motel. "Thank you all for coming out tonight, and I hope everyone has gotten to know each other properly." She winks, biting her lip and waggling her eyebrows. "I know this is a bit...unconventional. However, life is short. Eat the cake, buy the dress, sleep with hottie you just met, am I right?" A few laughs and whoops ring out from the crowd. "It's time to pick the keys, my friends. Ladies, please step forward and make a line."

I glance at Alyssa. She looks paler than a ghost who just saw a ghost. A knot of anxiety tightens in my chest, quickening my heartrate.

Oddly enough, I'm nervous.

I had no expectations going into the night, and I certainly didn't expect to see Alyssa Akins again—the girl who hasn't left my mind since she swiped right. Truth is, I didn't even want to come to this weird-ass key party. My buddy from work, Ike, encouraged me to give it a shot because I've been a bit of a hermit lately, too focused on work and family shit. I can't even remember the last time I got laid. Summertime, I think.

Now it's October.

Not that I need to fuck around all the time to be happy, but loneliness has been sneaking its way inside, and I figured a few drinks, some laughs, and a pretty girl in my bed might perk me up.

But now I'm nervous because the only pretty girl I want in my bed might be going home with someone else.

Alyssa fiddles with the fringe along the hem of her dress, sends me an uncharacteristically timid glance, and then saunters toward the island with the other eleven women.

Fuck me. Her ass looks delightful in that dress.

Hips swaying, hair bouncing, she settles into the line, coming in third.

My heart jackknives when the first girl—the insipid brunette from the couch—digs her hand into the bowl and fishes around for a set of keys. Deciding on her pick, she lifts them into the air and jangles them back and forth.

Bullet dodged. Not mine.

They happen to belong to Touchdown Dude, and away they go, collecting purses and coats as they shuffle toward the front door.

Inching forward, I watch as Tulip goes next, plucking out a new set of keys.

Also not mine.

A breath of relief spills out of me.

Then it's Alyssa's turn. I don't miss the way her eyes pan around the room, landing on me as I move a little closer and send her an easy smile.

She blinks a few times, inhales a deep breath, then glances down at the bowl of keys.

It almost looks like she's studying them. Light brown eyes skim over the bowl, narrowed and thoughtful, as if it's some sort of quiz and her mind is working to piece the answer together.

I hold my breath.

I wait.

And then she dives in, singling out a set of keys and latching onto them.

When she holds them up, Alyssa looks right at me—almost like she knows.

There's no way she could know, but I take the win and flash my teeth.

Fuck yes.

The red chili pepper pendant dangles from my keychain, the one my mom gave to me on my sixteenth birthday. It glimmers in her hand, the crimson charm glinting off the ceiling light like a smoldering victory.

I shuffle forward, watching the blush on her cheeks travel to her neck and the tops of her ears. As I close in, I raise my hand and snatch the keys from her loose grip. "Nice pick, Bugs."

"Fate must really hate me," she murmurs.

"Only as much as you hate me." I wink. The amount of hate is negative zero. "Ready to bounce?"

We're forced to leave the line so the next pair can be fatefully united, and Alyssa shoots me a squinty look over her shoulder as she searches for her clutch and peacoat. "I'm not sleeping with you...but for appearance's sake, we can leave together."

I follow her. "You sound so sure."

"Because I am."

"Bet I can win you over."

"In the thirty-second trek to our separate vehicles? It would take a miracle, but you're welcome to try."

She sweeps out the front door and races to the entrance of the condominium at double the speed, as if she's trying to chop a solid twenty seconds off her timeframe. I'm still shoving my arms through the armholes of my David Outwear Salvador leather jacket when she slips through the main door.

A crisp autumn breeze prickles my skin as the scent of smoky bonfires wafts around us in a cloud of burning leaves and possibilities. I'm hot on her tail, watching the way her hair catches flight and floats in an assortment of different directions, illuminated by the moon. Her shampoo overrides the smoke in the air, smelling citrusy. Like grapefruit or lemon sorbet.

Honestly, I don't need to sleep with her.

I'd never expect a woman to fall into bed with me just because a dumb party says we have to. There's nothing wrong with easy, meaningless sex every now and then if both parties are on board—but Alyssa isn't easy. That's what I like about her.

And I know sex with her would be damn far from meaningless.

What I *do* want, however, is to spend more time with her, so I jog up beside her with my hands in my pockets. She veers toward the Hyundai Kona, a flashy cerulean blue. The night we ran into each other at Lucy's birthday party, Alyssa drove me home in that car because I'd been a tad overserved. I remember it smelled like oranges and something feminine and powdery. A little like baby powder, but more floral. Musky and sweet.

Alyssa moves to the driver's side door and pulls out her keys.

I come up right behind her, my chest flush with her back, and cage her in with both arms. My lips dip to her ear as I whisper, "You say miracle, I say Pad Thai."

She freezes. Her head tilts slightly, cheek brushing my lips for a breath before a smile pulls on her mouth. It's involuntarily, gone in a blink, but it was there.

"I prefer my Pad Thai without the side of blinding aggravation," she mutters, but her words hold little fight.

I've already witnessed the surrender.

I take a step back, let her think on it for a minute. But when she just stands there, indecisive, my patience runs thin because Milwaukee chose to drop from seventy degrees to thirty faster than it seems Alyssa is capable of making a decision. "Listen, you shouldn't drive. You've been drinking. I'll drive you home, at least. Then you can stew in your regret, and forever wonder if you just gave fate the middle finger." I finish with a grin, "All alone and Pad Thai-less."

Her sigh falls out as a little plume of white. Shoulders deflating, she finally spins around to face me, folding both arms over her enticingly low neckline. "You've been drinking, too."

"Negative. My Coke was ninety-five percent Coke and five-percent well-water ice cubes."

"No way."

"Yes way. The point of the night was for someone to pick my keys so I could drive them back to my place."

Starlight illuminates a trace of hesitation in her eyes while she chews on her thumb. "Fine," she relents, straightening her spine. "You can drive me home. But you're not coming in."

I whirl around and stalk toward my neon-orange Camaro, knowing she's not far behind. A few seconds later, her heels click along the cement in rapid succession as she tries to keep up. "Fine."

"Fine," she repeats, a snap to her tone.

A smirk curls, a side effect of my small victory.

The wind whips me in the face as we approach my Camaro SS with all the bells and whistles. Header, exhaust, intake. Even a supercharger. I'm a bachelor and a mechanic, so it's easy to see where my leftover paycheck goes.

Alyssa noticeably slows her speed behind me with a sharp gasp. I pull open the passenger's side door and wait, all while she stares at the car like we're about to commit a felony.

"This is your car?"

"No, I stole it. Get in before the cops get here."

Her eyes pan up to me and hold for a beat before she crosses the rest of the way over to where I'm standing, my wrists dangling over the open door. "It's...nice," she forces out.

"And you thought it wasn't mine. Real flattering."

"Well, *you're* not nice. Easy assumption." Alyssa slips inside and falls onto the leather like she belongs there.

I rake my eyes over her, from her jittery expression to her creamy white thighs serving as a sexy contrast to the black interior. She tucks a section of cornsilk hair behind her pink-tinged ear.

Pink from the cold, or pink from the prospect of a late-night drive in my sports car with a guy she clearly has the hots for.

My bottom lip snags between my teeth for a drumbeat before I give the door a tap, then slam it shut. When I slide into the driver's seat, Alyssa inches back, gaze swinging over to me. In her eyes, I see it. I see the truth.

It's not the cold.

Pulling my keys out of my pocket, I toss them into the air one time before starting the engine, thanking my little good luck charm in the shape of a chili pepper.

Chapter
THREE

Alyssa

Dante plugs in his iPhone and pulls up a song on Spotify that has me second guessing everything I thought I knew about him.

"Head Over Feet" by Alanis Morissette.

Considering he told me once that his favorite bands were more along the lines of Sevendust, Chevelle, and Red, the song choice has me gawking at him as we careen out of the parking lot, the guttural engine growl hardly doing anything to overpower my shock.

Words die in my throat as I stare at him.

He glances at me once, then does a double take. "What?"

"You know what."

"Right." He nods. "You want me to take you back to *my* place. I figured."

I fill my cheeks with air and blow out a breath. "The song, Dante. Why are you playing this?"

He's staring straight ahead now as we cruise down the quiet stretch of road that's stripped of light. The smile he wears softens. "You told me it was your favorite."

Our ancient Tinder messages flash through my mind.

Dante: *Favorite song. Ten seconds. Go.*

Me: *I only need one. "Head Over Feet" by Alanis.*

Dante: *Interesting. Tells me a lot.*

Me: *Like...?*

Dante: *Like you won't be an easy one to get over. :)*

I wasn't exactly sure what he meant by that, but it filled my cheeks with warmth, and that warmth traveled into my chest, seizing my heart, too.

I liked him. For a blissful two weeks and four days, I liked him a lot.

Then he ruined everything.

Cool leather presses into my skin as I lean back in the seat, the scent of The Dreamer by Versace mingling with the rugged interior. My ego tells me to say something snappy, but I force my pride to deflate as I gnaw at the inside of my cheek. "Thanks."

This earns me another brief glance. "That sounded somewhat sincere."

"Because I'm somewhat surprised. I didn't think you'd remember our talks."

"Why? Because I'm a soulless asshole who 'stood you up?'"

"I guess."

Dante cups his clean-shaven jaw while his opposite wrist dangles over the steering wheel. He doesn't look at me as he says, "My dog got hit by a car that night. My fault. I knew the ring on his collar was loose but hadn't gotten around to buying a new one." He scratches at his chin with a joyless shrug. "The leash snapped off when he saw a squirrel, and he booked it into the street."

In an instant, *I've* become the soulless asshole.

A reply peters out on my tongue as I stare at him, his face half in shadow, half alight with moonglow. "I didn't know. I'm so sorry." It's as walls-down and vulnerable as I've ever been with him. I feel like crap for assuming the worst.

"It's fine. I tried to tell you, but you insta-blocked me."

"Yeah, I'm...sorry about that, too." Pulling my eyes off of him, I slink miserably into the seat and tug my unbuttoned coat around me. My throat stings as I choke on the residual shame. "I've been burned before. I jumped to conclusions," I admit.

He sniffs. "I get it. No big deal. Not like I gave you any reason to think I was anything other than a douchey Tinder prospect who found something better to do."

Actually, he'd given me plenty of reason to believe otherwise. He was kind, funny, charming.

Different from all the other guys I'd been chatting with at the time.

It was my own insecurities and bruised ego that had me clicking the block button without a second thought.

I close my eyes and release a long breath. "The last guy I dated was married," I tell him. And if that's not bad enough, I confess the second poisoned arrow to my heart: "To two separate women."

His attention snaps toward me for a beat before swinging back to the road. Running a hand through his cropped hair that's longer on top and shaved along the sides, he whistles with sympathy. "Shit, Bugs. That's fucking low."

Nodding, my eyes flutter open, and I drink in the expanse of dark road stretched out before us as Alanis croons from the speaker. "Why didn't you tell me the truth at Lucy's party?"

"The party where you immediately despised me? Thought about it, but the mood was a bit tense if I recall." The soft smile he sends me waters down his words. "I wanted to. Honestly, I wanted nothing more than to go home with you and explain everything. Have some drinks, start over. Even left my beanie in your car, hoping you'd bring it back to me since you knew where I worked."

I blink. "You did that on purpose?"

"That surprises you?"

Yes.

Well...*no.*

I don't know. Everything seems to be surprising me right now, including the notion that I want to invite Dante inside when we get to my condo. Have some drinks, make amends.

Maybe more.

"You made Lucy give it back," he adds with a mopey chuckle. "Figured I'd never see you again."

My chest pangs with regret.

A twinge of guilt.

But before I have a chance to explain further—to send him a flurry of apologies—Alanis suddenly stops singing. The interior lights dim. Even the headlights go out, and my stomach pitches when the car starts rolling to a slow stop in the middle of the road. My attention whips over to Dante, catching the look of irritation that claims his eyes. "Umm...?"

"Motherfuck."

"What's going on?" Without the heat pouring out of the air vents, a chill seeps into my bones, mingling with a pinch of anxiety.

"Goddamn alternator." The car stalls completely just as he manages to pull off to the gravel-laden side of the road. "*Damnit.*"

Dante slams his fist onto the wheel as I flinch in my seat, and a single car passes by. We both pull out our cell phones. I almost expect to find that neither of us have service for no apparent reason, and we're about to be stranded on a dark, desolate road, miles from civilization, while a twisted serial killer kidnaps us both and locks us in his basement, intent on keeping us as pets.

This is why I need more of a social life and less Investigation Discovery binges.

Luckily, we both have service. Dante calls a towing company, while I update my Instagram stories with a grainy selfie and an interactive multiple choice prompt that reads:

"All dressed up with nowhere to go because the car broke down on Highway 12. Who's gonna get me first? A) Escaped mental patient with a hook for a hand, B) The Matchmaker back from the dead, C) My own paranoia."

My red-tinged lips are pursed into a pout as I crinkle my nose for the camera.

Five minutes go by and *C* wins by an eighty-five percent landslide.

"Got a guy on the way," Dante says, pulling me from my social media distraction. "Sorry, this sucks ass. I swear I didn't plan this."

I shrug, flipping my hair over my shoulder. "I'm sure you did, but it's fine. I could use a little adventure in my life. It's been a while."

Lucy always tells me that there's a fine line between a disaster and an adventure and it's all about the people we experience them with.

Glancing at Dante, my smile holds more sweetness and less bite.

The grin he sends back is *all* bite.

Definitely an adventure.

***

We pile into the tow truck fifteen minutes later, Dante getting sandwiched between me and the portly driver. My senses are immediately assaulted by an odor that resembles a horrifying marrying of nutmeg and stale kitty litter.

I gag as I slam the door, my thigh smashing against Dante's.

"Where ya'll headed?" the driver wonders. "Amos' shop is two miles out."

"Cal's Corner," Dante provides. "I'm a mechanic there."

I twist my neck to glance at the man in the driver's seat wearing a grease-stained T-shirt that rides up his stomach, showcasing a prominent beer belly and a smattering of coarse dark hair that disappears into an unbuckled waistband.

Why is it unbuckled?

I don't want to know.

I don't.

Instinct has me scooting closer to Dante, and desperation has me moments away from burying my face into his armpit because it has got to smell better than this truck.

Dante glances down at me, my hair tickling his shoulder as the truck growls to life. "You good?" he murmurs, warm breath whispering against the top of my head.

My eyes lift, and I mouth the word, "No."

But then everything *is* magically okay because Dante reaches over and plants his hand along my knee, giving it a tender squeeze. Goosebumps case my skin. I inhale sharply and stare straight ahead, stilling to a statue.

"Name's Buck," the man says before immediately rambling off a story about his last tow experience, where he accidentally locked his keys in his truck and had to call a tow for his tow.

I reach for Dante's hand still cupping my knee.

We share another glance. Sage-green eyes twinkle back at me, lashes dark and curving, dimples framing full lips. I never noticed his dimples before. I'd always been too wrapped up in thinking about the next snarky comeback to ambush him with, that I failed to notice them.

I never noticed the fullness of his lips either, and now they're all I'm thinking about.

"Nice bird you got there," Buck says.

Blinking around Dante, the driver appears to have his eyes fixated on my bare thighs instead of out the windshield where they belong.

Apparently, I'm the bird.

Dante squeezes my knee again. "She's my wife."

"Yeah? Nice." Buck nods with approval.

I groan, falling against the seatback, my thighs squishing together so hard, I think they become one single entity.

"She's not all that nice," Dante quips before sending me a wink. "Kind of a pill, actually."

"A *pill?*" I parrot, tone scathing. My hand instantly pulls away from his.

"A bit high maintenance. She snores, too. The lung-rattling kind of snores. The kind that shake the bed like she's been possessed by something, and make me wonder if I'll wake up and find her levitating." His smirk is positively beaming. "And that mouth. It's either driving me crazy with her sass, or it's driving me *wild* with—"

I kick him in the shin with my stiletto, a makeshift skewer of red-hot loathing.

"—those awful sounds she makes when she chews food. Noisy chewers, man. Is there anything worse?"

Buck chomps on his gum obnoxiously loud. "Nope."

"She has some good qualities, though. Obviously, she's sexy as hell. And she's generous. One day, I came home to a houseful of stray dogs. A few dozen. Maybe fifty, I'm not sure. She picked up a coyote by mistake, but it was fine because she named him Flufferafugous and crocheted him this adorable pink sweater." Dante trails his hand up my leg, but I swat it away. "She's got a big heart. Don't you, Bugs?"

"I'm going to kill you."

Dante sighs, glancing at Buck. "She's feisty, but I love her."

"Bugs?" Buck wonders.

"Yeah. Short for Bugsy Marie, her given name."

"Kind of weird," he notes.

"No. It suits her."

I'm now pressed up against the passenger door, putting a sizable gap between me and the man on my left who is probably the reason I'll be sleeping in a prison cell come sunrise. My hand is curled around the door handle as I prepare to tuck and roll at the next stop light.

We turn into the parking lot of Cal's Corner five minutes later while Dante sends me a few soft, flirtatious glances that I ignore. My blood pressure is concerningly high, and there's no way I'm inviting him inside my condo now.

He's dead to me.

Alanis never happened.

The moment the tow truck shifts into park, I tug at the door handle a million times, but it doesn't open. I'm trapped. Buck takes his time collecting his keys and readjusting the waistband of his slacks as he makes an assortment of grunting noises.

"I'll get the door for ya, Bugsy," Buck mutters, exiting the truck and rounding the rear to my side of the vehicle.

I level Dante with a sharp, squinty-eyed stare of disdain as a moment of silence infects the space between us. "I hate you so much."

He ruffles his hair, gaze still teasing. "I was just messing with you."

"You were being a jerk."

"Where's your sense of humor?" he asks with a grin.

"It died the second you told him I snored. I don't snore. I'm a silent sleeper. What's wrong with you?"

"Maybe I like watching you squirm a little. Your cheeks turn all pink. It's cute."

"Sadistic."

The door pulls open, hinges squeaking as Buck extends a hand to help me out of the truck. Before I can leap into his arms, Dante gets up and starts shuffling over me to exit first.

"Ow," I wince when he steps on my foot.

"Sorry."

"Ow! What are you doing?"

He jumps down, hip-bumps Buck out of the way, and holds out his hand instead.

"Wow, so you're a gentleman now?"

"A sadistic gentleman. No one is perfect."

I ignore the baseless chivalry and climb down by myself, ankle twisting as I make a faulty landing on the cement. "Ow," I repeat, noticing my heel broke off. Now I'm going to be limping and shoeless on top of my simmering fury, all because I picked the wrong keys.

"You okay?" Dante wonders, reaching for me before I faceplant.

"Fine." Dodging him, I storm off toward the entrance of the shop, waddling like a furious penguin. Dante races to catch up after settling things with the driver and getting his Camaro dropped off near the garage. I watch as apology replaces the levity in his expression, his smile dissolving when he slows to a stop in front of me. My arms are folded, defenses flared. Cold wind sends my hair into a tizzy as I look away, refusing to make eye contact.

"Hey. I'm sorry."

He sounds sincere.

Oh well, I don't care.

"I was just playing around. Didn't mean to offend you."

"Can you open the door? It's cold."

A long sigh meets my ears, earning him a quick glance. He's sifting through his collection of keys, looking sorry and deflated. I'm forced to bite down on my tongue to keep any unwarranted forgiveness at bay—he has the eyes and disposition of a kicked puppy right now, but really, *I'm* the kicked puppy.

I don't care, I don't care.

Popping the key into the keyhole, the front door swings forward as a set of jingle bells chime to life, and Dante holds it open for me. I sweep through, my focus anywhere but him. He still smells really good, which isn't helping my cause.

"I'm just going to leave a note for Cal real quick," he says, moving to the reception desk and flipping on the lights.

"Kay. I'll order an Uber."

"Yep. Sounds good."

He says it like it sounds as good as going in for a daily root canal until the end of time.

Blowing a stray piece of hair out of my face, I pull up my Uber app and find a driver nearby as I slip out of my heels and lean my shoulder against the wall for support, my back to him.

My ankle hurts. Probably sprained.

The moment I finish the transaction, I feel him saunter up behind me, body heat warming my back. My skin puckers with more goosebumps as traitorous tingles dance up my spine. I gnash my teeth together, waiting for him to say something.

"Should I order a second Uber?" he asks gently, tone low and defeated.

He knows he blew it.

A shred of guilt stabs at my chest, and I wonder if I'm overreacting. He was definitely being a jerk, but I haven't exactly been a saint, either—my bitchiness was strong. And also underserved at the time. I stare down at the lock screen on my phone, which is a picture of me and Lucy singing karaoke a few weeks ago, our smiles bright, our arms wrapped around each other.

WWLD is my motto in life: *What would Lucy do?*

Sighing, I shake my head a little. "It's fine. We can share a ride and figure something out. My condo is a one-bedroom, but you can crash if you want." Blush inhabits my cheekbones. "I mean, on the couch. For practical reasons. I can drive you to get your car tomorrow at the shop."

"You can drive me in your car that you left at Vanessa's?" His tone is still soft and kind, but the playful edge is evident. "Totally practical."

Oh. Right.

Dante releases a sigh off my silence. "I can get my own Uber. It's not a big deal."

Finally, I pivot to face him, drinking in that still-sorry expression that has my heart fumbling around inside my chest. "Is that what you want to do?"

"Not in the fucking slightest. I want to spend more time with you." He shrugs, hands slipping into his pockets. "But I can. If I made you uncomfortable."

I drag my teeth along my bottom lip, our eyes holding.

He blinks, glancing down at the floor. A beat passes, then another. And then he's bending over to unlace his black boots. I watch as he toes them off his feet and slides them over to me, clearing his throat as he says, "Wear these. Sorry if they reek, but I'm not letting you walk across the parking lot with no shoes on."

My gaze zigzags between my naked, blood-red toenails and Dante's boots. "Oh...well, you don't have to do that. I'll be fine." I harness a small smile. "I've had lots of practice over the years. Bare feet seem to go hand-in-hand with drunken college adventures."

Half of his mouth curls up with a smile, but he doesn't back down. "Put them on, or I'll be forced to carry you."

A light chuckle falls out of me, followed by a breath of surrender. "Okay then." The boots are huge but warm as my dainty size-seven feet slide into the cozy leather lining. I'm sure I look ridiculous, even though the look in Dante's eyes as he gives me a full sweep has me thinking otherwise.

"You look extra sexy in my boots, Bugs," he murmurs, taking a slow step toward me. "Bet you'd look good in just my T-shirt, too."

A lump snags in my throat as my pulse revs.

He's rude, he's crass, I hate him.

My mind chants it over and over, but my heart doesn't seem to agree as it breaks into a gallop.

Dante's attention dips to my mouth when he takes one more step forward, until we're a hair's breadth apart. Electricity crackles. My eyes flutter, lips parting, and I wonder if he's going to kiss me. I wonder if I'm going to let him.

But the only thing he whispers is, "Uber's here."

I suck in a breath and glance over my shoulder, out the glass door. Sure enough, a silver sedan waits on the other side of it, the headlights flashing. Turning back to him, I nod.

He smiles. Soft and sweet. "Lead the way, Bugs."

Chapter FOUR

Dante

Her condo smells like roses and vanilla cake. There's a touch of hesitation in my gait as I slip inside, closing the door behind me. Alyssa flips on the main light, illuminating a cozy living space adorned in kitschy décor and splashes of aqua and blush. An ivory sofa with floral pillows sits in the center of the room, surrounded by contemporary knickknacks and crown molding lining both the ceilings and floorboards. A plush white rug greets my feet as I saunter farther inside in just my socks.

Alyssa is brimming with nerves. She lets her peacoat fall off her arms, tossing her clutch onto a rectangular side table. Nibbling her lip, she glances up at me as I face her with my hands in my pockets.

Shit. I'm kind of nervous, too.

"We can, um...order in some food?" she suggests, shuffling between both feet.

"Yeah. That works."

Slipping out of the clunky boots that swallow her right up, she bends to move them out of the walkway, giving me a prime view of her cleavage spilling out the top of her dress.

I suppress a groan.

I'm pretty sure the night is no longer going to go as planned since I decided to run my mouth and fuck over my chances with her.

Stupid.

I wasn't purposely trying to offend her, thinking she'd appreciate my attempt at humor. After all, I knew the driver was making her uncomfortable, and it's not like we'd ever see the guy again. I just wanted to lighten the mood.

That backfired.

Instead, I pissed her off and hurt her feelings.

I linger in the tiny foyer made up of a dozen cream-colored tiles and watch as she straightens a few feet away from me. She pushes her sunny blond hair out of her eyes before nodding at the couch behind her.

"I'll turn on a movie and pull up a food delivery app. Want something to drink?"

"Yeah, sure."

"Any requests? I have red wine, a few beers..."

"Beer is good. Thanks." Our eyes hold for another beat before she nods, then traipses over to the adjoining kitchen.

Alyssa returns with a full glass of wine, along with a beer that she hands me, as we both settle onto the couch and speak at the same time.

"So, I, uh—"

"Well, this is—"

She tucks a loose strand of hair behind her reddening ear and glances down at her wine, twirling it between both hands. "Maybe I should head to bed."

I don't need to look at the clock to see that it's early; likely still before ten p.m. And I don't need to be a rocket scientist to decipher that her statement was *not* a thinly veiled request for me to join her. Leaning back and dangling the beer between my spread legs, I try not to sound too desperate. It's hard because I want nothing more than to spend more time with her. Get to know her better. Fix whatever I broke. "You could. Or we could watch that show you like—Fear Thy Neighbor?"

She visibly shudders. "Our tow truck driver instilled enough fear in me for one night, thanks." A small smile crests as she glances up at me. "How did you remember that?"

"Why are you assuming I forgot about you? We spent a lot of long nights talking until sunrise. I remember everything you told me." Our shoulders brush together as I get more comfortable and prop my ankle atop my opposite knee. "Besides, most girls I talk to are into romcoms. Girly shows. Not neighbors murdering neighbors."

"Do you talk to a lot of girls on Tinder?"

I bite my lip.

Is she fishing?

Why yes, I think she is.

"Average amount."

"Define average."

"I'm a single, twenty-six-year-old guy who enjoys sex. You do the math."

Heat claims her eyes, pink flush blooming on her cheeks. "So, you're a fuck-boy."

I cringe. "I despise that term," I tell her. "I'm a connection man. If I make a connection, and the cards fall into place, I fuck. But...I don't fuck *just* to fuck. There needs to be a spark. Substance. Otherwise, what's the point?" Alyssa swallows, shifting her attention to her area rug while she taps her toes. My head tilts to the side as I study her. "Too blunt?"

She shakes her head. "No."

"What about you?"

"What about me? Do I 'fuck around?'" she wonders, lifting her chin to find my eyes for a split second before glancing away. She blows out a breath with a tiny shrug. "Not so much anymore. I used to date, but I haven't had time lately. It's actually been a while since I've...been with anybody."

"How long?" Hopefully, I'm not overstepping. Alyssa is hard to read, and I've already fucked up once. Another misfire will definitely put my ass in an Uber before the sun comes up.

"A year."

I chew on my cheek, my eyes narrowing thoughtfully. "Why do you seem embarrassed by that?"

"I'm not, I just..." Flustered, she tucks her hair behind both ears repetitively. "I'm not inexperienced."

I'm not sure why she thinks I'd care.

She could be a virgin, or she could have a thousand guys under her belt, and I wouldn't want her any less than I do right now.

My silence stretches for longer than preferred because I'm stumped on a response.

Unfortunately, Alyssa takes my non-reply as something else, and tries to backpedal. "Not that it matters. I'm not sleeping with you, so there's no need to fill you in on my *experience*. God, that sounded really desperate."

"No it didn't."

"It did. Sorry...it doesn't matter." Stuffing her hand between the couch cushions, she pulls out the remote and switches on the television, scrolling through her streaming apps. She lands on ID and searches for a show to watch. "Murder, it is."

A smirk lifts. "Should I be worried that you invited me over?"

"I do have a really high-end knife set. On sale at Macy's. I haven't used them yet, but they look sharp. Very effective."

"Noted. I'll be sure to sleep with one eye open tonight."

Alyssa settles back into the cushions, her body twisting toward me as she thinks on her next words. "Honestly, I've always been a crime junkie. I wanted to be a journalist..." She trails off, a shot of melancholy clouding her eyes. "*Want*," she corrects. "I still want to be a journalist."

The mood softens as my eyes skim her face. "You'd make a great journalist."

"What makes you think that?"

"You're outgoing, enthusiastic, witty, smart."

"Ah," she nods, smile stretching. "Overcompensating with the compliments now, I see. Cute. Well, thank you. I suppose those qualities do make up for the fact that I supposedly snore."

"Not really, but they help."

Please don't smack me. Please don't castrate me with your discounted Macy's knife.

Mercifully, I'm spared.

Even better, her smile doesn't dissolve.

I stretch my arms, itching to do the super subtle reach-around but play it cool, instead. "Tell you what. I'll give you one whole minute to insult me to your heart's desire. Lay it on me. No holding back." My eyebrows pop up and down as I wiggle my fingers at her in a way that says, "*Let me have it. Do your worst.*"

She scoffs. "So, two wrongs make a right?"

"Yes."

Her eyes narrow, lips puckering to the side as she debates the offer. "Fine."

"Great. Your time begins now." I start counting out loud.

Frazzled, she shifts closer, chugging her wine, our knees brushing together. "Jeez, okay. Um..."

"Five, six..."

"Stop counting. It's distracting."

"Eight, nine..."

"Ugh. You're...arrogant."

"Compliment. Try again," I breeze. "Eleven, twelve..."

"Crude, presumptuous, sarcastic."

"Still compliments. You're terrible at this game." I keep counting, waving my hand at her to continue while I take a sip of my beer.

"Oh my God, stop counting." Her eyes pan around the room, as if her picture frames and dusky-rose wall paint hold all the answers. "Um...you're probably messy. I bet you throw your clothes on the floor and leave your dirty dishes next to the sink."

"You have no proof. Overruled."

"You're mean. Kind of a jerk."

"False. I'm very generous, and I always reciprocate." Innuendo bleeds into the last word. "That I can prove."

She blushes.

I wink.

Somehow, we've scooted closer to each other on the couch, and when I drop my arm, it grazes her thigh. She swallows, fidgeting at the contact. "I bet you wouldn't call me. If something happened between us," she says, looking anywhere but at me. "I bet I'd never hear from you again."

This puts a stop to my countdown and has my smile slipping. There's a trace of earnestness in her tone that makes me feel itchy. I'm not offended, exactly, but I *am* kind of sad, realizing she actually believes that. And it's so far from the truth.

Maybe I am a little offended.

Taking a slow pull from my beer, I watch as her eyes dart back to me, her throat bobbing as she chews her lip. She sees me deflate and knows she touched a nerve. "Not true," I tell her. "You've got me all wrong."

"Do I?" she squeaks out.

"I could prove it if you wanted me to."

Indecision paints her face, but she manages a quick head shake. "I'll spare myself the heartache. Thanks, though."

Her eyes flare when she recognizes the admission hidden within her statement, and this puts the smile back on my lips. "You'd be heartbroken if I didn't call you? I'm flattered, Bugs."

"That's not what I meant. You're reading into things."

"I'm literally taking your words at face value."

She has no counter to my claim, so she flips on a crime show until the images flash across the screen, brightening the dimly lit room. "Stop calling me 'Bugs.'"

I don't say anything right away. I stare at her, drumming the bottom of my beer bottle against the edge of my thigh as my gaze skates across her face—cheeks tinged with makeup and a soft pink flush. Heart-shaped lips, full and pouty. Muted brown eyes that shimmer like copper pennies.

She's fucking gorgeous.

"Okay," I say softly, my voice dipping low. Rough with gravel. "Alyssa."

It might be the first time I've called her by her real name. Those three syllables echo between us, causing her to inhale a quick breath on instinct, like the sound of her own name is a foreign, intoxicating thing. Her knuckles turn white as she grips the spine of her wine glass and brings the rim to her lips, chugging the rest. A crimson kiss is left behind when she sets it beside her on an octagon table.

She glances at me again, then lingers in a way that feels sensual, arousing, and has me sweltering in my own skin. Then she pulls her eyes away.

I swallow, slicking my tongue along my top teeth as I study her. "You know, I kind of hate it when you look at me like that."

Flustered, she clears her throat. "The look of immense revulsion isn't the biggest ego boost, I know."

"Mm, right." I sniff. "I'm referring to the look where you're this-close to giving in, but then you second guess yourself." My gaze sweeps over her face when she glances back at me, and I tilt my head, a crease furling between my eyes. "Kills me."

A sharp breath leaves her.

I'm affecting her.

Good.

Alyssa adjusts the thin strap of her red dress as she swivels away from me and changes the subject. "Tell me the stupidest thing you've ever done."

I continue to stare at her, read her. There's a trace of softness in her eyes, her tawny irises shimmering with something curious. My mind races with a reply, but I'm so entranced by the way her tongue pokes out and slicks along her plump bottom lip, that it takes me a minute to form words. I force my eyes away and say, "Nothing. I'm a saint."

"I'm serious." A grin tugs at her lips, despite herself. "I feel like you can learn a lot about a person from their answer."

Close to a thousand stupid memories flicker through my brain because I'm definitely a liar. I'm far from a saint, and the amount of stupid shit I've done over the years could probably earn me some kind of feature in the *Guinness Book of World Records*.

A shout out, at least.

Still, I try to play it cool and pretend I'm perfect. "Nothing comes to mind. Sorry, Bugs."

"You're such a liar. Can I add that to your list of insults?"

"Nope. Your time ran out." I shrug, downing the rest of my beer and discarding the bottle beside me. "What a shame."

Somehow, Alyssa appears to be sitting two inches closer to me on the couch. *Witchcraft.* Our thighs are pressed together now, stealing my attention for a heady heartbeat. The image of her milky white thigh flush against my faded black jeans has my dick stirring to life.

Not that it's been dormant all that much since I laid eyes on her earlier, but I've tried to keep a handle on the situation. My jeans are snug, and my dick is big.

Don't want to scare her off.

Shifting in place, our knees knock together, and I swear I can feel the heat from her skin absorbing through the denim fabric. "Fine, I'll play," I relent. My hand falls off my lap in a slow-motion sweep, transferring over to her lap.

Whoops.

Alyssa tenses but doesn't pull away. She even does an impeccable job of keeping her eyes trained on me, and not on the way my fingers have a mind of their own as they graze along the hemline of her dress, gently caressing.

"Let's hear it," she murmurs, nearly a whisper.

I have a few options I could share. Some are embarrassing, which will earn me sympathy points, and some are downright hilarious, which will gift me with her sweet laughter.

In the end, I choose neither.

"The stupidest thing I've ever done, huh?" I glance at her. "I didn't find a way to track you down. I didn't look for you. I didn't do everything in my goddamn power to find you and explain what really happened after missing our date."

Her lips part, jaw dropping little by little as my words sink in. The breath she intakes is choppy. Flimsy.

Her chest heaves up and down as she blinks at me, a current of heat passing between us.

I swallow. "What's the stupidest thing you've ever done?"

I'm desperate to know more about her, eager to uncover her secrets. The beer has my blood buzzing.

She has my blood buzzing.

Alyssa's attention drops from my imploring stare to my mouth.

It's brief, it's fleeting.

But I notice.

In a blink, she answers the question by closing the gap between us and cupping my face between her hands. She inhales a sharp breath the moment right before our lips meet. We linger for a heavy heartbeat, my right arm curling around her, hand sliding up her spine and palming the back of her neck to keep her mouth a centimeter from my own.

I feel like I'm on fire. My pulse is in my ears, blood rushing south. Soft hair slips through the cracks in my fingers while her lashes flutter, her body trembling.

"This is the stupidest thing you've ever done?" My words fall out in a ragged breath, my hold on her tightening.

Nodding once, her gaze slips to my mouth again the second before she leans in and brushes hers to mine. It's hardly anything; the slightest graze.

Yet it's so fucking erotic.

I move forward to seal the kiss, but she inches back a fraction. She's teasing me, and the notion has me grinning through the lust. "Bet I could get you to do this stupid thing over and over again," I rasp, drawing my other hand up and cradling her jaw. My thumb drags down her bottom lip, smudging the remnants of her lipstick.

Alyssa lets out a whimper.

An actual fucking whimper.

My dick hardens to a steel rod, straining against my jeans. I lean in again, yearning for more contact, for another graze. A groan rumbles in my throat as I give her a squeeze and pull her forward until she's falling into my lap, legs straddling me. The groan morphs into a growl when my hips thrust up on instinct, my erection flush with heat between her legs.

Her dress is rolled up to the top of her thighs, exposing long, creamy legs that cage me in. She whimpers again, a sound I've burned into my memory, saving it for future bouts of "me time."

So goddamn sexy.

Our mouths lightly kiss, and I murmur against her lips, "I'm fucking dying to know what you taste like."

She flicks her tongue along my bottom lip and grinds into me. This girl has me so wound up, I'm literally about to come in pants. "Wine," I say, voice all gravel and rough edges. "You taste like sweet red wine."

With a flirtatious grin, she does the tongue-flick again.

"Berries," I add. "Something fruity."

"It's the lip balm," she murmurs, her hands in my hair, sifting through the strands and squeezing.

"Mmm. You don't taste like a mistake, Bugs." My own hands drop and latch onto her hip bones, our groins pressed together.

Her head falls back when she feels how hard she's made me, and the ecstasy on her face has me attempting to incinerate our respective clothing to ashes with only the power of my mind.

She releases a tortured sigh, like she needs more, like she needs it all. Her head pops back up, falling forward until our lips touch again. "Maybe we should find out."

Our eyes lock and hold, chemicals crackling. Inhibitions turning to dust. I pull her bottom lip between my teeth, giving it a nibble before letting go. "Maybe we fucking should."

No more teasing.

I drag my hands up her body until I'm fisting her hair with one palm, the other curling around her throat and holding her in a loose grip.

In an instant, my tongue is in her mouth.

Hard, fast, needy. Wet and sweet. Her moans burn through me like a blazing brushfire, and I can't get enough. I tug her head to the right, angling her mouth so I can plunge in deeper with furious, sensual strokes that strangle my chest.

Twist my heart into knots.

Have my dick *aching* to slide between her pretty thighs.

Alyssa kisses me like my dirtiest fantasies brought to life. She wants me, and she's not afraid to show me by the way her body melts into me as she sucks my tongue into her mouth.

Fuck.

Her hands trail down my chest, landing on my belt. The sound of a buckle tinkling as she unfastens me is a symphony to my ears, and the feel of her other hand squeezing my cock has me letting out a pornographic moan.

I watch her eyes bulge as we pull apart to catch a breath.

"Shit," she pants, still cupping me through the too-thick denim. "You feel...really big."

She strokes my ego as she strokes my painful erection. I can't help but smirk. "You want it, don't you?" I bury my face into the curve between her neck and shoulder, teeth nicking the sweet skin. Marking her. Making her mine. "I'll show you. Bet you'll be screaming my name in no time."

Moaning through her surrender, she continues to loosen my belt as I leave future bruises along the expanse of her throat.

"Dante?" she pants.

"Yeah?"

"I have a confession."

I bite the lobe of her ear as my hands explore her curves. "Go on."

"I don't really have chlamydia."

This has me inching back, my grin broadening. "Is this the Alyssa Akins guide to flirting?"

She nods, trying really damn hard to hold back her smile.

That's when my phone buzzes, lighting up beside us on the couch cushion, screen facing up.

We both glance at it, and it feels like someone dumped ice water down my jeans.

Tinder Tiff: *Wanna meet up tonight ;)*

A selfie accompanies the text. It's the busty brunette I've been chatting off and on with over the past week, partially clothed in hot pink lingerie, her tits pouring out the top of the scrap of lace.

Goddammit.

Alyssa freezes in my arms, the flush of desire on her skin heightening to an angry shade of red. She whips her head toward me, catching the flash of frustration lighting up my eyes. "Not a fuck-boy, huh?" Hurt paints her face, decorating it in disappointment.

And then she's climbing off my lap, putting a sizable gap between us as she inches the hemline of her dress back down her thighs.

Impeccable timing, Tinder Tiff.

Fucking wonderful.

I scrub a hand down my face, shaking my head. "She's nobody. I haven't even met her in person."

"Yet."

"Jesus, Bugs, do you really think I've been celibate for a year, waiting for you to text me? I talk to other women, yeah. Sometimes I fuck them. It's not a revelation."

Her eyes flicker with confliction—almost like the rational part of her brain understands completely, but the other part is still looking for an excuse to abort the mission.

She wants this, but she doesn't *want* to want this.

For some fucking reason.

Scooting farther away from me, Alyssa clears her throat and scratches her collarbone, attention panning to the rug beneath her feet, as if she's searching for her next move within the white wool fibers.

I inch toward her, not wanting this to spoil anything. "C'mon, don't pull away. I'm not with her right now—I'm with you. I'm exactly where I want to be."

She glances up. The confliction lingers, glimmering back at me in pools of pale brown.

And then my damn phone lights up again, buzzing with a notification. Tiff is sending me a slew of eggplant emojis.

Go. Away.

Grumbling with aggravation, I snatch up my phone and power it off, then toss it across the couch, wishing I could bury it under the floorboards.

But it's too late.

Alyssa jumps to her feet, mumbling something under her breath about getting tired. She even feigns a yawn.

"Alyssa," I try, collapsing against the cushions with defeat. "Stay."

I don't even sound desperate. I sound a little wounded, which I think surprises us both.

She hesitates, the candor in my voice catching her off guard. Then she forces a joyless smile, fidgeting with the ends of her hair.

"I'll, uh, grab you some blankets. Sleep well, Dante."

Damnit.

Alyssa practically runs out of the room, escaping down the short hallway.

The click of her bedroom door is like a hammer to my heart.

Chapter
FIVE

Alyssa

I lean back against my closed door, my heart in my throat.

I'm being ridiculous.

My cheeks flame with the remnants of my massive overreaction as I close my eyes and drag my fingers through my hair.

This is silly. I can't expect an attractive single man to *not* have sexy women with huge boobs blowing up his phone, just because I finally swallowed my pride and decided I wanted to sleep with him. He's not mine. In fact, I made zero attempt to make him mine, taking his singular misstep as a painful dismissal and blocking him from my phone with no context.

I never blocked him from my mind, though.

I've thought about him. More than I care to admit.

And now I had him, but I allowed petty jealousy to push him away again.

My mother's words echo through my mind on loop: *"You're the stubbornest girl I've ever met, Lyssy. It's going to bite you in the ass one day."*

Consider me bitten. Consider me chewed up and pulverized.

Blowing out a breath, I push up from the door and strip out of my dress, rummaging through my dresser drawers for a tank top and sleep shorts. The night is ruined, so I might as well curl up into a ball of depression and cry myself to sleep because I don't know how to *not* act like a basket case around this guy.

Hot pressure burns behind my eyes as I pull the tank over my head and flatten my hair back down. I step into my baby-blue shorts and shimmy them up my hips before collapsing forward on my dresser, head falling into my hands.

I hear rustling from the living room. Footsteps. The jangling of the door lock.

He's leaving, and I don't blame him.

I blew it.

Indecision races through me. I pull up on my elbows and glance at the door through the darkened bedroom. It's not too late to apologize, to beg him to stay, to invite him into my bed and salvage what I can from the evening.

It's not too late.

He's still here.

My heart kicks up speed as I gnaw on my bottom lip until it chafes.

Screw it.

Pushing up all the way, I jog over to the door and curl my hand around the knob, adrenaline rocketing through me.

Then I whip it open.

Shock steals my expression when I see him standing directly on the other side of it. His shoulder is propped up against the wall just outside my room, hands tucked inside his pockets.

He was waiting.

Anticipating.

Knowing.

My heart continues to pound like a bass drum between my ribs as we stare at each other, awareness so heavy, it feels like a third entity standing between us. My lips part, still bee-stung from our kisses, still tingling and wanting. Mossy-green eyes gaze down at me as he continues to wait.

But I can't move. My feet are frozen to the carpet, my muscles all locked up.

"Fuck it," he grits out. Dante takes two steps forward and grabs my face with both hands, pulling my mouth to his.

I moan with relief. With renewed passion. With heat, desire, and a touch of reckless abandon. Both of my hands clasp his neck, short nails digging into the skin, sure to leave marks. Our tongues collide. Hungry, demanding. Nothing is tame or gentle, and there's no holding back.

I need this.

I need him.

Dante walks me backward into the room until the back of my thighs are smashed up against the foot of my bed, our mouths still locked together.

God, he tastes good.

A trace of green apple from the beer, fused with peppermint gum.

My fingernails inch underneath his t-shirt, scraping up the planks of his rippled abs. Hard and rough, just like his kisses. Heady cologne assaults my senses, a masculine cloud of birch and cedar. My nails drag up and up, scratching at his chest until he groans into my mouth and yanks the shirt over his head one-handed, tossing it across the room.

I don't even have time to appreciate what my eyes are witness to. Moonlight brightens his muscled torso and inky tattoos as he reaches down to pull up my top, his movements as reckless and clumsy as mine. My arms lift, and the tank is tugged up over my head, my hair falling back down and into my eyes.

A big palm sweeps it back, fisting it tight, his other hand moving to my breast and massaging it through my satiny black bra. "Christ, Alyssa. You're fucking gorgeous."

My legs are no longer functional, giving out as I collapse onto the bed. Dante steps between my knees, and I take the opportunity to finish unlatching his belt, the buckle still partially loose from my earlier attempt.

He lets me. He makes no move to assist, only cradling my head between his hands and scraping his nails along my scalp.

I pull down his zipper, fingers shaky. I'm eager to see him, to feel him heavy in my hand, to taste him on my tongue. He groans when I push his pants down his hips and watch them fall to a halo of black denim around his feet. Then I tug his boxers mid-thigh, and his hard cock springs free.

Oh my god.

Sexy BEDTIME STORIES

He's huge. Thick and veiny, the base rimmed with coarse black hair. I take him in my fist, giving his erection a firm squeeze.

"Oh, *fuck*," he grunts, head tipping back briefly before dropping back down to watch me stroke him. "Mmm. You want my big dick, don't you?" Dante pulls my head closer, until my lips caress the wet tip leaking with precum. "Suck me."

My pussy throbs with need, drenching my panties. I open my mouth and take him inside without hesitation, laving my tongue around the head and tasting him. The sound he makes is primal. Devastatingly sexy. It only spurs me on, and I take him deeper, wrapping my lips fully around him.

"Fuck, Alyssa...*fuck*, that's good."

"Mmm," I hum, moaning as I suck him. My hands reach around to cup his ass as his hips thrust forward, slow and steady at first, then jerkier the faster I suck.

"That's it, sweetheart, take my cock. Mmm. Goddamn. Feels so fucking good."

I feel him in my throat with each thrust, his grip on my hair so tight it almost burns. I love giving head. There's always been something about it that turns me on more than anything else.

The power. The control.

It's intoxicating.

I'm certain he's going to come this way, but then he pulls out with a sharp grunt, as if the separation was painful to do. I gasp when he tugs my head back farther and bends down to kiss me.

My mouth tastes like him. Salt and musk.

Dante draws back and reaches underneath my arms to toss me backward on the bed, and the mattress squeaks and sinks beneath my weight. I watch him pull his boxers down the rest of the way before kicking his jeans aside and climbing over me, knees caging me in. A streak of moonglow seeps in through my open window, spotlighting the heat in his eyes as he crawls over me and slides his hands up my thighs to my hips, removing my sleep shorts.

"Fuck, you're beautiful," he murmurs, bending to scatter kisses along my skin as my one knee arcs up. He slips his fingers inside the waistband of my underwear and inches the scrap of black lace down my legs. "I'm dying to eat you."

My spine bows off the bed the moment he buries his face between my thighs with a primal sound of need. "Oh god...Dante..."

"Fuck," he says. "Keep saying my name like that."

His tongue plunges inside of me, pulling his name from my lips over and over again. I reach behind my back to unclasp my bra and toss it on the floor while Dante's hands sweep up my body and palm my breasts, flicking my nipples as he eats me out like he can't get enough. His moans are so visceral, it's as if he's enjoying this even more than I am.

Impossible.

I already feel my orgasm climbing. My core tightens as he sucks my clit and thrusts two long fingers deep inside me.

"You're fucking soaked," he grits out. "Taste so damn good." The slippery sounds echo around us as his fingers move in and out, fast and hard, his mouth relentless.

"Yes, yes, ohh, don't stop," I pant and squirm, clamping his head between my thighs.

"Gonna make you come on my tongue. Then you're gonna come on my cock."

His tongue is a weapon, punishing me. But holy hell, it's a gift, too, breaking me apart so beautifully, all I can do is beg for more. I fist his hair as his head bobs between my legs, and I throw mine back, my release detonating as he works my clit just right.

"Ohhh my *god*," I cry out.

"Fuck yes. Come for me, sweetheart."

I'm quivering beneath him, collapsing into a boneless heap atop the mattress as his tongue placates to sweet, gentle strokes, and his fingers slip out slowly.

My eyes are glazed over, clouded by a fog of lust, my chest heaving with labored breaths. I watch as he glides his glistening fingers between his lips to taste me, suckling them, then moaning as he pops them back out.

He crawls over me, shoving my legs back apart as the tip of his cock teases my wet entrance. "I'm gonna fuck you 'til you come again," he tells me, bending to nick the side of my jaw with his teeth. "I'm not gentle." Another bite, harder this time, right beneath my ear. "Something tells me that's exactly what you want, yeah?"

He's right.

He's absolutely right.

I claw my fingernails down his shoulder blades and pop my hips up, grinding my pussy along the length of his shaft. A smile pulls when he hisses through his teeth. "Only one way to find out."

He makes a growling sound, biting my throat again, then trailing his tongue along the little bite mark to soothe the sting. "Gotta get a condom."

Dante pulls off of me to pluck his jeans off the floor, and I draw to my knees, watching him through the shadowy room and bringing my hands to my breasts, palming them. I tweak my nipples and toss my head back, releasing a breathy moan as I wait for him to return. When I open my eyes, he's struggling with the wrapper, too distracted by my little show.

One of my hands trails to my pussy, the curls trimmed short and neat, and two fingers slip inside while my other hand still massages my breast. "Mmm," I whimper. "Want you. Hurry."

He tears the condom open with his teeth and manages to sheath it over his erection in point-two-seconds.

Then he pounces.

Before I can inhale my next breath, I'm being flipped onto my stomach and yanked up by the midsection until he's settled behind me, teeth latching onto my shoulder. "You're a fucking tease," he rumbles against my skin. "Gonna pay for that." He shoves me back down in a way that's careful yet dominating as my hands plant palms-forward on the mattress, and I'm positioned doggy-style.

Dante slams into me from behind.

I would collapse if he wasn't holding me up by the middle, one hand latched onto my waist in a white-knuckled grip.

Holy hell, holy shit, I think I just saw Jesus.

Stars and heavenly lights twinkle behind my eyes as he pushes in all the way, as deep as he can go, then continues to pound into me, over and over again.

He's huge. He's all-consuming.

It hurts, and I want to scream, and it feels so, so soul-shatteringly *good*.

I cry out, a roar of stunned pleasure.

"Fuck yes," he groans, thrusting in and out with quick, furious strokes. "Such a good girl, taking my dick. You feel so fucking good. So tight, so wet. Mmm...*fuck*."

He slaps my ass. Hard.

I buckle, faceplanting into the bed covers. I'm pulled up by the hair, my back flush with his chest as he continues to fuck me.

"You love it, don't you?" he rasps against my ear. "You love my big cock. Can't get enough of it."

"Yes," I moan pathetically, my tits bouncing as he reaches around to palm one in his hand. "Don't stop. Don't stop."

He stops.

But only to flip me around until I'm flopping backward onto the bed. He falls over me, shoves my thighs apart, and slides back in with a tapered groan. "Christ, Alyssa." Both hands fist my hair as he fucks me, lips hovering a whisper above mine.

I pull his face closer. Our mouths crash together, my legs wrapping around his waist, arms crisscrossing behind his neck. He drags one hand down my body to clutch my hip, anchoring me, as the other moves to my jaw.

Tongues collide. A dual of dominance. A war of lust, battling for control, strokes moving in time with his hips. He bites my lip, and I bite his. Our teeth crash together, hot and messy, as he sucks my tongue into his mouth, then nibbles on it before pulling away.

Drinking in a ragged breath, Dante stares down at me, pushing my hair off my forehead and drinking in my flushed face and bruised lips.

He slows a little.

Our eyes hold, our faces an inch away from one another.

A shot of intimacy swims between us.

This is rough and dirty sex, the definition of *fucking*, but something else is sneaking its way inside. It has my breath catching, and I can't look away. The crease between his eyes deepens, his gaze glinting with more than lust as a wash of moonlight brightens his face.

He blinks, long, dark lashes fluttering as he severs the hold. Picking up his pace again, Dante drops his head to my shoulder and ruts into me, grinding against my clit with his pelvis.

"Oh God..." My nails dig into his back, and my legs squeeze tighter around him. "You're all wrong for me," I whisper, fighting the moment. Fighting whatever that was.

"Bet you're all wrong for me, too," he bites back, face still buried in my neck.

"Funny how it feels so right."

He unravels my arms from his neck and slides them up the bed until our hands are clasped tight above me. Lifting his head back up, he doesn't seem to want to fight it. Dante locks eyes with me again until neither one of us can look away.

His strokes are hard but languid. Purposeful. Squeezing my hands, his hips sink into me, his cock reaching deep as my clit tingles with an impending orgasm. A rush of heat sweeps through me, peaking, unfurling, and I arc off the bed, seeking more friction.

"Come for me, Alyssa. That's it," he murmurs, his tongue flicking my parted lips. "That's it. Let it go."

I do. *God*, I do.

It's intense, mind-blowing, exquisite.

"Dante..." I chant his name which drives him wild, and he kisses me with the same intensity. Moans leave my mouth and fall into his as my body shatters with the most powerful orgasm of my life. I feel weightless and starry-eyed, drenched in bliss.

But he's not done with me yet.

Dante draws up to his knees and grabs my hips, lifting my ass off the bed as he plows into me, chasing his own release. "Fuck, that was so hot," he husks. "Watching you come. Watching what I do to you." He wraps my jellylike legs around his lower back to hold me up, his thrusts turning quick and uneven as he's about to come.

I'm boneless below him, my lips painted in a drowsy, lust-laced smile as I watch him finish through hooded eyes. His face twists with raw pleasure, jaw unhinging as his head falls back.

"*Fuck*," he groans, jack-knifing into me, the final stroke of his cock sinking deep and holding as he breaks apart.

We're both panting, breathing heavily, as Dante lets my legs fall back down and collapses over me, catching himself on his elbows. Our foreheads press together while his eyes close, his hard chest flush with my breasts. "Jesus, Bugs," he murmurs, a tiny smirk brimming to life. "Been waiting a whole year for that. Holy shit."

"Worth the wait?" I grin, still catching my breath.

"Five fucking stars. Would absolutely come again."

I hold him against me, pulling his face against my collarbone and stroking his sweat-slicked hair, still smiling. "You're falling for me, aren't you?" I wonder softly, fingers sifting through the dark strands. Vulnerability laces my question, overriding the attempt at teasing. All I can think about is the moment we shared while he was moving inside of me. Brief yet poignant.

I swallow, waiting for his reply.

Say yes, my mind pleads. *Tell me you're falling.*

Dante scatters soft kisses to my skin and whispers back, "Head over feet."

Chapter Six

Dante

She steps into the kitchen in only a T-shirt that reaches the tops of her thighs.

It's not my T-shirt, but she *is* wearing an assortment of purplish hickeys along her neck, all provided by me. And that's fucking hot.

I twist toward her from my perch at the sink as I rinse noodles off in a silver strainer. "Morning, Bugs. I made breakfast."

Alyssa yawns through a shy grin, stretching her arms over her head until the shirt rides up over her neon-pink thong. "Yummy."

Yummy, indeed.

My eyes latch onto the shadowing of bruises that decorate her hip bones in the shape of my fingerprints. Maybe I was too rough with her. Giving the strainer a shake, I drop it in the sink and swivel around to face her. "I, uh…didn't hurt you, did I? Last night?" There's thinly veiled concern bleeding into my tone because the last thing I want to do is hurt her—in more ways than one. "Sorry if I got carried away."

She parks her hip against the counter, showing zero regret for the way the prior evening unfolded. "My bruises and bite marks hurt as much as those claw marks down your back, I'd wager."

The claw marks chafe against my Henley.

My dick jumps to life in my jeans.

"Good." I smirk, turning back to the pasta. Rummaging

through her meticulously organized cabinets, I pull out a giant serving bowl and dump the noodles into it.

"Speaking of rough sex, what are you making?"

"Speaking of?" My eyebrow arcs with amusement as I send her a quick glance over my shoulder.

She smiles. "Yeah."

"I'm making Pad Thai."

"That looks like spaghetti." She sidles up beside me, leaning forward on her arms. Her nose scrunches up at the lump of spaghetti noodles and accompanying jar of marinara sauce.

"Well, noodles were the only ingredient you had on hand. Had to improvise."

"Cute." She grins.

She smells like me, and it does nothing for my growing erection. Light blond hair curtains her mascara smudges and a tiny bike mark near her jaw as her hip grazes mine. Alyssa's eyes lift to me while I toss the noodles in salt and butter, a dreamy daze glittering back at me.

Memories race through my mind of our intense sex marathon last night, causing my skin to heat and tingle.

We didn't stop at just once. Shortly after round one, Alyssa slipped beneath the covers and curled her body into me, her breasts pressed up to the planks of my chest, the crown of her head tucked right beneath my chin, legs tangling with mine. The scent of her hair and the feel of her warm curves against my skin as she grazed her fingertips up and down my arm did something to me. It felt so comfortable, so *right*, and the feel of her resting soundly in my arms had me turned on all over again.

Twenty minutes later, I fucked her for a second time. And then she put my dick in her mouth until I came down her throat quicker than I care to admit.

Fuck.

Alyssa is a complicated mix of stubborn sass, fiery passion, and a trace of timid sweetness. She matches my sarcasm and aggressive sex drive, but she also has this intoxicating femininity and mystery about her that has my heart wondering if I'll ever be able to get over her.

And that's a little fucking terrifying, considering I've hardly spent a full twenty-four hours with the girl.

My distracted thoughts have me accidentally pouring marinara sauce onto her countertop as I dish up my very Italian version of "Pad Thai."

"You missed," she notes, reaching for the paper towels.

"You're distracting me."

"Am I?" She wipes up the mess, then tosses the wad into her garbage can. "I'm not sorry."

The embarrassing breakfast I've whipped up seems a lot less vital when she hops up onto the counter and spreads her knees, flashing me her pink thong.

Such a fucking tease.

And insatiable, just like me.

I fall right into her trap like a chump, pushing the food aside and sauntering toward her open thighs until I'm perched directly between them. Her hands lift, landing on my shoulders as our eyes lock together. A soft smile pulls at her lips, something genuine—less teasing, more heart. It has my own heart teetering inside my chest. "Can I be honest?" I ask, dropping my forehead to hers. Vulnerability leaks out, which seems to be a common theme when I'm with her.

My question has her stiffening slightly, her grip on my shoulders tightening. "Of course."

I lean down and press my lips to hers. Just a featherlight kiss. "You scare me."

She inches back. "I scare you?"

"Yeah. A lot, actually."

Blinking a few times, her hands fall away, and she ducks her chin. I'm waiting for her defenses to flare, but only a mask of insecurity claims her expression.

"I'm a lot to handle...I know. *Too much*, according to most guys."

"That's not what I mean." It's evident she's been burned before, called *too much* by other men in a negative way, so I tread lightly. "You scare me because it's hard to think about a time when I won't be able to touch you like this. Kiss you, make you lunch for breakfast. Tease you, and watch you smile." *Jesus*—I sound whipped and delusional. I shake my head and swipe a hand down my face. "Jesus. That sounds whipped and delusional."

She clears the laugh from her throat. "It does feel different, doesn't it?"

Different.

That's a good word.

I've had plenty of one-night stands, and none of them have ever made me feel like this. None of them had me spooning the girl as we drifted off to sleep, impossibly entangled, and more at peace than I've ever felt before. None of them had me climbing out of bed the next morning and wanting to cook for her, eager to spend more time with her, desperate for another kiss, another electric touch, another conversation.

All of them had me leaving in the middle of the night with a noncommittal text that read something like, *"Had fun. I'll call you."*

Sometimes I had fun. Sometimes I called them.

But none of them ever had me craving the next time I would hear the way my name sounded leaving her lips.

"Yeah," I reply, a little breathless, still terrified, as I bend to brush another kiss to her mouth. "Different."

She flicks her tongue out, igniting a new firestorm. I open her mouth with mine, tasting minty toothpaste and exploring her warmth until we're both panting, and my hands are cupping her cheeks in a way that feels...*different.*

Pulling back with a little gasp, a hoarse whimper, Alyssa finds my eyes. Then she says, "I knew those were your keys."

I almost stop breathing. Pretty sure my heart actually peters out for a concerning length of time as I freeze, my head popping up with a baffled frown. "What? How?"

Her bottom lip snags between her teeth, her cheeks flushing a rosy pink. "The chili pepper," she murmurs. "You called yourself 'Picante Dante' in your Tinder bio, remember? I put two and two together. It wasn't hard."

I recall the way she studied those keys. Carefully sifted through them, plucking out mine like she somehow *knew*. It seemed ridiculous at the time, but now it makes sense. "Shit, Bugs," I say through a grin, grazing our noses together as I lean back down. "I knew you liked me."

She pinches her thumb and index finger together. "Little bit."

"More than a little bit." I drag my hands down her body until I'm clutching her hips, giving them a firm squeeze. "Admit it."

"Never."

"Bet I can make you."

"You can try."

Challenge happily accepted. I tug the T-shirt over her head until her full breasts meet my eyes, looking even more perfect in the shimmery light of day. A groan leaves me as I take them in both hands, palming them until her head drops back to the upper cabinet. She blindly reaches for my belt buckle, and it doesn't take long before my pants hit the floor and her panties are shoved aside, and a condom rolls over my cock until I'm buried deep inside of her.

We both moan, drowning in the feeling. The delicious familiarity.

I go slow this time as she winds her arms around my neck, holding onto me. Face to face, I pump my hips, glancing down at the way my thick cock fills her completely, sliding in and out. Slow and deliberate. I'm savoring the moment, trying not to let the erotic image spiral me to spontaneous orgasm. Her fingernails dig into the nape of my neck, and I look up, spellbound by the ardent look glowing back at me.

Alyssa leans in and nicks the side of my throat with her teeth. A love bite.

And I know, without a doubt...

I'm toast.

We spend a few hours being lazy, finding our way back to the bedroom and forgoing my overcooked spaghetti for more engaging activities. My face is between her thighs for a good portion of that time, satiating my hunger pangs. When noon strikes and I know I need to get home to let Diesel out, I reluctantly suggest we head out to pick up my car.

By one p.m., after a quick joint shower, an Uber drops us off in front of my shop.

Alyssa looks wary as her sneakers slap the pavement, her hair pulled up in a short, high ponytail. She gives it a tug, eyes flicking between me and the main entrance. "I can wait out here while you settle up."

I frown. "Why?"

"No reason."

Yeah, right.

That "no reason" is dripping from the lie like she shouted it through a megaloud speaker. "You're ashamed of me," I gather. "Nice."

"No, that's not the reason."

"So, there *is* a reason."

The sun is warm today, a contrast to yesterday's bone-rattling chill. It brightens her hair like a twinkling beam of light, makes her eyes sparkle with a semblance of apology. "I just…I don't want Lucy to know. Yet."

My boss' girlfriend, Lucy, just so happens to be Alyssa's best friend. Lucy is an *actual* beam of light; probably the most kindhearted girl I've ever met. There's no doubt in my mind she'd be our number one cheerleader if she saw us walk in together.

However, Lucy's not here.

She works the front desk Monday through Friday, saving her weekends for volunteer work and music gigs at wine bars and cafés.

I slow to a stop, stuffing my hands into the pockets of my day-old jeans. "She's not working today. Just Cal and the rest of the guys." Sighing, I squint up at the cloudless sky, trying not to feel offended that the girl I'm suddenly gone for wants to hide me in the shadows. "It's fine. I'll meet you by my car in a few and drive you to Vanessa's."

She doesn't get a chance to reply before I'm pushing through the main door, ignoring the way my heart wilts a little.

"Yo," I mutter to Cal when I see him towering over the reception desk, a beast of a guy, wearing his trademark scowl, a navy beanie, and angry tattoos. "Sorry I left you with extra work this morning. My alternator fried."

He looks up briefly. "All good. Ike took care of it first thing."

"Appreciate that."

I'm off every other Saturday, but I probably should have come in today to work on my own shit. I kind of feel like an ass, but more pressing matters awaited.

Pressing matters that don't seem all that pressing to Alyssa.

Cal's eyes are on the computer screen as he mumbles, "Alyssa coming in or not?"

I turn, watching her fidget outside the glass window, her back to the building. "Guess not," I say miserably, trudging forward. "She's ashamed of me."

"Understandable."

I smirk, despite the fact that I'm actually kind of broken up about it. "You're a dick."

"Far from an epiphany." Cal pulls up my invoice and straightens from the desk. "Car is good to go. Changed your oil, too."

"Thanks, man."

Jingle bells chime from behind me, pulling my attention over my shoulder. A jolt of ridiculous elation shoots through me as I watch Alyssa step inside, a bundle of nervous energy, her eyes on the floor. She tucks her lips between her teeth as she squeezes the strap of her handbag in a deathlike grip.

I grin.

"Hey, Alyssa," Cal greets.

"Hey." She finally looks up and squares her shoulders, her gaze zeroing in on me as a small smile crests. Then she glances over at Cal. "I'm here with Dante," she confesses.

Cal lifts an eyebrow. "I see that."

"We had sex."

"Heavily implied."

"Lots of sex," she continues, her voice rising in pitch, growing with conviction. "It was great. The best I've ever had. In fact, I want to do it again. Today. And I'm not ashamed of it. Not even a little."

She folds her arms across her chest as I gape at her, my jaw on the floor.

My boss appears unaffected by her uncensored tirade, but that's nothing new. He's basically unaffected by everything except for Lucy. He pulls the beanie off his head, ruffles his hair, then moves away from the desk. "Congratulations. I'll grab your keys, Dante."

He disappears into the garage.

Alyssa glances at me, her cheeks tinged pink. My silence thickens, causing her to shuffle between both feet as she tinkers with the edge of her shell-pink blouse. "Overshare?" she squeaks out.

I shake my head, blinking back at her. "Under share. You forgot to tell him about my impressive tongue dexterity."

Watching her squirm really is my favorite thing.

Blush continues to bloom on her porcelain cheeks as she steps forward, chin still tucked to her chest but eyes on me. There's something unguarded in the gesture, causing my skin to swelter.

She bites her lip, adding to the vulnerability. "I'm not ashamed of you, Dante. I'm not."

I swallow. "Okay."

"I just want to take it slow. Talk to Lucy, face to face. I've dated a lot, and I always jinx myself by running off and telling her every little detail, and then everything falls apart."

"You can tell her every little detail." I smirk.

"You know what I mean," she smiles back, stepping toe to toe with me and reaching for my hands. Giving them a squeeze, her expression softens. "Let's not rush this, okay? I'm feeling something for you. Something I wasn't expecting. I'm excellent at self-sabotage, so I want to take it slow."

I get it. Sort of.

Actually, I don't really get it, but I'm not one to overthink, so maybe this is a female thing.

I can be patient.

Our fingers interlace, and I lean down to press a kiss to her hairline. "Whatever you want, Bugs. But just so you know, Lucy will be excited about this. Promise."

"She thinks I hate you."

"No, she doesn't. She knows damn well you liked me from day one."

"That's your ego talking."

"My ego is astute."

Before I can steal another kiss, Cal plows through the service door. "Keys," he says, tossing them to me when I spin around. "See you Monday."

"Thanks, boss." He grumbles a goodbye before disappearing again, and I turn to Alyssa, her hands still clasped with mine. "How about we grab some actual Pad Thai? We can chill at my place and order in. You can finally meet my dog."

Meet my dog, meet my mattress.

It's a win-win.

I'm pleasantly surprised when there's not a trace of indecision on her face.

She steps back, nodding. "I'd love to."

Hell yes.

I never thought I'd go to a last-minute key party and leave with my dream girl. Alyssa Akins was the woman who would often worm her way into my subconscious; the one who got away. A missed opportunity that has always nagged at me.

It's funny because my mother used to tell me that second chances were just the universe's way of telling us that the timing wasn't right the first time around.

Something tells me it's finally our time.

I hold up my car keys, jingling them between my fingers. The little chili pepper pendant catches the light as it dangles from the keychain.

My favorite good luck charm.

Alyssa glances at it. Then she gifts me with a wide, genuine smile, the kind that reaches her eyes and has her whole face lighting up.

I toss her the keys with a wink. "You drive."

THE END

http://www.jenniferhartmannauthor.com

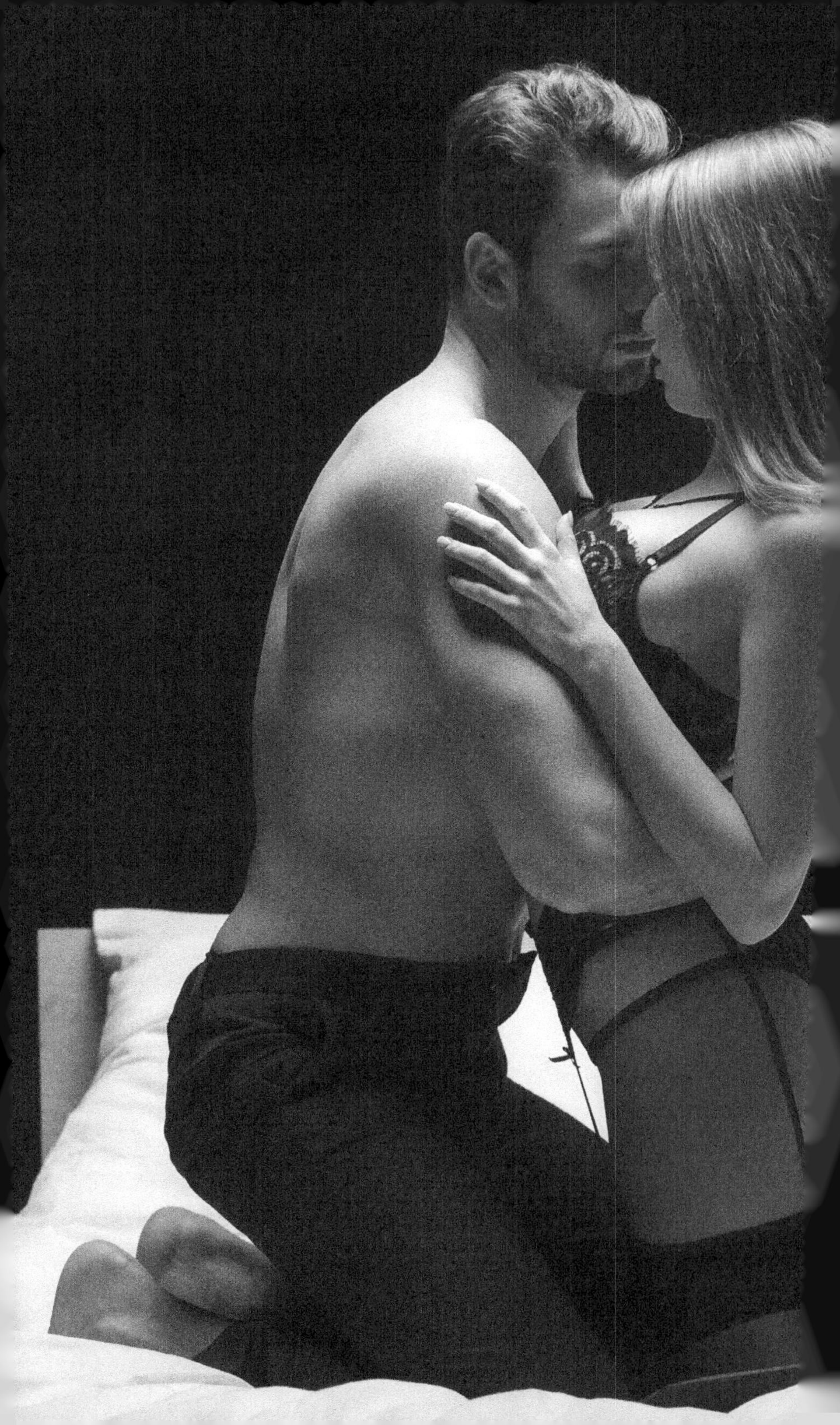

MR. JANUARY

K.K. ALLEN

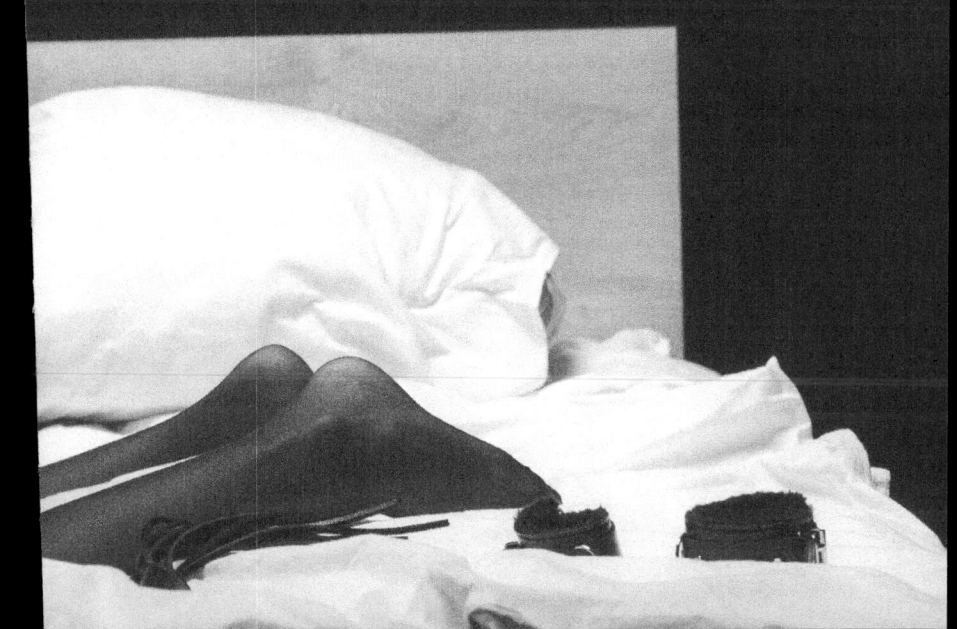

Chapter ONE

Lila

I've never sighed more with relief than I do the moment our plane touches down in Chicago. After a traffic accident caused me to miss my first flight in Asheville, North Carolina, and then bad weather caused my next flight to be delayed getting to my layover, I was beginning to think the universe was conspiring against me. Now, I'm finally halfway to my destination—to my new life in Seattle—where the grass will most definitely be greener. I'm starting to see the light.

Weight rolls off me like a steamroller as I make my way down the aisle, relieving me from the pressure, the noise, and the discomfort of everything I'm leaving behind. While leaving one police department for another, in a new state no-less, was a drastic decision, I know without a doubt it was the right one.

After checking the departure status of my next flight, I locate the private lounge reserved for my airline and head straight to the bar. I have two hours to kill, the need for a distraction, and a thirst that could rival the Sahara Desert. A stiff drink or two will do the trick.

There's only one other person at the bar. He's hunched over a full glass of amber liquid. There's a dark gray hoodie pulled up and over his head like he wants to be left alone, so I steer away from him, heading for the adjacent side.

"What'll it be, love?" asks the male bartender with a thick Australian accent. His name tag reads Sean.

I don't even have to look at the menu. Instead, I give him a pinched smile, trying desperately to mean it, and say, "Cosmo, please."

He nods and immediately reaches for a tumbler to start making my drink. I slip off my black jacket and lift my arms over my head to stretch. I shouldn't even be sitting after a long flight. I should be getting my steps in before my next leg of travel. But there's something so satisfying about a hard, cold drink in the middle of the afternoon when your only responsibility is to board a plane.

My arms fall from above my head, and I begin to stretch my neck, slowly rolling it in a circle. Ever since I was lead patrol sergeant in a high-speed pursuit two months ago and drove my car into the damn shooter to stop him, my body has been a mess of tight muscles, bruises, and sore bones.

"Damn, what is this, bar yoga? Can I join?"

My eyes snap to the man in the dark gray sweatshirt. The hood is still pulled over his head, but there's no mistaking his crystal blue eyes that roam the top half of my body in a lazy scroll. The man looks like he's on a mission to scan me into his brain like he has X-ray vision.

"Sorry," I tell him with a tilt of my head. "Class is full."

He quirks a brow. "Then I'll enjoy the view from here."

He leans back against his stool while swiping the hoodie from the top of his head, revealing a mop of long, wavy, dirty blond hair. A short layer of scruff frames a wide mouth with lips that look like they could happily bruise all the sensitive parts of my body.

He crosses his arms while narrowing his gaze at me, a challenge I'll happily accept. Luckily, Sean sets my drink in front of me before I have to. I pour all my focus into admiring the frothy pink cocktail while pinching the stem between two fingers then giving the glass a little swirl.

I try to ignore the man's eyes as I sip my drink. It's heaven on my lips and even dreamier going down my throat. When was the last time I had a drink? Two weeks? Three? Hell, I don't know. Between the demands of being a cop and my hunger for a promotion, I rarely found time to sleep.

I'm mid-sip when, out of my peripheral, I see someone sitting on the stool beside me. Call it my sixth sense from my profession, but I know it's the annoyingly dreamy blond. Why do all the assholes have to be hot? Of course, I don't know that he's an asshole, but his lazy flirtation hints him to be. Still, I should give him the benefit of the doubt.

"I'm bored." His words are flat, nonchalant. Like it's every day that he sits next to a stranger and confesses his state of mind. "Entertain me."

The corner of my mouth turns up with amusement. "Something tells me you're not easily entertained."

He raises his brows as his eyes flicker between mine. "And something tells *me* you'll find a way." He shrugs. "Tell me your deepest, darkest secret."

Laughter bubbles up my chest and out my throat before I can stop it. "And why would I tell a complete stranger my deepest, darkest secret?"

The corners of his mouth turn up even more. "That's precisely why you should tell me. Think about it. We don't know each other. We'll never see each other again after today. It'll be like counseling without the weeks of nervousness leading up to divulging the real shit."

Turning slightly to face him, I take a better look at the mysterious man sitting to my right. He's like a mix between a Ken Barbie, an Abercrombie model, and a mechanic. He's almost too perfect—with his fuck-me eyes and cocky smirk. Even his thick neck has me quelling the ache between my thighs. It all seems like a shallow guise to mask whatever he's buried deep down inside.

"Why don't we start with something a bit tamer?" I suggest. "Like..." I bring my drink to my lips while cycling through a mental list of questions. "What's your biggest fear?"

He barks out a laugh. "Hey, this was my game."

I pin him with my stare. "It's my game now."

There's a burn in my chest, and I'm not sure if it's from the liquid currency sliding down my throat or because of the way the gorgeous man smolders at me now. Maybe he's not used to the challenge. It wouldn't surprise me if most women fell at his feet, no questions asked.

When I set my drink down, I'm not immune to the heat in his gaze as it slips from my face to my lips then back up again.

"Public speaking," he admits. "I'm a private person for many reasons, but just the thought of standing in front of a crowd and delivering a speech or accepting an award makes me want to curl up into a ball."

I try to imagine the gorgeous man curling into the fetal position, vulnerabilities exposed, but I struggle to draw the picture. He looks far too confident and aware of his good looks to cower at any form of attention.

He quirks his brow like he's waiting for me to say something. "What about you?"

Nerves rattle my chest at just the thought of my biggest fear. It's no secret to my family and friends what it is, but I still hate talking about it. Mostly out of pride. *This was your question, you dummy.* "Heights." There it is. My first confession to a complete stranger, but he doesn't know the extent of my embarrassment, being a cop who's afraid of heights.

His brows pinch together. "Aren't you about to get on a plane?"

For some reason, his question releases some of the tension I racked up while confessing. "I am, but it's not the same."

He leans back, seemingly perplexed. "And just like that, I'm entertained." He leans forward, placing his elbows on the bar and resting his chin on top of his curled fists. "Please explain."

Heat rises up my cheeks. "Well, for one, I'm not the one flying the plane. Also, I always choose an aisle seat so I can pretend there isn't anything below me. But I think what helps the most is the fact that the odds are on my side when I fly. Besides, just because heights is my biggest fear doesn't mean I don't face it every now and then. It's never crippled me. My job simply wouldn't allow for that."

"What do you do for work?"

Alarm bells go off in my head. His questions are too personal. "If we're going to play this game, I think I should refrain from giving you stalking collateral."

His grin widens. "Fair enough. It's still my turn to ask a question though." He doesn't miss a beat. "Favorite sex position."

"The bridge."

His eyes widen like he's shocked I responded to that question at all. "What is that?"

I let out a laugh. "Like you don't have a book of sex positions tucked away in that horny brain of yours."

He flashes a grin. "Oh, I do. I just want to hear how you describe it."

For some reason, I'm not embarrassed at all describing it to him. "When a man is on his knees while I'm straddling him, then he picks up my hips and I lean all the way back." I curve my hand. "When I arch my back, the depth is explosive."

There's a glassy look to his narrowed gaze like he's trying to imagine what I'm describing. "You must be flexible."

"What about you?"

"I'm all muscle, sweetheart. I'm not flexible. But my hips are locked and loaded for gunfire."

I stifle a laugh. "I mean what's your favorite position? You have to answer your own question."

He pulls his drink to his lips before saying, "Upstanding citizen."

I nibble on my bottom lip while I attempt to imagine what's beneath his bulky sweatshirt. He must have muscles if he's able to hold a woman up like that to fuck her while standing. No man I've ever been with has been able to pull that off with me without tiring quickly. Maybe this guy is a football player, or a wrestler. Or maybe he just spends a lot of time in the gym.

"Favorite hobby?" I ask, aiming to lead us away from more sex conversations, but when I see a wicked gleam light up his eyes, I instantly regret not clarifying.

"Other than fucking?" He winks. "Water sports. Preferably slalom water skiing. Ever tried it?"

"Is that your question?"

He chuckles. "Is that yours?"

With that, I take an intermission, turn back to the bar and finish my drink just as Sean walks back over, making eye contact with both of us. "Another?"

Mystery man and I both agree to another which only proves dangerous considering the one drink has me buzzing really well. While Sean makes our drink, Mystery Man gets up to use the restroom. When he comes back, I can't take my eyes off him while he removes his jacket, revealing exactly what I was afraid of: six-feet-four-inches of pure muscle.

Now, all I can think about is how easily he could hoist me into his arms and fuck my brains out into tomorrow—something I clearly need after all this talk about positions. I've never been so sexually frustrated and aroused in all my life.

Somehow, after we get our second round of drinks, we end up playing the same game, asking each other random questions—mostly tame, sometimes completely inappropriate—and I find myself completely comfortable with this stranger who I'm looking forward to never seeing again.

I've lost count of my drinks when it's his turn to ask another question and he leans closer, his sexy mouth tipped up at the corners while his eyes rest on my lips. "Have you ever kissed a complete stranger?"

It's less a question and more an invitation, causing my next breath to be caught somewhere between my heart and my lungs. I manage to shake my head in response.

He leans closer, his lips only a few inches from mine. "Do you want to?"

Instinct has me shaking my head again while my heart pounds a million miles a minute. *Would he really kiss me if I said yes?*

The corners of his mouth tip up another margin as he leans in again. "Liar."

His husky words float between us like a threat, the whiskey he's been sipping on only adding to my current level of intoxication as it blows over me like an erotic haze.

"I think you do want to kiss me," he taunts like he's wedged into my brain, hearing all the dirty thoughts I've played over and over in my head since meeting him.

He's so cocky, it's infuriating. But damn, why does he have to be right? There's something so exhilarating about not knowing a single identifying fact about this man. He's just a stranger in a bar on his way to who-knows-where. And he's sexy as hell.

A thick hand wraps my upper thigh, and my normal reaction would be to remove it, but my curiosity is too strong, so I part my legs slightly instead. His eyes flash and stare down at the subtle invitation, then he slides his hand up another margin as if testing me. Again, I don't stop him, even if his meaty hand is teasing the bottom hem of my skirt.

His eyes snap to mine like he needs more permission than what I've already given him. So, I part my knees another margin, quivering when his calloused hands slip an inch beneath my skirt.

What is wrong with me? Who am I right now? Clearly, the cosmopolitans are getting to my head because never in my life have I flirted so openly with a stranger. But today, I'm not Lila Goldman, the new Lieutenant for the Seattle PD. I'm a mystery woman in an airport who very much wants to fuck a complete stranger. Which is exactly why I slip my hands around his thick neck, pull myself the final inch toward him, and skim his plush lips with a smile.

"How much time do you have before your flight?"

The man groans, his fingers sliding another inch toward my center. "I'm thinking about giving up my seat to someone on standby. There will be plenty of flights tomorrow."

My lips curl into a smile. "What an upstanding citizen you are."

His lids narrow at the term as his tongue darts out to wet his bottom lip. "What about you?"

There's a clear buzz in the air when my lips close the final gap to meet his. "Same."

Chapter TWO

Lila

It's too easy. He tells me to go change my flight first while he pays for our drinks, and since the flight I was supposed to be on is full, they are more than happy to swap my flight for one in the morning. When I'm done, I head straight to the airport hotel where Mystery Man and I planned to meet.

I'm fully aware of the risk I'm taking by agreeing to this rendezvous. I'm also aware that he has already gone through airport security so the only weapon he carries is that cocky ass grin permanently attached to his face. That, I can handle. And even with his thick, athletic build, my extensive self-defense training could take him if necessary. But my gut instinct tells me Mystery Man is harmless—physically, emotionally—and that's what makes this all so thrilling.

"I'll take care of this," he says huskily as he sidles up to me at the hotel counter while whipping out his credit card.

He doesn't try to hide the details on his card from me even though we've so much as decided to keep personal details to ourselves. But the name Samuel Waters is visible just long enough for me to lock it into my memory.

I quickly type out a text to my best friend.

Me: Samuel Waters. Chicago O'Hare Airport. Don't ask questions.

Then I tuck my phone away, biting down a smile at the story I'll be telling her later. She'll probably kill me, but it will be so worth it.

Samuel peers at me over his shoulder. "Everything good?"

I nod while shifting my carryon that rests on my shoulder. "Yup. Everything good with the room?"

"Here you go, sir." He flips back around to where the woman behind the desk is speaking. "Two keys." She slides a map across the counter next and begins to scribble all over it, showing us where all the amenities are. Gym, pool, arcade, business lounge. Like we care.

Finally, he thanks the woman, spins around, and takes the bag from my shoulders, adding it to his, then nods toward the set of elevators up ahead. "After you."

We step into the elevator, and he reaches over to push the number four. "I requested an inside room so you wouldn't have to worry about looking out the window, but they didn't have any. They did promise to make sure the curtains were closed, though."

His comment is almost more surprising than my decision to skip my flight to spend the night with a stranger. "That was... sweet."

He chuckles and shakes his head. "Trust me. If you knew me, you wouldn't be calling me sweet."

I lean back against the wall and laugh. "Yeah, well, I guess it's a good thing we don't know each other. I don't usually take risks like this."

His eyes connect with mine, an electricity running between us. "Then I guess this is something new for both of us."

I tilt my head. "You're not married or anything, are you?" I flush at the fact that I should have thought to ask that sooner.

But he shakes his head, giving me no time to question it. "No wife. No girlfriend." Then he grins. "Just you, Cosmo Girl."

Something about the nickname makes me feel giddy inside. Like I'm back in high school flirting with the high school quarterback.

"What about you? You married? Divorced? Kids?"

There's a tightness in my chest at the question. Perhaps, if I had stuck around North Carolina, two of the three would eventually be true. "No, no, and no."

He squints at me for a few beats, then shakes his head.

"What?" I ask him with a laugh.

"Nothing." He shakes his head again. "I'd love to know why a beautiful woman like you is single, but then you'll want to know why a drop-dead gorgeous man like me is single, and then we'll be crossing the line as far as info-sharing goes."

Laughing again, I nod. "You're right. We should refrain from those types of questions. We're just two single people in the right place at the right time."

There he goes smoldering at me again. "I like that," he says easily.

Jesus. The way Samuel looks at me like I'm a fresh piece of meat and he's a lion being held captive in a cage—I never want another man to look at me again if it's not like that.

The door to the elevator dings, distracting him from his meal and me from my predator. My chaotic nerves fill the empty space in the silence that follows. While I know exactly what I agreed to, I'm shocked that I'm going through with it.

Samuel takes my hand and leads me down the hallway a few doors until we get to Room 424. He taps the keycard against the plate and pushes the door open when he gets the green light. Seconds later, we're inside the hotel room—just a small room with a bathroom, television, and a king bed. The windows are completely blacked out, as promised, and I'm grateful that there's one less thing I have to worry about today.

He sets our bags down and slides his sweatshirt back off his arms and grins down at me. It's then that I get a good grasp on his size compared to mine. He's well over a foot taller than me and almost three times the size, if I were to guess. Maybe I underestimated my strength when it comes to this man. Because right now, I feel like he might just be able to suffocate me with one wrap of those thick arms.

I guess that's just a risk I'll have to take.

As if he can read my thoughts, he backs up against the opposite wall and tilts his head with narrowing eyes. "If I take a shower, will you still be here when I get out?"

How does he do that—make me feel so calm in such a strange situation? I step forward, once again feeling like I'm a completely different woman—one who packed her worries away and committed to enjoying this one selfish thing she's being offered— and I rest my palms on his chest while gazing up at his handsome face.

"How about I join you?"

His nostrils flare and his eyes blaze with a heat that matches everything I'm feeling in my chest. I'm an inferno, a wildfire, and it might just take all day and night to put out my flames.

He brings his thumb and forefinger to my chin, holding me there while he searches my eyes. Maybe he's giving me time to back out. Maybe he's calculating everything he wants to do to me. I'm not sure. But when his lips touch down it's nothing like it was back at that bar. This kiss is primal, hungry, vicious—but in the most intoxicating way.

His hands move to my ass, palming me firmly like he's laying all his intentions out right there. He's not going to be gentle—not in the least—but neither am I.

I slide my fingernails up his chest, just hard enough to leave a little indent, a trail of desire up to his neck then his scalp before I'm tangled in his long, disheveled locks. His groan rumbles between us as he pulls me closer, his hard cock digging into the skin just below my belly button.

He's so tall and strong, and he uses it all to his advantage. His strength locks me in as he towers over me, sucking the flesh from my lips with his kiss. His palms slip down my ass, just enough to grip me there before he hoists me up.

My legs wrap easily around his waist as he begins to walk us into the bathroom. I'm so focused on our bruising kiss, but I hear the shower turn on and then I feel him plant me on a cold, hard surface.

When his mouth detaches from mine, my eyes flutter open just in time to see him pull his shirt up and over his head, revealing the most defined body I've ever seen in my life. I run my hand over his cut muscles, unable to hide my awe.

"I didn't know bodies like this really existed."

The corner of his mouth tugs up into a pleased smile. "Thank my job for keeping me in shape."

My desire to know about Samuel Waters has suddenly quadrupled. "Let me guess," I purr while tracing the divots in his abs. "Football player."

He shakes his head. "Not since high school."

I stick to my previous guesses from back at the bar. "Wrestler."

He chuckles and slips down his jeans, leaving his red boxer briefs intact. "Unless you mean the way I'm about to wrestle you in that bed, the answer is no again."

I smirk, my finger instinctively moving to his elastic waistband of his boxer briefs, eyes drawn to the very clear outline swelling there.

"A fitness model."

He bites down on his bottom lip, drawing attention to the exact place where my mouth wants to be again. "No, but I did model one time for a charity thing."

The clues he's giving seem to be leading me in the right direction. I feel like I'm closer.

"A personal trainer?" I ask, still relying on my earlier guesses.

"No, but I do spend a lot of time in my gym at work."

That's when it clicks. I look up to find his amused eyes waiting for me to win the guessing game like he's proud of his profession. "You're a firefighter."

His grin lights up his entire face. "Ding ding ding. And the charity thing I modeled for was a calendar." He winks. "You can call me Mr. January."

Heat blasts my cheeks, but I don't know why. Suddenly, I'm more than insanely attracted to my mystery man. Not only is he hot as sin but he's a first responder, like me.

"Now you have to tell me what you do."

Panic runs its course through my veins. "I thought we didn't want to get too personal." But the moment I say it, I realize his question is only fair.

He narrows his eyes. "You started it."

"Fine," I say with a sigh, eager to get past the talking and back to kissing. "I'm a cop."

His eyes light up with a mix between intrigue and fear. "Oh, shit. Are you going to cuff me, Cosmo Girl?"

"It's your lucky day. I'm off-duty."

A dimple pops in his cheek, as if he could be any cuter. "I wouldn't call that lucky," he says while his fingers grip the bottom hem of my shirt.

I lift my arms, allowing him to pull my shirt up and over my head. "Yeah, well, I don't carry cuffs with me everywhere I go, Calendar Boy."

His eyes dip to my chest then flick back up to my eyes. "Would you cuff me if you did?"

"Depends." I tilt my head. "Would you give me a reason to?"

"Most likely."

With that, he takes hold of the waistband of my pants and yanks them just hard enough to remove them, even with my ass still flush against the counter, leaving me in just my bra and panties.

The door to the bathroom is closed and steam is already filling the room. He's in no hurry to get me into the shower. Instead, he plants himself against the counter and pulls me toward him to where his hard cock meets my center.

Firm hands continue to grip my waist while his gaze travels over me like he's planning his mission. Feeling impatient, I find the clasp of my bra and unlatch it. Samuel's eyes darken on my breasts as the fabric holding them falls away.

"Fuck me," he says on a breath. "Your body is unreal."

I smile, taking pride in how hard I work to balance my love for eating and my need to stay fit for my job. I've always loved my curves—my thick thighs, my ass that seems to jiggle in the mirror no matter how much cardio I do, and my small waist in comparison only draw attention to my thicker parts.

"I think," I say slowly while my arms wrap around his neck again, "you should stop gawking and start *doing*." The way I speak to him like he's one of my former patrolmen thrills me to my core.

Samuel isn't someone who needs to be told twice. His mouth lands hard on mine, molding our lips together and snaking his tongue into my mouth like he possesses every inch he's exploring. I use the kiss as an opportunity to strip him off his boxer briefs, peeling them over his firm ass and down his muscular thighs until he growls, rips his mouth from mine, and shoves them all the way down.

"Oh my." My eyes are wide on his monster cock. The length, the width—I should have known given the size of his body—but nothing could have prepared me for this.

He doesn't seem to notice my suspended disbelief while he strips me of my panties. I gasp as he pries my knees apart with his hands.

"Look at that pretty little pussy," he rasps, looking almost as taken aback as I was looking at his cock.

His palms move up and down my thighs, inching closer and closer to my center. His fingers are so close to touching me where I want him most. Just the thought of one of those thick digits entering me has me quaking with need.

He groans, like the sight of me physically hurts, then his lids flip up and his gaze locks on mine. "Ready to get wet, pretty girl?"

Chapter THREE

Lila

"Ready to get wet?"

My first thought is that he's going to touch me. Finally. He's been eyeing the prize for so long at this point that my arousal is practically seeping out of me and leaking onto the counter. I need his fingers, his cock, his mouth. I'll take anything at this point. But he doesn't touch me there. Instead, he lifts me off the counter then sets me down on my feet.

"Get in the shower," he growls. "I want to get a good look at you."

Peering up at him, I step away, not breaking eye contact until I turn around completely. It's a decent-sized glass shower with a door and a rain shower head. When I step inside, I leave the door behind me open and walk directly under the water.

I don't stop to look back at him. I don't need to since I can feel his heated gaze on me, watching the water soak my hair and run over my skin. I make a show of it, running my hands slowly up and over my breasts to my neck, then back down to the space between my thighs.

"Face me," he demands, the husk in his tone deepening with desire.

My body turns and my eyes lock on his through the fogging glass as I run my two fingers over my clit. His hand has his length in a chokehold, stroking it in perfect pace with my movements.

"Keep your hand there, pretty girl, and press your tits against the glass."

I step forward, gasping at the cold as my hardened nipples smash against the window, but I never stop circling my clit with my fingers.

"Come join me," I taunt before I dart my tongue out to lick the glass.

He groans and quickens his strokes. "Oh, I will. But I want to watch you come first."

"Come make me," I demand, already tired of his game.

His eyes narrow and he shakes his head. "Patience, baby girl. We have all night. Trust me when I say that you will be thoroughly fucked. But not yet. Right now, I need to see you fuck yourself." He quickens his strokes around his cock again. "Put your fingers inside of you."

I growl with frustration but do as he says, letting my wet fingers push inside my pussy and shuddering at the contact. With all this build-up, I feel like I could come any second. Knowing he's watching me, desperate for more, I don't hold back either. I pump myself full of my fingers until I feel the heat begin to build deep inside of me.

"Good girl," he husks while stepping forward until he's inches away from me, with just the shower wall separating us. He leans his palm against the glass, looking me in the eye as we both pleasure ourselves. "Are you getting close?"

I nod while everything begins to tighten below the waist.

His eyes squeeze together tightly before he nods. "Me too. Just tell me when."

In seconds, I'm warning him of my unraveling, shocked to find that he's right there with me, his seed spurting like a firing squad at the shower wall. And holy fuck, it's a like a Santa bag of a release. Neverending, in thick solid streams, one, two, three, then four times.

He doesn't waste another second entering the shower and pulling me to him in a passionate kiss, our bodies slick with water.

He pushes me against the back wall, his fingers slipping between my thighs and over my tight, quivering hole.

I'm still coming down off my high when he pushes two thick fingers into me. The fullness is nearly blinding as he sinks as deep as he can possibly go. "You have the prettiest little pussy, you know that?" he murmurs against my mouth. "So tight, I might as well fuck your ass."

His dirty words only turn me on more. "Is that where you want to take me? In my ass?" I murmur back.

He growls and grips my ass cheek, squeezing as he flicks two fingers deep inside me. "I want your cunt, your ass, your mouth. But as hard as I want to fuck you right now, it might hurt a little."

I shake my head. "You won't hurt me." I skim my nose along his lips. "I don't want you to hold back."

He groans and slips his hand from my ass up my stomach, between my chest, not stopping until he gets to my neck. His fingers press down slowly around me, and he squeezes just slightly. "You'll be sore tomorrow."

A wicked grin lights up my face. "Good."

Something grows hard between us, and I reach down to take hold of it. "Wow, Calendar Boy, you sure are blessed, aren't you?"

Amusement tilts his lips. "I believe you're the one who's about to be blessed, sweet girl. I'm just here to deliver."

Another orgasm bursts through me, pulsing around his fingers while he continues to jerk inside me. Even when I'm done, he doesn't pull out. Instead, he kneels before me, lifts one of my legs over his shoulder, and looks up at me with one telling gaze.

If I ever needed a warning more in my life, it's right then. I watch as he covers my clit with his mouth as his fingers continue their dance deep inside me. Jesus, I've never built up to an orgasm faster than I do that next one.

"You're spoiling me," I tell him with my next set of panting breaths.

He peers up at me with a smile, his lips soaked from my arousal and the shower. "As all good girls should be."

"Don't good boys deserve to get spoiled too?"

He nods. "Sure." "Then he shakes his head. "But I'm not a good boy. I'm bad." He stands and presses his lips to my ear. "And bad boys just need to get fucked."

He lifts me into his arms again, which I'm beginning to learn truly is his all-time favorite move, then he's carrying me back out of the shower, flipping off the water behind him, and then walking me into the bedroom.

When he flips on the overhead light, I laugh in surprise. "Afraid you'll miss something."

He grins and tosses me onto the bed, watching me land with a little bounce as he stands at the edge. "I only get one night with you. I'm afraid I'll miss everything."

As bad and dirty as Samuel Waters is proving to be, there's something else there too. A vulnerable side that he clearly masks with all his might. It doesn't stop me from wanting him to rail me into tomorrow. Actually, it has the opposite effect.

"Turn around," he commands. "Hang your head off the mattress."

I love how he commands me. For once, I'm not the one in charge and it's hotter than I ever expected. I spin around, so that my head is now hanging over the edge of the mattress, his hard cock hanging above me.

He reaches down with one hand while he holds himself with the other. Thick fingers glide over my breast before pinching my nipple between two fingers.

"Look at you," he says, his gaze darkening where my mouth waits open for him. "Salivating for me."

I reach for him, replacing his hand with mine and stroking him toward me. "You're so big," I rasp.

"Think you can take all of me?"

My eyes widen as they meet his, and I brace for his entry. "I'm sure going to try."

Chapter FOUR

Samuel

Her beautiful mouth stretches as I glide between her lips. With every disappearing inch, my pulse races faster. Cosmo Girl is a beautiful sight as she takes me. With her thick curves, heaving breasts, rose-colored nipples, and glistening pussy, she's a sight to behold as we work ourselves up to the grand finale of our little rendezvous. Because when I finally get to fuck her, I'm not going to hold back.

I knew from the second I laid eyes on her that I had to have her. It wasn't even the high ponytail that accentuated every detail of her almond-shaped green eyes and heart-shaped face, or the natural pout to her mouth that I couldn't stop imagining around my cock. It was the way she challenged me from the start yet glared back at me with the same fuck-me expression I knew I was delivering to her. But it wasn't until we started talking honestly and openly about sex positions that I began to wonder how I could get her alone.

I groan as her lips close around my throbbing length. She hasn't taken all of me yet, but with a few inches to spare, she's close enough. Rocking my hips, I keep my pace measured, slow. My size hasn't scared her away yet, and I'll do everything possible to help her acclimate. I'm not a complete asshole.

Every sound she makes in the back of her throat is a cherry on top of the pleasure I feel around her slippery mouth. It's the moaning between the gagging that has every muscle in my body clenching in anticipation of a release. But as much as I'm desperate to see myself decorate my beautiful companion with every inch of my seed, I'm enjoying this view far too much to let it end soon.

Her perfect tits, the bottom of her dark brown hair sweeping the floor from its high ponytail, her watery green eyes, and agonizingly sweet curves. If I had a type as far as looks went, she would be the ultimate definition of my dream girl.

"Think you can take more of me?"

When she nods my cock slips another inch down her throat. Fuck, I'm going to blow any second. "Gahh," I groan, desperate to hold on for a little bit longer.

She makes a choking sound with the back of her throat and then there's a pressure squeezing around the crown of my cock. "Fuck yes," I gasp, realizing she just swallowed around me. "Gag on me just like that again."

Her hand comes up, making a ring with her fingers around my base as she pulls me deeper. She swallows again and that's all it takes to unleash the surge of my release.

"That did it," I growl and rip my length from her mouth. As much as I love a good sploogeapalooza, I'd rather paint her pretty tits than her throat. Besides, we still have the rest of the night to look forward to.

I grab hold of myself just as my orgasm takes hold of my entire body. It only takes three strokes before my seed spills on her face and neck then chest. And if that's not sexy enough, her hand slips between her thighs like she's ready for more.

"One sec." I slip off the bed and walk to the bathroom where I run hot water in the sink. Then I grab a washcloth, soak it, then ring it dry before bringing it back to where Cosmo Girl hasn't moved an inch, her fingers still buried between her thighs.

I kneel to where her face is hanging off the bed and begin to clean her in all the places I spilled on her. Her eyes bat to mine like she can't believe the thoughtfulness. But as soon as I'm done, I spin her around and drag her to the edge of the mattress. I grab her legs and pull them on either side of my head so it's her ass that's hanging off now, then I bring my mouth down to where she glistens just for me.

"You're a beautiful girl, you know that?" I take a swipe of her pussy with my tongue to make it clear of what I'm referring to now, although I'm convinced there isn't a single inch of her that isn't laced with perfection.

"Sweet too," I add as I flick my tongue over her center.

She quivers and I growl while locking my arms around her legs to steady her.

"And so fucking sensitive."

I lash out my tongue at her again, this one lapping her back-to-front in one long and slow motion. "I'm going to devour this pussy. No mercy. You hear me, Cosmo Girl?" I lift my lids to meet her gaze.

She nods so fast like she doesn't dare miss the opportunity. "Yes, please," she begs.

I smile and lean down again. "Since you said please."

***

Lila

Holy shit, Samuel Waters was not lying when he promised to devour me. His tongue is like a metal detector searching every inch of land for that one nugget of gold. My pussy is his mine, there for his exploration.

He makes me come, repeatedly. First with his tongue and then with his fingers then again with his mouth paying special attention to my clit. I'm like a war zone, firing off in all directions, begging for mercy, begging for *him*.

He's just given me another orgasm when he stands up, his mouth shimmering with my arousal, his heated eyes scouring every inch of me, and his cock so hard and ready. Meanwhile, I'm already spent. He's taken every drop from my body. At least, that's how it feels.

My muscles are weak, my breaths feel labored, and all my energy is completely depleted. But looking back at Samuel—the intentions in his eyes, crystal clear—I can see that none of that matters. We're nowhere close to finished.

He's not immune to the sexual energy running between us. His breaths come hard and heavy, his abs working overtime, while he walks to his overnight bag and pulls out a box of condoms. Magnums, of course.

He tears open the box and rips open a package then rolls it expertly over his length.

"C'mere," he commands, when he steps back over to the bed.

But I can't move. I can barely think straight. All I know is that I've never experienced so many consecutive orgasms in my life. It was never even a goal. Now, I don't even know how I'll recover.

I groan and reach my hand out so he can help me up. He does, and as soon as I'm sitting in front of him, he's lifting me into his arms, wrapping my legs around his waist, and kissing me like I've deprived him of my lips all this time.

"What did I tell you?" he murmurs against my lips. "I told you I was going to devour you."

"And now I can't move a muscle."

He chuckles. "You don't have to, baby girl." He positions himself so his cock is budded up against my entrance. "I've got plenty of strength for the both of us."

A second wind blows through me at that moment. If I only get one night with this sexy man, I'm going to make it count. "Just do me one favor," I tell him.

"Anything," he rasps, and somehow, I know he means it.

I bite down on my bottom lip, fighting my smile. "Don't you dare go easy on me."

Amusement shimmers in his eyes. "In that case, you're going to have to tell me your name so I can worship you properly."

There's only a second of hesitation that halts me before I realize I already know his name, even if he doesn't realize it. It's only fair for him to know mine.

I reach between us, offering my hand. "Lila Goldman. Pleasure to meet you."

His amused expression transitions to a full-on megawatt smile. "Lila," he says with a flick of his tongue. "I like that." He takes my hand and squeezes it instead of shaking. "Samuel Waters. But you can call me Sam if that's easier for you to scream when I'm fucking you against that wall."

Laughing, I release my hand from his and tighten my hold around his neck. "In that case, *Sam*, I'll do my best to hang on tight."

I barely have time to take another breath before he's entering me in one long thrust. My eyes fly open at the instant pressure from a fullness I've never experienced before. It's a blinding intensity—like tubing down a rocky stream after a rainstorm. There's no stopping the rush, the obstacles, the direction. There's no getting off this ride. All I can do is hold on for dear life.

Chapter FIVE

Lila

My mind stirs before my body does that next morning. At least, I think it's morning. The sheets are warm, the room is pitch black, and my entire body aches at the slightest movement. It's like I was hit by a bus, yet I've never felt more relaxed in my entire life.

I don't want to move, but something deep inside me screams that I have no choice. When I attempt to stir again, my bare skin rubs the sheets, and that's when it begins to click together.

The airport lounge.

The cosmopolitans.

Samuel Waters.

The change in flight plans.

The hotel.

And then a string of orgasms so long I know I'll never recover.

When I shift again, that's when I feel the rock hard body beside me. While I might have made the best decision of my life to forego my flight to fuck a stranger, I know this has to be the end. The last thing I want is to stick around for Samuel to wake up so we can exchange an awkward goodbye before going our separate ways. I don't want that.

I don't want to exchange phone numbers or pretend like last night was something it most definitely was not. I just want to complete my one-way trip to Seattle and start my new life. I'm ready.

As quietly as I can, I tiptoe around the room, gathering my belongings before stepping into the bathroom to wash up a little and get dressed. Then I'm slipping out the door and into the hotel hallway with my overnight bag in my hand.

My heart is still beating fast when I get to my gate and sit in the waiting area while I wait for boarding. I'm early, so I tug my hoodie over my head and stare in the direction of the gate door to avoid looking at where I might accidentally spot Samuel.

By the time the airline starts to announce boarding, I'm convinced when I look back on last night, it will be nothing but a distant memory. I might even wonder if it was all just a dream. A hot, erotic, mind-fuck of a dream.

I shudder when I think about the way Samuel hoisted me into his arms and plunged into me like he couldn't last another second without me. The way he slid his hand around my neck and gripped me there while he bounced me on his dick until I came. The way he moved me to the bed and straight into my favorite position and then helped me arch my back so I could feel every sturdy inch of him inside me.

At least I've committed the entire night into my memory.

A sigh of relief filters through me when I make it onto the plane and into my seat. A middle seat since I switched my flight and everything else had been booked up.

I pull out my earphones and slip them onto my head, then connect the Bluetooth to my phone and start one of my favorite playlists.

It's all cute and fun until a large figure sits down in the aisle seat beside me. My entire body tenses, knowing exactly who just joined me before even looking at him.

Slowly, I turn my head to meet the eyes of none other than Samuel Waters.

"Really? Not even a goodbye?"

I blink harder like that will fix the very vivid mirage playing out in front of me. "I'm sorry." I shake my head. "Did you find a way onto my aircraft just to ask me that?"

The corner of his mouth pulls up in a sideways smirk. "Don't flatter yourself, babe. This is my flight, too."

Again, I blink at him, this time leaving my lids closed a few seconds longer. Maybe when I open them, he'll be gone. But when I find myself staring back into the blue eyes of Samuel Waters, I begin to register what he just told me.

"You're moving to Seattle?"

He nods. "Moving to Seattle, actually."

I blink back at him, wondering if I'm somehow getting punked. "Wait...*I'm* moving to Seattle." I tilt my head. "You're fucking with me, right?"

He chuckles and shakes his head. "I might have fucked you, sweetheart, but I'm definitely not fucking with you. Tampa didn't exactly work out for me, and Seattle wanted me. So..." He shrugs like moving is the easiest thing in the world for him. "Here I come."

I fight the instinct to roll my eyes. "Of course."

The arrogant smile on his face is enough to plant a tiny seed of resentment for my decisions. Isn't this how my luck always plays out? Everything follows me. And now, Samuel will be more than a distant erotic dream, he'll be a shadow—one that I now have to share a city with. And something tells me not even Seattle is big enough for the two of us.

"Excuse me," says a soft voice above us.

I look up to see a pretty woman smiling down at us, a young child standing beside her.

"I think these are our seats," she says, pointing to where Samuel is sitting. But as her eyes connect with his, something changes in her expression. She frowns slightly, then tilts her head like she recognizes him.

A sinking feeling weighs down my gut. Of course. He's probably fucked her too.

Samuel doesn't seem to share her recognition. Instead, he scrambles out of the seat and into the aisle. "Sorry about that. I was just saying hello to my friend here." He flashes another cocky smile at me. "Guess I'll see you in Seattle, Cosmo Girl."

Before I can say anything, he's walking down the aisle toward the back of the plane and the woman behind him is smiling at me, appearing flushed.

"I'm so sorry about that," she says. "I didn't mean to interrupt your conversation."

I wave my hand in the air. "It's no problem, really. I barely know the guy."

The woman ushers her son to enter our section of seats. "You get the window, Tate. I'm just going to be right here on the aisle, okay?"

I frown when I realize what's going on. "I'm happy to move to the aisle if you'd like to sit next to your son."

The woman's expression lights up. "Really? That's so nice of you. I mean, if you don't mind."

The little boy latches onto his mom's arm. "Say yes, mommy." She laughs. "Thank you so much."

I get out of my seat so they can filter into theirs, and then I sit back down in the aisle seat and buckle my seatbelt. "I'm Meadow, by the way," the woman says once she sits down. "And this is my son, Tate."

I introduce myself and then leave them so they can get comfortable. But something continues to gnaw at me long after we begin to taxi down the runway and I turn to the woman beside me.

"I'm sorry, I couldn't help but notice you look at the man who was sitting here earlier. Do you know him?"

The woman cringes a little before she nods. "He used to work with my husband." Then she laughs lightly. "Well, they were on this charity project together."

Something clicks. "The firefighters calendar? He was a model in it, right?"

She nods, her eyes lighting up like it's something she's proud of. "I was the photographer for it this past year. That man, Samuel, was in the calendar the year before my time."

"He was Mr. January."

Meadow flushes again and I wish I knew what was going on in her head. "That's right. My husband ended up taking his spot in the last calendar, though."

Confused at why Samuel left that part out, I tilt my head. "Why's that?"

Meadow searches my eyes like she's trying to figure out if I'm trustworthy or not. "Well," she says slowly. "Samuel is kind of known to be a troublemaker. He got fired before we started shooting and kind of left us in a bind." She frowns and then leans in slightly. "I don't mean to speak ill of him if he's a friend of yours."

I shake my head. "I don't know him all that well. Maybe that's a good thing." I give the woman a smile, hoping to reassure her that she hasn't crossed the line in any way.

She leans back in her seat and nods. "It's probably for the best. If it were me, I'd run fast and far away from Samuel Waters."

Her eyes meet mine again, a knowing twinkle in them. "But I can already see that you're not me, and from what I saw, he seems to be very intrigued by you." She shrugs. "Who knows. Maybe there's hope for Mr. January once and for all."

***

For now, you can meet Samuel Waters in Meadow and Asher's story, Fired Up. For more information, go to my website.

https://www.kkallen.com/

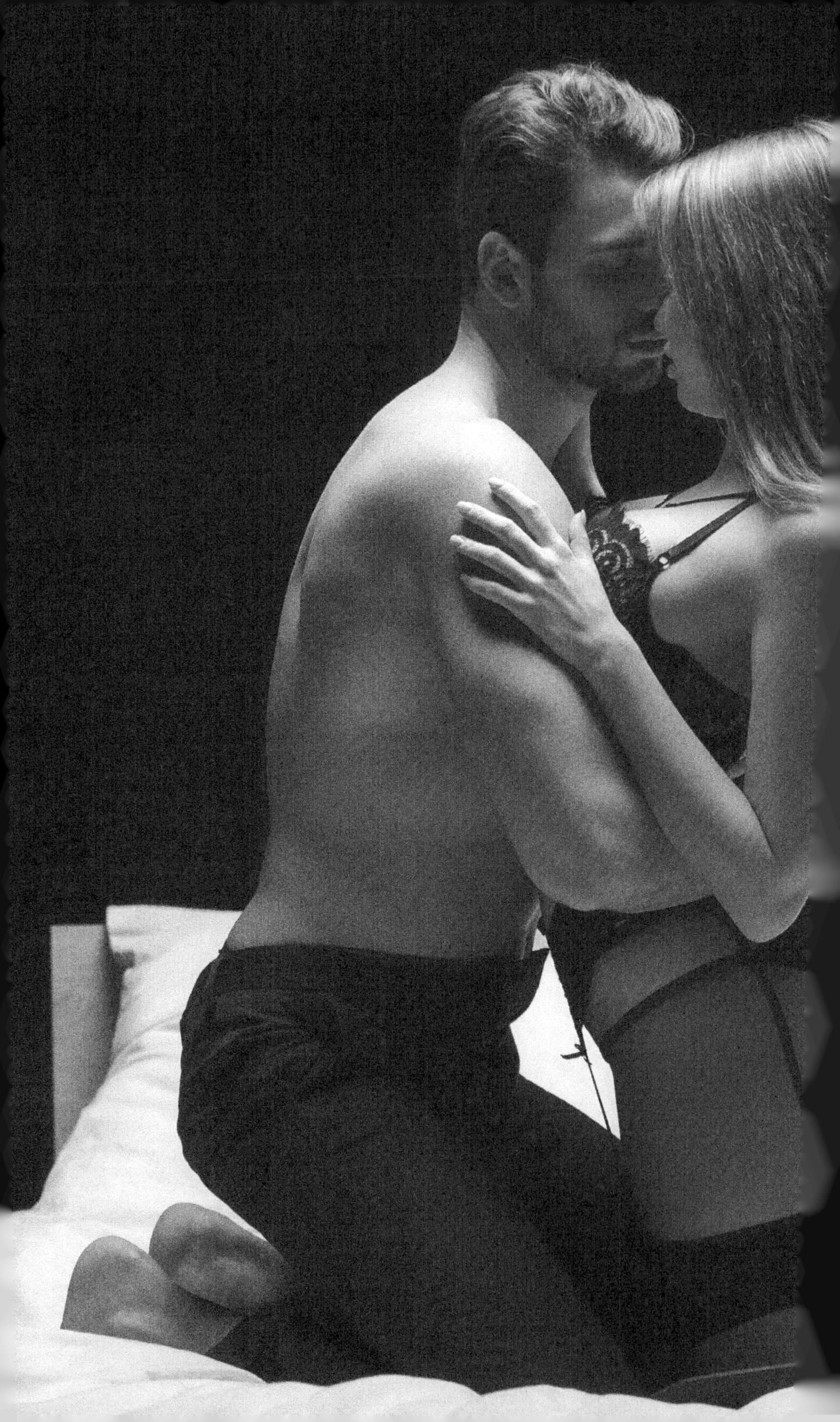

IOU

KRISTY MARIE

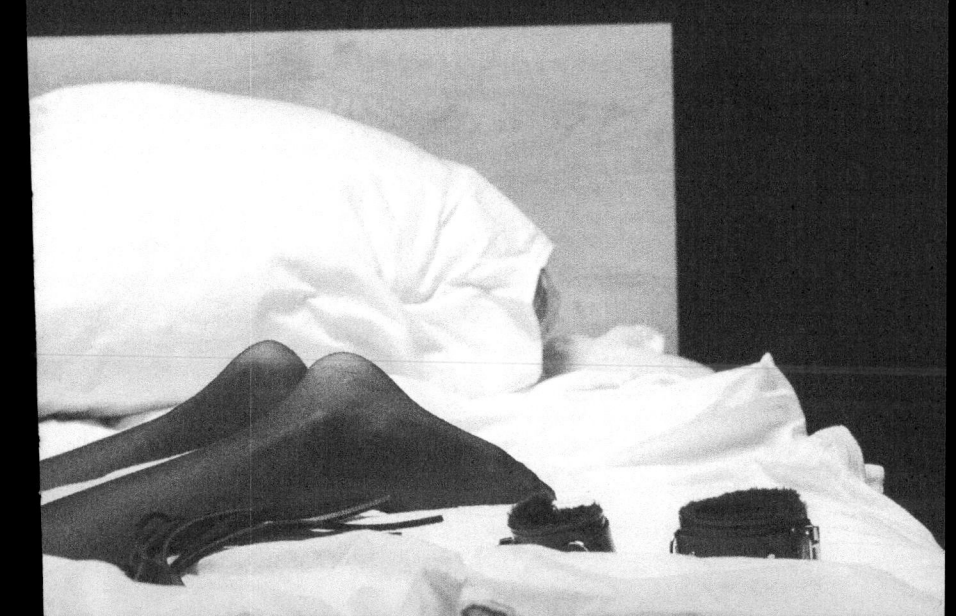

Chapter ONE

Ainsley

"I'm going to ask you one last time, Ainsley." Maverick's lips drop to the sensitive spot behind my ear, whispering threats that only my vagina cares about. "What did you do?"

"What did *you* do?" I retort as he crowds me, forcing me backward until the heat from the car scorches the backs of my thighs. "Leaving me alone was your mistake."

His body presses against mine as he leans into me, his breath fanning over my neck. Shivers break out along my skin, cascading all the way down.

"Is that so?"

I nod with a smirk that only he is infamous for. "I thought you knew better."

His eyebrow arches at my boldness. His hand slides along the goose bumps staining the base of my neck as his fingers disappear in my dark hair. My head falls back as Maverick pulls my head far enough back that I meet his eyes.

"I thought you'd know better than to play dumb." I can barely focus on his words as his breath fans over my pebbled skin. It sends a surge of excitement down my spine when he speaks again. "You're a smart girl, Ainsley, so tell me what happened to my car."

"I have no idea," I chirp, masking my voice to sound completely oblivious to the reason we're stranded and the fact that it's all my fault. "Maybe it's user error."

A growl echoes from his throat. He yanks my hair harder, making me smile. "User error, huh? You're saying the reason the gas tank is empty after I left *you* to fill it up is *my* doing?"

"I swear I heard the pump click," I chide, brushing my hands over his sculpted chest. Hills of muscle bunch beneath his shirt as I rake my hands over his pec. "I can't help that you let me drive so you could nap."

"Did you not pay attention to the gauge?"

"I did!"

I totally didn't. I was too busy singing.

His hand flies to my jaw, gripping it so firmly I think it may bruise. "Don't lie to me. My patience is thin, Ainsley."

"You don't say," I tease with a coy smile—one he ignores. "I'll be happy to put three seats between me and your sour attitude when we get to your brother's baseball game."

Surprise schools his features.

"I'll just kiss some poor guy that came alone on the kiss cam, and you can kiss the beer you won't drink."

That surprise vanishes and morphs into something much more sinister. He hauls me up, our fronts pressing together. My boobs strain against his sculpted chest as he holds me close, his heart pounding in sync with mine.

"No man will ever kiss what's mine."

"Better stake your claim, then," I taunt him, pushing him to his breaking point.

I want to see him break.

I want to be his undoing.

Just like he is for me.

"Time's tickin', Maverick." His eyes drag down my body, taking in every curve and dip. "Are you going to show me who I belong to?"

He stands quietly for a minute before a smile pulls up his lips. "No."

Well, I wasn't expecting that.

"I want to know why you think this was my doing."

Dammit.

He's not letting this go.

"I may have gotten distracted when you brought out snacks when we stopped." I wave my hands dramatically. "There, happy?"

"How much were those snacks worth to you?" he questions, leaning on the hood with his arms crossed across his chest. "One card or two?"

"Your cards don't scare me," I whisper, folding my arms over my chest.

"They should," he retorts with a smile.

"Don't play dumb, Mav," I start, already knowing this isn't going to end well. "You're not near as scary as you think. I'd try and tone it down some."

I knew those were fighting words.

I just expected they'd have a far different reaction.

His body pulls taut under my hands. His hands move to his back pockets with a smirk that I've seen too many times before.

A smirk that means he has a terrible idea.

One with my name on it.

"How did we end up here, Ainsley? On the side of the road in the middle of nowhere?" His eyes turn to slits. "And don't lie this time."

Maybe it's his plain black tee stretched snugly across his broad chest or the way his jeans are riding low on his hips—low enough that I can see his tattoos perfectly—that's fueling my confidence. Or maybe I'm just crazy.

"You ran out of gas," I lie, just so he'll act a fool.

I want him to come apart.

"The only one to blame for us being stranded here is *you*."

His eyes heat with frustration as he takes in the fact that I'm not admitting defeat.

"Fine," he barks, pushing off the hood and leaving me alone. "You can think about it while I call Triple A to get us out of here."

I won't, but I'll sure pretend.

I slip onto the hood, relaxing in the heat of the sun while he talks with roadside assistance.

"They'll be out in an hour," Maverick hollers from the driver's seat as I turn, finding his laptop open on the dash.

"What are you doing with that?"

"Working," he clips quickly.

"No," I whine, smacking my hands against the metal of his Mustang. "We have an hour."

He shrugs, his gaze focused on the screen. "Enough time to get through a few reports."

Sliding off the hood, I loiter in the open window, dragging a hand through his messy hair. "Or..." I cut a smile. "We could do something else."

His eyes fly to meet mine, curiosity flashing in them. "No."

"You didn't even hear my idea."

"Don't need to," he clips, settling back on his accounting lies. "If it's not work, we're not doing it."

"But we could have fun," I whine, tapping the pad of my fingers against the thrum of his pulse. "A lot of fun."

He doesn't even look at me, just shakes his head and continues typing.

What an ass.

"Fine." My shoulders rise and fall easily. "I guess I'll just have to play by myself."

Maverick groans and throws his head against the headrest. His eyes look to the sky, probably asking for strength, as he growls out, "Don't test me, Ainsley. You'll find out it's much more than you can handle."

Chapter TWO

Maverick

Twenty minutes later

I can't take much more of this.

It's too much.

Ainsley's spread over my hood like it's her damn throne, glancing back at me with lustful eyes and heated hate.

It turns me on all the same.

Settling my eyes on the laptop in my lap, I try to focus on the bullshit report I've already done.

I scan halfway over it by the time I hear *the* video.

"Ah, Ainsley." Groans flow through the open window, pulling my gaze to the only other person on this road. "Right there."

She wants me to spank her ass.

To bend her over this hood and take her body to my liking.

To wear the mark that signifies I've finally lost control.

How disappointed she'll be.

Ignoring her, I focus on anything but the sound of her toying with me.

She wants me to break.

She wants me to give in.

She won't win.

"Harder, Ainsley, harder."

My patience must snap because I sling open the door and get out, rounding the hood and yanking her small body until her center is lined up right where I want her.

"Ow," she coos, rubbing her bare thigh under her shorts. "That was too hard."

Her eyes fall to mine, and I drink in the sight of her. Sprawled over my hood, fanned out dark hair, lustful eyes, and a smirk that only I am notorious for.

Plucking her phone from her hand, I eye the video of us she's taunting me with, and dammit, if it doesn't make me hard.

She pushes up, her boobs brushing my chest.

I tip her chin to meet mine. "What game are you playing?"

"Play with me and find out," she taunts, a coy smile playing on her lips.

Sliding my other arm around her, I pull her close until she's in my arms and wrapped around my waist.

It was a fatal mistake.

One I learned too late.

Ainsley's lips press against that spot right under my ear that makes my dick strain against my jeans. It doesn't hurt worse than the self-control it takes to set her back down, though.

It's not that I don't want to fuck her on the hood of my Mustang. I do.

I just can't stand the thought of someone coming by and seeing her.

So, to be preventive, I'm not going to fuck her here, but when we get to this damn hotel, I won't stop.

"Cock tease," she barks, adjusting to the metal under her.

"Needy, are we?" I muse with a smirk.

"Insecure, are you?" she bites back, amusement coating her tone.

And this is why we work.

She's my brand of crazy.

Gripping her wrists, I pin them above her head, ignoring the way her shirt rides up, exposing a sliver of her toned stomach. Leaning into the crook of her neck, I revel in the scent of her—soap and utterly mine.

"Tell me, Ainsley," I murmur against the soft flesh under my lips. "How should I treat such impatience?"

The way her eyes close tells me plenty already, but it's too early to give in now.

"You know what I want," she deadpans.

"Now, you know I require a little more explanation," I tease, moving my gaze from her pert nipples back to her eyes. "I am a man, after all. I'm much more *visual.*"

The urge to roll her nipple between my fingers like it's my very own playing card weighs on me.

It's a hand that's given me the advantage.

A rarity.

One I'll never give up.

"Please, Maverick." Her plea falls on deaf ears.

"How's this?" Her breath hitches as I hover over her neck with my lips, never letting them reach where she wants them. "Is this enough?"

"You're being ruthless." She huffs, sounding breathless.

"I thought I was a cock tease," I question, moving my lips lower to her shoulder, where I lightly bite. She shudders under my hold, and a feeling of victory surges through me. "Which is it, Ainsley? Am I a cock tease or ruthless?"

"A ruthless cock tease."

Damn right, and it's killing me.

Sticking to my name, I tear my hands and mouth from her, taking a regretful breath. She pushes up with a conceited smirk that says she knew I'd do this, and she was simply waiting for it.

Walking away, I pace, hoping for strength not to fuck her for everyone to see.

"I wonder if the stranger I'll kiss at the ball game will kiss better than you," she taunts at my back and frozen stature. "Maybe I'll even get his number."

The hell she will.

Turning, I grab her arms and press them against the hood as I smash my lips to hers. They're soft and compliant against mine. She follows my lead, allowing me my feel of her sweet mouth.

I start slow, never once demanding dominance.

That is, until she taunts me again.

"Do you think he'll shut me up like that, too?"

A growl erupts from my chest as I ram her body farther up the hood. Kicking her feet apart, I step between them and press my lips against hers harder this time.

"No man will ever get to see you this way," I demand, moving my tongue along her lips, reveling in her taste of fruity gloss and gum. "You need a reminder."

A satisfied smile pulls up her lips as I pull back, extracting a marker from my back pocket.

"Where do you want it?" I ask her.

"I get a choice?" she coos, her smile only growing.

"No." Snatching her arm, I use my teeth to uncap the Sharpie I keep with me and start with her reminder.

"Tell me what your punishment is, Ains," I demand, going over her skin to make it stick. "What letter did I draw?"

She barely whispers but manages to get it right on the first try. "I."

"Next one."

Her hips buck as I move the marker by her boob as I spell out the next letter.

"O," she breathes.

"Last one," I promise with a smirk at her closed eyes. They don't open until I stand, awaiting her answer.

"U." It's a mumble, but the right answer, nonetheless. "IOU."

I smash my lips to hers at a rewarding pace. "Maybe the poor soul will be able to pay back all the IOUs this'll earn you."

She nods incoherently, never tearing her mouth from mine.

I manage to force out my final command within a second.

"Now get the fuck off the hood."

Chapter THREE

Ainsley

"Are you going to pout all day?" Maverick asks from the hood, where he's shuffling his poker cards just to annoy me.

"I'm not pouting."

"Is that why you're letting yourself burn instead of sitting under here where it's shaded?" I eye his pointed finger from under the large oak tree cascading over the hood, protecting him from sunburn.

I refuse to sit next to him.

Which is my reason for sitting across the highway right under the sun's blaze.

It's a bit childish, but so was he.

So, I'll play his game, just better.

"What you should be worried about isn't a little sunburn," I warn curtly, holding his eyes.

"Oh, yeah? What should I be worried about, then?"

"I'm so glad you asked," I reply sarcastically, folding my arms over my chest. "I looked up the seating chart for Cooper's game, and I am most definitely seated next to a guy."

I am completely full of shit.

I didn't look up anything but the weather to see if this heat would cool off. And, even if I actually wanted to check, they don't disclose that kind of information. So, I have no idea if my claim is true or not, but Maverick may buy it.

"Cute." He laughs before opening his arms, his cards still in hand. "Now, come play with me."

I decided to get a sunburn.

One that's around third-degree status.

Okay, that's a little theatrical, but it hurts all the same.

"Ainsley," Maverick barks, his eyes rising to the sky as if he's asking for strength. He definitely needs it. This won't end well for him. "I won't ask you again."

"You're going to have to come and get me." His eyes widen like he can't believe I'm making this hard for him. Newsflash: I make everything hard for him. Well, apparently, not *everything*.

"You don't want me to come and get you," he warns, already pushing to his feet. "It will be more than you can handle."

For some reason, my body betrays me and shudders.

"Now get up and come to me." The word slips off his tongue so easily that I think he might have misspoken. But the hardness of his jaw tells me otherwise.

"No." My shoulders rise and fall lazily as I look off into the vacant road for wherever the hell this confidence came from.

"No?" he muses, halfway across the street. He reaches me within seconds, and I instantly regret it. "I think I misheard you."

"Maybe we should get your ears checked."

Without a second more, my arm is snatched, and I'm hauled to his chest. "Maybe I shouldn't have given you a fucking choice."

His words don't scare me.

Nothing about Maverick Lexington frightens me.

He excites me, so that's why I press my chest against his, allowing my boobs to indent his prudeness. "You're right. That was your mistake."

A growl escapes him at my intrusion. "Come play with me."

"Make me," I challenge, bowing up to him. I can feel the heat of his breath on my face at our proximity. He smells of mint gum and aftershave. It's intoxicating in the best way.

Several arguments and a haul across the street later, I've found some relief under the oak tree with Maverick at my side. Poker cards span over the hood, with me already having the losing hand.

Checking my watch, I pipe up with a deal of my own before it's too late.

"Let's make this more interesting," I coo, hoping my offer is worth more than his hand.

His eyebrow crooks as he sets his set facedown.

"If the next card you put down is a two or a black five, you have to take off some form of clothing."

"Deal." He picks his hand back up, then throws down a damn black five without looking.

"Strip, Lexington," I bark, clapping my vindictive hands together. "Take it all off."

He nods but then moves over to my side, and his fingers slip under the strap of my tank top.

"I didn't say *my* clothes," I argue as I allow the elastic to fall.

"You said *clothes*." He moves to the other one, careful to miss my sunburn. Soon, my top is around my midsection as Maverick helps it below my bra. "You didn't specify whose."

"You know better," I chide as he sits back and takes in the view of me like I'm some portrait.

"Give better instructions next time."

Rolling my eyes, I make another bet.

"If you put down a diamond, you have to take off my shorts."

He nods, but this time, he looks at his hand, and a six of diamonds hits the pile.

See, I knew, secretly, he wanted this as much as I did.

He just likes to play games.

Too bad I'm the master.

"Lie down."

My back hits the hood, sending the pile astray.

Maverick doesn't cast it a second glance as he climbs up my body.

"You always have to fight me," he growls, his hands going to my hips, yanking me closer until we're lined up perfectly.

His fingers play with the button on my shorts as his breath fans over my neck. Shivers break out across my skin all the way down my spine.

"I just wanted to please you." My eyes roll back as he tugs down my shorts, leaving me bare in a bra and panties. He eyes the cloth covering me before his fingers dip under it and move it to the side.

"Trust me, your pussy pleases me."

With that, I push my hips down so he has no choice but to finger me.

A hiss rips through his chest as he's met with resistance. I can practically feel myself tighten as he adds another finger, stretching me.

"I want it swollen," he coos, scissoring his fingers like a starving man finally having his first taste.

"I want it dripping." My breath halts at his words.

"I want it ruined for any other man."

Chapter FOUR

Ainsley

"Ainsley."

He sighs into my mouth. "Are you still with me?"

A light humph falls from my lips as I revel in the feeling of his fingers moving inside me. It feels like heaven and hell all at once.

"What have you learned?" Maverick chides, working his fingers back and forth in my needy flesh.

"That you suck at Texas Hold'em?"

"Funny," he muses with a grim smile. "How about distractions aren't worth the price?"

"Anything is worth this price."

His lips turn up, showcasing his straight teeth.

"Well, enjoy it, because you won't get it for much longer."

I feel my disapproving groan bubble up. "Why not?"

"'Cause someone could drive by and see you like this—spread open and aching for me." My core clenches at the realization of what's really happening here. He's giving me control. He's giving in. For me.

"But, we can't have that, now, can we?" he ponders, immediately reminding me who's in charge—and it's not me. "No one will see what's mine."

Another finger intrudes my center.

"No one will touch what's mine."

Those fingers work back and forth, driving me into a frenzy.

"No one will take what's mine."

"Never," I promise, moving my hips to meet his fingers. The sound of my flesh smacking against his hand, along with my moans, fills the air.

We lie like this for what feels like forever until his fingers disappear from my core, leaving me empty and writhing.

"Why'd you stop?"

"Consider your IOU paid." He shrugs my shorts back over my bottom before fixing my top, too.

He helps me to my feet, holding me until I'm steady. It doesn't take me long until I'm level and whipping around so Maverick is pressed against the hood.

"Whoa," he chirps like he's not used to being the one controlled. "Playtime's over."

Not yet.

I still have thirty-four minutes.

The game is still on.

Pressing my hands against his chest, I back him up until his knees bend, and he's sprawled over the hood as I was.

I have to say, him at my mercy is a nice look.

"What have you learned, Mav?" I tease, throwing his earlier words back in his face. "Have we learned not to be a cock tease?"

His shoulders rise and fall carelessly. "No, but I'll think about considering it for the future."

Good enough.

Reaching for his shirt, he lets me slip it over his head and brush it to the ground.

It feels like it takes forever as he strips my tank top from my body. I would've preferred a much faster approach, like ripping it off, but that's just me.

After my shirt litters the hood, I drop his hands, licking my way down his ripped torso.

"What letter am I spelling, Mav?" I work my tongue under his belly button, awfully close to where he wants me. Now, it's *his* turn to be tortured.

"IOU, Ainsley. Don't play."

"Wrong answer," I breathe, dragging my tongue through the strip of hair that lines the ridges that dip under his jeans. "Two more tries."

His hips buck as he lies quietly, looking like a sculpted martyr.

"I," he forces through clenched teeth.

A light tsk falls from my smile-pained lips. "Not quite."

"O," he tries one last time and fails.

"I'm disappointed in you," I quip, moving my hands over his, bridging them over his head as he did to me. "How will you ever make it up to me?"

"Between your legs," he offers with a boyish smile.

"Is that what you want?" I question, matching his smile. "For me to reward you with pussy?"

His hands buck against my hold.

"Ah, ah," I tsk. "I'm in charge."

He nods as my fingers curl around the band of his jeans. Tugging, his hips lift, helping me with the buckle. I run my fingers over his bulge through the fabric, familiarizing myself with every part of him before I still.

"Tell me what I wrote, and I'll suck your cock."

His eyes flash with heated desire at my words. "What if I can't?"

"I suggest you think very hard," I scold, freeing his cock and wrapping my hand around the base. "I'll even give you a hint. You *blank* me."

A smile creeps up my lips as I thrash my tongue around his tip, which makes his head lift. "What's the word, Maverick?"

His arousal leaks onto my lips. Taking my thumb, I run it through the clear liquid before licking the rest off my lips.

Maverick moans, his head falling backward onto the brassy metal.

"Owe." He forces out the word I traced on his skin breathlessly. "I owe you."

As promised, I take his cock into my mouth, almost gagging at the intrusion. My eyes water as Maverick starts thrusting from beneath me, hitting the back of my throat.

I round the head of his cock at a punishing pace that has his hips lifting off the hood and his hands tangling in my hair.

"Do you think you deserve to come down my throat?"

His eyes gloss over at my words.

"In fact, I do." He shakes his head like a kid at Christmas. "I think I deserve it more than anyone here."

He looks around at the vacant street just to be an ass.

"Yep, I sure think so."

He's so damn cute I can't help but smile.

Or take his cock down my throat.

Fisting my hair in his hand, he controls the pace as he guides my head to his liking, which slows me down.

It's the sweetest surrender—my favorite type of submission.

"You're right," Maverick growls, thrusting harder as he grows close. "I owe you everything."

Chapter FIVE

Maverick

"You owed me this."

With one easy swoop, I take Ainsley in my arms and move us inside the car. Except, I don't set her in the passenger seat like I probably should. I sit her over my straining cock.

"Is that so?"

It's like she can barely form a coherent word as her lips move, but no sound comes out.

At her silence, a coy smirk crosses my face as I hum in dissatisfaction. Lifting her core from my aching front, a muffled groan escapes her.

"Your pussy doesn't please me as much as your praise," I state clinically, totally spouting off bullshit. There's nothing in this world that I love more than Ainsley's sweet cunt. "Use your words."

I beat her to it.

"Should I stretch you to your limit?" A gasp rocks her body, urging me on.

"Should I push you until you can't take anymore?" A groan masked by a moan escapes her. "Until you're begging for release that will never come because such behavior shouldn't be rewarded."

"I'm not sure you deserve to get off," I start, toying with the hem of her shorts. I move torturously slow as I unclasp the button providing my only barrier from taking her right here for everyone to see.

Shifting, I strip the shorts from her body and settle when I'm lined up with her burning entrance. Neither one of us talks as I push into her, fast and punishing. Just heavy breathing fills the car.

My pace picks up as she starts meeting me thrust for thrust.

My arousal leaks down her thighs as the sound of our flesh smacking together echoes over this backroad.

It's heaven if I'll ever know one.

"Harder, Maverick," she whines, needing more. I can practically feel the pressure building between her thighs. She's close, but it's not time.

"Come on, Maverick," she barks, her boobs bouncing relentlessly over my mouth. My tongue thrashes, searching for any ounce of a taste. "We're almost there."

She's right about that.

I've been close since the first time my fingers slid between her soaked folds.

"Just a little more," she groans, her hips slamming into mine with an urgency I've never seen from her before. "We can do it."

I ram my hips into her with a force I'm surprised to see from myself as her words rile me up. I'm not sure what game she's playing, but whatever it is, I don't care right now.

All I care about is staking my claim and finishing with the girl I love.

And so, I will.

Another punishing thrust hits her hilt, making Ainsley bite my broad shoulder in agreement. My groan comes out gravelly and unhinged.

I add two fingers, alternating between fucking her with my fingers and cock. Each thrust is met with a moan until we both are close to orgasm.

But I never give in to her completely.

I let her think I get close before I reel it back in.

It's too soon.

She wants to enjoy it, even if it is a game to her.

Snatching my fingers back, I plunge deeper into her heat, making her body shudder in my arms. Holding her close, I press my hands to her hips and control the pace to my liking.

She bounces on my dick like it's the last time she'll ever do so, and that's what does it.

"Home run!" Ainsley yells as she milks the very essence from us both. My claim runs down her fair thighs, making her a pretty mess.

"Game over," she coos, sliding into the passenger seat with a satisfied smile. Her hair is sex-mussed, and her body is heaving with pleasure. It's the most beautiful sight. "Nice playing with you, Lexington."

"What the hell are you keeping on about?" I bark, pulling my jeans over my ass, buckling the belt strewn over the backseat.

She sits quietly, allowing me to figure out her master plan all on my own.

"Were you trying to round the bases in an hour?"

She eyes me like that was common knowledge, and I'm the dumbest motherfucker on the planet.

"No," she deadpans. "I was trying to just jump your bones for fun."

A smile pulls up my lips at the mere fact that I love everything about Ainsley James.

Her snark.

Her fight.

Her mouth.

"I won and paid off an IOU all within an hour." Her arms fold over her chest proudly. "Isn't that brag-worthy?"

"You deserve all the praise." And I intend to give it all to her.

Until we hear it.

The damning sound of a truck passing by.

Except it doesn't pass by.

It stops and waits.

For us.

I'm in no way embarrassed.

Ainsley, on the other hand, is spazzing like she's on death's door.

"Go out there and deal with him," she bellows, attempting to cover her body with mine.

"Why?" I tease, arching a brow. "Isn't this what you wanted?" I drop my lips to her breast, sucking a nipple. My teeth scrape her soft flesh, causing her to smother a moan in my shoulder.

But I can't continue.

I can't go to jail today because an innocent man will die just for looking at her.

"Yeeesss." Her answer comes out as a moan.

"Game over, though, right?" I chide, pulling the last of her tank top strap into place. "You won, right?"

"In multiple ways."

I grin and leave her to finish calming down as I get the gas from the guy, who, thankfully, didn't see anything, before calling Cooper to tell him we'll be there within the hour.

"Now, what did we learn from this experience?" I tease as I slide back into the driver's seat. Her midnight hair falls in waves over her covered shoulder as she faces me.

"That you're a cock tease until the most inconvenient times." Such a foul mouth.

"Let's try again."

"That you'll always owe me."

***

If you loved Maverick and Ainsley, check out their full-length story, IOU, available now. For more information, go to my website.

https://authorkristymarie.com/

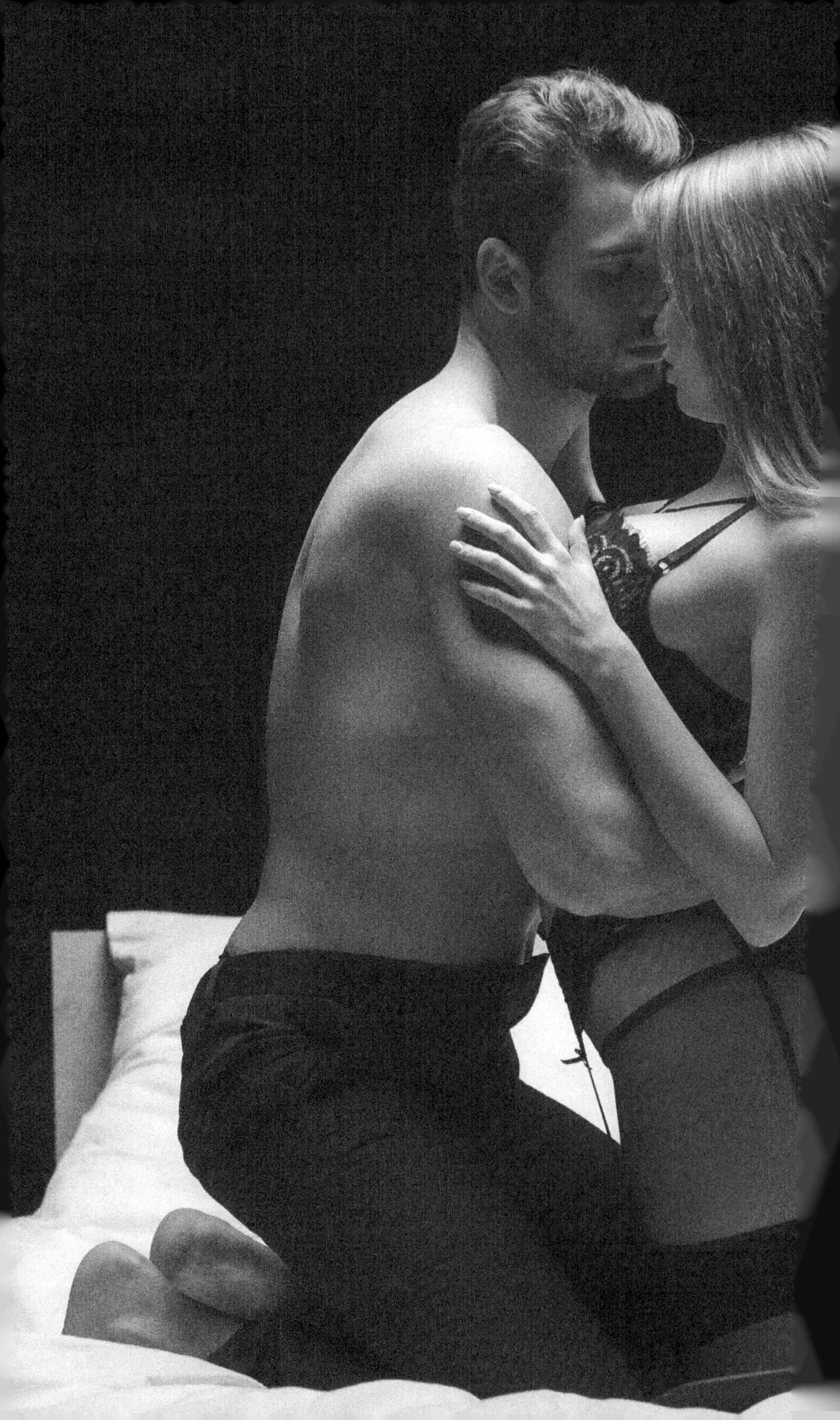

Bedding
THE BOSSMAN

LAURA LEE

A Bedding the Billionaire Story

Chapter ONE

Liam

The view of the Chicago skyline from our penthouse suite in the Maxwell Magnificent Mile is spectacular. It's a corner room, so in the daytime, you can see the sparkling blue water of Lake Michigan, but at night, you have the dazzling city lights. Being a luxury hotel heir certainly has its advantages. I may not have joined the family business like my little brother, Ronan, but I still enjoy the perks of free accommodations when I travel for my business needs.

"I just need a few more minutes, I swear," Avery's sexy rasp calls from the en-suite.

"That's what you said a few minutes ago," I tease.

"Yeah... well, I don't have the advantage of looking hot the moment I roll out of bed like you do."

I practically swallow my tongue as my beautiful wife steps out of the en-suite.

Fuck the skyline. The view from across the room is *much* better.

Avery is going full glam tonight with smoky eyes, red lips, and long dark hair curled into waves. But she's missing the dress I know she brought with her, not that I'm complaining. Her full tits are bare, and a lacy black thong is wrapped around her shapely hips. I groan as she crosses the room to her cherry-red stilettos and bends over to step into them.

Five years into our marriage, and the woman still takes my breath away every damn day. Despite her earlier comment, she *is* gorgeous first thing in the morning without a stitch of makeup, but when she's like this, I lose my fucking mind with desire. My wife has an affinity for designer lingerie and sky-high heels, and combined with her ample curves, I've never seen a sexier sight.

"Well, now we're going to be even later." Avery lets out a surprised squeal as I smack her bare ass before caging her against the window.

"Liam!" she moans as I cup her tits from behind and grind my erection into the crease of her ass cheeks. Avery's not especially tall, but with the five-inch lift her Louboutins give her, she's much closer to my height. "We don't have time for this."

"I don't fucking care," I growl as I bite the delicate patch of skin where her neck and shoulder meet. "I wanna have some fun with you."

"Trust me, where we're going, we'll have *plenty* of fun tonight."

I smile into her warm vanilla-scented skin, wondering for the hundredth time where she's taking me. The little minx is being annoyingly secretive about it. I do not know how she found the time to arrange any surprises. We did not plan this trip in advance. We flew to Chicago late last night for the sole purpose of extinguishing the publicity dumpster fire one of our clients started, but today is our five-year wedding anniversary, so we decided to stay an extra night before flying home to LA.

Our PR firm, Maxwell & Company, manages A-list celebrities and large conglomerates. The New York branch handles most of the corporations and moguls, while Avery and I babysit actors, models, influencers, and heiresses. It's a lot—you don't become a billion-dollar company without long hours and hard work—but my wife and I are hopeless over-achievers, so we make do. Plus, it helps that we fuck on any available surface as often as possible. Orgasms are better than any drug for stress relief if you ask me.

"Where are we heading to tonight?" I slide my hand down the center of her abdomen until I reach lace.

"Nice try." Avery's back arches as I rub her clit over the flimsy material. "I told you it's a *surprise*."

"Worth a shot." I laugh, moving to the side, rubbing the hem of her panties between my forefinger and thumb.

"Liam," she pants. "We should get going."

I slip beneath the lace, smiling at her reflection in the glass as she soaks my fingers. My girl is always so fucking wet and ready for me.

"We'll make it fast. But I'm fucking hungry, so you're going to put your hands on that window, throw your ass back, and let me devour my wife's pretty cunt."

"Is that so?" she challenges.

I grab Avery's arms, pressing her palms flat to the glass. "Don't move 'em, Avery. Just stand there, shut the fuck up, and look at the pretty lights while I make you come."

"You're such an asshole," she moans, wiggling her ass as I spread her thighs farther apart and drop to my knees.

We're on the forty-first floor with a wall of floor-to-ceiling windows, which is a huge fucking turn-on. The outer glass is mirrored, so nobody could *actually* see us right now, but Avery and I both get off on the idea of exhibitionism, even though it's not something we could ever do in reality because it wouldn't be good for business if we ran around creating our own scandals.

I bite her ass cheek, hard. "You fucking love that about me, remember?"

Avery moans and nods, her forehead pressed against the glass. "God help me, but I really do."

I grip her hips and angle her ass toward me, burying my face between her thighs. My wife is a squirmer, so I hold her still, alternating between lapping at her pussy and fucking her with my tongue. I close my eyes, breathing her in.

Everything about this woman is amazing.

We were never supposed to be more than an anonymous one-night stand, but when I found out one of the best publicists in the industry was looking for a job, the entrepreneur in me couldn't resist recruiting her. My business partner, Nick, headed up our efforts to get her on board. I couldn't risk her seeing me before she accepted the job, in fear that our hookup would cause her to decline our offer. Avery was fucking furious when she learned I was her new boss and that I had known exactly who she was when I picked her up at that club.

I had given her a fake name on the night we met, so she had no clue that the owner of Maxwell & Company was the same guy who gave her the best dicking of her life. In my defense, she gave me a fake name that night, too. It was obvious she was looking for a rebound screw to get over her douchebag ex's infidelity, so I ran with it. I sure as shit would not turn down the opportunity to fuck the hottest woman I've ever met.

When I made Avery an offer she couldn't refuse to move across the country to join our Los Angeles branch, I told myself my obsession with her had everything to do with her professional accomplishments. But the moment she walked into my LA office, I knew I had been bullshitting myself. I was equally obsessed with Avery Jacobs, the woman, and that obsession only grew over time. We fought over every little thing whenever we were alone together, but as I later realized, it was one giant game of foreplay. The moment months of tension between us finally snapped, and we fucked like animals all over my office, I knew I was never letting her go. It took her a while to get with the program because she's a stubborn bitch, but I'm a persistent motherfucker, so she never truly had a shot at resisting me.

I dive back into her pussy, groaning as her taste hits my tongue. "God, I love you so fucking much," I murmur, shoving my fingers inside her.

"I love you, too," Avery mewls as her pussy pulses around my fingers. Her moans fill the room, drowning out the noises from the air conditioner.

My dirty girl is so fucking loud as I eat her out, I smack her ass cheek. "You're supposed to keep quiet and watch the lights, remember?"

"Yes, sir," she whimpers.

"I mean it, Avery. Not a single word until I give you permission to speak, or I'm going to leave you high and dry. You're going to behave for me, aren't you?" I take my hand from her cunt, pinching her clit hard as I lap at her pussy.

"Yes," she moans. "No more words after this. I promise. Just please, make me come, you goddamn son of a bitch."

I chuckle against her slippery flesh. There is *nothing* submissive about this woman, but I'm a bossy shit, so whenever we're like this, I take advantage of her need to come as often as possible by going a little Dom on her ass. Sometimes literally, but we don't have time for anal prep right now.

"Good girl," I praise.

My good girl, I think as I bring her closer to the edge.

I flick her clit with my tongue, thrusting two fingers into her slick channel. I press my free hand on the small of her back, forcing her to bend forward even more. Avery braces herself against the windows, groaning as she comes apart so beautifully, breaking her vow of silence with a vengeance.

The moment her thighs begin shaking, I hold her still, licking her clean as she comes down from her orgasm. I don't stop until I'm certain she's fully sated, because I want my woman operating at peak distraction tonight. I want her to be so fucking consumed by the thought of how good my mouth feels and how sensitive her pussy is that she can't concentrate on much else.

I'm in a constant state of arousal whenever I think of her, so it's only fair to return the favor, right?

Chapter TWO

Avery

"Here we are," the cabbie says as he pulls in front of a tall building.

Like many downtown buildings, there's a row of businesses on the street level, with what appears to be condominiums on the upper floors.

Liam looks out the car's window, trying to piece together why we're here. I know it's driving him crazy that I'm withholding information, but surprising this man isn't easy, so I couldn't resist the opportunity on our wedding anniversary. The moment I knew we were heading to Chicago, I called an old friend of mine to arrange this. I can't wait to see my husband's reaction when he realizes where I've brought him.

"Thank you," my husband says as he swipes his credit card to pay the fare.

We exit the vehicle, and he places his hand on my lower back, guiding me to the sidewalk.

"What is this place, Avery?"

I point to the building's main entrance. "You'll see."

His lips curve into a smile. "You know I'm going to spank your ass for keeping secrets from me, right?"

"I'm looking forward to it." I lift my chin and wink.

The doorman, his face composed and serious, opens the door for us, ushering us into an opulent lobby. It's a cavernous space with a high ceiling, marble floors, and several small seating areas.

Each piece of art that hangs from the walls exudes a subtle amount of money and taste. The hush that fills the lobby is populated by whispers from the staff and a few well-dressed people who stand in small groups and converse among themselves. There's a reception area off to the left, which is where we head.

"May I help you?" the man behind the polished mahogany desk asks.

"Good evening," I reply. "My name is Avery Jacobs-Maxwell. My husband and I are personal guests of Weston Miller. He said you'd be able to direct us."

Liam raised a brow as I mentioned the well-known entrepreneur. "Well, now I'm *really* intrigued."

I was West's publicist back in New York before I left that firm and moved to California. Weston owns several successful clubs and bars in New York City. He recently started a new venture here in Chicago, but it hasn't been publicized because the nature of this business requires ultimate discretion. But what my husband doesn't know is that West is dating a good friend of mine, so I have the inside scoop.

"Ah, yes, welcome!" the man replies, fanning his arm out. "Please follow me to your private elevator."

"Thank you."

Liam and I follow him down a narrow hall, stopping in a private elevator bay. The man places a card over the sensor, triggering the golden doors to open.

He steps aside, allowing us to enter. "It's a direct lift, so once you hit the button, you'll be taken straight there." He nods at the selection of elegant masks hanging from the walls.

They're understated yet classy. Rich jeweled-toned velvet, black lace, and silk masks, some adorned with crystals, feathers, and other embellishments.

"Please help yourself to a mask if you'd like, and enjoy your evening at Sanctuary."

Liam gives me a quizzical look.

I smile as the man closes the door, trapping us in the small box. "Weston's new club," I explain, trying to contain my giddiness.

"So, your big surprise is taking me to a masquerade club?"

"Not exactly..." I bite my lip. "But it *is* a special club. Exclusive." I select a simple black linen mask from a hook and hand it to my husband. "Put this on."

Liam licks his lips as he takes the mask from me, bringing it to his face. After he's done, I slip mine on—this one ruby red satin with a lace overlay, watching him through the eye slits as I hit the button to start the elevator.

"What are you up to, Aves?"

My lips twitch. "You'll see."

A man in a crisp black suit is waiting for us when the doors part, holding a silver platter with a tiny velvet box atop it. Liam accepts the box as we exit the elevator.

"Welcome to Sanctuary." The man in black bows his head. "My name is Thomas, and I'll be your concierge for the evening."

"Thank you," Liam replies.

Thomas turns to me. "Ma'am."

I give him a brief nod, but my attention is already on my husband, who's admiring the box's contents. He opens it, revealing a gold key.

"What's this?"

"A key?" I reply with a smirk.

"No shit, smartass," he replies, leaning forward to kiss me before he hands Thomas the empty box.

I turn to the concierge. "Thomas, we've never been here before. Can you give us the run-down before we head inside?"

"It'd be my pleasure, ma'am." Thomas gestures toward the set of shiny double doors in front of us. A soft, thumping beat is coming through the walls, but the club must have some great soundproofing because it's barely noticeable. "Through those doors, you'll find the first floor of Sanctuary, which is designed for mingling. You'll find a full bar where we have a two-drink maximum and a dance floor. We have a strict no-play policy on the first level."

Liam takes a deep breath, giving me the impression that he's putting the pieces together.

"And there are other floors?" my husband asks.

"Yes, sir. There's also a mezzanine level, where you'll find a small seating area, along with several public play areas, then the private rooms are located toward the back. The key you hold will open your private room, courtesy of Mr. Miller. You'll find it stocked with the items your wife has requested. You can come and go as you please, or invite as many guests as you'd like."

"We're not really *guest* kind of people," I tell him.

Liam's hand flirts with the curve of my ass. Oh yeah, he definitely gets the hint now. "And the rooms offer full privacy?"

Thomas nods. "That's at your discretion, sir. Each room has switchable glass. When the switch is in the up position, the glass is frosted, giving you absolute privacy. With the switch facing down, anyone mingling on that level can view inside."

I can feel my husband's brown eyes boring into me, but I keep my gaze trained on our concierge.

"I think we've got it," I say. "Thank you."

"My pleasure," Thomas replies. "May I take your coats?"

"Yes, please." Liam helps me with my coat and hands it to Thomas. Then he does the same with his suit jacket, leaving him in dark slacks and a white button-up.

"If you need anything, please ask. Enjoy your evening." Thomas hands us a coat check ticket.

My husband's eyes fill with desire as he roams my curves in my little black minidress. "I've gotta say, you've surprised me, Aves."

"Good surprise or bad surprise?"

Liam ushers me toward the door, leaning into my ear. "Oh, sweetheart, it's a fucking *great* surprise. Shall we?"

Chapter THREE

Liam

Holy fuck, I'm pretty sure Avery snuck into my head and read my mind, because this is exactly what I've imagined whenever I thought about going to a sex club with her. My wife and I have no issue discussing our fantasies with one another, but exploring some of those fantasies in public is difficult with our chosen career in high-profile publicity. But here at Sanctuary, half the patrons are wearing masks like we are, so we blend in well. It couldn't be more perfect.

The main floor of the club is tastefully decorated and has a bar running along one side, with booths, low chairs, and sofas scattered all around. To the left is a dance floor, its floor-to-ceiling mirror tiles reflecting the lights that are beaming down on it. A single elevator is located toward the back, which I'm guessing takes you to the second level. I tuck the key I was holding into my pocket, licking my lips as I struggle to keep from devouring my wife right here and now.

She grins. "You really are surprised."

"I'm beyond surprised," I say. "How did you even hear about this place?"

"Weston is dating Heather." She shrugs. "She asked for a favor."

Avery's best friend back in New York is getting an all-expenses paid trip to the Bahamas in the morning.

"Well, lead the way, sweetheart." I fan my arm out.

"Let's get a drink." She pauses for a moment. "But remember, no touching until we get upstairs."

My heart races as we stride toward the bar. It's already packed, but we jam through to find a spot at the elegant marble counter. Avery sidles up to me, her curvy frame pressing into mine. Her full breasts are smashed against me, and her delicate fingers are slowly stroking the inside of my thigh, making my cock stir in anticipation.

"What happened to no touching?" I smirk.

Her delicate shoulder lifts in a shrug. "I can't help it. My husband is ridiculously sexy."

I'm laughing as another man in a crisp black suit leans across the counter, his eyes brazenly raking over my wife. Not that I can blame him. "What can I get for you, ma'am?"

His blatant ogling might offend a less secure man, but I know that my dick is the only one Avery's interested in, so this fucker can look all he wants. Besides, if this night goes as I'm expecting, he won't be the only stranger lusting over my wife tonight.

"I'll have a whiskey, neat." She glances over at me and raises an eyebrow. "And for you, my dear husband?"

I nod. "The same."

The bartender returns moments later with our drinks and swipes the card I give him for payment.

Avery swirls her liquor in its glass before downing it while I take a slow sip of mine.

Her hand returns to my thigh, giving me another subtle stroke. My cock twitches as her fingertip traces my pubic bone.

I lean into her ear. "Sweetheart, if you keep doing that, I'm going to bend you over this barstool and fuck you right here."

"Well, I guess I'd better stop. You know how much I *love* being a good girl."

I groan, discreetly adjusting myself. "You're the devil, you know that?"

Avery runs her fingers along my jaw. "Dance with me, Liam. Like the first night we met."

Hell, I'm not about to argue with her. I want this woman just as much as she wants me. But if she wants to take a trip down Memory Lane first, who am I to deny her?

I place my hand on the small of her back as we make our way toward the dance floor. My wife's hips sway seductively as we close in on the throng of dancers. Finding a spot against a wall, we stay just inside the dance floor, grinding against each other as if we're the only two people in the club, from one song to the next. My hands slide up her back, splaying out just under her shoulder blades. My fingers trace over her bare skin, enjoying the feel of her soft, warm curves. She grips my biceps, her fingertips digging into my muscles.

"I love you, baby," I say, my voice low and gravelly.

"I love you, too." She smiles. "Liam?"

"Hmm?"

"Are you okay with this? Being here?"

I trace her spine with the tip of my finger, smiling when she shivers against my touch.

"I'm *very* okay," I tell her. "I can't wait to check out our room."

Avery pulls me closer, hand sliding between us. "Me, too. Let's go upstairs."

I glance down to see her fingers curling around my thick bulge. She squeezes down on my erection and then releases it, her eyes staring into mine.

I nod, sucking in a slow breath. "Let's go."

We head toward the lift hand-in-hand. As soon as the elevator doors close, Avery is on me, her mouth devouring mine. The kiss is demanding and urgent, my wife's tongue sliding against mine in an erotic game of dominance. I'm about to fucking lose it when she breaks away, panting against my neck.

"Fuck, baby, I want you so bad." My hands cup her face, fingers tangling in her silky, dark hair.

The elevator dings and the doors slide open, revealing a hallway that leads to a small sitting area which is occupied by a trio of naked bodies moaning and writhing against each other.

"Damn, that's hot," my wife says, as I close in behind her, gripping her waist.

My cock throbs, my balls tightening in agreement. "Fuck yeah, it is."

The man is sitting on the couch with his pants around his ankles, thrusting into the woman on top of him, who's facing us. Her large breasts bounce as a second woman licks and sucks her light brown nipples, working her way down her torso.

The reverse cowgirl throws her head back in ecstasy, her screams of passion loud and raw, as the blonde, now on her knees, begins tonguing her clit while she's still getting pounded from the guy beneath.

Avery gasps as we watch the scene, her body rubbing against my erection as her chest strains against her tight dress.

My cock is tenting my pants, eager to be let out to play.

More moaning and the sound of skin slapping draws our attention to the enormous round bed off in the center of the room. It's surrounded by sheer netting, but you can see the couple on the mattress just fine, their bodies moving in perfect sync.

"Oh yeah, baby," the muscular man grunts. "You love taking it up the ass, don't you?"

"Give it to me, daddy," the voluptuous redhead replies as she's being fucked from behind. It's a little hard to tell with the netting, but it seems like she's fingering her pussy while her partner pounds her ass.

Avery's breath is coming hard, her chest rapidly rising and falling.

She turns to me, licking her lips. "We need to find a club like this back home," she says, her voice heavy and breathy.

"Agreed." My voice is gruff. "I want to bury my cock inside of you right now, Ave. Let's get to our room."

"Wait," Avery says as I take her hand, intent on finding our room. "How about we get started here while we watch the others?"

I look around, noticing the dozen other people playing with one another out in the open. Two couples are watching the same couple we were, while the rest of the patrons are standing in front of the transparent glass of two different rooms. The last room is the only one that has frosted glass, so I'm guessing it must be ours.

"Out in the open?" I ask. "You sure?"

Avery turns around, tugging at my belt. "I'm positive."

Again, who the fuck am I to argue with my beautiful wife?

Chapter FOUR

Avery

As soon as my husband's big, thick cock is free, I swipe the slit with my thumb before lowering to my knees before him.

"Fuck." Liam shudders as my tongue swirls around the tip, lapping up the salty precum before sucking him inside my mouth. "So good, sweetheart. So fucking good."

We've only been at this club for a little while, but I already know it's going to be one of the most memorable nights of our relationship. I also know I'm going to fuck my husband as many times as I can while we're here, so making him come is a big priority for me so we can move on to round two. Liam may be in his early forties, but lucky for me, the man has the refractory period of someone *much* younger. Out of the corner of my eye, I can see we're gathering our own little audience and it's making me even hotter. I lower my head, stretching my mouth to accommodate his girth as I take him in as deep as I can.

"That's it." Liam's fingers tangle in my hair, massaging my scalp as I bring him to the brink. He looks me right in the eye as he says, "Lower your dress, baby. Show these people those gorgeous tits of yours. Show them what only I get to touch."

I moan around him, my pussy clenching with need as I lower the straps of my dress until they're bunched around my torso. Liam's brown eyes glaze over as my exposed nipples perk up. He reaches down to pluck at them as I continue working his shaft with my mouth and hands, stroking and sucking, my tongue teasing the sensitive underside of his cock as he thrusts inside of my mouth.

Part of me can't believe we're acting out one of our biggest fantasies right now, while the other part is squirming with excitement, already on the brink of orgasm, knowing we're being watched. That other couples are getting off watching me and my husband do what we do best with each other.

"Baby," Liam moans, his voice thick with lust. "I want to paint those pretty tits with my cum."

I smile around him, sucking harder, stroking faster.

Just as Liam's balls tighten up, I sense someone stepping up behind me. "Such a beautiful couple." The voice is female, soft but commanding. "I'd love to see that, too."

Liam looks down at me, grinning. "You heard the lady, baby. Get ready to have your tits covered in cum."

He tugs on my hair, forcing my head up, holding it in place as he pulls his dick out of my mouth, taking over with his other hand.

This is so unlike me, but I'm getting so turned on because we're taking part in a live sex show along with the other patrons. I'm exposed, practically naked, and my husband's about to shoot his load all over my chest. It's almost too much to handle. Liam strokes himself until his cock gives one last pulse before coming all over my breasts in streams of hot, sticky cum.

I moan as the wet warmth covers me, coating my skin and sticking to my dress, but I don't care. This club is about pleasure, about freedom. And for tonight, I'm going to do whatever I want.

I moan, rubbing my fingertips into the sticky substance, bringing them to my mouth and licking Liam's essence from them.

"Mmm, you taste good."

"So do you, I bet. I'd love to find out for myself," the woman behind me says. "Are you two perhaps looking for a third tonight?"

I turn my face up to look at her. She's beautiful, maybe in her late twenties, early thirties. Her light brown hair is pulled up in a bun, and she's wearing a tight black pencil skirt and a white silk blouse with the buttons undone to her navel. Her small breasts are encased in a red lace bra, giving the whole look a sexy librarian vibe. But as enticing as the offer is, nobody gets to touch my husband but me.

"Thank you for the offer, but we don't share."

Her red lips form into a pout. "Pity. But good for you, honey." She winks before sauntering off to look through the viewing window of one of the private rooms.

"I need you in a bed," Liam growls before offering a hand to pull me back up to my feet.

I moan when he grips my hips, pulling me forward and burying his face into my cleavage. His stubble grazes my sensitive skin as he works his way down, his tongue leaving a wet trail on my flesh, licking right through his own cum. When he reaches a nipple, he latches on, sucking and nibbling as I whimper for him. Liam pulls his slacks back over his ass and digs through its pocket, producing the gold key from earlier.

"Shall we check out that room now?"

I smile. "Absolutely."

Chapter FIVE

Liam

I can't get the door unlocked fast enough as we approach our private room.

"Wow," Avery breathes as we step inside, flick on the dim lights, and close the door behind us. "It's beautiful."

The entire front wall is one giant glass window. It's frosted right now, but the switch our concierge mentioned when we first arrived is easily identifiable, right next to the window frame. With one flip, anyone could see inside. Avery marvels over the ornate four-poster bed covered in black silky sheets, the black leather chairs and the little table covered in a variety of fun items. The other walls are painted a soothing shade of gray, with erotic photographs in frames placed at regular intervals.

I nod, turning toward my wife, taking a moment to admire her. Her lips and breasts are glistening with my cum, her posture proud and confident. Even with massive sex hair and a tight dress bunched around her waist, she somehow still manages to look like a goddess. I can't believe I'm married to such a fucking knockout. My cock is already coming back to life, urging me to hurry and get her fully undressed.

"Fuck, you're sexy," I growl, picking her up in my arms, our mouths meeting in a hungry kiss as I carry her across the room.

Avery's body is an undulating, beautiful work of art as I toss her onto the bed and pull down her dress, tossing it off to the side. I tear the black thong away with one quick yank but decide to leave her shoes on for now. Her tits are a little red, the result of my enthusiasm. I squeeze one of her nipples between my fingers, and she hisses out a moan. I can't resist giving her other nipple the same treatment before leaning down to take a taste. Avery's fingers tangle in my hair while she parts her legs invitingly.

I kiss my way down her stomach, nipping lightly, taking time to taste her smooth, soft skin.

"Liam," she breathes, tugging on my hair even harder.

"Yeah?" I pull back with a grin.

"Let's give them another show." Avery inclines her head toward the frosted wall of windows.

I raise my eyebrow. "You sure you're up for that?"

"I'm sure." Avery sits up, sliding her palms down her breasts to her pussy, stroking herself. "Grab the toys I requested, then flip the switch to open the window."

I stand, heading over to the table where an assortment of brand-new sex toys are waiting for us. I smile as I take in some of our favorites: silk scarves, a jeweled butt plug, a cordless Magic Wand, and a generous array of flavored lube.

Fucking hell, my wife is amazing.

Avery watches me with her bright blue eyes, licking her lips, as I step out of my shoes, remove my socks, unbutton my shirt, and slide my pants and boxers down. I place everything on the chair, grab the items from the table, and walk back toward the bed. My cock's already rock hard again, twitching as it bumps against my stomach. Avery sits up and stares at it with a hungry gaze.

God, there's nothing hotter on earth than your partner looking at you like they want to eat you alive.

I throw the props on the bed and take her hands, pulling her to her feet. "Let's get you prepped, shall we?"

She doesn't need any direction as she turns around, grabbing on to two of the bedposts. I pick up the scarves and concentrate on breathing as I wrap them around my wife's wrist, securing her right hand to the post. She moans, her ass and pussy wiggling for me.

I give her a playful swat on the ass. "Behave, or I'll be forced to reprimand you, Ms. Jacobs."

Avery's red, swollen lips curve into a smile. "Oh, Mr. Bossman, I've been *a very naughty* employee. I think I *deserve* to be punished."

I chuckle as I kiss her shoulder, thinking about how far we've come. We still fight like cats and dogs—I think we're both far too stubborn and passionate not to—but these days, we don't bother denying it's foreplay. Avery is an equal partner in our PR firm now, but this little power play is a game we enjoy often. It's the only time my wife will let someone else take control, and I take advantage of it every chance I get.

I stroke her skin, taking a moment to trace my fingertips across her bare back. Avery tenses, goose bumps rising almost instantly as I take my time, working my way up the back of her neck. I pull the second knot tight, and she moans, her back arching, the scarves secure around her wrists. I lean forward, pressing my chest up against her back.

My cock throbs as I run my palms down her arms, cupping her hands and massaging them gently. "You good, baby?"

"Mmm, yes."

I run my tongue down her spine, licking and sucking along her skin until I reach her ass. I grab a cheek in each hand and spread her open for me. She bends her torso until her upper half is parallel to the mattress, giving me better access. Her pussy is already dripping wet, swollen, and glistening with her arousal. She's so beautiful, and watching her get turned on turns me on even more.

I stare at her slick pink flesh for a long moment, taking in the sight, then flick her clit with my tongue before sliding a finger inside of her. Avery groans, thrusting back against my hand, and I press my face closer, lapping at her juices, feeling her coat my lips and chin.

I pull back, adding a second finger. Avery's body is shaking with want as I continue to tease her. She whimpers as I remove my fingers, her pussy clenching at the sudden emptiness, but then she smiles when she sees me select a bottle of cherry-flavored lube.

I break the seal and flick the top open. "Let's add a little sparkle, and then we'll begin the show."

"Fuck," Avery pants as I drip lube onto her tight asshole, working it in with my index finger.

She wiggles her hips, pressing the circle of muscle against my digit. I press my open mouth against her ear and whisper, "You want me to fuck your ass while everyone watches you, Ms. Jacobs?"

"God, Liam, please."

I chuckle darkly, feeling as if I'm about to implode with lust. "Easy, baby." I wrap a hand around my cock, stroking myself lazily before removing the butt plug from its package.

Avery whimpers as I tease her with the tip, pressing it against her hole but not going any further.

"Remember, it's not coming out until you're screaming for me to replace it with my dick. And if you ask nicely, I might even let you come."

Avery groans, her body quivering with desire. "Please put it in, Liam. I trust you'll make it good. So, so fucking good."

"Such a good girl," I praise, pushing the tip of the plug past her tight muscle. "Trusting me to know what your body needs."

Avery hisses out a breath as the plug breaches the first ring. I hold still for a long moment, giving her time to adjust, then continue working it in, a little at a time. This plug is one of the larger ones, made to simulate double penetration. The first time I fucked her ass with one like this, I almost lost my load before I'd even slid fully inside. Once the plug is in place, a rainbow jewel winking back at me between two luscious cheeks, I cross the room until I reach the window.

"Last chance to back out."

"I don't want to back out," Avery insists. "I want them to see you love me. How well you take care of me."

Before flipping the switch, I adjust my mask to make sure it is still in place. Within seconds, the glass is no longer opaque, which does not go unnoticed by the people standing near the private rooms. A few people approach our room with obvious interest as my erection salutes them.

"Fuck, baby, we've already got an audience. Let's show them how I make you scream."

"God, yes," Avery says, squirming in her bindings.

"I'm going to make you lose your shit before I allow you to come. Understand?"

"Yes," she pants.

I lift my brows. "Yes, *what?*"

"Yes, *sir.*" Her toned calves flex as she lifts on her toes in her heels.

I grab Avery's hips and pull her into me. Her pussy's hanging right over my cock, so close I can feel her heat. I lean down, kissing her shoulder, and whisper, "Spread your legs."

I watch as she obeys, splaying her pussy lips. Her clit is already full and engorged, her hard pink nipples brushing against the sheets as she hovers just above them.

I run my fingers down the silky skin of her back, over the curve of her hip, and around to the front of her freshly waxed mound.

"Fuck, you're dripping wet, Ms. Jacobs."

"You get me so fucking wet," she moans, grinding against my hand. "Please."

I push two fingers into her cunt and she moans, her head falling forward. She grinds against my hand while I pump my fingers in and out of her, my palm pressing against her clit. I run my tongue up and down the curve of her shoulder as she rocks back and forth on my fingers, her cunt walls clenching around my digits. Avery whimpers again as I press my cock against the puckered bud of her ass. I tease her, rubbing against the toy, watching as her glistening pussy sucks my fingers in with ease.

"So greedy for my cock," I praise, pumping her pussy faster. "Greedy for my cum."

She lifts her head, her body trembling. "Yes, sir."

"Beg me for it," I command, flexing my cock against the plug, feeling it move inside her ass.

I watch as my wife begs me, as she becomes completely undone in front of my eyes. Her body shakes and trembles, pussy contracting greedily around my fingers. As she cries out in orgasm,

I feel a chill. I pinch her clit between two fingers, and she explodes, her pussy walls fluttering, her body jerking against my hand.

I utter a curse and pull my fingers out. I want to feel her coming around my cock so badly I bury myself to the hilt with one powerful thrust.

"Fuuuck," Avery and I groan in unison as I slide into her.

Her channel is extra tight from the plug, slick and hot around my cock as she takes me in. Her pussy is so wet, her body so ready, that I'm able to thrust in and out of her without pausing. I'm so turned on, I can barely control myself. I grip her shoulders, using them to pull us both back and forth, her body rocking against mine. Her arms stay tied to the posts, her ass cheeks spread, while I fuck her in front of the window. Her cries are almost loud enough to cover the moans coming from the voyeurs on the other side of the glass.

I am so, so fucking close to losing control, but I need Avery to come again first. I grab a handful of her hair and pull her head back, exposing her neck. I lick and suck on her skin, feeling the heat rush up my chest and into my cheeks. With my other hand, I pinch her clit between my fingers, and she screams, her pussy contracting around me. I lose myself in her pleasure, bucking hard as I grunt and groan, knowing I'll need to take her ass on the third round, because I can't hold off any longer.

"Please come inside of me, Liam. I need to feel you filling me up."

"Hold on, baby."

I fuck her harder, faster, pounding into her, my balls slapping against her ass. She's so tight and wet that I can't hold off any longer. I feel my balls drawing up, the tension rising in my body, coiling in my cock.

Her pussy contracts around me, the sensation pushing me over the edge. I come in a frantic rush, filling her with my cum.

"Fuck," I groan, thrusting until she milks the last drop from me.

I collapse onto Avery's back, my cock still buried to the hilt. I press a kiss to her shoulder and plant my hands on either side of her head.

Gazing out the window, I see that we've gathered a much bigger audience.

I press my lips to Avery's ear and say, "How was that, baby?"

"It was perfect," she says with a moan before I can even finish my question.

I chuckle. "We're not done yet."

Avery whimpers as my cock slides out of her pussy. "I can go as long as you can, Bossman."

I revel in the sight of my cum dripping from her spent cunt as I untie my wife, rubbing her wrists, before turning her toward me and placing a soft kiss on her lips.

"Such a good girl." I reach behind her back, placing a firm hand over the plug still nestled in her tight ass. "My perfect girl." I finger the plug, making her squirm with anticipation. "But I still haven't heard you beg me to fuck you *here*. So this is what we're going to do. I'm going to get on that bed, you're going to straddle my face, and I'm going to eat your delicious cunt until I'm hard again. Then, you're going to ride me, bounce on my dick until you can't take it anymore, and you're begging me to fill your ass. Then, *and only then*, will I remove this plug and give you what you truly want. Are we clear, Ms. Jacobs?"

Her eyes sparkle as she bites her lip. "*Crystal* clear, sir. I can't wait to get started."

Goddamn, I am one lucky son of a bitch.

Do you want more sexy billionaire stories?
Visit https://www.lauraleebooks.com/beddingthebillionaire to learn more about Laura Lee's Bedding the Billionaire world.

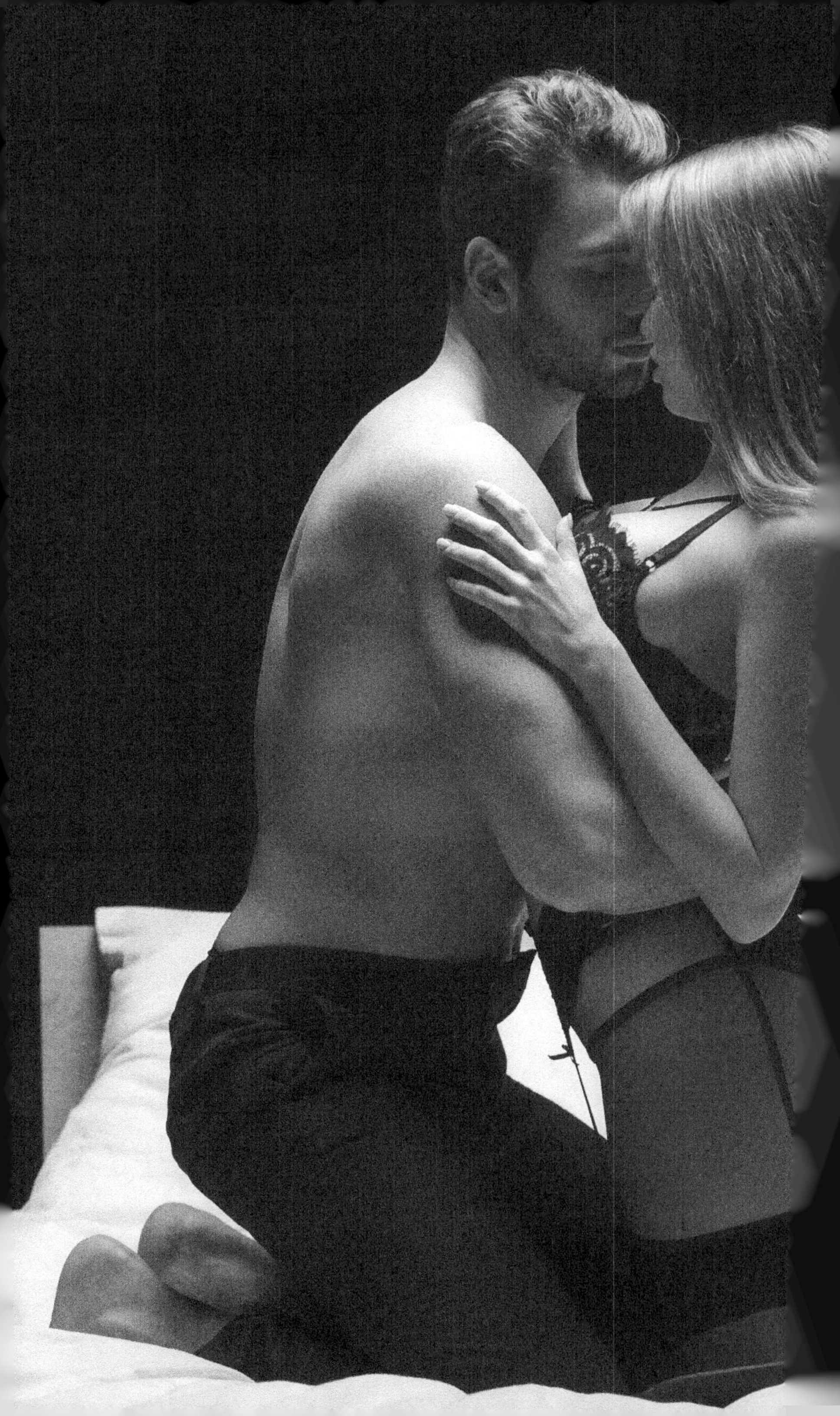

Beneath the Clouds

LAURA PAVLOV

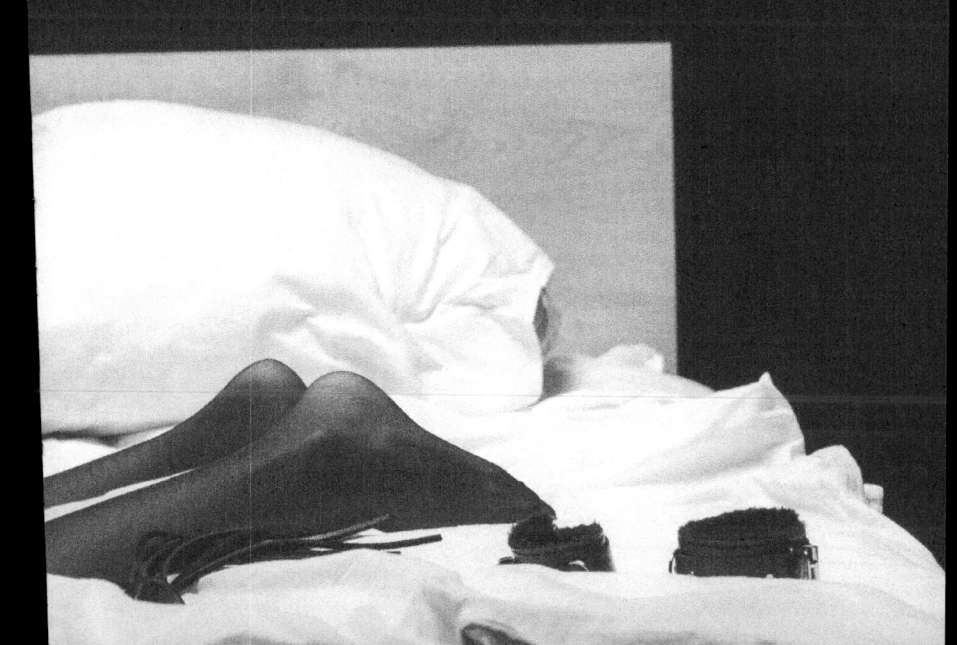

Chapter ONE

Brax

I sat behind my desk, pulling up a few listings for my next client. I owned the largest real estate company in Cottonwood Cove, and I was proud of the business I'd built over the last few years.

My desk phone buzzed, and I put my office manager, Callie, on speakerphone, hearing the holiday music in the background because Christmas was right around the corner. "Hey, boss. Frannie Peterson is here to see you."

"Thank you. Send her back, please."

Frannie Peterson was my younger sister's best friend. They'd been inseparable growing up. She'd left to go to college across the country at Yale, which had surprised nobody in town, as the girl was an overachiever and as type A as one could get. I hadn't seen her in a few years, because when she came back to visit her grandparents and my sister, she only stayed for a short time, from what I'd heard.

We'd never gotten along all that well, as my mere existence seemed to annoy her when we were growing up.

Most people loved me.

I was a friendly guy.

A good time.

The life of the party.

But Frannie was the exception. I'd promised my sister, Tessa, that I'd help her best friend find a new home, now that she'd finished law school and was moving back to town. I glanced down at the last text I'd received from my sister.

> **Tessa: Please help her find a house, and try not to kill one another. <praying hands emoji>**
>
> **Me: Hey, I'm never the one to throw the first insult. I'm always nice.**
>
> **Tessa: She seems to bring out your inner snark more than anyone. Be the bigger person, Braxy.**

I rolled my eyes just as a clacking against the tile floor had my head springing up. When she rounded the doorway, my mouth went completely dry.

The girl with auburn hair, a bigger-than-life personality, and more confidence than a professional athlete no longer wore a pair of overalls and her hair in a ponytail.

She was... stunning.

She'd always been petite, more than half a foot shorter than my six-foot height. But now, she wore a fitted pencil skirt and a white button-up with a pair of red stilettos, with a black dress coat slung over her arm. Her hair fell around her shoulders in loose waves, scarlet-painted lips that matched the color of her shoes, and dark brown eyes locked with my gaze.

"Frannie, hey." I stumbled over my words as I moved to my feet.

"Hello, Brat." She chuckled at the use of the nickname she used to call me.

"Ahhh... thanks for the memory, *Frownie*."

I came around my desk and gave her a hug. She smelled like citrus and honey, and she pulled away quickly before clearing her throat.

I motioned for her to take a seat in the leather chair across from my desk, and she dropped her purse and coat in the chair beside hers.

"It's been a few years. You look great," I said when I sat back down to face her.

"That's slightly sexist. I see you haven't changed at all."

Here we go.

The girl could take one word that I said and turn it into an argument. I'd always known she'd be the perfect lawyer. She got off on debating, and she was fucking smart, so she usually used her words to talk people into a corner.

But I'd never been afraid of Frannie, and I could handle myself just fine, which I was fairly certain had annoyed her.

"I just told Hugh that he looked great when he dropped by with coffee for me this morning, so nice try on the sexist assessment. It's called being friendly." Hugh was one of my best friends, and she'd grown up with him, as well. Obviously, I hadn't told him that he looked great this morning, because that would just be weird, but she didn't need to know that.

"I see you're still argumentative." She raised a brow.

"Not usually. But you seem to bring out that side of me."

She rolled her eyes. "Anyway... seeing as you own the largest real estate company in town, and I need a house, I guess we'll have to tolerate one another for a few days."

"We're both adults. I think we can handle it."

"I know one of us is an adult." She smirked. "When was the last time you drew a mustache on someone's face with a Sharpie while they were sleeping?"

I groaned. "I was thirteen years old, and you'd just told everyone at the pool that I liked to make videos of myself singing Jonas Brothers songs. You should have known better than to sleep at our house with Tess that night after pulling a stunt like that."

"You *did* make videos of yourself singing 'Burnin' Up'. It wasn't a lie. I walked in on you, and you know it." Her hands fisted in her lap.

"That didn't mean you had to go tell everyone."

"I told Jana Roberts because she was asking about you in the bathroom at the pool. I can't help it if she told everyone."

"Oh, that's rich," I growled. "Telling Jana Roberts, who'd I turned down the night before after she tried to force her tongue down my throat at a party, that you had some juicy gossip on me, was like pouring gasoline on a fire."

"Hey," she said, her voice remaining even but firm. "It's not my fault that you could never balance your many hookups."

"Careful, Frannie. You almost sound jealous."

"Please. Even if you were the last man alive, I would invest in the best vibrator money could buy and remain celibate until my dying days."

I barked out a laugh.

Did it just get hot in here?

Seeing those luscious full lips hissing at me and spewing out words like vibrator, had my dick going hard beneath the desk.

She was sexy as hell.

Still just as snarky.

And the last woman on Earth my dick should be reacting to.

"Great. Well, the feeling is mutual. So, let's just stick to the reason you're here. Tess is thrilled that you're moving back home. Let's find you a house, so we can be done with this."

"Don't threaten me with a good time, Brat." The corners of her lips turned up.

Goddamn, she was sexy.

When the fuck did that happen?

Chapter TWO

Frannie

It had been a long week of house hunting, and I'd spent every single day with Brax, as I'd been getting up early to get my work done in the morning and then spent my afternoons going on house tours. Even though we bickered, I'd be lying if I didn't admit that I was having more fun than I'd had in a long time. He was witty and charming and frustrating all at the same time.

We'd just seen three houses, and none were what I was looking for. He'd insisted on driving, just as he had every day, and his music was giving me a headache. I reached over and turned down the volume.

"Do you blare your music when you're with other clients?" I asked, crossing my arms over my chest.

He glanced over at me when he pulled up in front of the adorable cottage with more curb appeal than anything he'd yet to show me.

The final house we planned to see today.

He put the car into park and turned off the engine before shifting to face me. His dark, wavy hair reminded me of my childhood. Of the self-confident, older brother of my best friend who I'd had a ridiculous crush on through my entire adolescence.

I'd never known what to do with my feelings back then. I didn't have siblings. My parents had bailed on me early on in life, and I'd been raised by my much older grandparents, who did the best they could. But I certainly wasn't talking to them about boys and crushes and those types of things.

And the one time I'd worked up the nerve to tell him how I felt, he'd rejected me without a second glance.

Brax Clayborne may be the sexiest man I'd ever laid eyes on, but I wasn't a teenage girl with a crush anymore. I was a graduate of Yale Law School. I dated men now. Not boys who burped in your face, constantly teased you, and didn't have a serious bone in their body.

Although, I imagined he had *one* impressive bone in his body.

Being back in Cottonwood Cove took me back to a time when I wasn't in control of my emotions, and I didn't like it.

"I don't blare music with my other clients, and do you know why?"

"I can't wait to hear." I didn't make any effort to hide my irritation.

"Because my clients don't normally insult me each time we leave a property. You have walked in and out of the last three houses today, along with countless other houses this week, and you've called me names and acted like I don't know how to do my job."

I looked out the window as I processed his words.

I knew I could be difficult. I wasn't above owning it.

"Perhaps I should have been the one named Brat." I smirked, trying to make light of it, because he was right. I'd acted unappreciative, and he was doing me a favor by taking me around. He could have assigned me to one of his agents, but he was willing to walk me through each house and tell me the pros and cons. Even if they'd all been cons so far.

"You can't steal my nickname, Frownie." He laughed. "How about we start over?"

"I'm sorry." I sighed. "I didn't know I'd be coming back home. When I'd accepted the position at the firm based in the city, I'd thought I'd be moving into a high-rise in San Francisco. I'm just feeling overwhelmed with all that's happening."

His eyes softened. Brax had a big heart—there was no doubt about it. I wanted to hate him for a multitude of reasons. First off,

I didn't like that I'd had an intense crush on him, which had always made me feel out of control, and that only made me angrier. It wasn't rational, but it was the truth. And second, he'd been my first rejection—well, unless you count my parents bailing on me before I spoke my first word. But Brax was a different kind of hurt. I guess everyone gets rejected at least once in their life, right? You can't hate someone for not feeling the same way about you that you feel about them.

Clearly, I'd be the one to know that.

My father had left my mother to raise me on her own. They were teenagers, and he had no interest in being a father at seventeen years old. And my mother had left shortly after giving birth to me. She struggled with drugs and alcohol, from what I'd been told, and my grandparents had stepped up and raised me.

I'd always wanted to make them proud for the sacrifices they'd made for me.

"Tell me why you're moving back. Tess said you signed with some big firm in the city. Is your law firm all right with you living in Cottonwood Cove?"

"Yeah, Tess is so excited that we'll be able to hang out all the time now." I fidgeted with the strap of my purse, winding the leather through my fingers. "Gramps isn't doing well, and I know having me close would help my grandparents a lot. I can work remote most days, honestly. I'll probably go into the city once a week, and they have corporate housing I can stay in when I'm there if I need to stay overnight. I'm not a trial attorney. I mostly do the research to prepare the case."

"I'll bet you're a kickass attorney, Frannie. You always knew how to win an argument," he said, as his green eyes locked with mine. I sucked in a breath before forcing myself to look away.

"I don't know about that. My best arguments were always with you." I shrugged.

"Don't sell yourself short. You accomplished so much as a teenager with all your protests. Remember how you got our high school to offer almond and oat milk options to people who were lactose intolerant?" He tapped his mouth with his finger as a wide grin spread across his handsome face. "Even though, if memory serves, you weren't even lactose intolerant yourself."

My head fell back in laughter. "Well, Marcy Fitzpatrick was lactose intolerant, and she was too scared to say anything. The poor girl spent one too many afternoons locked in a bathroom stall in pain, and I knew it was time to do something about it. Sometimes people need someone to fight for them. I was just being Marcy's voice."

"Is that why you fought so hard to have a registered nurse on campus? No other public school had one." His tongue swiped out along his bottom lip, and I squeezed my thighs together in response.

No man had the right to look this good. His dark hair and mesmerizing green eyes were easy to get lost in. He had a chiseled jaw covered in just the right amount of scruff. He was lean with broad shoulders, and he oozed confidence just like he always had. It was just part of who he was.

Some of us were just putting on a show. A weak attempt to convince people that we had life figured out... but I was still just surviving most days.

"Timothy Brighton was diabetic. Did you know that?"

"Yes. He was in your grade, right?"

"Yep. We went to school together since kindergarten. I became a pro at being able to tell when his blood sugar was low. Did you know he ended up in the hospital in ninth grade from collapsing during P.E.? That's the day I made him a promise that I would fight to get him a nurse on campus. Why shouldn't he be entitled to a safe and healthy education like the rest of us?"

"I didn't know that." His gaze searched mine. "You always acted so confident and sure of yourself. I didn't know you were such a bleeding heart."

I knew he meant it as a joke, but his words stung. Just because I always pushed myself to accomplish things did not mean I had no feelings.

But I'd never been very good at being vulnerable or asking for help.

Life had blessed me with a thick skin.

"I didn't feel the need to explain my reasons for doing the things that I did back then because I knew they were the right thing to do. I never wanted to embarrass anyone. Neither of them would have pushed to have their needs met, so why should I call them out?"

"I guess I was just so used to you fighting for things, I never took the time to ask you why you were doing it. But I did always sign every petition you ever asked me to, didn't I?"

I let out a huffy breath. "You did. Even if you made me give you whatever cookies I had in my lunch every time I asked you for anything."

"Your grandma always made the best cookies, Frannie." He smiled, and my chest squeezed. "And, if I'm being totally honest, I think sometimes I just enjoyed getting you worked up back then."

Butterflies fluttered in my stomach. "Well, you were very good at it."

"Why do you think you wanted to help everyone so much? I mean, you were a teenager. Teenagers are notoriously selfish. Fucking up comes with the territory. But you were so focused and determined," he said, his gaze searching mine like he genuinely wanted to know.

"I don't know. I think, in a way, I was trying to prove I belonged here."

His eyes widened. "What? Of course, you belonged here. Hell, everyone in this town adores you."

I shook my head. "It's hard to explain. But growing up without a traditional family like everyone else, and the whole town knowing my parents didn't want me, and my grandparents having to step up to raise me—I guess a part of me always wanted to prove I was worth it."

He reached for my hand, catching me completely off guard. "I never knew you felt that way. You always appeared so sure of yourself."

"I got pretty good at putting on a show. I think it's easy to focus on the things you want to accomplish instead of dealing with all the hurts that lie beneath, you know?"

"Fuck, Frannie. I had no idea. I wouldn't have given you such a hard time. You were always the only girl in town who wasn't charmed by my shit, and I was pretty determined to change that."

Ummm... what? This was an unexpected admission.

"I annoyed you. You don't have to try to make me feel better. I'm good. I don't know why being back home is making me all emotional. Let's go find a house, okay?" I'd already said too much, and I wanted to end the conversation. It was getting too heavy, and I didn't like the way that I was feeling.

Vulnerable and out of control.

Those were two feelings I avoided at all costs.

And this man was the one person who could make me feel more than I wanted to.

Chapter THREE

Brax

Something had shifted between Frannie and I in the car, and we took our time walking through the cottage as she gushed about the home. I'd never realized that she'd had a hard time as a kid, and what did that say about me? I'd been so self-focused on the fact that she was always annoyed with me, I never took the time to think about what growing up without her parents must have been like for her.

I had the twins, Tess and Deaton. My brother, sister, and I were all really close, and Frannie never had that.

"I think this is the one," she said, moving back to the kitchen for the third time.

"You sure? You don't want to think about it for a day or two?"

She shook her head. A wide smile spread clear across her pretty face. "I know when something is right, and I don't second-guess that."

"That's something I've always admired about you. While the rest of us were constantly questioning our decisions, you always just sort of knew."

"Brax, you're one of the most confident people I've ever met. I hardly think you question anything."

"You'd be surprised. I question a lot of things lately." I stood in the living room as she took several photos and videos of the place and sent them to Tessa.

"I think since I opened up to you about all my insecurities, you should tell me at least one secret that nobody knows about you." She dropped her phone into her purse and came to a stop in front of me.

She was so fucking beautiful, I was having a hard time looking away.

"I'll tell you what. Let's head back to the office, write up your offer, and get it submitted, and then I'll take you to Reynolds' and buy you dinner and a drink to celebrate."

She raised a brow. "And what about these things you're questioning lately?"

"Let me get one cocktail in me, and maybe I'll share all my secrets with you, Frannie Peterson." I held out my hand to her, offering to shake on it, and she slipped hers in mine, and I tugged her closer on instinct. Our chests bumped the slightest bit, and I didn't miss the way she sucked in a strained breath.

"Deal," she whispered, before tugging her hand away and stepping back.

But I had the strongest urge to move back into her space because this pull that I felt toward Frannie was stronger than anything I'd ever felt before.

Frannie's new house wasn't the only thing I planned to talk about at dinner.

***

It had been a full day, and one of the best days I'd had in a long time. We'd submitted the offer to the listing agent, and they'd accepted her offer immediately. It was one of the easiest deals I'd ever been a part of.

I'd called Hugh and asked him to save a table for us as we were heading over. Frannie was stopped by several people once we'd arrived at the Reynolds', and my best friend and his fiancée, Lila, had both come over to give us a big hug before sending over a bottle of champagne to celebrate her new house.

"This day has been a whirlwind," she said. "I love the house, Brax. Thank you for taking me around today and working your magic with that lowball offer."

"I was happy to do it."

We paused to clink our glasses in cheers as we both took a long pull from the tall champagne flutes. Our server, Danielle, stopped by our table, and we placed our order before she stepped away.

"That champagne is delicious," Frannie said. Her tongue slipped out and swiped along her pouty pink lips, and my dick strained so hard against my zipper I had to slyly adjust myself beneath the table. "So, you've got your first drink going. Tell me what you question about your life, Brax."

Her voice was playful, but her dark, smoky eyes locked on mine, and I could feel her sincerity. We had a history. For whatever reason, I trusted Frannie.

I blew out a breath and set my glass down because I was driving, so I wasn't going to have more than a few sips. "I guess I'm questioning the way I've been living my life lately."

"In what way?"

"Well, you know, I like to have a good time. But lately, seeing Hugh planning his wedding with Lila, and Travis and Shay becoming parents... I don't know," I said, clearing my throat and looking away, suddenly feeling self-conscious about how serious this conversation had turned. My two best friends were moving forward in life, and it felt like I was at a standstill. "Sometimes I wonder if maybe it's time for something more."

"I get that." She smiled when my gaze found hers.

"How about you? Are you still with that neurosurgeon boyfriend?" I asked, holding my breath while I waited for her to answer.

Her brows cinched together. "I'm surprised you know about that."

"You're Tessa's favorite topic. And, if I'm being honest, I also ask about you often. Just always wanted to make sure you were doing all right."

"Thank you. I wouldn't have thought that." Her dark eyes softened. "Ted and I broke up almost a year ago. He didn't want the same things that I wanted."

"What did he want?" My tone had more bite than I meant it to.

"A companion when he wasn't working, which was not very often. And it really just came down to the future. Once he drew the line in the sand that he never wanted children, I suddenly got anxious, you know? I never thought I'd want those things, but hearing him say that he didn't, made me realize that I saw my future differently."

"I get that. We can all change our minds as we go." I looked up as our food was set in front of us.

We spent the next two hours talking as we ate and then went on to order dessert.

More talking. Like we had years to catch up on.

And somewhere along the way, we'd turned up the heat as she admitted that she had a crush on me. I was calling bullshit on that.

"You did not have a crush on me. Don't lie just to make me feel better about the fact that I'm the last of the three amigos to be single," I said. And for whatever reason, the longer I talked to her, the more comfortable I grew, so I gave fewer fucks about filtering what I said to her.

I was having a good time.

Hell, the best time I'd had with a woman—ever.

She was smart and funny and charming as hell.

Gorgeous and sexy and confident.

"I'm not the one making things up. You knew it, Brax," she said, her cheeks flushed.

"Are you fucking with me, or are you being serious?" I asked, because all the teasing had left her voice.

"I told you. You rejected me. Don't be an asshole and make me relive it." She reached for her champagne and took another sip, her dark gaze locking with mine.

"Frannie. I would never have rejected you. Tell me what you're talking about."

Damn, I wanted to kiss her. I raised a brow and waited for her to speak. I wasn't going to let her out of it because it seemed to be something that she was angry about.

"You were a senior in high school, and I was a sophomore. I came and sat with you at that bonfire. Tessa was off with her boyfriend, making out in the woods, and it was my first time having a beer, and you were lecturing me about being careful." She chuckled, but there was something in her gaze that didn't match the lightness in her tone. "I told you that I was fine and that I'd been looking for you. I was so nervous."

I wracked my brain, pulling that day from my memory. "I remember that night. You were buzzed, and I was pissed that Billy Rogers had given it to you. Yeah, I remember now. It had been overcast earlier, and you were telling me that you liked cloudy weather because you didn't feel like you needed to be outside having fun. You could focus on schoolwork. But you, in no way, shape, or form, said anything about having a crush on me."

I was fairly impressed that I remembered it so vividly.

She raised a brow. "I love that's what you remember. I do have a thing for cloudy days." She chuckled. "And you said that you preferred sunny days because you could be out on the boat. And then I told you that I had fun with you the last time we'd all taken the boat out on the water."

"Okay. I remember that now. And I said that I'd had fun, too." I narrowed my gaze and shook my head in confusion. "And that fucker Billy handed you another beer, and you and I argued about it. I told Billy that I'd fucking knock him out if he ever gave your or Tessa a drink again."

"Well, that part's a little fuzzy. I downed that drink and was trying to prove to you that I was not just your little sister's best friend. I thought the liquid courage would help. I'd liked you for a long time at that point."

"Frannie. I had no idea. You never acted like you liked me at all. I always thought you hated me, and it drove me crazy because I didn't know why."

She smiled. "Don't you remember that cartoon, *Hey Arnold*? There was that girl, Helga Pataki, who had a massive crush on Arnold, but she was super mean to him because she didn't know what to do with her feelings. I guess I was Helga."

I shook my head in disbelief. "I had no idea. And I do know that I sure as hell never rejected you, Frannie. I'd never do that. I always teased you back then, but I'd never be cruel."

She sipped the last of her drink. Cheeks flushed. Lips plump. Eyes on me.

"I remember telling you that I liked you when you drove me home, Brax. I know I said it because a weight lifted off my shoulders, and I was proud of myself for coming clean. But you just pretended like it never happened, and then you started dating Brigit a week later."

"Jesus, Frannie. That is not how it happened. You were drunk off your ass and saying all sorts of shit that night. You were talking about how you loved debating with me, and that you wanted to be a lawyer. But you also said that you loved vanilla raspberry cupcakes and SpongeBob. So how the fuck would I know you were serious about anything? Your words were slurring, and you kept laughing. If you recall, you said that you liked me, and I thought you were confessing to the fact that you didn't really hate me. I didn't know you meant it any other way. I told you I liked you, too, because I did. I swear to you, I didn't know you had a crush on me, Frannie."

She studied me for the longest time and then leaned forward. "Well, now you know, Brax. What are you going to do about it?"

Chapter FOUR

Frannie

I didn't know if it was the champagne or the fact that we were finally clearing the air. I'd hated Brax so much after that night because I was young and immature and didn't know what to do with all those feelings. And then Brax had started dating Brigit and never brought it up again. It hurt and felt like rejection, which fueled my anger toward him.

But hearing him say that he didn't know made me realize that I probably hadn't been very clear. I'd gotten drunk for the first time in my life and made a fool of myself. We were kids back then, and everything seemed bigger when you were a hormonal teenager.

And here we were, all these years later, revisiting it.

There was an attraction here that I wouldn't deny if he was willing to admit he felt it, too.

So, I laid out all my cards on the table.

"What am I going to do about it?" he asked, as he leaned across the table so his face was just inches from mine.

"Did I stutter?" I teased.

"What do you want me to do about it, Frannie?" His voice was laced with desire, his gaze hooded as he drank me in. "It's been a long time. How do you feel about me today? Right now? Because I sure as fuck know how I feel."

"I asked you first." I bit down on my bottom lip to keep from diving across the table and climbing him like a spider monkey. He was so damn good looking, and I still saw the adorably charming teenage boy that I used to long for. But now he was a man. A confident and sexy and smart man. One I was deeply attracted to, even all these years later.

"You want to know what I want?" he purred as his hand came across the table and reached for mine.

"I do."

"I want you, Frannie Peterson. Sure, you're fucking beautiful, and I'm attracted to you. But that's not it. That's not even half of it. I want to know about your grandparents and your job and your time away from Cottonwood Cove. I want to know about what you like to do on cloudy days. I want to know grown-up Frannie. Because I can promise you that dinner is not going to be enough. Not even close."

"I thought you liked the sunshine, Brax?" I teased, my heart racing at his words as I tried desperately not to react.

"I'd sit beneath the clouds with you any day. You light up any room you walk into."

"That was a little cheesy," I teased, but I could feel my cheeks were flaming because I loved every minute of this.

"I don't give a shit if it's cheesy. Because being with you, sitting here, it feels like it's important, doesn't it? Do you feel it?"

"I feel it," I whispered.

Brax held up his hand and handed his credit card to Danielle, and he just watched me as he waited. When she returned, he signed the credit card slip and placed his card back into his wallet.

"Come home with me, Frannie," he said, and it wasn't a question. It was a statement. Like he would do everything in his power to convince me to leave with him.

And damn, did I want to.

I'd always been cautious when it came to men. I had some deep-rooted trust issues, and normally, I'd never consider going home with a man after one date. Hell, this wasn't even really a date, was it?

It was a dinner with two friends.

Or were we even friends?

It was more of a business dinner, wasn't it?

"Don't do that," he said, as his gaze searched mine.

"Don't do what?"

"Doubt what this is. We aren't teenagers anymore, Frannie. There are no misunderstandings here. I may have been a dumbshit back then, but I'm not a kid anymore. I told you I've been struggling about what I wanted, trying to figure it out, and somehow, after just a week with you, it all seems so clear. When I wake up in the morning, I look forward to the day because I know I'm going to see you. It's you, Frannie Peterson. I don't want a one-night thing. I don't want to be friends or even friends with benefits. *I want you.* I'm smart enough to recognize what an amazing woman you are, and I'm not going to let you get away this time. So come home with me tonight, or don't. I'll be at your door tomorrow and every day after until you say yes."

And as much as I wanted to say yes, self-preservation won out.

"Let's see if you're a man of your word, Brax." I pushed to my feet, and we made our way out of the restaurant.

He opened the door for me, and I slipped into his car and pulled my seat belt into place as he moved into the driver's seat.

"Thanks for having dinner with me. How about breakfast tomorrow? We'll get the inspections scheduled for the house, and we can talk some more about us." He reached for my hand when he pulled in front of my grandparents' house and put the car into park.

I turned so I was facing him.

"About us?" I whispered.

"Yeah. This isn't over, Frannie. We're just getting started."

I unbuckled my seat belt and reached for him, and he pulled me over the center console and onto his lap. I moved a leg to each side so I was straddling him, and my hands tangled in his hair. He tugged me down as his mouth crashed into mine, and my lips parted in invitation. His tongue slipped in, and our kiss was desperate and needy. I moaned into his mouth just as his hand was on my thigh and the other on my neck, angling my face to take the kiss deeper. I'd never been kissed like this. His erection pulsed beneath me, and I ground up against him, tugging my coat off in frustration. He helped me remove it and tossed it onto the passenger seat as we both chuckled, because our lips never lost contact. My body was moving of its own volition now as I continued to grind against him, and his hands found my hips, rocking me up and down his engorged cock.

He pulled back, causing me to whimper as both of his hands moved to each side of my face. The moon shone from above, allowing just enough light to see the heat in his eyes. His breaths were labored, and his tongue came out to swipe along his bottom lip.

"Tell me what you want," he said, as he leaned forward and spoke against my ear.

"Touch me. Please." My voice was breathy and barely recognizable.

His hands traveled up my legs as they shoved my skirt up to bunch around my waist. He stroked over the scrap of lace between my thighs, and my head fell back. My back was pressed to the steering wheel, keeping our bodies ridiculously close.

"Is this where you want me to touch you?" he whispered, running his fingers up and down my seam as desire flooded. "You're so fucking wet. I can barely keep myself from flipping you onto your back and burying my head between your legs."

"Brax," I whispered as he shoved away the lace, teasing my entrance before one finger slipped inside. "Oh my gosh, please don't stop."

"Not going to stop, Frannie. Never going to stop."

He pulled my head back down, and his mouth was on mine. His tongue slipped inside, and he moved it in and out with the same rhythm of his finger. And then he added a second finger, and I gasped. My hands were on his shoulders, bracing myself so he could pump in and out of me, as our lips never lost contact.

His thumb pressed to my clit, and he rubbed little circles, and the most overwhelming throbbing sensation built between my thighs.

My breaths were coming hard and fast. I groaned into his mouth as I bucked faster, and Brax knew exactly what I needed.

Bright lights exploded behind my eyes, and my head fell back on a loud gasp as I exploded. My body trembled and shook and quaked as tremors rocked through me. I'd never experienced an orgasm like this.

He stayed right there as I rode out every last bit of pleasure.

When my breathing settled, and I looked back down at him, he pulled out his fingers and slipped them into his mouth, and my eyes bulged.

"I will never get enough of you, Frannie."

"Thanks for that," I said, my voice hoarse and unrecognizable. A nervous laugh escaped because I couldn't believe that I'd just climbed onto his lap in his car and had an orgasm while parked outside of my grandparents' house.

But I was done holding back. Done being afraid to take what I wanted.

And I wanted this man something fierce.

"Don't thank me. I'm just getting started."

Chapter FIVE

Brax

"Take me home with you," she whispered, as her fingers feathered through my hair, and I nipped at her bottom lip.

Seeing Frannie get off was the hottest thing I'd ever experienced.

And I only wanted more.

"You sure? There's no rush here. I'm not going anywhere. If you're not ready tonight or tomorrow or even next month, I'll be knocking at your door either way."

She smiled. "I believe you, Brax."

For whatever reason, her words did something to me. I wanted her trust, and she was taking a gamble that I was a man of my word.

She climbed back over the seat and buckled up, her hand finding mine as we drove the short distance to my house.

Once inside, I planned to give her a tour and make her a drink—whatever she wanted. But she surprised me by pushing off her coat and letting it drop to the floor before tugging my hand as soon as I closed the door. She pushed up onto her tiptoes to kiss me. My hands were in her hair as my mouth claimed hers immediately. I lifted her, and her legs came around my waist liked we'd been doing this for years.

Like she just fit here perfectly.

With me.

I didn't know what it was. Maybe it was our history. Maybe we just had a strong connection. Maybe the stars had aligned, and the timing was finally right.

But this felt like—everything.

I carried her to my bedroom and dropped her onto the bed as I hovered above.

"There's no rush, Frannie." My nose rubbed against hers.

"I'm tired of waiting for my life to start. I want this. I want you. And I don't want to wait one more minute."

She pushed forward and wrapped her arms around my neck, tugging me down. Our mouths sealed as my dick strained against the denim fabric of my jeans. I kissed her as I ground up against her.

My tongue tangled with hers, and I continued rocking against her as her legs wrapped around my waist.

I couldn't get enough of this woman.

How did this happen?

Just one week with her after all these years, and I only wanted more.

Our hands explored one another, and I found the hem of her shirt and slipped my hand beneath, climbing up her lean stomach as my thumb traced along the swell of her breasts.

I pulled back to look at her, her lips swollen from how long we'd been kissing. Dark eyes wild and full of desire. I unbuttoned her blouse one button at a time, pushing it open to expose her lavender lace bra.

"Fuck, Frannie," I growled, as I pulled the straps down her shoulders, sliding away the lace so I could wrap my lips over her hard peaks. I licked and sucked as she writhed beneath me, her fingers moving through my hair.

"Tell me you have a condom," she whispered. "I need you now, Brax."

I pulled back, my fingers tracing over her gorgeous tits as I nodded.

"I do." I reached into my back pocket and pulled a condom from my wallet while she sat forward and unbuttoned my jeans, shoving them down as my cock broke free.

"Wow," she said, which made me chuckle. I yanked the sweater over my head and dropped it onto the floor.

"You like what you see, Frannie?"

"I always have."

"Well, I've been dreaming about getting you out of this pencil skirt since you walked into my office." I motioned her to lie back as I kicked off my shoes, pants, and briefs and shoved them to the side. I reached for her hips, and in one swift move, I flipped her over onto her belly, and she gasped as laughter escaped her sweet mouth. I lowered the zipper and slowly slid the fabric down her body, taking my time to admire her perfect ass that donned a matching lavender lace thong. I unbuckled her bra and ran my fingers down her back before leaning down and kissing each cheek. "I should have been kissing your ass years ago."

She rolled over, a wide grin on her face, but her eyes were hooded, and her chest was rising and falling as I plucked the bra away from her and tossed it onto the floor.

"You're so beautiful," I whispered, unable to pull my eyes from her perfect body.

"You are, too." She sank her teeth into her bottom lip, and I nearly came undone right there.

I tore off the top of the foil packet and dropped it onto the floor, as well, before rolling the latex over my throbbing dick. She sat up on her elbows and watched.

"It's been a while for me," she said, her eyes searching mine as if she were nervous.

"It's been a while for me, too." I climbed onto the bed, her legs falling apart to make room for me. "But I don't think it's going to be a while for either of us after tonight."

She sighed, her eyes wet with emotion. "I think you're right."

I teased her entrance with my tip, and her back arched with anticipation. I stroked her with my fingers, finding her soaked.

"Please," she groaned as she rocked against me.

I slowly pushed inside, inch by glorious inch, and nothing had ever felt better. She was so fucking tight. I paused a few times, giving her a minute to adjust to my size, before I rocked all the way into her.

Her eyes were closed, and I looked down at her. "Frannie. Eyes on me, baby. I want to see you come undone."

Her eyes opened, and my hand moved to the side of her neck, fingers tracing along her cheek. I pulled out and then slowly pushed back in. We took our time finding our rhythm, our eyes never leaving one another's. Our breaths were the only audible sounds in the room.

And we moved faster.

Harder.

We both gasped and panted.

I pulled back to watch her, and my hand moved between us, knowing just what she needed. My thumb circled her clit, and she arched up in response as her hips bucked, meeting me thrust for thrust. My lips came down over her hard peak, and I flicked her nipple with my tongue, and that was all it took.

Her body started to tremble and shake.

And I fucking loved it. Loved watching this woman lose control.

"Brax," she cried out as her pussy convulsed around me.

I thrusted once more.

Twice.

And I went right over the edge with her a guttural sound escaping my lips.

Fucking ecstasy.

We both rode out every last bit of pleasure before I rolled onto my side, taking her with me.

I wrapped my arms around her and held her close.

And I was never letting go.

***

It had been three weeks since Frannie had returned to Cottonwood Cove. I'd helped her move into her new house, even though I wished she was moving in with me. We spent every night together, taking turns at each other's homes.

My sister, Tessa, had been surprised at first, but had embraced the idea of her brother dating her best friend.

I hadn't known what had been missing all this time. I'd felt like there had to be more to life over these last few years. And with one visit from Frannie Peterson, all my questions were answered.

So, for now, we'd live in our own homes, and we'd date.

When she spent the night in the city, I went with her.

We still had our moments where we argued—hell, it was part of our charm.

We bickered. We laughed. And we loved hard.

It was almost Christmas, and we were down by the cove, even though there was a light layer of snow on the ground. This had always been one of my favorite places to go. So, we'd bundled up and walked downtown to get hot cocoa, enjoying how festive the town was this time of year. Then we'd walked down to the water. To a private spot we used to come to as kids.

"Do you remember this place?" I asked as I helped her to settle onto a log that sat a few feet from the water.

"Yes. Isn't this the place where we went to the bonfire?" She rolled her eyes, but I saw the corners of her lips turn up.

"It is. But I was just a teenager back then, and too stupid to recognize what was right in front of my eyes."

"And now?" she teased.

"Well, now I'm a man, and I'm still a little stupid about a lot of things." I chuckled, and she leaned forward and gave me a chaste kiss. "But not when it comes to you."

"Oh, yeah?"

"Yeah, Frannie. So, we're back here now, and I'm going to do it right. I know we haven't been together long, and it's too soon to move in or take the next step, but I plan on doing all those things with you. But for tonight, there's just one thing I need to say."

"Say it," she whispered.

"I love you, Frannie Peterson. I probably always have. But the way I feel about you now... it's indescribable. Even the cloudy days are my favorite now. Thanks for coming home and showing me exactly what I've been missing."

A tear streamed down her cheek. "Thanks for finding me a home, and thanks for being my home, too. I love you. And I can't wait to take every step with you."

I wrapped an arm around her shoulder and pulled her close, my forehead resting against hers. "Are you going to boss me around every step of the way?" I chuckled.

"Damn straight, Brat. Wouldn't have it any other way."

"I wouldn't either, Frownie."

And my lips found hers.

I kissed her like it was forever.

Because I knew in my gut that it was.

THE END

Thank you so much for reading! Do you want to catch up with everyone in Cottonwood Cove? Start the series today! Lila and Hugh's story is LIVE. For more information about Into the Tide and all my books, go to my website.

https://www.laurapavlov.com